The Heart of a Vicar

OTHER BOOKS AND AUDIOBOOKS
BY SARAH M. EDEN

THE LANCASTER FAMILY

Seeking Persephone

Courting Miss Lancaster

Romancing Daphne

Loving Lieutenant Lancaster

THE JONQUIL FAMILY

The Kiss of a Stranger

Friends and Foes

Drops of Gold

As You Are

A Fine Gentleman

For Love or Honor

The Heart of a Vicar

STAND-ALONE NOVELS

Glimmer of Hope

An Unlikely Match

For Elise

A Regency Romance by

SARAH M. EDEN

Covenant Communications, Inc.

Cover image © Mark Owen / Arcangel

Cover design copyright © 2019 by Covenant Communications, Inc.

Published by Covenant Communications, Inc.
American Fork, Utah

Copyright © 2019 by Sarah M. Eden
All rights reserved. No part of this book may be reproduced in any format or in any medium without the written permission of the publisher, Covenant Communications, Inc., P.O. Box 416, American Fork, UT 84003. The views expressed within this work are the sole responsibility of the author and do not necessarily reflect the position of Covenant Communications, Inc., or any other entity.

This is a work of fiction. The characters, names, incidents, places, and dialogue are either products of the author's imagination, and are not to be construed as real, or are used fictitiously.

Printed in the United States of America
First Printing: June 2019

25 24 23 22 21 20 19   10 9 8 7 6 5 4 3 2 1

ISBN:978-1-52440-861-9

To Karen Adair,
for keeping me going through countless ups and downs;
we've laughed together, cried together, celebrated together,
and I don't know what I'd do without you

ACKNOWLEDGMENTS

THANK YOU TO:

James Woodforde, a parson in the English countryside, whose diary, kept from 1758–1802, offered incredible insights into the day-to-day experiences of clergymen in the 19th century.

Alexis Sorenson at The Quarry climbing gym for showing me the ropes (literally) and helping me discover a previously unknown love of rock climbing.

The team at Anglican Pastor for such detailed information on rites, rituals, beliefs, and services, as well as kindly and patiently supplying answers to a long, long list of questions.

Theodore Maynard's 1919 compilation of historical drinking songs.

Samantha Millburn and the team at Covenant for tireless hard work, attention to detail, and a love of story that shines in every book they produce.

Pam Victorio and Bob Diforio, an incomparable team and the greatest support an author could hope for.

Annette Lyon and Luisa Perkins for Tuesdays.

Ginny Miller for proofreads and supportive feedback.

Liz Swick for keeping things running behind the scenes.

Paul, Jonathan, and Katherine for being the best.

CHAPTER ONE

Nottinghamshire, England
October 1816

According to his brothers, Harold Jonquil was born a vicar. And when one was *born* something, one learned to act well the part.

He stood outside the church doors, as he did every Sunday, offering the appropriate nods of acknowledgment to his parishioners as they left, pretending as though interacting with dozens upon dozens of people didn't take every drop of reserved energy he had. He didn't struggle to interact with people as much as his brother Corbin did, but it was still a battle. He never entirely knew what to say, falling back again and again on an authoritative recitation of scripture or sermons, hoping no one would realize how inept he really was. That near-constant uncertainty was exhausting.

He accepted the various comments on his sermon, whether expressions of praise or criticism, with solemnity. He neither smiled nor frowned; a vicar, he had come to learn, was meant to be a study in neutrality, ever calm, ever rational, ever dependable.

Ever exhausted.

Ever boring.

His oldest brother, Philip, stepped from the church. Philip had been born to be an earl, yet no one could convincingly argue that he fit that mold at all. He was flamboyant to the point of absurdity, his mannerisms so overdone that he was rendered rather ridiculous, and not the least interested in hiding his thoughts and feelings behind a neutral mask. Philip's behavior inspired annoyance in at least one of their brothers. Why was it earls could fill their roles in nearly any way they chose but vicars could not?

Philip's wife, Sorrel, walked at his side, one arm through his and the other firmly gripping her cane. She had suffered horrific injuries in an accident many years earlier. Though efforts had been made to restore some of her mobility and to relieve the constant pain she endured, she was not, and likely never would be, truly whole.

She had often been absent from services over the past year. Sorrel had endured two very difficult and ultimately heartbreaking pregnancies and was in the midst of another, though few beyond the family knew as much. Her already fragile body was struggling. Not to mention the house party at Lampton Park, the family seat, about six weeks earlier. The gathering had taken a toll on Sorrel, one from which she hadn't recovered. Indeed, she seemed to be struggling more.

"I am pleased to have you here this week, Sorrel." Harold offered a dip of his head. He'd found over the years that it served as a good general gesture, one suitable to most any occasion, and it saved him the difficulty of trying to think of the correct thing to do when he was already worn down.

"I do hope you mean to bestow a blessing on our heads, Your Grace." Philip bowed deeply from the waist, addressing Harold in the way one would an archbishop.

Harold's older brothers were forever doing that: making sport of his adherence to the protocols of his profession and insinuating that he had excruciatingly lofty goals, when, in actuality, his only true aim was to not be a complete failure.

"*You* are more deserving of a curse," Sorrel told her husband in her usual tone of mingled amusement and impatience. She loved her husband—no one who spent any amount of time with the two of them could doubt that—but she, of all the people in the world, allowed Philip the least leverage for ridiculousness. She was, thus, one of Harold's favorite people.

Despite Philip's mocking, Harold maintained his equanimity, as always. "Do send word if any of your tenants or any member of your household has need of me. I will, of course, do all I can to discover those needs on my own."

This was the relationship a vicar was meant to have with the finer families in his parish. Doing one's duty as a man of the church required open communication with all in the area. His request was met with the usual response: Philip rolled his eyes, and Sorrel promised to tell Harold of anything he ought to know.

They made their way up through the churchyard. Harold watched their progress, concerned for his sister-in-law. As vicar, he ought to be helping in some way, but he didn't know how. He wasn't a doctor. He could offer thoughts from holy writ or writings of various religious scholars, but he had found over the past year that she was not comforted by that.

Mr. Pearsely, who had been the vicar in the years Harold had grown up in this neighborhood, had been a calming influence, serene and composed. When he had visited the Park after Father's death, Mr. Pearsely had brought with him a degree of peace no one else had. Harold had watched that influence transform Mater, calm her, comfort her. A vicar was meant to be a source of tranquility. Harold wanted to be that in the lives of the people he served, but inwardly, he was often in turmoil, stumbling his way through his life's calling.

Philip and Sorrel were the last to leave the church. Harold's duties were complete for the moment. He closed the chapel and made his way toward the nearby vicarage with neither haste nor sloth.

A few of the area children ran around the road, laughing and calling to each other. They paused in their game as he passed.

"Good afternoon, children," he said with a dip of his head.

"Good afternoon, Mr. Jonquil," they answered almost in unison.

Behind him, he heard their playing resume. If only joining in a game of chase were considered appropriate for a man of his profession. He liked to run but didn't get to very often. And children could be endlessly amusing. He stepped up the narrow footpath leading to his humble front door. He'd often thought of adding flowers to the path, perhaps a larger shade tree to allow the parlor window a bit of reprieve from the afternoon sun. But the vicarage itself had suffered neglect under the previous vicar. He needed to see to repairs and upkeep before spending his minimal funds on expenses that were comparatively frivolous. If only the course of study at university had focused a bit more on the financial and temporal aspects of this profession, then Harold might have had a better idea how to juggle it all.

He pushed open the door and stepped into the narrow entryway. The arched passage beyond framed the equally narrow stairwell lit by sunshine spilling in from a generously proportioned picture window at the first landing. The same arching detail framed the four doors leading off the open space at the foot of the stairs. It was not a large home nor a fine one, but there was something very pleasing in its detailed simplicity. Once he had addressed the peeling plaster and cracked windows, the fireplaces that smoked, and the roof that leaked no matter how often he patched it, the home would be nearly perfect.

The aroma of Mrs. Dalton's beef stew filled the house. His housekeeper was a gift from heaven itself. She cooked mouthwatering meals on a thin budget. She did not object to the sparse second-hand furnishings and out-of-date decorations he had inherited from his predecessor, nor the drafty, neglected spaces. Best of all, she was not a gossip.

Harold plucked his hat from his head and tossed it on the hat rack. His outercoat joined it. He stepped into the spill of sunlight from the window. Eyes closed, he took a deep breath, filling himself with the sounds and smells of this house that had so quickly become home to him. He pulled off his jacket and hung it over one arm, then unbuttoned the cuffs at each wrist. *Much better.* Once he had money enough, he meant to have shirts made that didn't constrict his arms so severely. Enduring the starched collars and cravats was bad enough.

This vicarage was small compared to the parsonages and vicarages in which several of Harold's classmates at Cambridge now lived. He didn't mind. The living was a comfortable one, or would be once he'd set the house to rights. How did vicars with smaller livings than his ever afford even the most basic care of their homes? Surely there had to be a better approach. He only hoped that years from now, when all was set to rights, he might have income enough, if he were fortunate, to raise a family of his own, provided they were frugal. And it was the living his late father had hoped would be his. Living and working here had always been part of the plan for him.

The tiny kitchen sat just to the right of the stairwell. He could hear Mrs. Dalton working inside. Interacting with the entire parish every Sunday after services was draining, but the time he spent one-on-one with Mrs. Dalton filled him again. She was a joy. He bit down a smile as he began whistling a tune he'd learned during his early years at university.

He leaned a shoulder against the kitchen doorframe and sang gustily to the closed door.

"Some people think distill-e-ry drink
Is wholesome, neat, and sheer,
But I will contend to my life's end,
There's nothing to tipple like beer."

From inside the kitchen, Mrs. Dalton laughed heartily. She pulled the door open and, to Harold's surprised delight, took up the chorus.

"For I likes a little good beer;
And I will contend

To my life's end,
There's nothing to tipple like beer."

"You know that one," Harold said with a grin. "I was so certain you wouldn't have heard it."

"Your knowledge of tavern songs is very extensive." She motioned him into the kitchen. "But so is mine."

"It's not the most vicarly of repertoires," he admitted.

Mrs. Dalton lowered her voice and spoke conspiratorially. "I like it. I'd not want you to actually be a tippler, and I know for certain that you're not, but it's a fine thing being able to be a bit absurd now and then."

Absurdity was something in which a vicar ought not indulge. But in the privacy of his home, with only his dear, discreet housekeeper as witness, he could allow it and enjoy it.

He laid his coat over an obliging stool. "One of these days, my dear Mrs. Dalton, I will find one you haven't heard before."

She pointed her wooden spoon at him. "You've not managed that in all the time I've been here."

He snatched up a hot currant bun from the worktable. "I know an awful lot of drinking songs," he warned her. "This challenge could last decades."

She crossed to the fire, where the pot of stew simmered. "I grew up in a tavern, Mr. Jonquil. I doubt there's a ditty I haven't heard." She ladled a bowl of stew and handed it to him. "Carry it to the dining room, and eat there like you have manners."

He held the bowl near his chin and sipped his stew. "What if I'd rather stay in here and sing inappropriate songs with you?"

She snapped a kitchen towel at him. "Behave."

Harold winked at her and took another spoonful. "Heavenly, Mrs. Dalton. Absolutely heavenly."

"Having a vicar declare my cooking heavenly! Now, that's a fine thing." She turned back to her work a moment before a knock echoed off the front door.

"Ah, lud." It was a rather unvicar-like word, but the most appropriate one for the occasion. He was jacketless. His sleeves hung open. His cravat loose. He was eating in the kitchen, standing up, having challenged his housekeeper to a competition involving songs about liquor.

Act well your part; there all the honor lies. Father had said that so often when Harold was young that it was etched on his very soul.

Act well your part. Harold was doing a poor job of it at the moment.

"I'll answer the door," Mrs. Dalton said. "You set yourself to rights."

"Thank you." He left his bowl on the worktable, grabbed his jacket, and hurried into his study directly across from the kitchen, snapping the door closed behind him.

A small circular mirror hung beside the door. He used it to straighten his cravat. He buttoned his waistcoat, then smoothed it once more. He buttoned his cuffs, inwardly groaning at how uncomfortable they were. He pulled his jacket on and tugged it into place. A quick adjustment to his hair made him entirely presentable.

He took a quick breath, then stepped into the open area at the foot of the staircase, preparing himself to present an image of easy and dignified interaction.

Mrs. Dalton was only just closing the door. No one had come inside.

Harold passed under the arch and joined her in the narrow entryway. "Do we not have a visitor after all?" He didn't manage to entirely hide his relief.

"A note's come from the Park." She held out a folded bit of parchment.

Leave it to Philip to wreak havoc on Harold's life even from afar.

He took the note and opened it.

Your Eminence,

At least he hadn't addressed it to "Holy Harry." All Harold's brothers had been calling him that for years. He hated it, and he didn't actually *hate* many things.

I write to you with news of great significance and possible concern. I also write with a question of a deep spiritual nature.

Harold doubted that.

Speaking hypothetically, if word were to reach me that visitors to the neighborhood are soon to arrive and I am absolutely certain their arrival will cause our otherwise stoic vicar to have a stroke, is it my spiritual duty as the patron of this parish to inform the archbishop before or after I break the news of our vicar's tragic demise to the poor gentleman's mother?

Philip never did do anything in the most efficient, direct, or somber manner.

"Have you heard of any new arrivals in the neighborhood?" he asked Mrs. Dalton.

She shook her head. "'Course, I don't spend my time chatting with the gossipy women in town."

He returned to the note, hoping Philip eventually got to the point.

Further, if my very welcoming family wishes to have the new arrivals to dinner soon after they return to the area and I extend an invitation to the vicar to join in the friendly gathering and he subsequently dies, would his death be an eternal mark on my soul? I only ask because watching our vicar topple over at the sight of the very person who shoved him into a nearby stream years ago might be worth the exchange.

Harold's heart stopped.

Please advise as to my best course of action for being both entertained and secure in my already shaky claim to salvation.

Yrs. etc.

Ph.

The person who shoved him into a nearby stream.

Harold knew precisely who the expected visitors were. His heart dropped to his shoes. He attempted to swallow past the lump suddenly forming in his throat.

Sarah Sarvol had, years earlier, during a previous visit to the neighborhood, sent him toppling into the rock-filled tributary. That was the last time he'd seen her but certainly not the last time he'd thought of her. Until that horrible day, she'd been his dearest friend, his closest confidante. More than that, she had been and still was the only woman he had ever loved.

Sarah Sarvol. He wasn't the least ready to see her again. He doubted he ever would be.

* * *

Liverpool

Sarah was in England for the first time in years. The familiar smells and sounds and chaos of Liverpool enveloped her as she walked at her brother's side along the docks. Her legs were grateful to be back on solid ground again after weeks at sea. Her heart soared higher with each passing moment.

I am back to stay. She had lived most of her life in America, but this felt like home. If she tried to explain the pull to anyone, she would most certainly fail. It was indescribable but undeniable. She and her brother, Scott, were relocating to England permanently, but home to Mother would always be America.

As the press of people on the dock grew closer, more tumultuous, Scott took hold of Sarah's arm. "Don't want you wandering off again."

She shook her head. "I was six years old when I did that. I would like to believe I have developed better judgment since then."

"You are much older now," he said quite somberly. "I understand matronly ladies are generally quite wise." Scott liked teasing her far more than any older brother should.

"Wise and occasionally violent," she answered. "So you would do well to watch yourself."

He smiled. "You like my teasing; admit it."

She tucked her arm more cozily through his. "You had best get all your jesting out of the way now. Our uncle hasn't a sense of humor." It was one of the things she remembered most vividly about the gentleman whose estate her brother would soon inherit.

Scott gave her a concerned look as he wove them through the crowd toward the line of carriages. "Can you endure it? A somber household might very well render you miserable."

She smiled up at him, allowing a hint of a laugh. "When have you known me to be miserable?"

He squeezed her arm. "Not ever."

"Well, I don't mean to start now."

Scott led them to a waiting carriage. The well-dressed man standing in front of it shook his extended hand. "Welcome back to England, Mr. Sarvol. Miss Sarvol."

"This is Mr. Clark," Scott told Sarah. "Our uncle's man of business."

She nodded her understanding. Much of the coming weeks and months would be filled with matters of business. Scott had worried about that, warned her of the very real possibility that she would spend a lot of her hours alone while he was educated and put to work. She hadn't the least concern about that. He was not a neglectful brother, and she was not one who needed to be entertained. She made her own happiness; she always had.

They were soon situated inside the carriage, Sarah facing forward, as was proper, the two gentlemen on the bench facing her. The carriage rolled forward, swaying and rumbling. How very tired she was of travel. The sea journey had been uneventful but long. The next leg, from Liverpool to

Nottinghamshire, would not take as long, but it was likely to be even more uncomfortable. Still, she could endure it. They were, after all, going home.

"How is our uncle?" Sarah asked.

"Frail," Mr. Clark said. "It will be good to have young Mr. Sarvol here for what time the elder Mr. Sarvol has remaining. That will allow the transition of ownership to be smoother."

Scott listened with brows drawn. "We would have come sooner, knowing he is poorly, but arrangements took longer than expected."

"The last few weeks have made a noticeable change in him." A heaviness filled his tone, which was devoid of tenderness. Few people liked Uncle Sarvol, not even his family. "Had he been this frail when I last wrote to you, I would have urged greater speed."

"Is Uncle Sarvol pleased that we are coming?" Sarah knew it unlikely but held out some hope.

"He has grumbled a great deal," Mr. Clark said. "He did, however, order the small study adjoining the library to be converted into a bedchamber for you, Mr. Sarvol."

Scott tossed Sarah an amused and confused look. "Off the library?" he repeated.

Mr. Clark nodded. "He wishes you to always be near the place where you will be working."

Sarah kept her expression serene despite the urge to laugh at her brother's odd arrangement. "How very exciting for you, Scott."

He chuckled. "I'm not afraid to work. The more I know about the estate, the better."

"And what will I be doing while you are chained to your ledgers?"

"You swore to me you would find plenty to occupy your interest."

She hadn't meant to cause him worry. "I am to be a permanent part of the neighborhood now. I mean to begin calling on our neighbors as soon as they initiate the connection—I do remember what I learned about the intricacies of interactions in this overly complicated kingdom."

Mr. Clark watched them with widened eyes. She had been told before that she was a bit exhausting. She also knew with perfect clarity that the silliness she and Scott indulged in was often confusing for those more accustomed to solemnity.

"You are not a stranger to the families around Collingham," Scott said. "I doubt they will wait even an entire day to make their calls; then you will be free to visit them as often as you like. The last time we were here, you were hardly at Sarvol House. Perhaps some of your friends are still in the neighborhood."

Mr. Clark unwound a length of twine from around a stack of documents. "If we could, Mr. Sarvol."

Sarah bit back a grin she knew Mr. Clark would not appreciate. It was simply odd to hear her brother addressed so formally, and by someone who was likely at least ten years Scott's senior. She needed to grow accustomed to it though. Everything was more formal here. And soon enough, her brother would be a gentleman of importance and position, and she would be mistress of his household. She would likely need to learn to be a little less ridiculous.

Mr. Clark and Scott dove into their discussion of land, investments, and tenants. Sarah's thoughts wandered.

She had made some wonderful friends during their previous visits to their uncle's home, just as Scott had said. But her previous visit had been filled with one person in particular: Harold Jonquil. Sweet, kind, handsome Harold Jonquil. They'd talked of dreams, futures, hopes. They'd walked around their families' gardens and out along a stream branching off the Trent.

She'd fallen top-over-tail in love with him in the full-hearted way only a starry-eyed sixteen-year-old girl could. He'd even kissed her on her last day in England, right before telling her he wouldn't ever write to her or accept any letters she sent him in a tone that indicated he would likely forget all about her the moment she set foot on the ship returning her to America.

His rejection had been thorough and precise, and he'd broken her heart.

He had been about to begin his clerical studies that long-ago summer. He would be a vicar by now, though only just, likely working and living in a distant parish, having entirely forgotten about the lovesick young lady he'd last seen running away, weeping. If he thought of her at all, it was likely with amusement.

Memories of him would be a little difficult when she first arrived in Collingham. He had a large family, and at least two of his brothers would still be living in the neighborhood. The difficulty wouldn't last long. She loved the area and the people there. She looked forward to making new memories now that she was grown enough and happy enough to move on from her disappointment.

She would make a new life for herself in her brother's household and forget Harold Jonquil had ever claimed even the smallest corner of her heart.

CHAPTER TWO

Nottinghamshire

SARAH WAS MORE THAN READY to be done traveling. As they passed through the town of Collingham, the nearest hamlet to Sarvol House, relief very nearly surpassed the nervousness she felt.

The carriage passed familiar lanes and houses, places she remembered well. After some time, she spied Farland Meadows, the estate where her cousin Bridget had lived. In the distance, the roof of Lampton Park, the grandest estate in the neighborhood and the Jonquil family home, rose above its surroundings. Many mornings and afternoons had been spent walking those grounds with Harold. They'd been bending the rules of propriety; they'd known that perfectly well, though nothing untoward had ever happened. The closest they'd come to anything scandalous was that disastrous kiss before she'd left.

To her surprise, she felt only the smallest twinge of regret seeing Lampton Park again. She ached for the girl she'd been and the dreams she'd had. But life hadn't been terrible since then. Most of her memories of this neighborhood were pleasant. Not all her memories of *him* were unpleasant.

The carriage turned off the main road toward Sarvol House. Nothing had truly changed on the familiar lane, though the trees that lined the side of the lane were taller, a little older. Her last visit had been in the summertime when the trees and shrubs were thick with leaves and the flowers were blooming in riotous color. But even in the shades of autumn, the surroundings were comfortingly familiar.

Mr. Clark had ridden ahead of them during this last day of their journey. Only Scott and Sarah sat in the traveling carriage, and Scott watched the landscape with the same expression of mingled anticipation and nervousness she felt.

"It will be strange being here without Father," he said.

"It is strange being *anywhere* without him." She hadn't yet grown accustomed to him being gone, despite the passage of almost two years. It hurt less acutely, but it still did not feel normal.

Scott slipped from his side of the carriage to hers and pulled her into a very brotherly side-hug. "Have I thanked you enough for undertaking this adventure with me? I couldn't imagine how lonely this new life would be without you here."

Lonely? She rolled her eyes. "Though it pains me to say as much, you are a rather exceptional gentleman—personable, friendly, and, as it turns out, the future owner of an estate in this neighborhood. I haven't the slightest doubt you will have no difficulty making the acquaintance of a great many people. 'Lonely' is not a state you need worry about finding yourself in, whether I am here or not."

"Well, I would miss you, regardless of the fact that I am impossibly handsome."

"I never said you were handsome."

He narrowed his eyes at her. "I think it was implied."

"Sisters aren't allowed to think their brothers are handsome. We are absolutely required to view you as obnoxious for all our lives."

"Obnoxiously handsome?"

She shook her head, grateful for his antics. She was more nervous than she was willing to admit. Being able to laugh with him helped tremendously.

The carriage turned as the drive looped back, offering a very impressive view of the red-stone house, with its twin bay towers and many chimneys. Three rows of narrow windows, evenly distributed and perfectly symmetrical, dotted the walls. The stately trees framed the picturesque sight. It was not so large and impressive as the house at Lampton Park or even Farland Meadows, but it was a fine and lovely estate.

"Are you ready to take all of this on?" she asked her brother.

"Ask me in a few weeks when I've had a chance to better understand what 'all of this' entails."

They rolled to a stop under the small front portico. The front door opened, and two lines of servants spilled out, fanning out in opposite directions, forming a V that joined at the doorway.

She felt Scott take a deep breath.

"Everything changes once we leave this carriage, doesn't it?" His attention didn't waver from the formidable scene.

"We are still together. We are still family. That doesn't change, Scott. That will never change." She sat forward and turned ever so slightly to face him. "Together we are equal to whatever lies ahead of us. I know we are."

He smiled. "Remind me of that now and then, will you?"

She gave a quick nod. Her brother was of an optimistic disposition most of the time, but he sometimes doubted himself. She had considered it her job from childhood to cheer him. "I will remind you of it so often you will say, 'For heaven's sake, Sarah, you are drowning me in encouragement.'"

He laughed silently. "I have said that a time or two, haven't I?"

"A time or two or three or four."

The carriage door opened. A footman stood at the ready to hand her down.

Heart pounding with anticipation, she scooted to the edge of the bench, moved to the door, and placed her hand in the gloved hand of the footman, carefully setting her foot on the step and making her way to the graveled ground below.

The servants watched her; some smiled, some seemed curious, and some were quite obviously eager to be getting on with their work rather than enacting this ceremony. Sarah saw among them many familiar faces, including the butler and housekeeper, Mr. and Mrs. Tanner. They were older now, likely approaching the age when they would need to be pensioned. Selecting a new housekeeper and butler would fall to Sarah. She wasn't entirely certain how to go about accomplishing that. Certainly someone in the neighborhood could explain that when the time came. People were generally willing to help.

Scott was quickly beside her. The servants offered their bows and curtsies, and then Mr. Clark stepped from the front door out into the afternoon light and motioned them inside with an efficiently worded welcome.

Mrs. Tanner followed them through the front door, instructing maids to take Sarah and Scott's outer things.

Sarah studied the familiar vestibule, with its tall ceiling and flat columns against either wall. "Did Uncle Sarvol have the walls rehung?" She didn't remember them being lavender.

"He did," Mr. Clark confirmed. "Only last year."

"The portraits have changed as well." She didn't see the one of her father that had hung amongst the others. Her cousin Bridget no longer had a portrait there. Even Uncle's portrait was gone. Instead, she was greeted by faces she did not recognize, stern people in clothing far out of date, sometimes by centuries.

"These are the previous masters and mistresses of this house," Mr. Clark said. "The senior Mr. Sarvol had their portraits placed here in recent months."

"Has he changed a great many things of late?" Scott asked.

Mr. Clark nodded but not in a truly firm manner. "Room colorings, portraits, moving around some furniture."

Scott gave Sarah a look of curious confusion. She had no more answers than he did. The house had not changed at all in the many years they'd been visiting. Even Uncle's wardrobe had remained unchanged. Why was he suddenly undertaking such upheaval?

At the end of the vestibule, two staircases led upward, one on either side. A vast hall spread out between this entryway and the remaining rooms of the house. Sarah had always loved this particular spot. Two large doors sat directly ahead, behind which was a grand ballroom. When she had last visited, she'd stood in the empty, dusty ballroom, imagining herself dancing with a handsome gentleman. By the end of her visit, her dreamed-of partner had a very real identity. As she'd sailed back to America after his thorough rejection, she'd sworn off golden-haired gentlemen. Life was far less complicated without them.

"I am certain I speak for my brother when I say I would very much like to rest for a time after so long a journey." She turned toward Mrs. Tanner, walking just a step behind them. "I haven't the first idea where I am meant to go though. I certainly hope I am considered to have outgrown the nursery."

Mrs. Tanner held back a smile. English servants, Sarah had discovered on previous visits, were quite stoic when interacting with their employers. To have brought even that hint of amusement to the very proper housekeeper's face lifted her spirits tremendously.

"I will show you, Miss Sarvol." She addressed Scott next. "Yours will be the room off the library, the one that, in the past, served as a secretary's office."

Scott nodded. "I know the room you're speaking of and can easily locate it."

Sarah could have as well. The library was on the ground floor, adjoining the ballroom. The secretary's office—Scott's bedchamber—sat just off the library. It boasted a door leading directly onto the back terrace. That would allow both privacy and freedom. Her father had been fond of that little room. He told her once he'd spent many an evening in there reading while his father worked in the library.

Scott leaned closer to her and said quietly, "Once you know where your bedchamber is, draw me a map so I can find you."

She shook her head at his absurdity. "I am certain it is with the guest chambers or in the family wing. I'll be easy enough to locate."

He made his way through the door to the library. Sarah turned toward the grand front staircase. All the bedchambers were above the ground floor. Mrs. Tanner, however, made her way to a low doorway between the library and the music room. She opened the door and watched Sarah with obvious anticipation.

Was she meant to go that way, then? She only vaguely remembered that doorway being there. It couldn't have led to any area of significance.

Beyond the doorway, she came upon a narrow stairwell, the plain and unassuming kind nearly always used by servants to navigate the house quickly and free of the interference of the family. A single window near the top lit the space. She spotted no wall sconces or candelabras. The space would be dark at night.

"Up this way, Miss Sarvol." Mrs. Tanner sounded truly apologetic.

"Could we not use the main staircase?" Sarah asked. The family bedchambers were accessible that way.

Mrs. Tanner shook her head. "This is the only connection to your chamber."

The only one, and it was a servants' staircase? This could not be a guest chamber. No architect would design such a thing. No hostess would resign a guest to such isolation.

"Is this a servants' room, then? I don't wish to see anyone tossed out of her room." Not to mention the oddity of being placed in a room reserved for a servant when she had arrived in full anticipation of being mistress of the house soon enough.

"This serves as the governess's rooms when there is one." Mrs. Tanner must have sensed Sarah's bafflement and disappointment. "It is a fine space, though; far larger than is usually reserved for a governess. And you will have a great deal of privacy."

"This is the only way to reach the room?" she asked again. The stairwell they'd used was dim and confined. *Privacy* didn't quite describe the arrangement. It felt far more like exile.

"The room does have a connection with the nursery," Mrs. Tanner said. "And the nursery is accessible from the main staircase. But this is the most convenient means of reaching the govern—your bedchamber."

They reached the top of the stairwell. Sarah was motioned through another small door. It was a very good thing she was not a terribly tall person.

The room that lay beyond the doorway was small, but it did not appear to be a bedchamber. A fireplace blackened by years of use sat against one wall. The opposite wall could not have been more than ten steps from it. At the far end was a small window, through which shone a shaft of much-needed sunlight.

"What room is this?" she asked.

"Some of the governesses have used it as a dressing room or a sewing room. One even had a small table and chair placed inside and took her meals here rather than in the nursery."

Sarah's heart dropped a bit. "Am I expected to take my meals here?"

"No, Miss Sarvol, though you certainly may if you wish." She motioned through a doorway on the adjacent wall. "Your bedchamber is through here."

Sarah moved warily across the threshold. The chamber beyond was finer than she had anticipated upon hearing "governess's rooms" and after seeing the tiny sewing and dressing room. It was nicely proportioned for a bedchamber that belonged to neither the master nor the mistress. The blue silk hanging on the walls, a very light, soothing shade, was a bit worn but was still in good condition. The fireplace was larger in the bedchamber than in the room she'd just passed through. It would offer much-appreciated warmth during the cold English nights.

"There is not a lot of furniture in this room," Mrs. Tanner acknowledged, "and none of it is new, but you should have all the necessities."

The necessities. That was a very good descriptor for the decorating style in these two rooms. A bed. A changing table. A bedside table. A clothespress. There was nothing else, not even a chair. The walls were even bare. The little adjoining room had been entirely empty.

A maid set Sarah's portmanteau and hat boxes on the floor beside the clothespress. A footman came in close on her heels with Sarah's traveling trunk.

"I haven't a lady's maid," she told Mrs. Tanner. "My mother judged it best that one be obtained here."

"I'll make certain a maid is available to help where needed until Mr. Sarvol approves the hiring of a lady's maid."

That likely wouldn't take too long. Though Uncle Sarvol had lived alone for a long time and had probably all but forgotten about abigails, the demands of a lady's toilette, and the impossible nature of a lady dressing herself in the complicated fashions of the day, a lady's maid was considered a necessity. Once he was made aware of the lack, all would be seen to.

She was soon alone in her sparse and quiet bedchamber. It was not ideal, but it was hers. She would make adjustments over time, making it more and more her own. And as soon as Scott was able to accompany her, a gentleman being necessary for the earliest visits, she fully meant to begin finding her place in the neighborhood as well.

"This is going to be perfect." Speaking the words out loud made it seem more possible. "It'll be just perfect."

CHAPTER THREE

Harold had lived in the vicarage for more than a year and, in that time, had never once been invited to dinner at Lampton Park when his mother wasn't in residence, despite his house sitting very near the Park, it being tied to the estate.

He wasn't offended—vicars ought never to be offended—but he was shocked when an invitation arrived to join his oldest brothers for a family dinner later that week. Mater had been in Shropshire for more than a month.

If Philip and Layton were requesting his presence without being forced to by Mater, it could mean only one of two things: either he was needed in his clerical capacity, or they meant to torture him. He might not mind so much that they heckled and tormented him if he could be at all certain they at least *liked* him.

He whistled as he went down the stairs. The days were growing shorter. The light spilling through the stained-glass window on the first landing grew dimmer earlier. Soon he would have to decide how many additional candles he could use without being indulgent or frivolous. A vicar should be frugal, after all. There were so many things a vicar ought to be.

"I know that tune," Mrs. Dalton called out from the kitchen.

He peeked his head in. "I wasn't issuing a challenge this time; I simply cannot get that ditty out of my head."

She rocked slowly in her chair by the low-burning fire. "You ought to suggest the choir sing it for mass on Sunday."

His heart clutched a moment at the thought. Mrs. Dalton didn't mind his idiosyncrasies, but if anyone else knew of them . . . *Act well your part.* "I likely should try harder to fill my mind with hymns instead. I'd be far less strange if I did."

"Strange ain't a bad thing."

When one meant to dedicate his life to being a respectable vicar, strange was a bad thing indeed. "Speaking of strange," he said, "I likely should be on my way to my brother's home."

Mrs. Dalton quietly laughed. "The young earl is unique, isn't he?"

"He is, indeed."

"Before you go, there's something needing attention that's too high for me to reach." She rose from her chair and motioned him back into the open area at the foot of the stairs. "This one will be a challenge."

"You said that last time."

She pointed to a high corner above the stairs. "We've a cobweb I can't get wiped up, and it's driving me mad."

He eyed the offending cobweb as well as the surrounding area. There was no way to place a ladder in the right location, neither did he have access to one that would be tall enough. Standing on a chair didn't work well in the middle of a staircase. Besides, chairs and ladders were incredibly uninteresting ways to accomplish the thing.

"I told you it would be a challenge," Mrs. Dalton said.

"I accept." He pulled off his jacket and hung it on the newel post. "I'll need a dust rag."

She pulled one from the pocket of her apron and handed it to him. "Best of luck to you, Mr. Jonquil."

He struck an overly confident mien. "I don't need luck; I have skill."

"You also have a house neglected by its previous owner. Don't think I'm not aware you've nearly spent yourself into the parish poorhouse making repairs here."

That was decidedly true, but he had no desire to dampen the excitement of the moment with those concerns. "I've tested the sturdiness of these things often enough to know they're sure." He took the steps two at a time, studying the cobweb above. At the first turn in the staircase, he began planning his route. The sill beneath the stain-glassed window. The banister. The lip of the wainscoting. He could manage this.

He unbuckled and slipped off his black leather shoes. They were decades out of date but had been left in the house by the previous occupant and, in a fortuitous turn of fate, fit him. He'd been surviving on a curate's income. Even now, as a vicar with an old and damaged vicarage, he was watching every penny. If only a clergyman's income were adjusted to account for the expenses incurred in the upkeep of the vicarage. Still, somehow, others managed it. So Harold kept his struggles and frustrations to himself, determined to prove to the world—and to himself—that he was capable of bearing the burdens of this position.

He set his shoes in the corner of the landing. They worked well enough for making calls and seeing to duties, but he'd found over the years that given the choice between climbing in his bare feet or climbing in his inflexible shoes, he did best to choose the former. He tucked his stockings into the shoes and rubbed his hands together in gleeful anticipation, then he tossed Mrs. Dalton a look of eager anticipation. "This is the best part."

"Taking your shoes off?" She liked to tease him about this oddity of his. Truth be told, he had a lot of them.

"Climbing."

He tucked the cleaning rag into the front of his waistcoat. With the tips of his fingers on the lip of the window and his toes on the sill, he pulled himself up. He set his other foot against the banister as he repositioned his hands to better hold himself. With quick, careful movements, he shifted one foot from the banister to the lip of the wainscoting. He kept the fingertips of one hand firmly gripping the top of the window. He laid his thumb over his fingers, pressing down on his fingernails to help keep the pads of his fingers in place despite the narrowness of the window frame. With the other hand, he pulled out the dust rag and stretched upward. A swipe made short work of the offending cobweb.

Harold made a quick assessment of the area directly below him, then hopped back onto the landing and spun about to offer a bow.

"You must have caused your mother no end of anxiety, climbing about like that."

He laughed as he sat on the nearest step and snatched up his shoes. "She wasn't privy to most of my climbing adventures. When I was little, I was considered a very valuable member of what we termed the 'Jonquil Freers of Prisoners,' a scheme we brothers concocted to help each other escape the nursery when our governess or tutors were punishing us."

"You helped your brothers break rules?" Mrs. Dalton pretended to be horrified. Nothing actually shocked the woman. "Perhaps you weren't born a vicar after all."

Perhaps not. What would his parishioners, his family think if they knew that though he managed to be the vicar he was supposed to be when undertaking his duties, he couldn't seem to help indulging in his undignified oddities when he was within these walls?

Harold had his stockings and shoes on once more. He walked down the stairs to where Mrs. Dalton stood and offered her the rag he'd used.

"You'd best pop your jacket on again, Mr. Jonquil. You've a family supper awaiting you."

It would be unvicarly of him to admit that he wasn't looking forward to it. Of all the members of his family, only Mater never laughed at him or mocked his efforts to be a proper and respectable vicar. She wouldn't be there to stop his brothers from mercilessly tormenting him.

"Don't fret, sir," Mrs. Dalton said. "If the evening proves too miserable, you can always climb out a window."

"Let us hope it doesn't come to that." He made his way under the arch leading to the front door, steeling his resolve to endure whatever lay ahead.

From behind him, Mrs. Dalton said, "Thank you for vanquishing the cobweb. I never could have reached it."

"I enjoyed doing it, though I shouldn't have."

"Why not?"

He stopped with his hand on the doorknob. "Vicars aren't meant to scale walls." *Or dread spending time with their families*, he silently added. *Or go about with rowdy songs in their heads. Or wish they could tuck themselves away instead of being out among people all the time. Or dread standing before the congregation to deliver a sermon.*

The walk to Lampton Park was not an overly long one, and the weather was fine. He had ample time to settle his thoughts and firm his resolve. Philip and Layton would be obnoxious—they always were—but he would remain unruffled.

By the time the Lampton Park butler showed Harold into the drawing room, he had summoned the look of mingled concern and contentment he'd practiced for so many years. He'd learned to exude calmness of mind and certainty of purpose whether or not he felt it.

His two oldest brothers and their wives were in the drawing room already. Layton stood beside Philip near the fireplace. Marion, Layton's wife, sat on a sofa beside Sorrel. Layton and Marion's children would not, it seemed, be joining them. Philip wore his usual dandified attire, but the others had also dressed quite formally for what Harold had assumed was a simple family dinner.

Marion spotted him first. In typical fashion, she welcomed him warmly and energetically.

Philip was quick to seize control of the discussion. "I hope you've not come with a sermon already in mind," he said. "I have a brilliant idea for a topic."

Layton bit back a laugh.

Harold refused to be nettled. "I have no intention of sermonizing at a dinner."

"What, not even a quoted psalm or an expounded-upon bit of holy writ?" Philip asked in theatrical shock.

"You had best send for Dr. Scorseby," Layton said. "I think Harold might be ill."

This was the point when Sorrel usually told them to be nice. But she sat silently beside Marion. She wore a look of pain Harold had seen on her face too many times.

He ignored his brothers and moved closer to her. "How are you this evening, Sorrel?" He wanted to ask after her well-being in greater detail, but there was a fine line between showing concern and being nosy. He never could be sure how to manage the thing. Erring on the side of caution had always seemed best, but he worried it made him seem insincere in his inquiries.

"I am sorely tempted to summon a footman to carry me in to dinner rather than walking there myself," Sorrel said.

Philip immediately moved toward her. "You're feeling that poorly? Scorseby said if things grew worse, you would need to be off your feet for the remainder of—"

"Do not get fussy, Philip. You know I cannot bear it when you get fussy."

His look of concern only grew. "I have reason to be fussy. We both know how very risky this is and the difficulties you are facing."

"Not now, Philip." Sorrel's whisper was tense and insistent. "Let us try to enjoy the evening."

Marion had taken hold of her hand and patted it reassuringly. "Take heart, Sorrel. Philip will be off to Shropshire in the morning, and I solemnly vow not to be the least bit fussy while he's gone."

Harold turned his attention to his oldest brother. "You are to be away?"

Philip nodded a touch too solemnly. "And I hope you will offer your most heartfelt prayers for my safe journey."

"I always do."

Philip laughed. Why did he always laugh? Harold was forever the object of his brothers' ridicule. It was disheartening.

"It seems our dear Arabella and young Lieutenant Lancaster mean to make things between them more permanent," Philip said. "I've been given the honor of standing in for our father, whom she would have asked, were he alive, to stand in for hers."

Arabella Hampton had grown up in the neighborhood, alongside them all. She was something of an adopted sister to the brothers and had served as Mater's companion for some time now. She was to have her own happy ending, it seemed.

"Will Mater be returning after the ceremony?" Harold asked. He missed his mother.

Philip nodded. "And we mean to haul back Charlie's battered and beaten body as well. So if you could prepare a eulogy, that would be helpful."

"Why must you be so morbid?" Marion asked in tones of horror. "His broken bones are nearly healed now. You make it sound as though he is a lifeless heap."

"I'm not entirely convinced that isn't what I will find when I get there," Philip said. "Mater may have been lying to us all these weeks."

"She hasn't been," Harold said.

All their eyes were on him after that pronouncement.

"Have you developed the second sight?" Philip asked. "How very pagan of you."

"It's more likely he had a revelation from on high," Layton said. "That is the way of things when one is treading the path toward sainthood."

Those two were insufferable when they were feeding off each other's absurdity.

"I wrote to the vicar of that parish," Harold said. "He has kept me apprised of Charlie's recovery."

Some of the jesting melted from Philip's expression. "And you didn't think to share with us the information you were receiving?"

"Dr. Scorseby made a very thorough report when he returned," Harold reminded them. "We all knew perfectly well that Charlie was recovering."

Layton's gaze narrowed on him, not in anger but curiosity. "What did you learn from this vicar?"

"That Charlie's spirits were a bit dampened by the experience but that he was recovering well. That Mater's presence improved his outlook. That Mr. Lancaster was not neglecting him. And that prayers for Charlie ought to focus on his patience during the recovery as he was not in danger of succumbing to his injuries."

"For future reference, Harry," Philip said, the annoyance in his expression reflected in his tone, "this additional information would have been appreciated, as the rest of us, not gifted with a personal messenger service from the church, have been doing a great deal of guessing these past weeks."

He could have shared what his colleague had passed along, but his efforts would have yielded only laughter, mockery, and, inevitably, dismissal. He knew the pattern too well by now to not anticipate it.

"What time did you tell our guests to arrive?" Sorrel asked Philip. "If I am to sit through a long and, no doubt, prosy meal, I would prefer to begin sooner rather than later."

Guests?

Philip was focused on his wife once more. "If you aren't feeling equal to—"

Her stern look stopped him midsentence. He held his hands up in a show of surrender and turned away. There was not often tension between the couple, but Harold had seen hints of it lately.

Approaching footsteps sounded in the corridor. The house was large enough that the arrival of carriages was not always audible. The mysterious guests had, it seemed, arrived. Sorrel would be granted her "sooner rather than later" request after all.

Harold slipped a bit away from the others. This was not his home, and thus, it wasn't for him to greet new arrivals. He'd found in the time since taking over parish duties that keeping to quiet corners while his more prestigious family members undertook their duties worked best for everyone. He could have a moment's respite from the mask his duties required he wear, and they would forget about him long enough not to pick at him.

Sorrel allowed Philip to help her stand. The brace that had been fashioned for her shattered hip had necessitated a change in her wardrobe to dresses that fit very loosely through the middle. The cut meant that most people likely could not tell that she was pregnant, though she was far enough along that if not for the design of her gowns, it would have been obvious.

Harold had been told early on by Mater, not because he was family but because he was the vicar and the outcome of this pregnancy was likely to be as devastating as the last two. He needed to be prepared to perform the various rites, should the child live long enough for him to do so, and to be on hand should Sorrel not survive the ordeal.

He understood the *what* of his duties should the worst occur, but the *how* of comforting, calming, and reassuring felt horribly elusive. Mr.

Pearsely would have known how. So would Father have. Harold had far less confidence in himself.

Layton tucked Marion's arm through his and joined his older brother at a proper distance from the drawing room door, ready to greet whomever had been invited.

Why hadn't Philip told him this was more than just family? Harold didn't mind interacting with people, but he appreciated warning. Their brother Corbin was always afforded that kindness. Harold needed it as well. Vicars weren't supposed to wish people to Hades, but there were times when being around people was just too much and he found himself doing exactly that.

Patience is a virtue. Endurance is a necessity.

The butler stepped inside and announced the new arrivals. "Mr. Scott Sarvol and Miss Sarvol, of Sarvol House."

The air in Harold's lungs turned solid. *Sarah. Merciful heavens. Sarah is here. Sarah.*

How was that possible? He'd heard for the first time on Sunday that she was expected. Why had word not reached him that she and her brother were in the neighborhood now?

Philip had planned an ambush. Harold's oldest brother had missed his calling; he ought to have been Wellington's right-hand man. They'd have ended the war with Napoleon far sooner but with far less dignity.

The butler stepped aside, clearing the doorway. Time slowed. Harold's heart pounded in pained anticipation. Years had passed since last he'd seen her, yet he could clearly picture her in his mind. Dark hair pulled up in a loose knot at the nape of her neck. Golden-brown eyes eagerly taking in all the world around her. A pert, upturned nose he had once, to her horror, described as adorable. She had, those long years ago, been the most tenderly pretty girl he'd ever known. She was likely now an unparalleled beauty.

Two shadows crossed the threshold, then stepped inside the drawing room. Harold spared only the briefest glance for Scott before his eyes found Sarah and refused to wander from the sight of her.

His brother Stanley's wife had been declared a diamond by Society during her Season. Athena Windover, who had attended Mater's house party a few weeks earlier, was praised in much the same way. Sarah Sarvol made them look dowdy by comparison. Perhaps it was simply that Harold had always found brunettes more attractive. Perhaps it was his younger self remembering how very much he had loved her.

Curse Philip and Layton, arranging this without giving him the least warning.

The six of them exchanged formal greetings, Harold keeping himself at a distance, trying to settle his thoughts.

Philip swung his quizzing glass on its ribbon, a sure sign he was about to undertake something ridiculous. "I know it's been a few years, but I'm certain you both remember the second-to-youngest of us."

He turned toward Harold. So did everyone else.

Drat.

He braced himself, forcing the calm neutrality he'd worked so hard to present over the years. Inwardly, he shook. How he hoped he wouldn't be expected to speak. Everyone would hear the trembling in his voice.

"I do remember him," Sarah said pleasantly enough, with no indication that seeing him again affected her at all or even really mattered much.

"Welcome back to the neighborhood." Harold hadn't the first idea how he managed the sentence whole with only the slightest catch in his voice.

Sarah Sarvol. At Lampton Park. His mind couldn't seem to reconcile it.

Sarah simply nodded and turned back to face the others. "It is good to see you, Layton," she said.

Layton's brow creased. His lips turned down, not in anger but something far closer to sadness. "You look so much like Bridget," he said quietly.

Sarah clasped her hands in front of her, glancing at her brother, then Philip. No one said anything. Harold didn't know what could be said after that observation. Bridget was Layton's late wife, who'd died tragically young shortly after their daughter had been born. Sarah was her cousin.

Layton hadn't looked away. "She was about your age when—" He cleared his throat. The hint of a smile he offered was stiff and forced. "Sarah, this is Lady Marion Jonquil, my wife."

Sarah pulled in a sharp breath. "You've married?" She sounded both amazed and overjoyed. "Oh, Layton. I'm so very happy."

She threw her arms around him. For a moment, Layton looked shocked. But just as quickly, his expression lightened, and he returned her embrace. He looked at Marion and mouthed, "Americans." Marion grinned in response.

Sarah had once embraced Harold with that same jubilant enthusiasm. He had nearly collapsed from the shock of it. That moment along the banks of the Trent was still one of his favorite memories. He thought of it often.

"Release our poor cousin, Sarah." Scott laughed out loud, shaking his head. "Uncle Sarvol's warnings obviously fell on deaf ears."

Philip watched him with curiosity and asked the very question hovering in Harold's thoughts. "What were his warnings?"

Sarah pulled away from her unexpected embrace, grinning from ear to ear. "He said I was to make particularly sure that I set aside my American manners and summon, instead, a more proper English mien. He seemed entirely convinced I wasn't capable of it."

Philip tapped a finger on his chin, eyeing Layton with immense curiosity. "Now, what would give him that impression?"

She wasn't the least offended. Harold remembered well that aspect of her personality. She was one of the happiest and most optimistic people he'd ever known.

"Uncle Sarvol also issued a warning to Scott." She tossed her brother a teasing look. "He said we would be dining tonight with the most influential family in all of Nottinghamshire, and one of the most important in the kingdom."

"What warning came along with that pronouncement?" Philip was clearly enjoying the conversation.

Scott answered. "I was told to make absolutely certain I did nothing to convince any of you that I am an idiot, as that would reflect poorly on the Sarvol family."

Sarah returned to her brother's side and slipped her arm through his. "So, Scott will do his best to suppress any idiotic tendencies he has, and I will attempt to be less American than my accent would indicate I am, and we will hope for the best."

A grin split Marion's face. "Oh, I do like you, Sarah Sarvol. We are going to get along excellently."

"I suspect we will."

Sorrel leaned in closer to Philip. "I need to sit down, dear."

In a flash, Philip had the butler announce dinner and then moved quickly and carefully from the drawing room, Sorrel holding fast to his arm and her walking stick. Layton walked hand in hand with Marion. Sarah kept her arm through Scott's.

They all left, not one of them noticing Harold had been left behind. The moment Sarah slipped from sight, he pushed out the breath he'd been struggling with.

For years, he'd wondered what would happen if he ever came face-to-face with Sarah again. She had been crying the last time he had seen her. It was an image he'd not been able to entirely clear from his thoughts, despite the passage of so much time. He'd worried she would still be hurt or angry. He'd played out this moment in his mind so often. Would she rage at him? Laugh? Would she cry again?

The reality of their reunion was both worse and far better than what he'd imagined. She hadn't more than glanced at him. She'd hardly noticed him there, and she certainly hadn't seemed burdened by memories of what had transpired between them. She was fine.

He swallowed against an unexpected lump in his throat.

She was fine.

Why, then, did he feel as though he would never be fully fine again?

CHAPTER FOUR

Harold Jonquil had changed. Sitting in the church, listening to his sermon on Sunday, she knew there was something fundamentally different about him. The alteration went beyond the fact that he was taller than he'd been when last she'd seen him, which was saying something, considering he was a Jonquil and Jonquils were known for being noticeably tall. It was also more than his being grown up now rather than being nearly so. It was more than how withdrawn he'd been during dinner at Lampton Park.

Something was different in his expression, in the way he held himself. He had always been more private and quiet than most would guess, but now he was distant. Aloof.

But it was more even than that. He was not the same person. She didn't know how else to describe what she was seeing.

He had told her often of his desire to join the clergy and have a parish of his own. He'd spoken of building people's faith, of touching their lives, of doing good in the world. He had not necessarily been eloquent in those long-ago, very personal discussions, but he had been passionate. There was no fervor in his words or expression now. Not an ounce of it.

What happened to you, Harold Jonquil?

How many times had she told herself during the journey here that she would put him from her mind? He had rejected her thoroughly and soundly. Why, then, was the mere sight of him, changed as he was, enough to tug real regret and mourning from her heart?

Beside her, Scott struggled to stay awake. Uncle Sarvol, on his other side, had been asleep for long minutes. Few in the congregation seemed to truly be listening. That was not entirely unusual, even when the sermon was delivered with feeling and ardor, but this was not the way she had imagined Harold taking on the mantle he'd so long worked toward.

"I could make a difference," he'd once said. "I won't have a title or a place in the government. I won't have a say in the law or the movement of armies. But the things I do each day will have a real impact on real people living real lives. It will matter."

Why, then, did it not seem to matter any longer? *He* almost looked bored.

Perhaps part of her grief grew from the fact that she shared those dreams he'd spoken of. She too wished to do good in the lives of the people around her. Serving and helping, touching people, changing the world in small but real ways had defined her longed-for future as well. It was still what she wanted. He seemed to have lost that fervor.

A few pews ahead and across the middle walkway, Layton's little girl, Caroline, whom Sarah hadn't seen since she was a baby, craned her neck enough to look back at Sarah. She must be six years old by now.

Caroline twisted so she faced fully backward, then curled her fingers around the back of her pew and rested her chin on top of her hands. She smiled at Sarah, a little shyly, a little hopefully. The girl had not been at Lampton Park for the dinner Sarah and Scott had taken there. Though Sarah knew her, she was likely a complete stranger to the sweet little girl.

Caroline's thick golden curls and bright-blue eyes declared her a Jonquil as little else could. But the child had her mother's small, upturned nose and all-encompassing smile. Seeing her, Sarah missed her cousin. Bridget, despite being eight years her senior, had been dear to her, a combination of older sister, beloved friend, and desperately needed confidante.

Layton noticed his daughter's distraction. He twisted a bit as well to see what had so captured her attention. His eyes fell on Sarah. She couldn't say if his smile was one of apology or tempered censure. He nudged his daughter forward-facing once more. The movement caught Lady Marion's attention. She, with a little bundle of her own resting against her shoulder, one remarkably well-behaved despite being at the usually disruptive age of somewhere between one and two years old, glanced back at Sarah as well.

Sarah mouthed an apology and received a bright smile in return, one that set her mind at ease. Layton had been as open and kind and dear to her as Bridget had been during every visit Sarah had made to Nottinghamshire, except for the last one. Bridget had died shortly before then. Layton had still been deeply in mourning. He'd seen no one, spoken to no one.

The slightest pause in the droning on of Harold's sermon caught Sarah's attention. She glanced at the pulpit. He had, in fact, paused and was, to her horror, looking at her. She wasn't being disruptive. Indeed, she'd not made a sound. It was hardly her doing that Layton's family had taken it in turns to look back at her.

Sarah folded her hands on her lap and lowered her eyes. Half the congregation was asleep. A good many of the younger congregants were squirming in their pews. Harold was making little to no attempt to capture anyone's attention, let alone "build their faith" or "touch their lives." She had sat perfectly quiet—and *awake*—through the entire thing, and he was lobbing a look of disapproval at *her*? It seemed Harold Jonquil was not done humiliating her; at least the misery he'd caused years earlier had been inflicted in private.

She didn't look up again as he droned on. When the time came for communion, she kept to her pew. One ought not approach the vicar for so sacred a rite when one was having uncharitable thoughts about that vicar.

The congregants began filing out once the service was over. Sarah sat beside Scott, silently bristling. Years earlier, Harold would have shared a conspiratorial smile with her over something as inconsequential as a child shuffling about during services. He'd even spoken about his wish that Sunday mass be a little more personal and less dreary. Had he become precisely the kind of unapproachable, uncaring vicar he'd decried all those years ago? She hoped not. He might not have loved her in the end, but she had cared deeply for him. A part of her still did.

Scott leaned his head a touch closer to her. "Should we wake Uncle?"

"If we leave him here, I might be able to spend the remainder of the day somewhere other than my bedchamber." Uncle had proven a bit too sharp-tongued; she had kept to her rooms much of the past two days.

Scott sighed. "I do not understand why he is so unkind to you. He was never this unwelcoming before."

She laughed. She couldn't help herself. "Did you never wonder why I didn't join you and the rest of the family for dinner when we visited in the past?"

His forehead creased. "You were too young."

"I am only a year younger than you are, you dolt."

He frowned. "I hadn't thought of that."

"I was not forbidden from joining, but Father thought it best to not subject me to his brother's unpredictable temper and propensity for insult. Bridget often joined me in the nursery. She was not unaware of the sort of person her father was, especially toward girls and young ladies. 'He finds us a waste of time,' she once explained. I preferred not to waste my time being treated that way, something Father convinced me was wise."

A group of young women, likely somewhere near sixteen or seventeen years of age, passed by the pew, blushing deeply and staring openly at Scott. That had happened quite often over the years. Sarah found it endlessly entertaining. Scott, though certainly not vain, seemed to enjoy it as well.

He rose. "Good morning to you all."

One of them spoke. "You have an accent."

"On the contrary." He flashed them a winning grin. "*You* are the one with an accent."

Giggles and ever-broadening smiles followed.

"Do you live here now?" another member of the group asked.

"I do." He bowed a little.

The giggles grew almost frantic, and the girls undertook a swift departure.

"It is unfair to torture them, Scott," she said. "Especially on a Sunday inside a church."

"Nonsense. That was the most interesting thing that occurred in here all morning."

Sarah rose, shaking her head in frustration. "I do not know what happened to Harold Jonquil. He never used to be a prosy bore. Quiet, yes, but not tedious."

"People change, Sarah. It is one of the few unavoidable facts of life." He glanced at their uncle. "Of course, some people simply become more of what they've always been."

"More cantankerous, you mean?"

"More sleepy." If any of his eager admirers had still been nearby, they might have actually swooned at the grin he tossed her. "Perhaps if we make enough noise, Uncle will wake on his own."

It was worth trying. The chapel was very nearly empty. The last of the congregants were at the door, making their way outside. Sarah held her Book of Common Prayer out beside her and let it drop on its face to the flagstone floor. It landed with a thud that echoed off the stone walls and pillared, pointed archways. Uncle stirred a bit but didn't awaken.

"I almost hate to wake him," Scott said. "A fellow doesn't get to nap that deeply very often."

"Unless that fellow happens to live here, and then he is afforded the opportunity every Sunday." Sarah had seen enough sleeping forms and not nearly enough surprise to tell her the sedative quality of the sermon was not new.

"Perhaps we could hire Morris dancers," Scott suggested.

"To deliver the sermon?"

"No." He laughed. "To wake our uncle. Though Morris dancers delivering a sermon would be exciting, and very English."

"For all we know, exciting sermons might be outlawed in this country," Sarah warned him, assuming a very stern tone. "You will get us stoned if you're not careful."

"Perhaps the stoning could be delayed until next week's services. Everyone would stay awake for that."

Sarah pressed her palms together in a pose of pious solemnity. "And that would be a miracle worthy of recounting for generations to come."

Scott laughed deeply. Sarah turned to look at Uncle Sarvol, wondering if he had awoken. It was not her uncle, though, who seized her attention but Harold standing in the middle aisle only a few pews back, looking at her.

Would the sight of him ever not send her heart into frantic spinning? She tucked it away, telling herself not to be overset. She could acknowledge that he was still quite handsome and that the young gentleman she had known had, with his kind heart and attentiveness, rightly captured her girlish heart. But she didn't need to fall to bits over this transformed version of him.

"Mr. Jonquil," she said.

"Miss Sarvol." He offered a very stiff dip of his head. "Were you in need of something?"

An explanation for the enormous change in him would be nice.

She kept her expression unconcerned. "Our uncle has fallen asleep, and we are debating the best method of awakening him."

Harold eyed her uncle. In sober tones, he said, "Have you tried a gentle nudge?"

"An excellent suggestion," Scott said. "We will try that."

Harold nodded and walked toward the pulpit. Under his breath, he added, "It ought to work at least as well as Morris dancers."

Scott turned wide eyes on Sarah and whispered, "He heard."

"We'd best hurry home before the stoning begins."

Scott nodded. "I will fetch Uncle's wheeled chair and think of a means of awakening him while you make good your escape. He's not as likely to forgive *you* for disrupting his sleep."

That was truer than it ought to have been.

She picked up her prayer book and slipped from the pew. She turned to face the back, intending to leave quickly. Her feet, however, refused to make the short journey. She stood rooted to the spot.

Talk to him, her mind insisted, even as her heart shouted its objections.

Apparently, her mind was in charge. She turned and faced the pulpit. Harold had collected some papers and was just then descending the steps. She moved slowly in that direction. He spotted her quickly but looked neither intrigued nor surprised. He wore the same expression he had throughout his sermon, throughout the dinner she'd taken at Lampton Park. She felt almost as if she were looking at a painting of a vicar rather than a living, breathing person.

She stood at the end of the first pew, and he stopped in front of her.

"You left so soon after dinner at the Park that I hadn't the opportunity to speak with you." It was something of a clumsy beginning to a conversation, but it was the best she could manage. She was not usually tongue-tied but certainly was in that moment.

"I had not yet finalized my sermon," he said. "I needed to return home to complete it."

She could accept that, though it struck her as not entirely true. "You did always hope to be granted this living. The timing proved better than you feared it would."

He gave a solemn nod. Did he ever strike any expression other than this bland emptiness? It just was not the Harold Jonquil she had known . . . and loved.

"Are you happy in your situation?" she asked out of genuine curiosity. No matter that she'd had no lasting role in his happiness; she still wished it for him.

His posture remained stiff and pious, his expression unchanged. "One is not made happy by one's situation but by one's choice."

He couldn't even answer her simple question without a pious bit of preaching.

"Are you happy?" she asked again.

He raised an eyebrow whilst lowering the corners of his mouth. That was a new expression since last she'd seen him. It might have suited a stuffy old cleric, but it served only to make him appear more severe and less approachable, two things a shepherd of a flock ought not be.

Harold didn't seem inclined to answer.

She chose a different topic. "Did Lady Lampton go to Shropshire with Philip? She was not here today."

Harold shook his head. "Her health does not always permit her to leave home."

Sarah had wondered if that was the culprit. The young Lady Lampton had spent the entirety of the dinner party with a vague look of discomfort, sometimes giving way to one of obvious pain. And though her gown hid it well, Sarah had not missed the fact that the countess was in expectation of a new arrival. "I do not know her well. Do you think she would object to me calling on her?"

Harold adjusted his papers and prayer book. "She is all that is proper and will receive you graciously."

Sarah only just stopped herself from rolling her eyes. "I did not mean would she object *socially*. I was concerned that receiving visitors might have a negative impact on her health."

"That, I do not know." Everything about him spoke of a desire to flee. Other than that final, fateful encounter on the banks of the stream of Lampton Park, he had never before seemed eager to be away from her.

That hurt more than it should.

She tried not to think on the change, so she returned to the topic at hand. "When you have called on your sister-in-law, has she seemed improved by the company or drained by it?"

"I do not often call on her," he said.

That was unexpected. "But her health is fragile; you have said as much yourself. You are not only her brother-in-law but her vicar as well."

Somehow his demeanor grew even more austere. "I am not unwilling to do my duty. They have sent for me when I have been needed."

When I have been needed. It was a very distanced approach to serving a parish. "Provided you aren't 'needed' when you have a sermon to complete, I suppose."

"Or when I am corralling Morris dancers," he said dryly. It was the first bit of humor she'd seen in him, a rare sign of life in this stone-cast version of him.

She very nearly smiled. "You have to admit it would liven things up significantly."

He stepped past her. "Sermons aren't meant to be 'lively.'"

"Then I would say today's was bang up to the mark."

He turned back around. "Are you lodging a complaint, Miss Sarvol?"

"I am expressing confusion," she countered. "I expected . . ."

"Expected what?" The question was the tiniest bit hesitant.

"More," she said. "More of the vicar you ought to be."

No one hearing him in the past could have felt anything but hopeful and eager in anticipation of the good he would do and the compassion he would show. And now, if his own telling was accurate, he did his duty when called on to do so but kept to himself otherwise. She hoped her impression was wrong.

"I do not claim expertise," she said, "but I do know what I would wish a vicar to be."

"I am not it?" His tone was unreadable. His expression looked almost confused.

"I don't know yet," she admitted. "I've not seen anything that would indicate you are." She surprised herself with the admission. Were he any other person, she would have kept her comments to herself. But Harold Jonquil—her sweet, kind Harold—ought to have been more than he had become. Did he not remember the weeks they had spent together? The dreams they had told each other of?

"Perhaps, Miss Sarvol, you would—you would do better in this role than you feel I currently am." The stiffness of his response added a degree of arrogance that pricked at her further.

"I believe I could do a good job of vicaring," she said.

That golden brow pulled ever lower. "Are you issuing a challenge?"

She hadn't been, but seeing a bit of fire rise in him, she found herself unwilling to disabuse him of the assumption. "Are you accepting?"

He returned to that infuriating calm that so ill-fit him. "A vicar's duties can only be performed by one ordained—"

"Not all of a vicar's duties require ordination. I would go so far as to say some of the most important do not."

"And those are the matters on which you mean to challenge me?"

She watched him, wanting to know how he truly felt beneath the veneer of solemnity. The Harold she had known would have laughed, then he would have accepted the rather absurd dare simply as a bit of fun and a chance to serve the people around them. *This* Harold seemed to consider it only as a matter of pride.

Serving and helping her neighbors, coming to know them on a personal level, was the best way she knew to make a place for herself among them. She had intended to do that anyway. If she could ruffle Harold a little *and* be of help to her neighbors, it seemed a fine way to begin her time in Nottinghamshire.

"Yes," she said. "Those are the matters on which I mean to challenge you. Serving your flock. Seeing their struggles. Leading in matters of compassion. Filling the myriad needs in the area."

"You can do that better than I can?"

She shrugged slightly. "That is what we intend to discover, is it not?"

Her determination clearly caught him by surprise. Did he not remember her at all? She'd always been a bit too stubborn and energetic for her own good.

"You do realize I will simply keep seeing to my duties. I am already filling the role you will be attempting to sort out." He almost seemed to be warning her.

"I don't appear worried, do I?"

His gaze narrowed. "You didn't used to be this headstrong."

This time, she actually did laugh. "I was absolutely this headstrong. You were simply not this indifferent."

He quirked that eyebrow again. She suspected she was going to grow to either dislike that particular expression or find it endlessly amusing.

"Very well," he said as though it truly didn't matter in the least.

"Is there to be a forfeiture to the winner?" she asked.

"Gambling is hardly in keeping with the dignity of a servant of the church." His mouth twisted in disapproval.

And there was another look that was new since last she'd seen him. She didn't care for it either.

She offered a dip of her head and an abbreviated curtsy. "I look forward to our competition, Mr. Jonquil."

"And I do not expect to particularly notice, Miss Sarvol."

The sally was well delivered, likely more so than he realized. He didn't care enough to take notice, but she still cared deeply enough for him to wish to see him happy, fulfilled in his work, living a full life. It seemed things were nearly as lopsided between them as they'd been that long-ago day on the stream bank. She cared; he didn't.

She tipped her chin up and slipped past him, moving all the way to the door of the church and out into the churchyard without slowing or looking back. Uncle Sarvol was nowhere to be seen, no doubt having been taken home by one of the servants, but Scott had waited for her at the gate.

By the time she reached him, she was fairly shaking. Years' worth of trying not to think of the dreams she had once entertained were proving insufficient in that moment. She had, it seemed, been less than honest with herself. She didn't love Harold any longer, at least not this new version of him, but her heart had not truly healed.

She would take up the challenge she had not intended to issue. She would carve out a place for herself in this neighborhood and, perhaps in doing so, finally close the chapter in her life that had begun so many years earlier in this same corner of the world with a young gentleman who, she feared, no longer existed.

CHAPTER FIVE

AT THE TOP LANDING OF the vicarage staircase, a portion of the banister doubled back on itself, creating a section that was twice as thick and twice as sturdy. It was tucked a bit behind a bend in the wall, making it inaccessible to anyone unable or unwilling to do a bit of climbing and balancing. Harold was more than capable of both. That corner had become his thinking spot over the past year, precarious though it was.

He sat there Sunday evening, unsure if he was more confused or upset. Sarah had been in the neighborhood less than a week. Mere days. Yet she had declared him a poor excuse for a vicar, insisting she could and would do better than he at the very duties to which he had dedicated his life. He'd made a study these past years of what a vicar did and was. He had learned to do and be precisely that. Now she was dismissing him as quickly as his brothers had.

Only three people in all the world had ever expressed unfettered faith in him as a future man of the cloth. His father, who was no longer there to offer reassurance. Mater, who was temporarily too far away for one of her encouraging talks. And Sarah.

Now even she has declared me a failure.

He harbored so many doubts in himself. To his frustration, he needed reassurances. Being so utterly without them was undermining every bit of confidence he'd struggled to gain, amplifying every uncertainty.

Mrs. Dalton came up the stairs, spotting him as she turned the corner at the first landing. "What's happened to send you into your corner?"

He rolled his shoulders, careful not to upset his precarious balance. "A difficult encounter with . . . a parishioner."

She remained on the landing below, placing her halfway between the ground floor and the one he was perched beside. She leaned back against the frame of the stained-glass window. "Someone suffering? Or someone complaining?"

"Complaining," he said. "According to this particular person, I am doing a poor job as vicar."

"And that matters to you, does it?"

"Doing a good job matters to me very much." If being a vicar was who he was and he was terrible at it . . .

She shook her head. "I meant that this particular person thinks poorly of you."

It did matter. She had once laid claim to his heart. Truth be told, that organ was still not whole. Part of him doubted it ever would be. He had loved her too deeply to recover entirely.

"I don't know if I want to prove the assessment incorrect more as a means of producing evidence that I *am* a good vicar," he said, "or because I really want to—" He stopped himself.

With an almost wicked grin, Mrs. Dalton finished for him. "To have the satisfaction of hearing this person admit to being bacon-brained?"

He winced at the accuracy of that. "Rather unbecoming for a vicar, isn't it? Which makes me wonder if maybe I *am* as inept at this as I was told I am."

"C'mon, then." She motioned him over. "I'll lend you a mother's ear since your mum ain't here right now. Hop down."

A mischievous impulse seized him. "Hop down?" He twisted so his legs hung over the open area of the stairwell, his hands on either side of him.

"I didn't mean for you to do exactly that," she insisted. "You'll break your neck."

He wiggled his brows. "Prepare to be amazed."

He lowered himself slowly so he hung from the top of the banister. One hand at a time, he moved to the bottom of two adjoining rails, then, hand over hand, moved himself to where the stairs turned.

Mrs. Dalton likely didn't fully appreciate how hard climbing was when one couldn't use one's legs. If not for his regular clandestine trips to the nearby ruins of an old abbey, where he climbed the familiar rock walls to his heart's content far from witnesses and prying eyes, or the abandoned chapel he'd climbed during his years at Cambridge, or even the exterior walls of Lampton Park when he was growing up, this wouldn't have been as easy as it was.

Only two rungs down the now-downward-sloping banister, he set his feet within an easy distance of the rising stairs below him. He released his grip and dropped softly onto an obliging step.

Mrs. Dalton swatted at him. "I think you enjoy giving me heart palpitations."

"Does not my singing voice manage that already? Palpitations of the most enjoyable variety, of course."

She shook her head. "You're trouble, you are." She often pretended to be annoyed with him, but her eyes gave her away. Mrs. Dalton enjoyed his company. He treasured her for that. Few people liked having him around.

She motioned him to walk with her. He tucked his hands in his trouser pockets. He often went without a jacket in the house. It was more comfortable and far easier to climb about.

"Now, what is it you've been accused of neglecting?" Mrs. Dalton motioned him into the kitchen. That was her domain and the place he most often went now for company and conversation. He hadn't fully anticipated the loneliness of being a vicar. Though he was most at home in smaller groups and felt most comfortable when not required to speak, he still missed being around people. He still longed for company.

"I was told I need to do better at serving my flock. Seeing their difficulties. Compassion. Meeting needs."

To her credit, Mrs. Dalton looked properly surprised. "That's most of what a vicar does."

He nodded, dropping onto the stool by the fire. "Everything outside of the rituals and rites of the office. It was a blow, I tell you."

"I figured as much when I saw you in your corner."

He met her eyes, expecting laughter or mockery. He saw none. "Have I told you how much I appreciate that you don't laugh at those parts of me that aren't as refined as they ought to be?"

"M'father was one of the best men I ever knew," she said, "and no one would have described him as refined. I don't need that in any person to see worth in him."

Her words helped. She, at least, would value him while he worked to be more of what he was supposed to be. He examined his upturned palms and the heavy calluses created by years of climbing. These were not the hands of a vicar. Did anyone else notice? Did it bother them?

"So this person who complained," Mrs. Dalton said, "can I know who it was?"

There seemed little harm in that. She wouldn't go about whispering in everyone's ears. And she might help him sort the whole mess out. "Miss Sarvol," he said.

Her brow pulled in thought. "Mr. Sarvol's niece who's just come from America?"

He nodded. "She's visited often over the years. We're near enough the same age that we've known each other more or less all our lives." He didn't intend to speak of their attachment and tenderness during her last visit, nor confess to the kiss they'd shared and Sarah's reaction to it. "She apparently has been unimpressed since returning."

"Mere days ago," Mrs. Dalton added drily.

"Yes." Harold stood and paced away. "I pointed out that she hadn't been here long enough to know how I was performing my duties. She was unmoved. Indeed, she went so far as to issue a challenge, insisting *she* could do better serving and tending and, outside of rites and such, being a vicar than I. I don't know whether to be more upset, amused, or . . . or worried."

Mrs. Dalton made a sound of pondering. He paused in his pacing to look at her.

"I think you ought to accept the challenge," Mrs. Dalton said.

He laughed a little, mostly in exasperation. "I will do just as I told her I would: continue as I have since being made curate here and now vicar. She would soon see that I do a fine job despite her current doubts."

Mrs. Dalton nodded.

"I am a good vicar." The declaration sounded more like a question than he would have liked.

"You are," she answered.

"Despite my propensity for drinking songs?" he pressed with a smile.

"The songs I can overlook. Climbing the walls like a spider . . . that's a little less excusable." That she grinned immediately afterward told him all he needed to know.

"You are a gem; do you know that?"

"I do." She spoke with a firm confidence he wished he possessed. Too many years of being mockingly called "Holy Harry" had undermined his certainty in himself more than he cared to admit. "I believe good will come of this odd contest, Mr. Jonquil. Having another person doing good in the area certainly won't hurt anyone."

That was true. He nodded, feeling surer in his course of action. "This will be a good thing."

"And it might keep you from climbing out onto that banister again." Mrs. Dalton shuddered. "I don't know how your mother survived seeing you doing things like that."

"Just don't tell her I'm still doing it, and I think we'll be fine."

"My word of honor." She nodded to him. "Now, you go think of some good deeds you can do, knowing what you know of the neighborhood—something Miss Sarvol hasn't had the chance to learn yet—so you can get first crack at this competition of yours. That'll give her pause, I'd dare say."

It would, at that. And it might offer him a much-needed bit of confidence, something that was far too often lacking.

* * *

Once a week, the parish choir met at the church to practice their hymns for Sunday services. Harold always attended, though he did not participate. Being present allowed him to show his support for their efforts while enjoying the soothing strains of their music. He brought along his portable writing desk and sat in a pew, working on his sermons or correspondence. It was a good arrangement all around.

That week, on the day of choir practice, he'd spent a good part of the afternoon at the abbey ruins, a thirty-minute ride from Collingham. Climbing helped him work out his frustrations. But he'd been there longer than he'd expected and returned with barely enough time to clean himself up and get to the church.

He fortunately arrived before anyone else, as he was meant to, and opened the church. He'd cut that too close.

He lit the candles near the doorway and a few surrounding the pews, giving light enough for him to set his portable writing desk on his usual choir-night pew. He whistled as he made his way toward the chancel to light the candles there. For the length of a few bars, he didn't think about the tune he'd chosen, then the truth of it penetrated his thoughts: "Good Ale for My Money." He was whistling a tune about ale. In the church.

"Act well your part," he reminded himself, then silently added, *you clodhead.*

After a moment—a silent one—he had the lamps and candles lit. This was one of his favorite moments in the week. The chapel was quiet and peaceful. The flicker of candlelight glittered on the stained glass high above in the clerestory. He stood alone in a building where his family had stood and worshiped for centuries. In these quiet moments alone in the chapel, without the pressures of his responsibilities or the requirement to talk to endless streams of people when he was overwhelmed and tired, he felt peace. He felt a connection to generations of his family that was hard to explain. He felt almost as if they were there as well, silently surrounding him. Supporting him.

Philip and Layton would have harassed him for the rest of his life if they had the first idea that he thought such things. They didn't understand what it was like to need the reassurance that came from imagining his family buoying him up and hoping they were proud of him.

Would Father have been proud? His gaze turned, as it so often did, to the family pew and the spot where his father had always sat. Father and Mater would likely have preferred to sit together, but with so many young boys to keep an eye on, most of whom had had a tendency toward rowdiness, they'd needed to adopt a more strategic arrangement.

Harold had usually sat on his father's left side. He still sometimes found himself expecting to smell Father's shaving soap when he entered these walls. He still half expected to hear his voice. Harold had adopted a habit when he was very young of bringing a bit of paper and a lead pencil with him on Sundays. He would scratch out questions for his father, then pass the bit of parchment to him. Father always wrote out an answer, no matter how silly the inquiry. Sometimes Harold asked after unimportant things. Sometimes his questions were far more serious. Still, Father answered. He'd always answered.

But his place on that pew was empty now. It had been for half of Harold's life.

"I wish you were here," he whispered. "I have so many questions, and I don't have anyone to answer them."

Silence. And an empty pew. That was all he had in that vulnerable moment.

There was a reason he didn't sit there during these choir practices. The music was and ought to be joyful. He did not wish to attach his grief to it.

He made his way to his writing spot. He'd not even sat down before Mr. Felt, who acted as head of the choir, stepped inside.

"Good evening," Harold said.

The usual nod answered. "Good evening."

Harold took his seat and opened his portable writing desk. That night, he meant to work on his sermon. He had set his Bible and Book of Common Prayer next to him on the pew when the sound of jovial voices floated in. The rest of the choir had arrived.

Harold stood once more and turned to face them as they made their way toward the choir stalls. They saw him and dipped their heads.

"Good evening," he said to the group as they passed. He received a near-unison "Good evening" in response.

They passed on to their places, and he retook his seat. Usually, they began rehearsing directly, warming their voices with various vocal exercises. This time, however, they launched into a discussion.

He didn't pay them much heed; they didn't need his interference. His responsibilities required him to talk often enough that he appreciated those moments when he could silently fulfill his duties.

An unmistakable American accent entered their conversation. "I do sing, but I can see that all the seats in the choir are occupied."

Sarah. Harold's head snapped up. He didn't have to search for her. Other than Mr. Felt, she was the only one not sitting.

"My goal, though, is to assist with the music in whatever way would be most helpful," she continued. "Simply tell me what I can do."

Helpful. Sarah was beginning her campaign. He ought not to have been surprised.

"I could use help organizing," Mr. Felt said. "There's so very much to arrange and prepare. Someone to keep hold of the music, hand it out, and collect it, to arrive a bit ahead of services and set the music in the stalls. That would allow a smoother transition on Sundays."

It was far from the enjoyment one would have participating in the singing when that was what she'd wanted to do, but Sarah showed no signs of disappointment or reluctance. She was, after all, filling a need, which was part of their wager.

"These are the pieces we are singing this week." Mr. Felt gave her a small stack of papers. "These"—he handed her another—"we will perform the following Sunday. And these"—he added more still—"are for the week after that."

Sarah nodded. "I'll give them this week's music. Let me know when you are in need of the next."

She did exactly as she'd offered, placing a sheet of music on the various stands throughout the stalls. She moved about with a bounce in her step. How well he remembered that about her. She always seemed to be anticipating something exciting. "Like a watch that is always fully wound," Father had once said to describe her. He wasn't wrong. It was infectious. Even when he'd been discouraged, she'd lifted his spirits with her ceaseless cheer and energy.

Sarah greeted several of the choir members by name, though they were not people she was likely to have met during her previous visits. She had already made friends. He lowered his head to hide his smile. She had always been affable, sometimes to a fault. He'd admired that about her; *she* didn't feel overwhelmed just talking to people.

With the music dispersed, she stepped away from the choir stalls and into the nave. Mr. Felt began the musical part of the evening. This was the point when Harold generally lost himself in his work, the music soothing and pleasant, even if there were many starts and stops and a few sour notes. They were preparing to do their duty just as he was undertaking his. Working while they were working dispelled some of the isolation he felt.

This week, however, there was a distraction. Sarah didn't content herself with sitting in the first pew, directly in front of the choir. She sat in the pew across from his, separated only by the aisle that divided the nave down the middle. Her eyes were on the singers, but he didn't for a moment think she wasn't aware of his presence. He could hardly have been more aware of *hers*.

He glanced in her direction a few times. Each time, her not-quite-hidden smile grew a little. She was enjoying this and clearly thought her participation was a victory for *her* in their challenge.

"I am here offering support as well, you will notice." He kept his eyes on his paper, though he wasn't writing anything.

She didn't answer but kept watching the choir. He didn't say anything else as the practice continued. She didn't either, at least not to him. Mr. Felt requested the next sheet of music, and she quickly obliged with words of praise for the singers, the sincerity of which could not have been mistaken.

"Lovely," she said, pausing in front of them all. "Simply lovely. I do hope I will be permitted to come listen to you practice every week."

Smiles beamed forth.

Sarah turned to Mr. Felt. "In exchange for offering whatever help you need, of course."

"You are welcome any time, Miss Sarvol."

She bobbed a little in place and held the music sheets against her chest. "I will not disrupt any longer." After another quick smile at the singers, she returned to the pew she had occupied before, the one directly across from him. She listened for a moment as the choir worked through a difficult section of the piece, then bent over her stack of music sheets and carefully arranged and piled them.

She set the stack beside the third piece the choir meant to rehearse that evening. With a look of absolute pleased contentment, she returned her gaze to the stalls.

Choir night was usually Harold's most productive. Yet, that evening, he was accomplishing absolutely nothing. Sarah continually pulled his attention, as she'd done every day of her family's previous visit to Collingham. He'd watched for her in crowds, aware of her every time she was present, thinking of her when she wasn't. Truth be told, he'd thought of her often in the years since.

After a long moment, she rose. She didn't move toward the choir stalls but took the few steps to his pew. Without a word, she sat beside him, not so close as to be touching or particularly intimate in their arrangement but certainly near enough for conversation.

His heart leaped immediately to his throat. Their most recent conversation had ended in this ridiculous competition. The one before that had ended with a kiss and him being sent sprawling against rocks and water and into years of regret.

"Mrs. Hightower says they are taking on more complicated arrangements," she said without preamble. Apparently, she wasn't as wary of discussions as he was. "A number of the choir members are feeling overwhelmed."

He hadn't heard as much; he'd certainly not seen any signs of it, and he was with them every week. "They always do fine."

She didn't argue. "Mrs. Gibbons says Mr. Felt has been choosing more complicated pieces because he worries that their offerings have not been good enough."

What had given Mr. Felt that impression? "They are always very good."

"Some of the choir members wish he would return to the simpler pieces, as they enjoyed those better. Others, though, are appreciative of the opportunity to expand their abilities. There are whispers, especially amongst the altos, that if the music grows too difficult or the choir is not afforded the occasional easier or more familiar pieces, some of the members may stop participating."

He turned toward her. "How many are thinking of leaving?" The choir was not in need of Sarah joining their ranks at the moment, but they weren't so large as to be able to lose more than a member or two.

"Enough that Mrs. Hightower is concerned." Sarah's eyes were on the choir, though she spoke low and directly to him. "Mr. Gibbons, who I am told has been a member of the parish choir longer than anyone, shares her worries."

He had seen no such signs of discontent despite having been present for every rehearsal for more than a year. "How did you hear of this?"

She leaned closer, eyes still forward, and whispered, "I discovered a shockingly effective means of learning things about people." She made a show of looking about the chapel as if afraid she would be overheard revealing her secret. "I *talk* to them."

The unfairness of that pricked at him. He spoke to people all the time, no matter that it was harder for him than it was for her. And he spoke to them in his uncertainty and his exhaustion. "I talk to people as well, Sarah."

She eyed him sidelong, and he realized what he'd said.

"*Miss Sarvol*," he corrected.

The choir's voices soared into the uppermost rafters of the church, forming an impressive and soothing chord.

"They are very good," Sarah said. "I hope they do not let their discouragement get the better of them."

"They add something wonderful to the Sunday services," he said. "Music has the ability to reach people when words cannot."

She looked over at him. "Do you really feel that way?"

"I have always appreciated music," he said. "You know that. We spoke of it often."

"We spoke of a lot of things, *Mr. Jonquil*." She rose. "Not all of them proved to be true."

He was afforded no opportunity to respond. He likely couldn't have, even if she'd remained sitting beside him for hours. There was an accusation in her words he didn't deserve. He'd never been dishonest. Indeed, he'd worn his heart on his sleeve with her, something he hadn't done before. Or since.

He looked to Father's spot on the Jonquil family pew. What he wouldn't give to be able to pass a note to his father now.

Mr. Felt had turned to face the pews, his gaze falling on Sarah. "How was that? This is a difficult piece."

"It was simply lovely," she said. "The height of the refrain a moment ago reached the very heavens, I am certain of it."

Looks of relief touched all their faces. Watching that transformation, Harold realized for the first time how tense they usually appeared. Perhaps they truly were as strained as Sarah had indicated.

"We do have one more week to practice it," Mrs. Hightower said, sounding both grateful and concerned.

Sarah slipped over to the pew she'd been on originally and picked up the as-yet-unrehearsed music. "Oh, we often sang this one in the congregation I grew up in. I did not realize our two countries had this hymn in common."

She held the papers to her chest, smiling broadly at the singers. "I am so pleased that you will be singing it."

"The arrangement is very simple," Mr. Felt warned. His words were for Sarah, but his gaze darted to Harold.

"The message is best served with simplicity." Sarah moved to where Mr. Felt stood. "As Mr. Jonquil only just said to me, music has the ability to touch people in ways nothing else can. I have no doubt that your efforts on this piece will do precisely that."

Very nearly in unison, every eye turned to Harold. Never before had he been asked to comment during a choir rehearsal. Not once. He hadn't the first idea the appropriate things for a vicar to say or do in this circumstance.

Was he meant to offer technical advice? Approve or disapprove of their choice of music? Simply nod and agree? He could guess, but he might be wrong.

He cleared his throat. Had that sounded as awkward as it had felt? Everyone was watching him in anticipation. He hazarded a look at Sarah, fully expecting to see mockery—he received that often enough from his brothers—or triumph, considering she was managing a more helpful interaction with the choir that night than he was. Instead, she watched him with what could be described only as hope. She gave him an earnest little nod of encouragement.

But what was the appropriate thing to say? He didn't want to do anything incorrect or inappropriate.

"Your music is beautiful every week," he said. "It adds greatly to our services."

Mr. Felt still looked concerned. "This song"—he indicated the one Sarah still held—"really is *very* simple."

"Holy writ does equate simplicity with sincerity." Surely referencing the Bible was permissible for a vicar on any occasion. "I do not believe you need to consider it a flaw in your offering."

That did not fully alleviate Mr. Felt's look of concern. "Our piece *this* Sunday will not be simple at all."

Harold's attempts to help had made things worse. Why was it he so often failed to do the good he wanted to do? He tried so hard to fulfill everyone's expectations but continually fell short.

Referencing the Bible had not helped a moment ago, but it was all he could think to do. "We are instructed in the New Testament to expand upon our talents. Choosing music that challenges your abilities would certainly be fulfilling that duty."

Mr. Felt looked back at the singers. "Perhaps a combination of difficult and simple pieces would be our best approach."

He received enthusiastic agreement, especially from the alto section. A conversation ensued in which various suggestions were made for musical pieces, some falling into the familiar and simple category, others clearly meant to increase the members' skills.

Harold sat once more, breathing a sigh of relief. He'd managed to say something helpful, and now he could return to quietly listening to the music. Choir nights were usually his easiest, the one time he fit his responsibilities: sit quietly, get his work done, enjoy the music. He didn't have to pretend. *This* night had not gone as planned.

As the choir discussion continued, Sarah quietly collected the music they'd been practicing and handed out the final piece. She slipped silently from among them and returned to the pew across from his.

"Perhaps we can avoid a mutiny now," she said.

He nodded. He'd nearly used up his allotment of words for the day. He was exhausted instead of rejuvenated. Would even choir night be draining now? He didn't know where he would find the energy to keep going when his endurance inevitably ran out.

"I believe supporting and encouraging the efforts of the parish choir is a task a good vicar would see to," Sarah added.

He understood perfectly what she was hinting at. "I have been supporting them every week since taking on the duties of this parish."

She was undeterred. "The challenge isn't who does a task and who doesn't. It is who does it *better*."

He hadn't a ready response, at least not one he was willing to give. He had stumbled through his attempts to offer the right response to Mr. Felt's inquiries. He'd been present for nearly countless rehearsals, and yet, until Sarah had pointed it out, he had been unaware of the difficulties rumbling beneath the surface.

He was a good vicar. He told himself that again and again. If only someone, himself included, truly believed that.

CHAPTER SIX

Philip had left for Shropshire several days earlier. Before departing, he'd asked Harold to look in on Sorrel now and then, concerned that she would overtax herself. Harold had readily accepted, grateful for a way to be of help.

He made his way to the small informal sitting room at Lampton Park. Sorrel was there, seated in an armchair near the hearth, shielded from the heat by an embroidered fireplace screen. It would have been a very cozy scene, except she sat alone, the only person in the large room. Her gaze did not appear to be on anything in particular. She hadn't any sewing in her hands or a book to read. She simply sat, alone and still.

Perhaps loneliness ought to have been as big a concern as her health. Harold knew what it was to feel alone; he knew the way that pierced a person.

"Good afternoon," he said.

Sorrel looked up. A very quick smile flashed over her face, one that spoke far more of obligation than true pleasure. Harold had come to know Sorrel well enough over the nearly two years she had been his sister-in-law to not be the least offended. She was as reserved as Philip was flamboyant. And her history had taught her to guard herself against the possibility of being hurt, particularly by those who professed to care for her. Family was kept as much at a distance as strangers, sometimes *more*.

"I hope you do not mind that I have come to call," he said as he crossed to where she sat.

Her expression didn't change in the least. "Did Philip require this of you?"

Harold preferred not to lie, though he knew Sorrel would not be terribly pleased with his answer. "We both know your husband's propensity for worrying about you."

She pushed out a puff of air. Her gaze returned to the fire. "Worrying about me has become his primary profession this past year and more."

"Our father was a worrier," Harold said.

Sorrel looked at him once more.

"I mean that in the best sense," Harold clarified. "He cared deeply for those he loved and dedicated himself to their well-being, but it meant he often worried."

"*Often* is not the same as *constantly*," Sorrel said.

"Mater's health was not so fragile as yours."

Her mouth tensed. "I am not fragile."

"I did not mean to imply that you were." He was not very good at this. What kind of vicar couldn't manage the most basic words of reassurance? "One is not defined by one's health."

"Spoken like someone whose health is not poor."

A maid came inside carrying a tea tray. The housekeeper moved at her side, watching both the tray and Sorrel with concern. The tray was carefully placed on the side table. The maid curtsied.

The housekeeper lingered, her brow pulled as her eyes searched Sorrel's face. "Is there anything else I can do for you, Lady Lampton?"

Sorrel shook her head.

The housekeeper remained a moment longer, not looking the least reassured. That set Harold to studying Sorrel a bit more closely himself. The tension in her face was unmistakable. Harold had assumed it was the result of her frustration at being "checked on." He suspected now that what he was seeing was pain.

Her suffering had increased tenfold during her previous pregnancies. Was she struggling again?

Her complexion had always been pale. Yet she looked almost colorless, spots of heat on either cheek only adding to her pallor. Philip hadn't specified that he wished the doctor sent for if Sorrel was less than well. But she needed medical care. The family knew all too well how quickly her circumstances could turn tragic. They were also well aware of her prickliness.

She shook her head. "I know that look, Harold. I call it the Jonquil Furrow, and it is infuriating."

"As one who is regularly the recipient of the Jonquil Grin of Mockery and Derision, I believe I have greater room for complaint than you."

"Did your brothers inherit that look from your father as well?" Sorrel asked.

"No. He teased and jested, but he never did so at anyone's expense."

"I wish I'd known him." Sorrel spoke quietly, sincerely, with real regret.

"He was an exemplary gentleman." One Harold hoped he would have made proud. He knew with perfect certainty that his father would have been disappointed in him if he didn't make every effort to help alleviate Sorrel's suffering. But what could he do? He had no expertise in the area of medicine, neither did his efforts to offer words of reassurance generally prove fruitful. "Will you please allow me to send for Dr. Scorseby?"

She rubbed at her temples. "Sending for the doctor only makes Philip fret more."

"Yes, but Philip is not here."

The smallest hint of a smile pulled at her lips. "Holy Harry is encouraging me to keep secrets from my husband?"

Of all the people who ever called him by that much-disliked moniker, only Sorrel ever said it in a way that actually made him laugh. "I am simply looking for more reasons to pray for Philip's soul, as doing so brings me an *un*holy degree of satisfaction."

"Are unholy prayers actually heard?" Sorrel asked.

"Lud, I hope so."

Sorrel smiled at him, the sight made more amusing by its rarity of late. "I suspect your brothers underestimate you, Harold."

"I suspect you're right." He allowed a lopsided smile. "Someday they'll realize as much."

"I hope they do," she said. "They are a bit blockheaded on some topics."

"It is a very good thing you are not." He quite pointedly didn't look at her.

"You are saying I ought to admit that sending for Dr. Scorseby would be a good idea?"

He didn't answer. He didn't think he needed to.

"You're right, of course." The admission clearly caused her some regret. "I've been thinking all morning that I ought to ask him to come by, but doing so feels like admitting that— that I'm—" She took a breath. "I wanted things to go so much better this time."

"I will send for the doctor," he said. "And you can tell yourself that, in true Jonquil fashion, I am fretting and worrying more than is necessary."

"You are generally sensible, Harold. I cannot excuse away *your* concern."

He appreciated the confidence but felt compelled to be completely honest. "Jason is the sensible brother."

She actually snorted. "No, he's not."

Harold was grateful to see her spirits lightened, however minutely. Encouraging that change seemed his wisest course of action. "Which one is Jason, then?"

"Stubborn," she said.

He rose and moved toward the door, though he continued speaking with her. "What about Corbin?"

"Gentle."

That was absolutely accurate. Harold addressed the footman standing in the corridor outside the sitting room. "Please have someone from the stables ride to Dr. Scorseby's home and ask him to call upon Lady Lampton at his first opportunity."

A nod preceded the footman's departure.

Harold turned back to his sister-in-law. "So, we have a stubborn brother and a gentle brother. What is Layton?"

"Compassionate," she said. "Though he struggles to extend that compassion to himself."

Harold sat once more, intrigued by her perspective on his family. "And Stanley?"

"Noble, sometimes to the point of being a little obnoxious."

Harold laughed; he couldn't help himself. "What about Charlie?"

"He is still becoming the gentleman he will be," she said.

"At the moment," he clarified. "How would you describe him *now*?"

"Lonely," she said. "Heaven knows he has a great many friends at university and scattered around the kingdom. But here, among his family and in this neighborhood, he is rather alone. I believe it is why he finds himself so often in mischief when he is here."

"Boredom?" Harold had wondered as much.

She nodded. "And I believe it is why he so eagerly accepted Mr. Lancaster's invitation to join him in Shropshire. It gave him something to do and someone to spend time with."

Harold would not have thought of that when describing his younger brother, who was always so personable and lively, but thinking on it now, he could not deny there was truth to the assessment. "What about Philip? Who is he?"

She didn't answer. Her brow pulled low. She pressed her lips together, emotion shaking her chin. The tiniest sheen of tears filled her eyes.

He hadn't meant to cause her pain. The topic had seemed to be an enjoyable one. How was it he continually took the wrong route in his conversations?

"Which brother am I?" He would rather endure a potentially less-than-flattering assessment than to push forward with a topic that was making his usually unflappable sister-in-law cry.

She didn't even have to think. "Adrift."

"Adrift?" Of all the things she might have said, he would not have guessed at that.

She nodded, just as confident in her answer as she had been when she'd offered it a moment earlier.

Adrift. She made him sound as though he had no idea what he was doing. Of all the brothers, he had known the longest who he would one day be. The family had fashioned a nickname for him ages ago based solely on what he was meant to become. *Adrift* hardly seemed the right word.

"I've upset you." There was the regret he'd expected to hear a moment ago. "I didn't intend to."

He waved it off. "I was simply surprised, is all." It was, of course, not all. He didn't wish to dig too much deeper into her assessment. "I have had my character evaluated before, but that was never the descriptor that was decided on."

"What was decided on in those instances?" she asked.

He borrowed a page from Philip's book and chose a light response. It seemed the right approach. "My brothers usually chose 'pious' or 'sanctimonious.' A young lady I once danced with at an assembly insisted on 'boring.' Another young lady has recently settled on 'indifferent.'"

Sorrel watched him more closely. "What young lady said 'indifferent'?" Bless her, Sorrel sounded offended on his behalf. His brothers would only have laughed.

"Is there anything I can do for you while we are waiting for the doctor?" he asked, avoiding her question.

Worry entered her expression once more. "Do you promise not to tell Philip?"

He narrowed his gaze. "Are you asking me as his brother or as your vicar?"

"Does it matter?"

He smiled. "No. I don't plan to say anything either way."

"Then you will have my undying loyalty." She took a deep breath. "I really need to lie down. I feel less sick when I do, and my pains stop. I was embarrassed and, I'll admit, a bit too proud, to ask any of the footmen to carry me up."

"Are you not able to walk?" That could not be a good sign.

"Not without a struggle. It is taking all the strength I have to simply sit here without collapsing or crying or . . ." She sighed.

"Say no more." Harold rose once more. "Allow me to carry you up. I do have your undying loyalty, after all."

She silently accepted, more than a little embarrassment in her expression. He lifted her into his arms, and she hooked her arm around his neck. Sorrel was lighter than she ought to have been, considering she had only a few short months remaining until she reached the time of her confinement.

"I do not like the idea of you being here alone while Philip is away," he said. "Allow me to stay here in the house or send for Marion. There ought to be someone here so you needn't be bothered by anything you don't care to be bothered by."

"Marion will tell Layton, and Layton will tell Philip the moment he walks in the door." Sorrel made quite an effort at sounding annoyed, yet there was a longing in her tone. Philip's tendency to fret ruffled her feathers a little, but she clearly missed him and found comfort in the reassurance of his affection.

"I am willing to remain," he repeated, "but you might find that having another lady here would be more comfortable, even if she is likely to tattle on you."

"Philip will sort it out either way," she said with exhaustion. "He sees far more than I wish he did."

Harold didn't need directions to Sorrel's bedchamber. She now claimed the one Mater had used all the years Harold was growing up. He knew every twist and turn, every room of this house.

He carried her inside. "The bed or the settee?"

"Bed, please," she said. "I am hoping I might actually be able to sleep."

He set her down. "I will pull the bell for your abigail. She can see that you are prepared for the doctor's visit."

Sorrel slumped against the pile of pillows. "Thank you, Harold."

"My pleasure, Sorrel." It truly was. It was a pleasure to be of help, to offer comfort. "I will send for Marion. And I will stay until I know if there is anything Dr. Scorseby needs me to do."

"Thank you."

"You are very welcome." Few things brought him as much satisfaction as helping people. Knowing he'd made a difference for someone he cared for as much as he did his sister-in-law meant a lot.

"Do you know, Harold, the footman who has carried me about in the past is quite strong, yet he struggles more with the task than you did?"

Harold folded his arms across his chest. "I would say that footman of yours is not so strong, after all. You, my dear sister, are very light."

She shook her head. "I'm really not. You are simply surprisingly strong. You are a mysterious sort of vicar, Holy Harry."

He let out a pent-up breath. "You have no idea."

CHAPTER SEVEN

Sarah hadn't seen Scott all week, beyond the occasional glimpse down a corridor. Truth be told, she'd seen hardly anyone at Sarvol House, not even the servants. She hadn't been assigned a particular maid to help her each day nor given the opportunity to interview and hire one of her own. Whichever of the chambermaids was available in the mornings and at bedtime was sent to quickly assist her. It was not a feasible arrangement long-term.

Though Scott would not have begrudged her a lady's maid, this was not his estate yet and he was not the one who made those decisions. She needed to ask her uncle.

He would be in the library. He was always in the library during the day, requiring Scott to be there as well. Sarah hadn't been privy to their many discussions but assumed there was a great deal her brother needed to learn in order to one day be master of this estate.

She slipped from her bedchamber and down the dim, narrow stairwell. The large entry hall was empty, the impression only emphasized by the sparse and unfamiliar portraits that hung there. Once upon a time, this space had been warm and inviting, the walls covered with portraits of family members greeting new arrivals and residents alike. Now it was merely an echoing cavern. Once Scott was master of the estate and she was in a position to dictate some aesthetic changes, she meant to see to it that the house felt welcoming again.

The door from the entry hall leading into the library was open. She hesitated. Uncle made her so uneasy. He had never physically hurt her, but he could be viciously unkind.

Sarah rallied her courage, then stepped through the bookcase-lined doorway and into the library. It was not so large as some, encompassing only a single level, but the bookcases stretched from floor to high ceiling. A short rolling ladder was necessary to reach the uppermost shelves. The room was dark, the rugs and tapestries heavy, yet it was not an uninviting space.

Her uncle sat in his wheeled chair at the round table in the middle of the room. Mr. Clark was with him. Scott, however, was nowhere to be seen. She hadn't intended to make this request without him there to take her side.

Mr. Clark rose.

Uncle glared at her.

"I apologize for the interruption," she said. "I have a matter of business I had hoped to discuss."

Uncle made something like a growl. "Proper ladies do not discuss business," he muttered.

His physical health was not good, but his voice certainly still functioned. And he was even more gruff than he'd been before. No matter that he had always been a difficult and often unkind person; she suspected he was far worse now because he was a little miserable. She could be patient with him.

"This is a matter pertaining to the household staff," she said. "That falls within the acceptable scope of a lady's concerns."

Uncle scowled. "Are you criticizing how I run my household?"

Be patient, she reminded herself. "I am in need of an abigail. I did not bring one with me from America, knowing I would be more likely to find an appropriate choice once I was here."

"And I am to pay that expense, am I?"

She wasn't certain what to say. The expense of personal servants was always borne by the household. She was not asking for anything extravagant. She knew with certainty that Uncle Sarvol had a valet. She was relatively certain Scott did as well.

"Adding a servant to the household is not an extravagance. Indeed, chambermaids must be spared now to assist me, which causes difficulties for the staff."

Uncle's expression hardened. "If the staff are neglecting their duties, I shall have to have a very stern talk with Mrs. Tanner. I expect more of her."

Sarah had meant only to explain the necessity of an abigail, not turn Uncle against the servants. They certainly didn't deserve to be blamed for the havoc Sarah's arrival had caused.

"They aren't being neglectful."

He narrowed his gaze on her. "You said they were. Are you lying to me?"

"No. Not at all."

His aged hands quivered as he took up a paper. "They're managing, then. No need for further expense."

This was not going well at all. "I need a lady's maid. I cannot even dress myself without one."

"I thought you Americans were supposed to be independent." The words spat from him. He had spoken very little to her since her arrival, and all of it had been tinged with annoyance, but this was the first time his voice had dripped with enmity. "You are not my daughter. You are not my heir. I have made room for you in this house. Do not make me regret that by being selfish as well as wasteful."

She looked to Mr. Clark, hoping for some explanation for this unexpected attack. The secretary simply stood quiet and waiting. There would be no help from that quarter.

"While you are here," Uncle said, "I have another bone to pick with you."

He did?

"I've heard that you've been traipsing about the neighborhood making a nuisance of yourself."

"I have heard no such rumor."

Mr. Clark gave a subtle shake of his head, the gesture clearly one of warning. Her attempt at humor, apparently, was likely to make things worse.

"Bridget knew her place. She stayed home and out of everyone's way." He pointed a trembling paper at her. "You'd do well to learn that yourself."

"I've only left to attend church, visit a tenant in need, and assist the parish choir in their rehearsal. Nothing in that is inapp—"

"She also didn't argue." Spittle shot from his mouth. "This is my house, and you are here as a poor relation. Do not forget that."

He shook his head back and forth, tiny repetitive movements more like a twitch than a gesture. His gaze, however, never moved from her face.

"I don't understand why you are so angry with me." It made no sense at all. "What have I done?"

His wrinkled lips pressed together. His nostrils flared with a breath. "Bridget never should have married Farland."

"Farland" was Layton Jonquil's future title.

"*They* decided that."

Sarah had helped the young couple get messages to each other, but she hadn't forced nor even suggested the match.

He slapped his papers on the table once more. "You cost me my daughter. Consider yourself on very thin ice."

Retreat seemed her best option in that moment. "I will just be in my room."

"That would be wise." His eyes returned to his papers.

Mr. Clark motioned her away, not in dismissal but in clear concern. She slipped from the library, her mind spinning. Her uncle's behavior was decidedly different, even threatening. Putting distance between herself and him was wise.

She took the narrow stairs toward her room. Perhaps being assigned the isolated governess's chambers had been a blessing in disguise. Uncle could not navigate this dark and secluded stairwell. He couldn't reach her here, so he couldn't hurt her. She couldn't imagine the staff would do his bidding for ill. Heavens, she needed to make certain they didn't too often do *her* bidding; simply mentioning them had turned her uncle against them.

She stepped into her bare sitting room, trying to reclaim a sense of home. She would be living here for some time. This space, her tiny corner of the house, needed to be her haven. She could not change her uncle's disposition or anger, but she could give herself a place of peace.

I make my own happiness. I always have.

Houses this size often had discarded bits of furniture and decorations tucked away. She would wager the attics contained a few items she could put to use. She set to work.

The attics proved relatively easy to find. She moved around the dusty space, looking over the various offerings. A dinged and scratched Queen Anne table desk. Another small table, one plain and rough-hewn. It had most certainly been used by a servant rather than having served a purpose in a public room. It was a good size for the location Sarah had in mind.

What else?

Behind a muslin-draped crate, she found a small stack of paintings. She carefully set them upright before looking through them one at a time. They were all familiar, though she could not identify the subjects of every single one. Most of these had, as of her last visit to Sarvol House, hung in the entryway. Her father's portrait would be among these.

She found it near the back. Despite the ill-advised, haphazard way it had been stored, the painting was undamaged. She didn't have to give it even another moment's thought. Father's portrait would go with her to her rooms. She found another of her and Scott, painted during a visit when they were very young. It was small and would easily fit above the mantle in her little personal sitting room.

At the very back of the stack was a portrait Sarah knew the moment she saw it: her cousin Bridget. She knelt in the dust and looked into that well-known face. Despite many years difference in their ages, she and Bridget had been friends. Sarah had rejoiced when Bridget and Layton had decided to marry. At the time, Uncle had been within a breath of promising the hand of his only daughter to an old and lecherous man. Through letters Sarah had clandestinely delivered between Layton and Bridget, Layton had offered himself as an alternative. He was heir apparent to a barony, in possession of a very comfortable income, and, unlike Bridget's other option, not a horrible person.

Bridget and Layton had been married shortly before Sarah had returned to America. Sarah never saw Bridget again; she died not long after Caroline was born.

She sat a moment on the dusty floor and simply looked into that dear face. Bridget had been such a kind and loving person, so very different from her father. Layton's tender affection for her had endeared him to Sarah. She would love him like her own cousin for all his life in gratitude for the happiness Bridget had known during their all-too-brief time together.

She set Bridget's portrait with the other items she meant to claim for her rooms, then went to find someone who could assist her.

Fortune was on her side; she passed the housekeeper on her way to her isolated stairwell.

"Forgive the interruption," she said, knowing the woman was always quite busy. "There are a few items I've found in the attics that I would be ever so grateful to have in my rooms, but I know I cannot bring them down on my own. Would you be so good as to send a footman—whenever one can be spared—to collect the items and bring them down for me?"

"Of course, Miss Sarvol," Mrs. Tanner said with a quick dip of a curtsy.

"But, please, do not pull them away from any of their duties," Sarah insisted. "I do not wish to add any burdens to the household."

Far from annoyed or put out, Mrs. Tanner smiled a little. "It will be seen to, Miss Sarvol. And it will be our pleasure."

Within a half hour, Sarah had all she had claimed. The housekeeper even sent a maid in with a few more items, having grasped quickly what Sarah was attempting to accomplish: a tablecloth—not new but in good condition—for her tiny dining table, an inkwell with a bit of ink, a couple of quills, and a small stack of parchment, as well as a chipped but lovely pitcher and bowl for her washstand.

"Thank you so very much," Sarah said. "I meant to make this space a bit more personal and pleasant, but I wasn't entirely sure how to go about it."

The housekeeper nodded. "These additions will help." Her glance around the nearly bare room was a bit embarrassed. "I know this isn't the finest room, but it seemed best. You have your own corner of the house, space all to yourself, where no one will . . . bother you."

Ah. Mrs. Tanner had selected this room for her and not out of neglect or disapproval but to protect her. "I am convinced I will love these rooms once I've had a chance to make them my own."

The housekeeper nodded but looked only a little reassured. "Do let me know if I can do anything else to help you put things to rights in here."

"I will."

Despite the effort required to get the items to her room, setting everything out took only minutes. Sarah hung the portraits on whatever nails were already in the walls. In time, she would decide on a more permanent location and ask the servants to provide her with nails in the right locations. This would do for now.

There was but one thing left to set out, an item that had been in her bedchamber in America for six years. She had packed it very carefully, afraid it would not survive the sea journey otherwise, and had checked it on her very first day at Sarvol House but hadn't pulled it out. She'd needed the perfect place for it first.

Sarah opened her traveling trunk, which was functioning as a bench at the end of her bed, and pulled out a frame. Sandwiched between two pieces of glass was a small pressed bouquet of wild flowers. Some were delicate, others bold. Reds and yellows and purples sat against dark-green leaves and pale-green stems.

How well she remembered the day she'd received the humble but tender offering. She had been walking along the banks of the Trent with Harold, something they had done so often during her last visit. He had paused now and then to pick a sprig of flowers, adding it to the collection in his hands.

Just when she thought it couldn't possible grow any larger, he had spied a determined spray of pale-yellow flowers growing out of the side of an old stone bridge. He'd been unable to reach them.

"They'd be perfect," he said, eyeing the taunting blooms with a fervent expression.

"What you have now *is* perfect," Sarah said, wanting to reassure him.

He shook his head. "I'll need you to hold these." He placed the bouquet in her hands, and then, in what would shock anyone who knew the staid and proper vicar now, pulled off his jacket and hung it over the side of the bridge. He pulled off his boots next and set them beside his jacket. His hat and gloves joined the other discarded items. She nearly fell over in shock when he pulled his stockings off as well.

She held to the flowers as tightly as she dared, not wanting to bend or break any stems, and watched as he climbed over the side of the bridge and moved with careful, heart-stopping movements, his toes gripping the thin ledge of stones, all the way to the flowers he sought. Possessing a nimbleness a cat would have been hard-pressed to summon, he picked a few sprigs, then made his way back to where she stood. With a hop and a flourish, he was back on his feet beside her, slipping the flowers in with those she held.

"Risking your life—no matter that your mother will love the flowers—hardly seems necessary." She remembered pressing the flowers to her nose and taking in the wild and sweet aroma.

"The flowers are for you, my darling Sarah," he'd said. "And it was, I assure you, well worth it."

Her heart had been fully and wholly his in that moment. She'd thrown her arms around his neck and embraced him, something no proper English young lady would have done. She hadn't been able to help herself.

How clearly she recalled his smile, both tender and amused. He'd held her hand, the one not holding his flowers, and walked with her for the remainder of that afternoon.

She had been so deeply happy. These flowers, flattened between glass, their colors faded and muted, were all she had left of those blissful days. The blooms did not, however, bring her any sorrow. They simply transported her and lifted her and gave her a brief moment to reflect with both nostalgia and longing on what might have been.

CHAPTER EIGHT

Scott appeared in the doorway of Sarah's miniscule sitting room, a look of anxious anticipation on his face. "Fetch your bonnet, Sarah. We've been granted a reprieve."

"What—?"

"I've managed to convince our uncle to allow us to attend the festival today, but I cannot guarantee he won't change his mind if given the opportunity." He crossed swiftly to the door of her bedchamber. "Where is your coat?"

"In the armoire." She followed him. "Uncle is allowing us to go?" She had attempted to obtain his approval the day before and had received for her efforts a thirty-minute lecture about remembering her place and being grateful for his generosity in housing and feeding her. She'd been called a number of unflattering things and had, in the end, simply given up trying to change his mind, just as she'd stopped inquiring about an abigail after his chastisement on that topic a few days earlier.

Scott pulled open the doors of her clothespress and snatched out her coat. "I mentioned to him that all the important local families will be in attendance and that I wished I had a better connection with the masters of those estates, as that would be beneficial to the future of this one." He set the coat in her hands and grabbed her bonnet off the top of her bureau. "Mr. Clark subtly concurred, further pointing out that the future master of the Sarvol estate ought to be seen attending a fair designed specifically to benefit the poor, that it would assure the neighborhood that I meant to be a responsible keeper of my inheritance. Uncle, to my shock, then agreed I ought to attend."

"*You* ought to attend." She shook her head. "He did not give me permission, then."

"I told him I meant to take you with me, then left before he could say anything." Scott plopped her bonnet on her head, a little askew, ribbons hanging limp around her.

"I am not wearing the right shoes for an outdoor festival."

"Then grab them." His sharp tone set her aback. He closed his eyes and pushed out a tense breath. "I'm sorry. I just cannot bear to be in this house any longer, never leaving that blasted library, listening to him drone on and on about things he thinks I am too thickheaded to understand. I never go anywhere and never see anyone, including you, and I cannot endure it any longer without some kind of reprieve."

She wrapped her arms around him and gave him a quick hug. "I can change my shoes in the carriage."

He nodded. "A good idea."

She pulled her shoes from the bottom of the armoire, then grabbed his hand, pulling him from the room and down the stairs.

"If today goes well, he may allow us more freedom moving forward," she said. "That would be a godsend for both of us."

"It would, indeed."

They reached the entryway. Scott caught the footman's eye. Most of the staff had gone to the festival. "Is the coachman here still?"

The footman nodded.

"Would you tell him that if he will hitch up the carriage and take Miss Sarvol and I to the alms fair, he can remain for the festivities without earning the ire of his employer? And if a stable hand is here yet, he could act as tiger and participate in the fair as well."

The footman watched with widened eyes. "Would you be in need of a footman, by chance?"

Sarah nodded eagerly. "I may very well purchase enough items, in the name of aiding those in need, of course, that my brother would be quite burdened by them. Having a footman at the fair somewhere—he needn't keep to our side—would be a welcome guard against desperation."

Scott motioned the footman away. "Let the butler know before you take word to the stables. We'll wait under the front portico and depart as soon as everyone is ready."

"Thank you, sir." The footman rushed off.

Scott grinned at Sarah. "It seems we are to liberate more than merely ourselves today."

"I did challenge our good vicar to a competition of saintliness," she said. "I am hopeful the footman's freedom will be a point in my favor."

They stepped outside, closing the door behind them. Uncle was unlikely to find them and rescind his permission if they were outside.

"I still cannot believe you did that." He laughed though. Sarah's heart warmed to hear it. Scott was not so cheerful as he had once been. "We wonder why, being from America, we are looked on as uncouth, then you declare *to the vicar* that you are a better vicar than he is."

"This isn't just 'a vicar,'" she said. "This is Harold. You knew him nearly as well as I did. Are you not struck by the change in him?"

Scott nodded in acknowledgment. "He was always more sedate than his brothers, at least when it wasn't just the two of us, or the three of us." He motioned to her. "But he does seem to have become . . . standoffish or a little pretentious or something." He shrugged minutely. "Whatever the change, it is unfortunate. A vicar can do a lot of good simply by allowing himself to be human."

"Precisely." Hearing Scott express the same thoughts that had driven her to enact the admittedly mad wager helped her view of the matter. "And I do not think he is happy. Harold ought to be happy."

A softness, one tinged with just a bit too much pity, entered Scott's eyes. "For a time, I thought his happiness and yours would be more closely tied together."

She could feel the hot blush creep up her neck. "That was not to be. But that doesn't mean I want him to live a miserable life or not be fulfilled in the work he has chosen. I assure you, I have recovered from my disappointment where he is concerned."

"Father worried about the attachment he could see growing in you. We, none of us, believed it could end well."

She swallowed against a sudden, unexpected lump in her throat. "Everyone could see how naïve I was?"

Scott didn't answer immediately. Why the hesitation?

"Harold was in no position to make any connection between you permanent," he said after a moment. "And you would soon be leaving for another continent, not to return for years. There was no hope of anything permanent between you."

"That is not necessarily true. We might have written to each other until he was in a position and of an age to make an offer."

Scott shook his head. "The gentleman's code forbids raising expectations that are unlikely to be fulfilled for years, if at all. Harold would have known as much. *I* knew as much, and I am an 'uncouth American.'"

She didn't at all like the idea forming in her mind. "Then he must have realized from the beginning that there would be no lasting connection between us."

Scott nodded, though he seemed to regret the truth he was sharing with her.

Sarah didn't know whether to be upset or simply heartbroken for her younger self. "You believe he led me on?"

Scott shook his head. "He was careless, and he ought not to have been. But I do not believe he intended to deceive you."

"Intended or not, he did."

Scott put an arm around her and squeezed her shoulders. "Father spoke of stepping in, of insisting you not continue spending time with Harold."

She felt more than a little humiliated at that revelation. "We thought we were being very . . . discreet about the time we spent together."

Scott laughed quietly. "You were, but Father kept a very close eye on both of us. He worried, knowing we were the proverbial fish out of water."

"Why did he not say anything about Harold's misrepresentation, then?"

Scott gave it a moment's thought. "I think because he knew, in *this* house, you were alone and miserable, and that being away from here saved you from our uncle's unkindness. He wanted you to have some joy in your life."

"It didn't end joyously," she said quietly.

"I know. And I am sorry."

She closed her eyes a moment and breathed through the rush of heartache she felt. Harold had *never* intended to pursue further the connection between them that he himself had actively forged. She hadn't realized the impediments. But he had. He had known what was coming, and he had hurt her anyway.

"Can you promise me, Sarah, that you are not pursuing this competition in order to wound him a little because he wounded you a lot?"

She looked at him once more. "He could be doing so much good in this parish, but he keeps himself aloof and distant from the people he serves. There is a sense of duty in his interactions but no indication of dedication. If I can prod him to see how much more he could do and be, that will benefit the people who live here, people among whom we mean to live. Harold

Jonquil wounded me more than I have let on, but that injury is not my motivation in this."

Scott nodded. "Then you give him a fight to be remembered."

She grinned, her heart instantly lighter. "Oh, I intend to."

CHAPTER NINE

Sarah had never attended an alms fair before. In fact, she suspected Lady Marion, who was credited with organizing the effort, had invented it. With the harvest complete, the hiring and mop fairs over for the year, and winter fast approaching, it had seemed to that enterprising lady a fine time to gather the people of the local area together to benefit those among them who were in difficult straits.

Outside of the end purpose of the fair, it was really no different from every other local fair Sarah had attended. Stalls filled the large field, each offering temptations of various kinds: food, drink, entertainments, trinkets, and baubles. A portion of what was spent at each stall was to be donated to the poor box at the church.

Children and families rushed about. Joyous laughter filled the fair.

"This is so much better than being confined to Sarvol House," Scott said. "I think we both needed this."

Sarah and Scott wandered from stall to stall. They bought meat pies and apples. Scott purchased an embroidered handkerchief from Mrs. Gibbons, who sang in the choir, for Sarah.

"This is beautiful," Sarah said. "Did you do the needlework?"

Mrs. Gibbons beamed. "I did, though Mrs. Carter provided the bits. Seeing as we aren't keeping the money spent on the baubles, she didn't want us ending this fair poorer for having helped."

"This will be perfect to carry with me on Sundays," Sarah said, indicating the handkerchief once more. "I will hold it while I listen to you sing."

Mrs. Gibbons leaned in closer. "I do not know what you said to Mr. Jonquil, but his support of the simpler pieces of music has taken a weight off our minds, I'll tell you that. We could hardly manage the complicated things Mr. Felt thought the vicar required."

Sarah squeezed her hand. "I am happy to have helped, and I hope you'll tell me if there's anything else I can do."

"Mrs. Jones, she's a tenant at Lampton Park, has just had a baby, and the poor thing has the colic," Mrs. Gibbons said. "With Lord Lampton away and the dowager too and young Lady Lampton not feeling well, the poor Jones family has no one to help, though they're struggling."

"Will Mrs. Jones be upset if I mention to Mr. Jonquil that she is in need of some help? I do not wish to overstep myself or give offense."

"I'd not think so. They're not proud people, the Joneses, though that's all the more reason for stepping in *before* they ask: they're likely to wait too long and land themselves in deep water, indeed."

Sarah nodded. "I will make certain Mr. Jonquil hears of this need."

Mrs. Gibbons smiled broadly. "Are you to be our messenger to the vicar?"

Sarah laughed. "I will happily serve in that role, though I certainly hope it does not prove necessary often."

She and Scott moved along past a few more stalls. A sideways glance revealed that her brother was struggling not to laugh.

"And what has you sputtering?" she asked.

"This battle of the vicars. You, sister, appear to be winning handily."

She made a show of being quite proud of that. "I told Harold I would. He ought to have believed me."

"I ought to have believed *what*?"

She spun, staring in the direction of that horrifyingly familiar voice. Harold stood on her other side, watching her with his now-characteristic unreadable expression.

Scott answered on her behalf. "My dear sister has discovered a need in your parish and has secured the promise of a very helpful informant to relay any other needs of which she becomes aware. And she was thanked for being the 'messenger to the vicar.'"

Anyone else might have been offended. Harold actually looked a little hurt. *Hurt.* She hadn't been expecting that, and she certainly didn't wish to cause him pain.

"People are coming to you with their concerns?" he asked.

"No. I am going to them. I am asking them how they are faring, what concerns they have, if their neighbors are well."

"I talk to them regularly." Confusion filled his eyes. "I really do, but no one ever tells me any of these things." His brow drew together in thought.

Was he truly pondering her suggestion? She was rather unaccustomed to that. Her mother had not placed much weight on her view of things. Father had been more willing to listen, but her understanding of matters that concerned him had been limited. Scott was kind but didn't often seek out her opinions. Uncle considered her an unwanted and inconvenient poor relation. There was something so blessedly uplifting about having someone take her seriously and truly listen to her. That the "someone" doing that was this altered Harold made the moment even more unexpected and, in a way, even more welcome. Her long-ago Harold would have done precisely this. Perhaps he was still there, hiding beneath the surface, somewhere.

Into the silence between them came a voice unknown to Sarah, one clearly belonging to a member of the working class. "Challenge the strongman, Mr. Jonquil? Penny a try."

Sarah looked in the same moment Harold did. A man she felt certain was the blacksmith stood inside a fenced-off section of the area. Several large bags of something that looked quite heavy lay on the ground beside him. Standing a touch closer to the path the fair goers trod was a second man, younger than the blacksmith but closely resembling him. His son, perhaps.

"No, I thank you," Harold said without pausing for more than the length of a breath.

"For a fine cause, sir," the son pressed.

Harold shook his head.

"You could challenge him, vicar," a child hovering nearby said. "You could try."

Another child added her voice to the first.

"Go on, Mr. Jonquil," the man at the next stall encouraged.

"Go on," another man tossed out.

Harold's posture stiffened. He shook his head firmly.

"Go on," a shout came from the crowd.

The gathering was not asking for much. A comical and lighthearted competition with arguably the strongest man in the area would entertain and, Sarah felt certain, endear Harold to his parishioners, all while raising funds for those in need. Could he not see this was a perfect opportunity to gain a bit of their trust and faith?

If only he could understand that reaching out to his parishioners involved more than the few words exchanged on the steps of the church on Sundays. Here was an opportunity for her to help not only his parishioners, but she could help *him* as well.

She turned to the blacksmith and his son. "I will challenge the strongman."

At first, they simply looked confused. Then, in near perfect unison, grins began creeping across their faces.

"You're a tiny thing, Miss Sarvol," the blacksmith said. "I suspect you'd be easier to lift than any of these bags."

"It seems to me," Sarah said to the crowd watching her with amused interest, "our blacksmith is afraid he will be bested by 'a tiny thing.'"

The blacksmith laughed heartily. His son had not stopped smiling. Many in the crowd chuckled as well.

Sarah pulled her reticule open and produced a penny. "A penny a try, I believe you said."

The blacksmith's son nodded.

She turned to the crowd, which was growing quickly. "I will pay the forfeit for the attempt, but who will pledge a penny if I can best him?"

The laughter returned, louder now. Absolute joy filled their faces. They talked and jested among themselves, guessing the chances of her succeeding, which they all seemed to consider absolutely nonexistent.

"Come now." She let her laughter show in her smile. "Someone must have some faith I can be triumphant."

"I'll give a penny if you win." Mr. Felt, who led the choir, appeared at the front of the gathering.

The blacksmith laughed heartily. "Anyone else care to toss a penny into the pot?"

"I'll offer a ha'penny," another member of the choir said from within the crowd.

Soon she had offers from all around, the total growing. Sarah hazarded a glance at Harold. He watched her and the gathering with uncertainty.

"A vicar supports a worthy cause," she said quietly, knowing he would hear her even with the pledges continuing to be shouted.

"I have never heard of a vicar participating in feats of strength." Again, though he clearly disagreed with her, he had not dismissed or belittled her. That part of his character had not changed. She'd needed that these past years.

"We are up to half a guinea," the blacksmith said, eyes wide. "I didn't think we'd earn that much all day."

"I'll pledge a guinea," Scott said. "I have full faith in my sister."

The crowd roared with laughing approval.

"Go on, then, Miss Sarvol," someone called. "Show our strongman who's mightiest."

Sarah set her reticule in Scott's hand, then slipped off her coat, which he held as well. With a show of dignity too overblown to be believed, she moved to the spot where the blacksmith's son stood. She placed her penny in his hand.

He motioned her into the fenced area with a shoulder-shaking laugh.

The blacksmith smiled a bit uncertainly. "What do we do now, then, miss?" he asked under his breath. "You can't actually lift more than I can."

"I know it," she said, "and they all know it. But we could secure a guinea and a half for the poor here in Collingham. I suggest we not squander the opportunity."

He thought a moment, then, face clearing, nodded. "I'll defer to Miss Sarvol," he called out to the crowd. "She can begin by lifting this bag here." Rather than indicating one of his heavy sacks of grain or any of the large rocks brought over for the competitions he had anticipated, the blacksmith motioned to a small burlap sack that, if Sarah had to guess, likely held the man's lunch.

Sarah rubbed her gloved hands together as if limbering them up for the task. She approached the bag slowly, examining it from several directions. With a deep breath, she took hold of it. Knowing the point of this particular exhibition was to entertain those who had gathered around and to give them a bit of a laugh for their generosity, she pretended to struggle with the bag, making a show of calling upon all her strength before at last lifting it up.

The crowd cheered.

She set it down once more, feigning exhaustion.

"Your turn, papa," the blacksmith's son called out.

The blacksmith borrowed a page from her book and put on the same show, grunting and wincing with effort he absolutely was not expending. He yanked his hands, grasping the top of the bag every which way without lifting the bag one bit from the stool it sat on. With a comically dejected posture, he conceded defeat.

A roar of approval filled the entire fair. A great many of those in attendance had watched the pretended competition play out. Sarah dipped a curtsy to the crowd, receiving enthusiastic applause. She turned to the blacksmith, who she knew would forever be a favorite of hers.

"Thank you for this," she said. "These funds will help many."

His eyes shone with approval. "You're a good 'n, Miss Sarvol. We're lucky to have you here."

His words touched her, likely more than he knew. Her uncle's criticisms echoed in her head too often for her to feel fully secure in her place in this neighborhood. "If ever you hear of a need I can help with, I hope you will tell me."

"I will, at that," he said. "And if ever I can do anything for you."

She pretended shock. "Why would I, the strongest person in Collingham, need assistance with anything?"

He laughed, a deep, rumbling laugh that proved contagious.

Sarah stepped from the competition area back into the crowd, who were delivering their pledged coins to the blacksmith's son and pausing long enough to tell her they'd enjoyed the lighthearted display.

As the crowd dispersed to enjoy the other offerings at the fair, Sarah's eyes caught Harold's once more.

"I do believe that is a point in my favor, Mr. Jonquil," she said.

"Performing theatricals with the blacksmith is not one of a vicar's duties." He spoke with confidence but not arrogance, a distinction she found encouraging.

"Isn't it, though?"

His gaze narrowed. "You think it is?"

"You are meant to be part of their lives," she said. "That includes fairs and moments of lightheartedness. That means being willing to do unexpected things if doing so means you are helping them."

"I do help them."

"Mrs. Jones could use your help," Sarah said. "She has recently been delivered of a baby who is struggling. There are other Lampton Park tenants who are concerned about their well-being in the absence of your mother and brother and your sister-in-law's ailing health. And reiterate your approval to the choir, as they are still unsure of it. And find a way to help at this fair, as it is a rare opportunity to connect with the people you serve while supporting so worthy a cause. Those things, Mr. Jonquil, are decidedly among a vicar's duties, and they are real and needed now."

"Let us see what else the festival has to offer," Scott said quietly, offering his arm.

She accepted it and, holding back an unexpected and entirely unwelcome rush of emotion, walked away.

CHAPTER TEN

Harold couldn't think back on that morning's sermon with anything but misgivings. He hadn't been so unsure of himself during a sermon since the day he'd first stood at the Collingham pulpit, attempting to deliver a message he was neither prepared for nor, if one were being a stickler, qualified to give. Neither of those things had been true today. Why, then, had he been so shaken with misgivings?

He tried to tell himself his uncertainty arose merely from having worn himself to a thread the day before. The alms fair had been an unmitigated success—he was happy about that—but being around so many people for hours on end, interacting, and constantly reevaluating his efforts had drained every last bit of energy from him. Crowds and gatherings were always that way. But a vicar was expected to be actively involved in such things. It couldn't be avoided.

And as Sarah had proven, simply being present wasn't enough. Seeing to the needs of his parishioners, being part of their lives, required he be more outgoing in his interactions, more involved. No matter how hard he tried to perform well his duties, she always managed to make him feel completely inadequate. That had weighed on him as well as he'd stood at the pulpit.

To make matters worse, he was now on his way to Lampton Park, where he would be spending the evening with his brothers. If not for the fact that Mater was at the Park at last and Harold hadn't seen her in weeks, he might have sent his excuses.

Upon arriving, he assumed what confidence he had as he stepped into the drawing room. It was a very formal space and might have been intimidating, if not for the large family portrait hanging above the fireplace. Father looked just as Harold remembered him, with his legendary quiet smile and a hand set tenderly on Mater's shoulder. Philip and Layton, no more than seventeen and sixteen years old, stood on either side of him. Jason and Corbin sat on a bench to Mater's left. Stanley sat in a chair at Mater's right, one of his hands in hers. Little Charlie sat on her lap, leaning back against her. Harold, a mere ten years old when the portrait was painted, sat on a footstool just in front of Mater, his head resting against her knees.

It was the last portrait ever painted of them, a moment in time Harold so often wished he could reclaim. Father had died not long afterward, and nothing in Harold's life had been entirely right since. Sorrel had said he was "adrift"; perhaps she wasn't entirely wrong.

"I suspect he is trying to decide on a topic for sermonizing while we're all together." Philip's voice cut into Harold's distraction.

He hadn't the patience at the moment for Philip's usual mockery. "I know my topic; I'm simply wondering who among you will actually listen."

Charlie, seated on a settee by the tall windows, laughed. "Philip won't listen, that's for certain."

Philip pressed a hand to his heart. "I am wounded. My tears will utterly ruin my cravat, then my valet will have both your necks."

"He wouldn't attack an invalid, would he?" Charlie motioned to his cane.

Harold thought Charlie had all but recovered from his injuries. Had he heard incorrectly?

Philip sighed dramatically. "I have one person in this household who is quite healthy but insists he is not and another who is falling to bits and won't admit it."

"Perhaps I should sermonize on patience," Harold casually suggested.

Philip looked at him, a laugh in his eyes. Had his humor actually met with his brother's approval? That seldom happened. Then again, a vicar was not meant to engage in the kind of ridiculousness Philip specialized in. Harold reminded himself of that. He wanted to do better.

He turned his attention to the rest of the room. Corbin and Jason were there, though neither brother lived in the area any longer. Their families did not appear to be present. This was not, then, a simple family gathering.

"Will Stanley be joining us?" Harold asked.

Philip shook his head. "He and Marjie are coming at Christmastime. It's too far a journey to ask him to make twice so close in succession."

That was sensible. "And Layton? Is his journey too treacherous as well?" Layton's estate neighbored this one.

Again, Harold received a barely hidden laugh. He'd managed to stay appropriately somber for less than a minute. Philip was not a very good influence, especially when Sorrel was not present.

"I suspect our dear brother's very persuasive wife has convinced him to bring the entire brood along," Philip said. "That takes time."

"And patience," Harold added with a solemn nod. "Seems *he* doesn't need my sermon." Lud, he'd done it again.

Seize a little solemnity, dunderhead. Act well your part.

"Is Mater not here?" Harold didn't see her.

"She is at the dower house," Philip said. "She'll come over in a bit. We have some business to see to first."

"We do?" Jason joined the conversation for the first time. Though Harold was a vicar and ought to have been more staid than the others, Jason was of a more serious nature than anyone else, though the happiness he'd found in marriage had lightened him considerably. "Has something happened?"

"This is more of a preparatory discussion," Philip said. "Father always said planning ahead was key to avoiding disaster."

Disaster? Every brother present was watching Philip closely.

"We should retire to the library," he said. "That seems the best place to undertake this."

"This sounds serious," Jason said, moving to Philip's side.

Philip didn't contradict the assessment.

Corbin stood as well, moving toward the door. Charlie struggled a little but was on his feet after a moment.

"You needn't strain yourself, Charlie," Philip said. "You don't have to join us."

Charlie didn't manage to entirely hide his disappointment.

Harold could clearly hear Sorrel's voice in his memory. The youngest of the brothers, in her assessment, was lonely. Leaving him out of whatever Philip wished to discuss would only add to that. Certainly, his presence wouldn't hurt.

"If this concerns the family, it concerns Charlie," Harold said.

They all looked at him, surprised. Was it so odd that he would speak up on behalf of the youngest of them?

In a turn of events more shocking even than Harold's interjection, Corbin spoke up. "Charlie should come."

Philip eyed Charlie with both surprise and amusement. "It seems you have finally reached adulthood."

"It's about blasted time." Charlie all but marched from the room, slowed only by the need for his cane. "To the library, brothers."

"He jumped from grown-up to in charge rather quickly, didn't he?" Philip observed.

Corbin laughed quietly and followed in the youngest's wake. Jason shrugged to Philip and did the same.

Philip met Harold's eye. "Are you seeing this? You might need to preach on the topic of humility. Charlie seems to have lost every bit of his."

"It's about blasted time," Harold tossed back.

Philip laughed out loud, making no attempt to hide his amusement as he had a moment earlier. "Are vicars allowed to say 'blasted'? Should I be drafting a letter to the archbishop?"

"Don't worry about that. Sarah Sarvol has likely already sent several letters of complaint."

Philip tossed him a curious look. "Has she criticized your efforts?"

"She insists she would make a better vicar than I." Harold wished he could say she was wrong. "She actually issued a challenge."

"She declared war?"

Harold shrugged. "In a way."

Philip grinned as they walked down the corridor toward the library. "Did you know, when I first met Sorrel during that house party at Kinnley, she declared war on me?"

"She did?" He hadn't heard this. "Over what?"

"I was, in her estimation, a poor excuse for a gentleman. Truth be told, going head-to-head with her made those weeks some of the very best of my entire life. A gentleman needs a challenge and a chance to reexamine himself."

All Harold seemed to be doing lately was reexamining. He didn't particularly care for what he was finding. "Did you learn anything in your reexamination?"

Philip nodded. "I learned she was right, and I learned my life was infinitely better with her in it."

The others were waiting when Harold and Philip stepped into the library.

"Thank you for informing me of the Joneses' struggles," Philip said as they crossed the room. "Mater means to check on them regularly, and I will make certain they have all they need."

Harold had looked in on the Joneses himself. He'd also sent word to Philip of the difficulties there. He was glad to hear that family would be looked after.

"And that seems a point in your favor in your war with Miss Sarvol."

"Except, she was the one who told me about the situation. So she wins again."

Philip barely kept his grin tucked away.

Harold sat on a high-backed chair near the fireplace. Philip sat on the sofa. There was only barely enough room for all of them. Layton would have to pull a chair over. Had Stanley been able to attend this informal meeting, they'd have been hard-pressed to find a spot for him.

"Layton and I have already discussed much of this," Philip said, "so I think we can begin without him." He turned to Charlie. "If that meets with your approval, of course."

"I'll allow it," Charlie said with a smirk.

Philip smiled, but the look of amusement didn't last. "Thanks to Harold's efforts, Sorrel agreed to be seen by Dr. Scorseby while I was away. He has given her strict instructions to remain off her feet for the remainder of her pregnancy. Should things not improve, she will be confined entirely to bed. This is not unexpected; we have experienced this twice before."

The bantering tone of a moment earlier was gone entirely. Everyone knew how the previous walks down this difficult path had ended. All their hearts had broken for Philip and Sorrel.

"Sorrel herself is not doing well this time around," he continued. "Scorseby fears for her well-being as well as the child's." Philip leaned forward, elbows on his legs, hands clasped in front of him.

"Being off her feet will help though?" Jason pressed.

"We are hopeful that it will preserve her health and strength."

"But not the baby's?" Corbin asked.

Philip shook his head. "There is no reason to believe anything will be different on that score than the last two times." He took a heavy breath. "We will see Sorrel through this; I refuse to believe otherwise. But we cannot do this a fourth time. Neither of us can bear it again. It is time I began planning for the reality that I will not have an heir."

This was a heavy topic of discussion, for certain.

"A family of seven brothers ought to have no worries on the matter of inheritance," Philip acknowledged, "but our situation is not so simple as most. There is the matter of the Farland title and estate."

"Layton is inheriting that." Charlie's brows pulled in concentration.

"Not if he is my heir," Philip said. "Father and Mater's marriage arrangement stipulated that the two titles not be folded into one another. The oldest son would inherit all of Father's lands and titles. The oldest child who was not heir to Father would inherit Mater's land and title."

Very few titles in the kingdom were eligible to be inherited by a woman. Indeed, they could likely be counted on one's fingers. Mater happened to hold one of them: the Farland Meadows barony. Had the eldest Jonquil sibling or even the second been a daughter, she would have inherited Mater's title and the Farland estate. That had fallen to Layton.

"If Layton inherits from Philip, he loses his claim to the Farland title and lands," Jason said, wearing what the brothers had always called his "barrister's face." "It would pass to the next in line."

Corbin shook his head firmly, repeatedly.

Jason's tone grew firmer but somehow kinder as well. "You are older than I am."

"By ten minutes." Corbin sounded more than a little anxious.

"The law puts a lot of store by those ten minutes," Jason said.

"I suspected Corbin does not wish to inherit Farland," Philip said, "and Layton and I don't particularly want to push it on him if it will make him miserable. But we don't know what choice there might be."

Everyone watched Jason. He had the better grasp of these things. "Most likely, there is nothing that can be done. He can refuse to use the title or assume possession of the estate, but I don't know that anyone else could take it up in his stead. It is marginally possible he would be permitted to abdicate, depending on the exact details of the letters patent. I won't know until I've looked it over."

"If he is able to refuse, that would leave the estate to you," Philip pointed out.

"And you suspect I don't want it either."

Philip raised an eyebrow.

Jason dipped his head in acknowledgment. "Mariposa inherited land here in England as well as in Spain. Her brother has an estate I am helping him see to. I have my barrister's practice I don't particularly wish to give up. If abdicating is an option, I'd consider it as well."

"This wouldn't come into play until after I stick my spoon in the wall," Philip said. "You'd be quite old and worn down by then, and young Santiago would not be so young anymore. He would have full control of his estate."

Jason didn't appear entirely convinced. "Should relinquishing our claim on the Farland inheritance prove possible, and should both Corbin and I choose to do so, that brings us to Stanley."

It was Philip's turn to shake his head in dismissal. "Stanley is finally happy, ensconced as he is in such a quiet and remote corner of the kingdom. Assuming the Farland title would mean regular trips to Town to take his seat in the House of Lords. It would mean being a gentleman of significance and influence in the neighborhood. He would have no peace. I cannot imagine he would be the least bit happy in that role."

This was growing complicated.

"Harold, then?" Jason said.

Everyone looked at him. Panic surged, but he pushed it down. He steepled his fingers, a strategy he employed whenever feelings of panic or being overwhelmed threatened to make his hands shake. "My aspirations lie with the church. I cannot even imagine relinquishing that." Indeed, no effort had ever been made to train him in the running of a vast land holding or to make governing decisions as a member of Parliament.

"A seventh son and we're discussing my position as heir." Charlie shook his head. "This ought to be the headline for the *Times*. I don't imagine this has ever happened in the history of England."

"I don't know about that," Harold said. "Our ancestors were more fond of fratricide than we are."

"This will end in murder, will it?" Charlie laughed.

"*There* is your *Times* headline," Philip said with a grin.

Even Corbin laughed, something he seldom did out loud.

The feeling in the room lightened. Though Harold wasn't certain Charlie's comment would have met with the scrutiny of either of the archbishops, he couldn't help thinking breaking the tension had been needed.

"Jason, will you look into the letters patent?" Philip asked.

"Of course."

"And, Corbin." Philip turned and faced him. "You don't have to make any decision anytime soon. Think on it. I know you are perfectly happy at Havenworth, and I would never ask you to leave that behind. But your little William would inherit from you, and that might not be a bad thing. Edmund will certainly carry on with Havenworth, and happily."

"I'll consider it," Corbin said.

"The chances are very slim of abdication being possible," Jason said, "but I will consider my position should Corbin be permitted to relinquish his."

"And we all know Holy Harry never stops considering his role in the church," Philip said.

His first inclination was to object to the hated nickname, but seeing smiles pop up around the room, he decided to let it go. They were all worried and their minds heavy. Having reason for levity was a blessing in that moment, even if it meant being the target of their humor.

"Can we do anything for Sorrel while we are here?" Jason asked, motioning to both himself and Corbin. They had often acted as one entity over the years.

"Drop in to her bedchamber before you go and chat with her a bit," Philip said. "She doesn't enjoy being isolated, and the worry is taking a toll."

"Is it taking a toll on you as well?" Harold suspected he already knew the answer.

"I've reconciled myself to losing another baby; I'm not pleased or even content with what is coming on that score, but I have prepared myself for that inevitability." Philip leaned forward once more, rubbing his face with his hands. "We came horrifyingly close to losing Sorrel the last time. Scorseby says the risk is greater now." His voice dropped to something closer to a whisper. "I can't even bring myself to think about it."

Losing Sorrel would shatter Philip; Harold knew without a doubt that it would. The previous vicar had failed utterly in supporting Layton through the loss of his first wife. What if Harold failed Philip as monumentally should the worst happen?

"Perhaps the heavens will provide a miracle," Harold said.

Philip didn't look up. "Miracles are not always heaven's plan."

"I know," Harold said gently. "But we can hope."

Philip pushed out an audible breath before rising. "Mater might very well be here by now. We had best go greet her before she declares us all the worst sort of sons."

"Maybe Layton decided to show up as well," Charlie said with a quick grin. "He's likely in the drawing room now, solidifying his place as Mater's favorite."

"Only one way to find out." Philip motioned them out. His expression was jovial, but his eyes were not. He, who was always the most light-hearted of the group, was inwardly crushed by the weight of his worries.

CHAPTER ELEVEN

Sarah hadn't the first idea how Scott convinced their uncle to lend them the carriage for the afternoon—the second time in a few short days—but she thanked him again and again.

"We both needed to get out of the house," he said as they rode up the drive at Lampton Park.

"Why did you settle upon this particular destination?" Sarah still had not entirely recovered her equilibrium from her last encounter with Harold. She wasn't certain she was ready to see him again.

"I had limited choices," Scott said. "Mr. Hampton makes our uncle seem magnanimous by comparison, so I'd rather not call there. Mr. Finley was a cad when we were there last, and I haven't heard anything to indicate that has changed."

Sarah pretended to be offended. "You know I have a preference for cads."

"You jest, Sarah, but Mr. Finley is the sort even scoundrels look at and say, 'That man is a scoundrel.' Finley Grange ought to be considered a plague house to anyone who cares at all for the safety and well-being of a loved one or"—he looked at her pointedly—"herself."

She reached across and squeezed his hand. "I remember enough of Mr. Finley that I have no desire to call on him. I promise you."

Scott nodded, the gesture one of relief.

The carriage came to a stop.

"Having eliminated Hampton House and Finley Grange," he said, "I had three remaining choices, including Carter Manor. But while Mr. Carter is a fine sort of gentleman, he's older enough than I that we don't have a great deal in common." Scott set his hat on his head once more.

"Which left Lampton Park and Farland Meadows," Sarah finished the thought for him as she adjusted her gloves.

"Lampton is older than I but not by very much." Scott looked a little nervous. "All the brothers are fine company. Chances are the family from the Meadows is here anyway. I thought we would enjoy spending time with the Jonquils more than anyone else."

If only he knew that she was not particularly keen on spending time with one Jonquil in particular. He upended her and confused her. What she needed now, as she was beginning this new chapter in her life, was certainty and reassurance.

The carriage door opened, and Sarah was handed down. Scott emerged behind her. He hooked his arm through hers as they walked toward the front door.

"The Dowager Countess has returned home, I understand," Sarah added. "I adore her."

"*Everyone* adores her," Scott said. "I felt more at home at Lampton Park than I ever did at Sarvol House. At the moment, I suspect that will still hold true."

"Uncle makes his home uninviting," Sarah said. "Lord and Lady Lampton took great pains to do just the opposite."

"And they succeeded."

The very proper Lampton Park butler showed them in. Scott provided him with a calling card which, as was proper, the butler took to wherever the family currently was.

"Do you suppose they will be at home for us?" Scott asked out of the corner of his mouth.

"If they aren't, we will be left with the unenviable task of deciding what message we ought to receive from that."

"Offense," Scott said firmly. "We absolutely must take tremendous offense should that happen."

She grinned. "We could kick up a row decrying our poor treatment to the entire neighborhood."

"We would be labeled 'those mad Americans' and would become quite the anecdote in local lore for generations."

"Let's do it," she said.

Scott laughed. She loved that he was so easily and willingly entertained. No matter the heaviness of life, she found in him the lightness and joy she needed.

The butler returned. He dipped his head. "If you will follow me, please."

"Seems we will not be afforded the opportunity to complain bitterly this time, dear sister." Scott twitched an eyebrow. "We could anyway, if you'd like."

"Perhaps next time."

They were shown to the formal drawing room. Sarvol House was a fine estate, but it paled in comparison to Lampton Park. Everything about the Park was regal and impressive, yet it was still so inviting and comforting. One never doubted this was a home that housed a family who loved one another. Sarvol House had never felt that way. The changes Uncle had made in the years since Sarah's last visit only added to the discomfort one felt within its walls.

The dowager countess stood nearby. She looked just as Sarah remembered her, though perhaps a little older. She still wore black, as she had in the more than ten years since her husband's death. Yet there was nothing in her smile or eager countenance to give the impression of one drowning in grief.

"Sarah Sarvol." The dowager spotted her, and pure joy filled her face. "And sweet Scott. Oh, I've not seen the two of you in years." Without warning, they were both engulfed in an embrace. "You've grown up so much. It has been far too long since you were here."

Sarah grinned, pleased with the warm reception. Then she saw the hint of emotion in Scott's face, and her heart seized.

The dowager held him a moment longer. "It has been too long, Scott. I have missed you. Letters are simply not the same."

Letters? Had Scott been writing the dowager? At least someone in the Jonquil family welcomed letters. Harold had been quite clear all those years ago that he did not care for correspondence, at least not from *her*.

"I cannot tell you how much I have valued your letters. They have been like manna." Scott hugged the dowager again. He was very seldom emotional. Sarah didn't know what to make of it.

"Please have a seat," the dowager invited. "The boys will be back in a moment."

Scott sat beside the dowager, looking twelve years old again. Sarah sat across from them, watching with surprise and curiosity. There was an unmistakable familial note to her brother's interaction with their hostess.

"I was so sorry to hear about your father's passing," the dowager said. "And to travel so far without your mother must be difficult."

"We miss her, of course," Scott said. "But she would not have been happy leaving the only home she has known."

"Losing one's home is a difficult thing for a lady." She spoke as one who knew. Her attention turned to Sarah. "How are you managing? Your role must be terribly undefined at the moment."

That was a remarkably succinct explanation. "It is a touch awkward."

The dowager turned to Scott once more. "I remember all too well your sister's tendency to tuck her worries behind a very determined flavor of optimism. Are things more difficult than she is letting on?"

Scott's shoulders drooped a bit. "It is worse than I anticipated."

"Is it? Your letters indicated you were bracing yourself for a great deal of misery."

Scott truly had been writing to her. Why had he never said as much? Sarah and her brother were as close as two siblings could be, so near in age they grew up almost as twins. Surely he had at some point considered that she might appreciate hearing about the Jonquil family.

Then again, she had not been entirely forthcoming with him. She had not told him in any detail what had happened with Harold. Perhaps they didn't know each other as well as she had always thought.

"Our uncle is unhappy, and he works very hard to make certain everyone else is as well," Scott said. "He is demanding and insulting, and he is particularly unkind to Sarah. I don't know how to stop him from being so vicious to her."

"He was unkind to little Caroline when she was a small child, thankfully too young to have any memory of it," the dowager said. "Layton eventually stopped taking her to see him. It was better for her to grow up without a grandfather than to be mistreated by him. For a very brief time, we thought he might have been softening, but it did not last."

Scott shook his head. "I wish I could say I am surprised that he would unleash his vitriol on a child, but I am not. He is a thoroughly unpleasant person. I find myself wondering how Sarah and I will endure living in his home for whatever time he has left. It could be years if he keeps holding on."

Sarah felt the blood drain from her face as a wave of cold realization swept over her. Could she live for years in her uncle's home, in that drafty, isolated corner of it, forced to decide between being entirely alone and being castigated?

"If there is ever anything you need," the dowager said, "please come call, either here or at the dower house. I know Philip and Layton are older enough than you that you were not particularly close friends during your visits, but those few years' difference mean very little now that you are all grown. And I have so few of my sons with me now; I will happily act as surrogate mother whenever you are in need of one."

"I will accept your offer," Scott said, taking her hands in his. "Expect me to arrive unannounced on your doorstep at inopportune moments."

The dowager smiled kindly. "I hope you do."

Sarah wasn't entirely certain she hadn't been forgotten. She had always been fond of the dowager and had been received with unwavering kindness and joy, but Scott, it seemed, had found in the dear lady something of an aunt and substitute mother. Sarah pushed back the tiny twinge of jealousy, reminding herself that Scott was lonely too and that the dowager appeared to long for her own children. They would be good for each other, even if Sarah did not appear to have a true place in their connection.

Voices floated in from the corridor, deep, rumbling, shockingly similar voices. The brothers, no doubt, were about to step inside. Mater's eyes shifted to the drawing room doors, an eagerness in her expression that spoke volumes of her adoration for her boys.

"This room is about to be a lot less peaceful," she said with amusement.

"It's the way you like it, I'd wager," Scott said.

The dowager laughed. "You aren't wrong."

The brothers came in a moment later. Heavens, the resemblance between them all was a bit startling. Seeing so many of them together made it impossible to miss. Tall and lean, golden hair with varying degrees of curl, blue eyes, identical smiles. And at the moment, a well-hidden but visible heaviness in their eyes.

What had happened? Her attention turned to Harold—old habits were difficult to overcome—but his neutral expression offered no clues.

The dowager rose and motioned to Scott and Sarah. "We have visitors."

"So we do." Philip offered a bow so flamboyant Sarah couldn't hold back a laugh. "A pleasure, dearest neighbors. We welcome you to our humble abode."

"Abode, yes," Sarah said. "Humble . . ." She narrowed her gaze and shook her head.

Philip grinned in response. She had always loved his cheerful, easily amused personality. "This one is definitely my favorite."

Scott pressed an open-fingered hand to his heart. "You wound me, my lord."

Philip scratched at his chin. "Are Americans allowed to call anyone 'my lord'? I am almost certain it was forbidden by the treaty ending our war."

"Which war?" Sarah asked a bit cheekily. "Our two countries did have another one quite recently."

Philip nodded. "And yet we've managed in the last minute to not shoot each other. It is a miracle of international proportions."

"Perhaps the key is that Sarah and I were born here," Scott suggested, matching Philip's exaggerated tone of solemnity. "We have a divided loyalty."

"Or we are simply exemplary people," Sarah countered.

Philip laughed. He turned to two of his brothers. "Corbin, Jason. I am certain you remember Scott and Sarah Sarvol. Charlie, you might not remember them from their last visit."

"How young do you think I am?" Charlie scoffed.

"Perhaps what he thinks you are is forgetful," Sarah suggested with a twist of her mouth.

Charlie's look of offense melted into amusement. "Or mutton-headed."

She nodded solemnly. "Older brothers do have a tendency to be rather bacon-brained when it comes to their younger siblings."

"Do we now?" Scott said.

"Yes," Charlie and Jason said in unison.

Corbin simply smiled.

Philip assumed a woeful expression. "I am a man at a mark, and my own family are wielding the weapons."

"That the truth is a weapon is not our fault," Harold tossed in.

Sarah was pleasantly surprised. Harold hadn't often participated in his brothers' banter, even years ago, but she would have assumed this new version of him *never* did. She was glad to be wrong about that. Combined with the fleeting glimpses she'd had of half-formed smiles, Sarah held out some hope that he was happier than he seemed.

Harold crossed to his mother. With a look of tenderness that would have melted even the hardest of hearts, he took her hands in his. "You were gone a very long time, Mater."

She smiled softly. "Did you miss me, Harold?"

"I always miss you when you are away."

She pulled him into a hug, as affectionate as the one she had offered Scott and Sarah but with an added air of fierceness. "Thank you for your determined correspondence with the vicar in Shropshire. Knowing you were aware of us helped me feel less overwhelmed."

"Knowing Charlie wasn't going to die helped me feel less desperate." He squeezed her once more before stepping back. "And having you back helps me feel less alone."

It was a moment of vulnerability that tugged fiercely at Sarah's heart. His parishioners and neighbors received staid, methodical interactions. One never forgot one was seeing *a vicar*. So often, though, what one needed was a fellow human being walking the difficult path of life.

There was not time to contemplate the sight, as chaos erupted in the very next moment. A flurry of skirts and golden hair rushed across the room, shouting, "Grammy! Grammy!"

The dowager was nearly knocked off her feet by a little girl throwing herself against the lady's legs.

"You're home, Grammy!"

"Caroline." The dowager lowered herself to the girl's level, pulling her into her arms.

"You were gone so long," Caroline said. "Why were you gone forever?"

"Charlie hurt his legs and arm. He needed me to look after him."

Caroline stayed in her grandmother's arms but turned to face the rest of the room. Her gaze settled on Charlie. "You hurt your legs?"

Charlie nodded. "Broke them both."

Good heavens.

"Like Aunt Swirl?"

Charlie didn't seem to know how to answer that. "Not exactly the same."

"Are your legs better now?"

"Mostly."

Sarah had been struck by Caroline's appearance that first Sunday; she still was. The girl reminded her so very much of Bridget, despite having Layton's coloring.

"This lot have been making disparaging remarks about older brothers," Philip said to Layton. "You weren't here to defend us, so I had to simply endure it. A sore trial, I assure you. And Miss Sarvol added fuel to their fire. I was outnumbered."

Layton, who had always been his older brother's partner in mischief, just shook his head. "Keep me out of it," he muttered and took a seat a bit apart from the others.

Philip watched him a moment before turning a concerned, questioning gaze on Lady Marion, who held her little boy in her arms.

"Something is weighing on him," she whispered. "I haven't sorted out what yet. But I will, mark my words."

"I learned long ago never to doubt you." He reached for his nephew, who reached back eagerly. The transfer was quickly made from mother to uncle. "Good afternoon, Henry. Have you had a good Sunday?"

Henry grabbed Philip's lower lip and giggled.

"I cam't talk wif your han im my mouf," Philip said.

The little boy only laughed harder.

"Twoublemaker," Philip added.

Caroline pulled away from her grandmother and moved to where Charlie sat, climbing onto the settee beside him. "I'm sad that you hurt your legs. Did Minus know?"

Who was Minus?

Charlie grinned. "I was with Minus when I hurt my legs."

Fear pulled at Caroline's features. "Did Minus break his legs too?"

Charlie pulled her up close to him. "No, sweetheart. Minus was fine."

Caroline sighed quite audibly. She tucked herself up against her youngest uncle and turned to face the room. "Mama," she called to Lady Marion. "Can we play a game?"

"What game?" Marion asked.

Caroline looked back at Charlie.

He shrugged. "A guessing game, perhaps?"

"Please, Mama." She turned her baleful eyes to Lady Marion. "Please."

Sarah couldn't help a chuckle. "How can you resist that sweet face?"

"Alas, I can't," Lady Marion said. "If you can convince your uncles to play, Caroline, you are welcome to do so."

Caroline hopped off the settee and spun about, looking at them all in turn. "You'll play with me, won't you? Papa's boys always play with me."

"We're never given a choice," Charlie tossed out.

Caroline's gaze stopped on Scott. "Who are you? You aren't one of Papa's boys."

"My name is Scott," he said. "I live at Sarvol House." He looked at the dowager. "Does she know where that is?"

"Vaguely, I'm sure." She smiled at her granddaughter. "He is not one of your father's brothers, but he is an exemplary gentleman."

Caroline smiled a little shyly. "Will you play with us?"

"Of course."

She clasped her hands together and looked back at Lady Marion. "They'll play with me." Her gaze shifted to Sarah but did not remain. "Can we play 'Yes and No'?" Again, the same movement of her eyes, quickly looking at Sarah, then away.

"Of course, sweetie."

Caroline turned toward her father. "Will you play, Papa?"

"Not today," he said. "But I will watch."

Caroline pouted but accepted the answer. "Uncle Flip, will you play?"

Philip bounced Henry on his knee, making faces at the little boy. "Only if Henry can play with me."

"He can't hardly talk," Caroline said, shaking her head.

"I'll have to do the talking for us, then." Philip pulled Henry up against him, rocking the boy back and forth with his face pressed beside his.

"Have you thought of something for us to guess?" Caroline asked.

Philip tipped Henry's head up and down in a nod.

Caroline bounced in place. "Is it a person?"

"Yes," Philip answered solemnly.

"A girl person?" Charlie jumped in.

"Yes."

"As old as Grammy?" Caroline asked.

"Your grandmother is not old," Philip was quick to reply.

"That isn't a yes or no answer," Harold said.

"Ah, but it is the correct answer," Philip said.

Everyone in the room laughed. Even the dowager took the teasing good-naturedly. How Sarah adored this family. One couldn't help being happy among them. Scott joined in the fun, asking questions of his own. The guesses grew more outlandish, which only made the game that much more entertaining.

In the end, she and Scott spent over an hour with the Jonquils, a longer-than-usual unplanned visit between neighbors. She wished it could have lasted several times as long.

Sitting at her tiny table in her antechamber that evening, taking her very lonely meal, she thought longingly on the estate not too far distant where the loving family were all together, laughing, and happy. Uncle Sarvol had commandeered Scott's full time and attention the moment they had returned. And she had been, as always, relegated to her rooms. Alone.

CHAPTER TWELVE

Harold guided his pony cart up the narrow lane leading to the vicarage, deep in thought. Philip's words the day all the brothers had gathered to discuss titles and inheritance weighed on his mind. He had full confidence his brothers would work out the legalities, making certain both estates were well cared for and no one was rendered truly unhappy by the arrangements. Harold's thoughts were on Sorrel and Philip.

He had called on his sister-in-law that morning on his way out to the abbey ruins and was worried by what he'd seen. She'd been nearly colorless. Her spirits hadn't been entirely dampened, but she was clearly not well. Philip had been in the room with them through most of the visit, and there was no mistaking his anxiety over Sorrel's condition.

She was too far from her time for the baby to survive if born now, but no one seeing Sorrel could doubt she was reaching the end of her endurance. There was no foreseeable happy ending, and it was tearing at Harold's heart.

He'd been at a loss to know what to say. As he often did when feeling out of his depth, he'd quoted what scriptures and sermons he'd thought applicable. What else did he have to offer? But he'd caught sight of Philip's annoyed expression and had fallen into silence.

He would give it greater thought, think of a more efficacious approach. He didn't wish to disappoint or fail in his duties. There simply had to be a way of offering comfort that he hadn't found yet.

He turned toward the vicarage gate, intending to go directly to his study to pore over his sermon. The more he studied it during the week, the less nervous he was on Sundays.

A tiny huddled figure at the gate, however, stopped him. *Caroline.* What was she doing here? He didn't see Layton or Marion nearby. They might be inside but certainly would not have left her outside on her own.

He hopped down from the cart and hunched down in front of her. "Sweetie?"

She looked up at him, worry in her big blue eyes, the stain of tears marring her cheeks. "I thought this was your house."

"It is. Did you come to visit me?"

"I'm lost." She took a shaky breath. "And I'm scared."

"Oh, sweetheart." He scooped her up. His forearms were a little sore—he'd climbed longer and harder than he usually did—but she was so tiny and light that she gave him no difficulty. "This is very far from home for you."

"I needed to see her." Caroline wrapped her arms around Harold's neck, tucking herself up against him.

"Whom did you need to see?" He rocked her a little in his arms, troubled by the continued catch in her words and breaths.

"The lady who played with us."

He thought a minute, trying to sort it out. The answer struck him quite suddenly. "Miss Sarvol?"

She made a noise of confirmation.

"Did you go looking for her alone?" he asked.

"Mama is with Papa because he is sad."

Why was Layton sad? Harold shook off the question. Caroline's situation needed addressing first.

"Do they know you went on this outing?"

"No." The poor girl sounded so very miserable.

"Does your nursery maid?"

"No."

Her absence had likely been noticed by now, and he would wager the household was frantic. "We had best go back to the Meadows, sweetie. They will all be very worried."

"Please, Harry. I need to talk to the lady. I need to go see her."

"I'm certain your mama would take you to see her."

Caroline held more tightly to him. "Please. Please. I *need* to go."

He could not countenance leaving Layton and Marion to worry over their daughter, but Caroline's franticness was unmistakable. Something about seeing Sarah was of paramount importance to her, and she would likely run off again in an attempt to make the visit if he didn't help her now.

"I am going to ask Mrs. Dalton to go to the Meadows to tell your mama and papa that you are spending the afternoon with your favorite uncle."

She kept her arms around his neck but leaned back a little to look up at him. How long before she would be too grown for him to hold her this way?

"Am I your favorite niece?" she asked.

He smiled. "I have two nieces now, dear."

"I have *seven* uncles."

Harold laughed. That quick wit was a Jonquil trait. The girl was her father's daughter, for certain.

Harold held tight to her as he walked through the gate and up to the door of the vicarage. She tucked herself up against him once more, so trusting and affectionate.

Mrs. Dalton was in the kitchen when they stepped inside. "What's this?" she asked, her gaze settling quickly on Caroline.

"Don't tell her I broke the rules," Caroline whispered.

He patted her back. "Would you be so good as to take word to Farland Meadows that Caroline is with me and that I will bring her home after we've had a little adventure together."

Mrs. Dalton nodded. "If you're to have an adventure, you'd best eat something first. I've made meat pies."

"Meat pies? You're a saint, Mrs. Dalton." His stomach rumbled loudly, agreeing with his assessment.

"I know well your love of meat pies. If I ever needed to bribe you to do something, I'd bake dozens and dozens of them."

"And I would accept." Harold looked to his armful. "Would you like a pie, sweetie?"

She nodded. He set her on her feet, and she approached the worktable. Mrs. Dalton offered a reassuring smile and motioned to the tray of pies. "Wrap three in a napkin: one for yourself and two for your uncle."

"Two?" Caroline's eyes went wide.

"He loves meat pies, to the point I sometimes worry about him."

Caroline's lips twitched a little. "We could bring him meat pies at the church on Sundays. He would like that."

Mrs. Dalton nodded solemnly. "He'd stand at the pulpit, eating, and forget all about us."

"And I wouldn't share," Harold tossed in. "And your uncle Flip would cry because he loves meat pies too, but he wouldn't have any, and I wouldn't even feel sorry for him."

Caroline giggled, then set earnestly to work selecting their traveling food.

Mrs. Dalton moved to Harold's side. In a low voice, she said, "One of those meat pies was your lunch for tomorrow. The pantry's a bit low on supplies."

Harold nodded. They were always a bit low on foodstuffs. "We'll think of something. We always do."

"Soup again," she said. "I can make that stretch."

"I'm sorry you have to. If you worked for anyone else, you'd know some ease instead of this struggle."

Mrs. Dalton looked a little offended. "I've a talent for this type of struggle. I'm good at it."

"I know you are, and I am deeply grateful for you."

She accepted the combined compliment and apology with a nod. "Is there anything else I ought to convey to Mr. Jonquil and Lady Marion?"

"Tell them Caroline is safe, and I will explain it all when I bring her home later today."

She nodded firmly and left without further comment or delay. Mrs. Dalton could be depended on.

"Shall we take the pony cart?" Harold kept his tone light and excited. The Meadows was a good distance from the vicarage. Caroline had likely been wandering for quite some time and was, no doubt, worn thin.

She nodded. "We can eat our pies in the cart."

"An excellent plan."

It proved a little tricky to eat and direct the pony at the same time, but by keeping his pace slow, he managed it. They were well fed and whole when they arrived at Sarvol House.

His very simple pony cart looked rather out of place in front of the stately façade of the large house. The fact that feeding his little niece meant he himself would be hungry the next day only emphasized his lowered situation. He did his best to keep the state of his income and stability hidden. Humility was a virtue a vicar ought to embrace, but being *humiliated* seemed to him to take the experience a bit beyond the mark. Other clergymen managed to not starve on their small incomes; he would find a way as well.

He lifted Caroline to the ground, then took her little hand in his. The butler answered the door after a moment.

"Mr. Jonquil and Miss Jonquil for Miss Sarvol, please," Harold said, supplying the butler with his card.

They waited in the entryway while their card was delivered.

"Papa sometimes sends a footman to the door with his card when we visit people," Caroline said. "So does Flip. Why do they do that?"

"Because it is easier and more convenient," he said. "But I do not have a footman, so I hand over the card myself and wait."

"Oh." She looked around the entryway, curious but quiet.

Harold hadn't been inside Sarvol House in several years, and it had changed. The walls were a more garish color, the portraits far older than what had once hung there. He couldn't help comparing it to the feel of the Lampton Park drawing room. That space was enormous and might easily feel cold and rejecting, but the soft palette and the inclusion of family items, chief among them the family portrait, made the space inviting, unlike this.

Long moments passed. Harold wasn't certain why Sarah hadn't responded yet. He had intentionally included Caroline in his request to see her, knowing she was more likely to be at home for his sweet little niece than for him.

Caroline was growing antsy beside him, her brow pulling in concern.

"Do not fret, sweetie," he said. "I am certain Miss Sarvol will be delighted to see you if she is able."

It was not the butler who returned, however, but the housekeeper. Odd.

"Forgive the delay," she said. "Miss Sarvol does wish to see you both, but there is some difficulty in arranging for a place where she might do so."

He had never heard of that particular impediment arising in this situation. "We certainly do not require the formality of the drawing room if it is unavailable. The sitting room or library or even the back terrace will be sufficient, I assure you."

The housekeeper shook her head. "Mr. Sarvol does not permit her the use of—" She cut off her explanation, seeming to remember it was bad form for a servant to speak ill of the master of the house. "It is unusual, but would you be willing to be received in Miss Sarvol's private sitting room? Having Miss Jonquil with you will address the intimacy of the setting. We could, of course, supply a maid to sit in the room if you prefer there be one."

He shook his head. "I believe Miss Jonquil's presence will be enough, provided the door is left open."

The housekeeper looked immediately relieved. Clearly, Mr. Sarvol's stinginess when it came to the use of public rooms did not meet with her approval. "This way, please."

She led them into the large entry hall, then motioned to a doorway to the right. They followed her through it and into a dim, narrow stairwell.

Why were they being brought to Sarah's sitting room via the servants' stairs?

At the top were only two doors, one of them ajar. The housekeeper stood beside it, a clear indication that it was their destination. Caroline's grip on Harold's hand grew tighter. This visit was important to her, but it also clearly made her nervous.

They stepped through the door and into the smallest sitting room Harold had ever seen in a grand house like this one. He would wager the housekeeper herself had a larger receiving area. The room held mismatched furniture serving a variety of functions, everything from a writing desk to a worktable to a small bookshelf. An unusual space.

Sarah stood in the middle of the room. Her welcoming gaze settled very quickly on Caroline. "I am so pleased you came to see me. I have only the one chair, though, so we will have to ask your uncle to stand during our visit."

Both Sarah and Caroline looked to him. "I believe I am equal to the challenge," he said with a dip of his head.

Sarah smiled. He'd always liked her smile.

"Caroline was most anxious to see you," Harold said. "I do not know if she would prefer to do so in private." He looked to his niece, willing to step from the room while they spoke if that was her preference.

But she shook her head. "Don't leave, please."

"Of course not, poppet."

Caroline took a breath and slipped her hand from his. With short, measured steps, she moved closer to where Sarah stood watching and waiting. The poor girl appeared to be shaking. What had her so very nervous?

"Would it help if we sat?" Sarah offered. "I can move the chair to the window, and you can sit on the sill."

Caroline nodded silently. The adjustment was made. Harold lifted Caroline onto the sill. Sarah sat in the chair, facing her.

"Did you wish to simply talk, dear, or was there something in particular on your mind?" Sarah asked gently.

Caroline watched her, worry tugging at her features. Tears began to pool in her eyes.

Sarah glanced at Harold. All he could do was shrug. He hadn't the first idea what was weighing so much on the little girl's mind and heart.

Sarah took one of Caroline's hands in hers. "You needn't be afraid to ask me anything, sweetheart. And you can tell me whatever might be on your mind. If you want to simply sit here, that is fine as well. And you may do so anytime you wish."

Caroline studied Sarah, an earnestness in her little face. She clearly wished to believe she could press forward with whatever she'd come to say. Sarah, however, was not well-known to her.

Harold slipped beside Caroline and set his arm lightly about her shoulders. They were both facing Sarah now. "You can trust Miss Sarvol, Caroline. I give you my word."

Caroline took a deep breath. She swallowed audibly. "Are you—?" Her voice didn't rise above a whisper.

Harold gave her a quick squeeze.

"Are you my mother?" Caroline asked.

Of all the things she might have asked, that had never occurred to Harold. Caroline's mother had died when she was an infant. He was certain Caroline knew as much.

"Your mother?" Sarah repeated gently.

Caroline pulled a miniature from the pocket of her blue spencer, one slightly too big for her little hands. She showed it to Harold. "Papa said this is my mother. And it's her." She motioned to Sarah.

The portrait was of Bridget, painted when she was likely about Sarah's age. There was, indeed, a remarkable resemblance between the two. Harold hadn't realized how much until that moment.

He turned Caroline's hand enough for Sarah to see the miniature. Sadness filled her face on the instant.

"Oh, my dear Caroline." She set her other hand atop the one of Caroline's she already held. "That *is* a painting of your mother. I would know her anywhere. She was my cousin and my dear friend."

"But this looks like you." A hint of argument entered her tone but not belligerence. It was an insistence that rang with desperation. "It looks exactly like you."

"Have you noticed that your father's brothers look like each other?"

Caroline nodded.

"It is because they are family. Your mother and I were family."

Caroline lowered her head, her eyes on the portrait she held. She didn't say anything. Harold looked at Sarah just as she wiped a tear from her eyes.

"She really is dead," Caroline whispered, agony clear in every syllable. "I thought maybe—I wanted to meet her." She dissolved, not into gentle tears but weeping. Harold took her in his arms and held her fiercely. Her little body was racked with soul-crushing sobs as he held her.

Sarah rose and stood next to him. She set her hand against Caroline's back, rubbing it in small circles. Tears fell from Sarah's eyes as well. He remembered with perfect clarity how deeply Sarah had mourned her cousin's passing all those years ago. She had arrived in England so soon after Bridget had died, missing seeing her again by less than two weeks.

Hesitantly, Harold set his other arm around Sarah, holding both the girl and Sarah in what he hoped was a comforting embrace. He met Sarah's eyes. The grief he saw there pulled at him fiercely.

"I didn't know she was going to ask that." He spoke as close to silently as he could.

"The poor, sweet girl." Sarah spoke as quietly as he had.

For long moments, they stood there, the two of them in Harold's arms. Was he helping? He hoped so. Caroline's crying grew quieter, less desperate, whether because she felt comforted or because she was exhausting herself, Harold didn't know. After a time, she lifted her head enough to look at him only briefly. Her red, swollen eyes and damp cheeks broke his heart anew.

"Will Mama be upset?" she asked, sniffling.

"She will be sad that you have been sad," Harold said.

Caroline wiped at her face with the palm of her hand. "She will think I don't want her to be my mama." The tears began again.

Sarah spoke before he could. "She will not think that at all, Caroline. She knows that you love her, and I know she loves you dearly. Wanting to meet your mother does not change any of that."

"I don't want her to be sad," Caroline said.

"And I don't want you to be sad," Sarah said. "Would your heart be happier if I told you stories about your mother? I knew her very well."

Caroline nodded quickly but minutely. There was a nervousness to her eager response.

"I have a portrait of her," Sarah said. "Bigger than the one you brought. She was younger when it was painted, so she looks a little different."

"It's here at your house?" Caroline asked.

"It is in this room," Sarah said. "See if you can find it."

Caroline's eyes widened. She shifted a little in his arms, looking around the small space. Harold set her on her feet. She stepped away and began her search.

Only Sarah remained in his embrace. Propriety dictated he should drop his arm, but she wasn't pulling away, and he was surprised at how reluctant he was to let her go. Having her there again, holding her, felt like coming home after years of wandering.

Sarah leaned her head against him. His heart pounded ever harder. "I wondered why she looked at me so strangely when I saw her at Lampton Park. The poor dear must have been so confused."

"All of this must be a lot for one so young to make sense of."

Sarah looked up at him. If he was not mistaken, there was some fondness in her eyes. "You always were good with children, Harold, careful of their often fragile feelings. I am pleased to know that has not changed."

He was not at all prepared to hear such a compliment. "Are you granting me a point in our competition?"

A smile blossomed. "I suppose I must, though I doubt you brought her here for that reason."

"To be honest, I hadn't given our competition a single thought since seeing Caroline at my front gate."

"And it did not enter my thoughts even once after the housekeeper announced that the two of you had come to call." Sarah shook her head. "If neither of us remembers that we are in this battle of abilities, how is anyone ever to be declared the winner?"

She leaned into his embrace once more. He felt her take and release a deep breath, the sound filled with comfort and ease. She had once told him she felt peaceful when she was with him. He had always been happier in her company than anyone else's. If only life had taken a kinder path.

"This is her portrait," Caroline called from across the room. "I know it is." She pointed up at a painting Harold knew to be Bridget. He had grown up here, after all. She had been his near neighbor, though older than he. In the portrait, she was likely sixteen or seventeen years old.

Sarah slipped from his arm and moved toward the little girl. A sudden, deep urge to call her back, to reach for her seized him. She'd felt so right, so natural in his embrace. Comfortable. At home. His heart remained partial to her, no matter that he tried to deny it. He cared for her still. Enough so that he had, without thought, tossed propriety to the wind and held her for an exceptionally long time. He was not exactly setting a good example for his parish. Yet he couldn't fully regret holding her. Sometimes he felt he would never escape the contradictions that lived inside him.

At Caroline's side, Sarah pulled the portrait off the wall and set it on the floor, leaning it against the side of the empty fireplace. The two of them knelt in front of it.

"Her hair is brown like yours," Caroline said.

"Yes. But your nose is exactly like hers," Sarah said.

Caroline leaned closer, studying her dear, departed mother's face.

"You have her smile as well. I noticed it straight away on the day we played our games at your uncle Philip's house."

Caroline looked at her. "Mama says I have a beautiful smile."

"You most certainly do." Sarah set an arm around Caroline, tugging her nearer. "Your mother knew me from the time I was a tiny baby. I visited her often. Did you know she lived here when she was a little girl?"

"In this room?"

Sarah shook her head. "No, but in this house."

Harold chose to give them a little privacy. Sarah was doing more to assuage Caroline's grief than he could have managed.

He slipped into the nearest doorway, only to realize it was not the one that had brought them in from the narrow stairwell but was the doorway to her bedchamber. As sparse as her tiny sitting room was, this room was barer still, the lack of furnishings and wall hangings more obvious in the larger space.

When he made to step back into the sitting room, his attention was claimed by a small frame on the mantel. Beneath the glass was a pressed bouquet of flowers. Flowers he was absolutely certain he had given her during her last visit to the neighborhood. Flowers he had offered as a token of his very real, very tender affection for her.

He could not possibly forget that afternoon or that bouquet. He'd added flowers as they'd walked, expanding the offering a little at a time. When he'd fetched the final sprig from the side of a stone bridge, he'd felt certain she was impressed. That was a heady feeling for a young gentleman, especially one who had been the butt of nearly every joke he'd heard over the course of his life. The enthusiastic embrace he had received in gratitude for the flowers had left him walking on clouds.

He often thought of that day and that moment and how very happy he had been. He'd assumed Sarah had forgotten all about it. But she had not only kept his flowers but had preserved them as well and now displayed them in her bedchamber, the only decoration in that room.

He slipped back into the tiny sitting room, confused and upended. He had assumed after all that had happened and her pointed disapproval of his efforts as a vicar that any tender feelings she might have once had for him had long since dissipated.

But she had smiled at him.

She had stood in his arms.

And she had kept his flowers.

CHAPTER THIRTEEN

Fully confident Mrs. Dalton had informed Layton and Marion that Caroline was safe and looked after, Harold drove his niece, along with Sarah, to Lampton Park that evening instead of the Meadows. Seeing Caroline's heartbreak, he had pieced together the likely reason for Layton's matching heaviness.

Sarah's arrival was revealing some painful, unhealed wounds in the Farland Meadows family. Telling Marion and Layton the full reason for Caroline's disappearance and the heartbreaking scene he had witnessed might not be wise. But keeping it from them didn't seem the right answer either.

If Father were still alive, Harold would have brought the matter to him without hesitation. He hesitated to bring the difficulty to Mater, not wishing to burden her or cause her grief, but he didn't know what else to do. He didn't want to be wrong in his approach, not with a heart as dear as Caroline's hanging in the balance.

"We are visiting Grammy?" Caroline broke her silence as they turned off the Lampton Park drive and down the smaller one leading to the dower house. Though the sun was hanging quite low in the sky, there was light enough to see their destination.

"Yes, as well as Flip and Swirl and Charming." The entire family loved the odd little names she had for them. Though she didn't use them exclusively any longer—she had all but outgrown calling him "Holy Harry," though he was often still "Harry"—they continued using them when speaking with her.

"Mama says Aunt Swirl is ill." Caroline looked up at him from her place on Sarah's lap. "Is she ill?"

Harold nodded. "I'm afraid she is. Dr. Scorseby has said she needs to stay in her bed nearly all the time. She must be quite weary of being in her bed, don't you think?"

She nodded firmly. "I wouldn't want to have to stay in my bed all day." She twisted a little and looked up at Sarah. "May we see her in her room? She will like to have me visit her."

"We will ask your uncle Philip if your aunt is feeling well enough for visitors."

"Did you know Flip when he was a boy like you knew my papa and mother?"

Sarah nodded. "I knew all your uncles and both of your grandfathers and your grammy."

Caroline bounced a little, her excitement at odds with her earlier lowered spirits. "Did you know Arabella? She lived here for a while, but then she started to love Minus, and she went to live with him."

Sarah looked at him. "Arabella *Hampton*?"

Harold nodded. "She lived at the Park for a time, acting as Mater's companion while Mater was making the transition to the dower house. It was her wedding Philip left to attend in Shropshire."

"Her wedding to 'Minus'?" Sarah's eyes danced with amusement.

He smiled back. "Linus Lancaster," he explained. "His sister is the Duchess of Kielder. Another sister is the Countess of Techney."

Caroline jumped back in. "And his other sister is Charming's worst enemy."

Sarah looked from one of them to the other. "Truly?"

Harold hadn't been present for much of the house party where his younger brother and the duchess's youngest sister had met, but he'd heard enough reports of it from Mater to know the lay of the land. "Charlie and Miss Lancaster are equally *un*fond of each other. They argued a great deal and generally disliked each other, and, I daresay, when they parted company, neither of them was particularly brokenhearted about it."

"That doesn't sound like him," Sarah said. "He was quite easy natured when I spoke with him yesterday, very like the Charlie I knew before."

Harold acknowledged that with a slight nod. "Miss Lancaster managed to wriggle her way under his skin quickly and entirely."

They pulled up in front of the dower house. Eventually, it might not feel strange visiting Mater here instead of at the main house. Did it feel as odd to Mater?

Caroline whispered something in Sarah's ear. Sarah nodded, urging Caroline to turn to him.

"If Sarah and I go ask Uncle Flip if we can visit Swirl, Grammy won't be sad, will she?"

" Grammy will, I hope, be happy enough to visit with me that she will not be sad that I am the only one coming inside."

Caroline furrowed her brow, mouth turned down in a fierce frown. "Of course she will be happy to see you. Why do you think she wouldn't be?"

He chucked her under the chin. "Sometimes I forget."

"You shouldn't," Caroline said firmly.

Sarah's gaze turned very pointed. "You really shouldn't, Harold."

"I have accumulated ample evidence over the years to know I am not anyone's first choice companion." He was "Holy Harry." He was no one's favorite.

"There was a time, Harold, when we were each other's first choice."

Sarah had begun tugging at his heart again. Watching her so tenderly comforting Caroline, laughing with her, smiling, Harold saw snippets of the young lady he'd loved so dearly when he'd been younger. A young lady who had saved his flowers.

"What happened?" he asked quietly.

She didn't look away. "Everything fell apart." Her tone was soft but burdened.

"Harry." Caroline whined his name. "We need to see Aunt Swirl, and you need to see Grammy."

Sarah looked away and held out her hand to Caroline. They walked hand in hand in the direction of the main house. Harold watched them a moment.

"Everything fell apart." She'd sounded so regretful, so mournful. Did she wish as much as he did that things between them had turned out differently?

He shook his head, dismissing the unanswerable questions. He had enough to sort out without trying to make sense of all that. He pulled his gloves and hat off as the housekeeper led him to the front sitting room. The dower house was not large; he didn't have time to fully collect himself before his arrival. Mater greeted him with an embrace, something he appreciated likely more than she knew. With her, he never doubted himself. That could not be said of any other person, including himself.

"What has brought you around, Harold?" She motioned him to the sofa, sitting with enough room for him to sit beside her.

He set his hat and gloves on an obliging table and took the seat she offered. "I have been presented with a question I don't know how to answer." A weight settled in his stomach. "My brothers would mock me mercilessly if they heard me say that."

"Well, I am not your brothers, and I am not laughing."

Thank the heavens for Mater.

"I will remind you that I am no theologian," she said.

He shook his head. "Not a doctrinal question, a personal matter."

Her brows popped up in interest. "I had wondered how everything was with Sarah back in the neighborhood. Do not think for a moment I was unaware of your attachment to her during her last visit."

"No, not that." He swallowed against the thickness rising in his throat. "This isn't to do with her—Actually, it does involve her, but not in the way you think."

"Now I am intrigued." Mater turned a bit to look more closely at him. "What has happened?"

"Caroline asked me to take her to visit Sarah today—*Miss Sarvol*, I mean."

Mater smiled in amusement. "Call her Sarah, Harold. I know that's how you think of her."

"A vicar ought to be proper and appropriate."

"And a son ought to be a son before a vicar when speaking candidly with his mother," she countered.

Yet again, his attempts to conduct himself correctly proved wrong. More and more, he wondered if he'd ever manage to do the right thing the first time rather than bumble his way through things.

"Tell me what happened with Sarah," Mater pressed.

"Caroline wished to see her, so we called." Harold didn't know any better way to explain except directly, though he knew it would distress her. "Caroline asked Sarah if she was her mother."

Mater paled and grew very still, looking away from him.

"She has a little miniature of Bridget that looks shockingly like Sarah."

"I did notice the resemblance when she called on Sunday," Mater said quietly.

"Sarah was very sweet when she explained the actual connection, but Caroline was shattered. I've not ever seen her cry like that, Mater." He ached again at the memory of her agony. "Sarah told her stories about Bridget and showed her another portrait of her. I believe Caroline feels a little better, but I am certain she is still grappling with her grief and disappointment."

Mater nodded. "And you are wondering what to tell Layton and Marion."

"Precisely." Harold pushed out a breath. "I suspect Layton is struggling with Sarah being here. She is a reminder of a difficult period in his life. Knowing his daughter is so heartbroken would only add to his burden."

Mater pressed her clasped hands to her lips, gaze unfocused as she thought. "I did notice he was more distant, but I could not sort out the reason why. I ought to have realized."

"I don't want to add to his grief nor increase the weight Marion is no doubt carrying, but I do think they need to know what Caroline is struggling with."

"You are absolutely correct," Mater said. "They need to know, but knowing will hurt."

He rose and paced away. "A vicar is not meant to cause pain but to relieve it. No matter what I choose, someone will be hurt by this."

"You did not choose an easy profession, Harold. You did, however, choose an important one."

He turned to face her once more, horrified that he could feel emotion building behind his eyes. "What if I chose wrong?"

Surprise and worry tugged at her expression. "Are you doubting your choice?"

"Increasingly." He'd not made the admission out loud until now. "I am realizing I don't know my parishioners as well as I ought. I know some of their circumstances but not their worries and hearts. I have been Philip and Sorrel's vicar during both of their recent losses and haven't on either occasion known at all what to say or do; I certainly don't now. Layton and Caroline are grieving, and anything I do will only add to it."

He stopped at the far window.

"I grow so nervous and overwhelmed in conversations, even with my own brothers, that I ramble on. They laugh at my tendency to revert to holy writ, insisting I'm being sanctimonious, but I often don't know what else to do. It's easier to quote other people's words than to offer up my own. It's also safer."

"You are offering *me* your own words," Mater pointed out.

"That is different."

"How?"

His reply stuck a moment. "You like me. I'm not a joke to you." He was to everyone else. "Half the congregation sleeps through my sermons while the other half, I am certain, listens only so they can accurately mock me afterward. I recently learned the choir has been operating under the false assumption that their efforts do not meet with my approval. And increasingly often, I find myself wanting to do things or say things that are not becoming of a man of the church."

"What sort of things?" Mater sounded genuinely concerned.

"Nothing scandalous or indecent, I assure you. But undignified." He dropped onto the window seat, letting his shoulders slump. He rubbed his palms together. He'd stayed much longer at the abbey that day than usual. A few of his calluses had torn, and his hands were sore. "Do you remember when I was little and I used to climb trees and walls and—"

"And literally everything?" Mater grinned. "I was convinced you were going to fall and break your neck before you even left for Eton."

He couldn't share her humor. "I still do that. Climb things, like the abbey ruins outside of Collingham. Even inside the vicarage. Mrs. Dalton finds it amusing, but we both know I'd lose what respect I have in this parish if I did any such thing in public. And I'm beginning to suspect there is little enough of that respect as it is."

Mater didn't comment further but simply watched him.

"I often think of that time Father took me to Astley's Circus in London when I was eleven years old, not long before he died, and I left utterly fascinated with the idea of joining Astley's and doing daring feats on horseback."

She smiled. "He told me about that. We both decided we had best not tell Corbin, as he was likely to be horrified for the horse." Corbin had always been very fond of animals, horses in particular. "Neither of us thought your interest was a fault, though, or a reason for concern."

"Not in an eleven-year-old boy, no," he said. "But now and then, I have the strongest urge to save up for a proper horse and find a quiet meadow somewhere to try to learn a few tricks. I am an adult now, and a vicar. St. Paul insisted that a grown man, especially a man of the church, must leave behind childish things. If I can't manage that, maybe I'm not meant for this life after all."

"Personally, Harold, I do not think any of these things truly makes you unsuitable to serve in your chosen capacity," Mater said. "I am far more concerned at the level of doubt you have in yourself. That is a far greater impediment than a desire to climb a wall or learn to stand on a moving horse. Part of your role as a vicar is to give hope to those you serve. You cannot do that if you have no faith in yourself."

"What reason have I for faith in myself?" he asked. "I see evidence to the contrary every day." He was horrified at the emotion he heard in his words but could do nothing to hold it back. "I feel as though I am fighting a battle to convince myself, and every day, I lose more ground."

Mater stood and crossed to him, joining him on the window seat. "It seems to me, my sweet, loving Harold, that you need to spend some time deciding who you are and what you wish to do with your life."

"But this was always meant to be my life. I am Holy Harry, born a vicar, quoting scripture from my cradle."

She sighed. "I cannot tell you how many times I have told each of you boys these past couple of years to stop listening to each other. You are all rather fatheaded."

For the first time since beginning this unintended confession, Harold smiled, however fleetingly. "Which of our parents do we have to blame for that?"

She laughed. "Both, I am afraid. Especially when we were younger. But your father, in particular, gained the wisdom he needed. By the time you boys joined our family, his judgment was reliably sound."

"And he always said I was meant for the church."

Mater shook her head. "No, he didn't."

That was not at all how Harold remembered things.

"Your father once said to me that you, more so than most of your brothers, had a great many choices available to you. We both agreed that your kindness and compassion coupled with the fact that you were never happier than when you were helping and serving others meant you could, should you choose, make a wonderful vicar." She took his hand in hers. "And we saw you climb the side of the house, for heaven's sake, and balance on one foot out on the old stone bridge. You were fearless and curious and adventurous. My sweet boy, the church was never your only option. Your brothers simply took too much delight in teasing you, and you took their words too much to heart."

"Then I did choose wrong?" His heart fell clear to his toes. Had he set himself on the wrong path entirely?

"I think, perhaps, the issue is you didn't *choose* at all."

He rubbed at his face, weary to his very bones. "What do I do now? How do I sort a mess of this magnitude?"

"With patience," she said. "And time. And hope."

He looked to her. "And help?"

She threaded her arm through his. "Your life is important to me. *You* are important to me. I want to see you happy. And not merely happy in appearance, Harold, but in your soul, the way you ought to be. Happy in yourself and happy as yourself, your true self."

Though nothing was at all certain—indeed, he felt more uncertain than he had when stepping inside the dower house—Harold felt a flicker of hope that he hadn't even realized was missing. Mater had always done that for him, given him a firm foundation when the world around him swirled in chaos.

"And do not worry about Layton and Marion," Mater said. "I will talk with them."

He hated that he was handing over a duty, however unofficial, to someone else, but he didn't know what else to do.

Sorrel, it seemed, had been right.

He was adrift.

CHAPTER FOURTEEN

"Did you know my mother liked to sing?" Caroline had been peppering her uncle Philip with questions for a solid fifteen minutes, all on topics he might or might not have known about her late mother.

"Yes, she did," Philip said. "And she had a very pretty voice. She and your papa both sang in the parish choir. That is where they came to know each other so well."

"Did you know her nose was like mine?"

He tapped the tip of that adorable little nose. "You do look like her, Caroline. And she was a beauty."

"Cousin Sarah says my mother was very kind."

"She was," Philip said.

Sarah looked to Charlie. He sat comfortably in a nearby chair, watching Caroline with a grin.

His gaze shifted to Sarah. "It is good to hear her talk so happily about Bridget." He spoke too quietly for Caroline to overhear. "I think it'll do her good."

"I believe you're correct in that." Having seen the pain in Caroline's eyes at wanting so desperately to know her mother, Sarah was certain that was precisely what the dear girl needed: to feel a connection.

"Did Swirl know my mother?" Caroline asked Philip.

"No, poppet, she didn't."

Caroline's eyes widened. "I could tell Swirl about her."

Philip hugged her. "Next time you visit, if your aunt is awake, I think she would love to hear everything you have to say about your mother."

Her brows tugged low again. "I wish she wasn't so ill."

For the length of a heartbeat, he didn't answer. Then, his voice breaking the tiniest bit, he said, "I wish that as well."

Sarah didn't know all the details of the young Lady Lampton's situation but knew she was in rather dire straits. She wished she were better acquainted with the lady and could offer greater help and support.

A clamoring from somewhere down the corridor echoed through the sitting room. They all turned and looked in the direction of the door. A moment later, a young lady, likely very near Sarah's age, with the coloring of a Jonquil but not a bit of the height, flew into the room.

Her eyes settled immediately on Philip. Posture resolute and determined, she declared, "Your brother is an idiot."

Philip appeared not the least shocked. "You will have to be more specific."

Charlie snorted, earning a glare from the still unnamed young lady. He pressed his lips closed and hunched low, as if attempting to hide inside himself.

A young servant stepped inside next, one dressed quite casually, and walked with absolute self-assurance. He met Philip's eye with a smirk one did not generally see exchanged between classes in England.

"Where's your captain, Pluck?" Philip asked the bold young man.

"Mrs. Captain left him at home, Your High and Mighty Lordship."

Philip nodded solemnly. "Because he is an idiot, by chance?"

"I can't say he ain't, sir."

Captain. Stanley was the brother in the army, the only one of the Jonquils Sarah had not yet seen. This beauty, then, was Stanley's wife. She was shockingly beautiful and quite petite. She was also rounded in the middle in a telltale way.

"Fallowgill is a long journey from here, Marjie," Philip said. "I cannot like the idea of you making the journey without Stanley. Not that you aren't capable nor that Pluck wouldn't look after you. I just know Stanley is frantic with worry."

Marjie—that was the name Philip had given—tipped her chin upward in a show of defiance. "I doubt he has even noticed I left."

Philip gave her a dry look. "Trust me, dear sister, he has noticed." He turned to the servant, Pluck. "Have Mrs. Jonquil's things been taken to whichever bedchamber Mrs. Beck thinks best?"

"Yes, sir."

"And do you imagine any other members of the Fallowgill household will descend upon us soon?" Philip asked a bit out of the side of his mouth.

Pluck's smirk tipped to one side. "I'd wager Cap'n is only a day behind us."

Philip nodded. "Thank you for seeing her here safely. I trust you remember where the kitchen is and can arrange for yourself a bite to eat."

Pluck snapped a smart salute, spun on his heel, and marched from the room. He was an odd sort, but Sarah liked him already.

Marjie looked around the room. "Where is Sorrel?"

"She is in bed," Philip said. "Scorseby has ordered it."

Marjie crossed to Philip. "How bad is it?"

"She and the baby are both in very real danger," Philip whispered.

Marjie reached out and set a hand on his arm. "May I see her?"

"She is likely sleeping, but you can certainly look in on her."

She and Philip both left the room. Caroline was sitting on Charlie's lap, talking his ear off. Sarah wasn't at all certain what she ought to do. The family had visitors and chaos and difficulties. While she had enjoyed the rare moment of interaction—she'd had little enough of it lately—she knew it was time for her to leave.

She rose and faced Charlie. "Do you think Philip would mind if I asked for a carriage to be called? It is a long walk to Sarvol House."

"Not at all," he answered earnestly. "He'd probably bellow at me all evening if he heard I let you leave without summoning a carriage."

She smiled. "For your sake, I'll ask for one."

Charlie laughed. Caroline took hold of his face and turned him to face her once more, apparently wishing for his undivided attention. "And she sang in the parish choir," Caroline said.

Charlie nodded, his eyes not wandering from her again.

The little girl felt better now, but she likely had a difficult road ahead of her. She had a mother to grieve, despite having never known her. Her last uncle at home, beyond Philip, would soon live somewhere else and wouldn't be available for the chat she was so eagerly undertaking.

Stanley and his wife were, apparently, having difficulties.

Philip might very well lose both his unborn child and his wife.

Layton had been noticeably unhappy when last she'd seen him.

The Jonquils were a family in crisis.

She was not in a position to truly help, though she longed to. And in the midst of that longing was a quiet wish that she belonged here at the Park with these people she cared about so deeply and that Scott could live here as well. Neither of them could endure their uncle's home much longer.

Unbidden into her thoughts came the remembered feel of Harold's arms enveloping her—not years ago but mere hours earlier. When Caroline had pulled from his embrace, Sarah had fully intended to do the same. But she couldn't.

Harold Jonquil had, when they were younger, shown himself capable of assuaging her feelings of loneliness and rejection with little more than a glance. The times he'd held her, she had felt deeply needed and loved and cared about. In his arms, she had never doubted she was important to someone.

That afternoon in her miniscule sitting room, she'd felt that reassurance again in a way she hadn't in years, and she'd been unable to pull herself from it. There was an aching familiarity in his embrace. For those few minutes, she had allowed herself to indulge in the dreams of the home he had inspired in her younger self and marvel at how quickly they returned when he showed himself to be the Harold she had known.

He had such a capacity to love. If only he still allowed himself to do so.

CHAPTER FIFTEEN

Sorrel eyed the gathering of ladies. "Then Lord Percival said, 'I wish my family were more dignified, like the Jonquils.'"

Around the room, four Jonquil ladies and Sarah all burst out laughing.

"Your boys have all of Society hoodwinked," Marion said to Mater.

Sarah had, during this visit, been invited to refer to the ladies more informally. She appreciated the change. For one who hadn't any family nearby other than Scott, whom she seldom saw, and Uncle Sarvol, who rather despised her, feeling a closer connection to her neighbors helped her feel less alone.

"I've watched Philip do an uncanny impression of a seedy inn keeper, complete with unkempt appearance and dirt-smudged face," Sorrel said. "No one would think him dignified after that."

Marjie, whom Sarah had learned was not only Stanley's wife but Sorrel's younger sister, pretended to be shocked. "The impeccable Lord Lampton smudged and unkempt? Scandalous!"

Sorrel laughed weakly. She was clearly not well but was alert and personable. Sarah hoped that meant her situation was improving.

Marion jumped in. "I happen to know the future Lord Farland walks about his house in his shirtsleeves and trousers without even his shoes on to add the slightest bit of respectability."

"Shocking!" Marjie said with a smile in her eyes.

"I can improve upon that," Mater said. "I once found the current Lord Cavratt, whom I will always consider part of this family, hanging from the kitchen garden gate by his trousers. I had to rescue him."

They all laughed again.

"When was this?" Marion asked.

"Last week," Sorrel tossed out dryly, bringing on another round of room-wide laughter.

Mater swatted at her playfully. "It was ages ago. He was so sweet and so embarrassed."

"I believe I can best all of you," Sarah said.

They looked to her with both amusement and doubt.

"I have heard Harold Jonquil swear."

No one seemed to know whether to laugh, deny the possibility, or simply sit in mute shock.

Sarah couldn't help but grin. "He would have been ten or eleven years old. The brothers were out on the east lawn playing bowls. Harold and Scott were teamed together, and Stanley and I were challenging them. Harold was a single good throw from capturing victory when Philip, Layton, and—" She had to think a moment, trying to recall Lord Cavratt's Christian name; he hadn't been Lord Cavratt at the time of this incident after all—"and Crispin came running through at break-neck speed and scattered the bowls in all directions."

She had the ladies' rapt attention.

"Harold looked over the destruction wide-eyed, then, clear as day, swore at his quickly departing brothers. Stanley burst out laughing; I truly thought he would suffocate, he was laughing so hard. Harold, poor soul, was horrified. If he'd had a shovel nearby, I think he would have dug a hole and climbed in."

"What did you do?" Marion asked.

Sarah smiled at the memory. "That was the moment I stopped being afraid of him. He might have been only ten years old, but he was, until then, a little intimidating. Hearing him say a slightly naughty word made him seem more like an actual person.'"

Marion and Marjie laughed.

Sorrel smiled, obvious amusement showing alongside her exhaustion. "I firmly suspect there is more to Harold than meets the eye."

Oh, there was. Depth none of them ever saw. Pain he kept well hidden. A capacity for love even he didn't seem to recognize.

"The flowers in your hair are lovely, Sarah," Mater said.

Sarah reached up and brushed her fingers over the small deep-purple blooms she'd tucked into twists of her hair. "Scott gave them to me. He had them left in my room this morning."

Finding the humble handful of plum-colored flowers, which Scott must have obtained from a conservatory, it being winter, she had been touched and reassured that he had thought of her.

"Dear Scott," Mater said fondly. "He always was a thoughtful young man."

A quick knock on the door preceded the arrival of the housekeeper. She gave a quick curtsy. "Begging your pardons, ladies, Mrs. Jonquil has a visitor."

The only person in the room who would be referred to that way was Marjie. She looked at them all, confusion clear in her face. She, after all, did not live in the area. Who would be visiting her?

In the next instant, Stanley stepped inside. Despite his use of a cane, his was the posture of a soldier.

Marjie stood, slowly, and turned to fully face him. She sat nearer the door than anyone else.

The room was silent. Everyone watched with bated breath. Would Stanley be upset? Would he decry her decision to leave, the danger she had courted, the difficulties she had caused him?

He released an audible breath. "Marjie," he whispered in a voice of utter relief.

Marjie watched him, sadness in her eyes. "I am rather put out with you."

He stepped closer to her. "I know." No defensiveness or sharpness entered his reply.

"I have reason to be," she added.

He stepped closer still. "I know."

Tears sprung to Marjie's eyes, spilling over on the instant.

Stanley set a hand softly on her cheek, brushing the tears away. "I love you."

Marjie closed her eyes. "I know."

Stanley pressed a lingering kiss to her forehead. Marjie embraced him. He kept one hand firmly gripping his cane; he obviously needed it to maintain his balance. His other arm slipped around his wife, holding her to him.

It was so tender a moment, Sarah could have cried. It transported her years into her own past to an idyllic stream not far distant and the gentle embrace of another of these Jonquil boys. How sweet Harold had been, how very tender and affectionate. For that short time, she had felt as treasured as anyone with eyes could see Marjie Jonquil was.

Stanley didn't release his wife, and she didn't release him. But he looked out over the gathering of ladies. "How are you, Sorrel?" he asked.

"I have certainly been better," she answered. "If I am truly fortunate, I have quite a few long, miserable weeks ahead of me."

"Is it wrong to wish you misery?" Stanley asked.

Sorrel shook her head weakly. "I am wishing for it myself."

He turned his attention to Sarah. "I had heard you were returned to the neighborhood. It is a pleasure to see you again."

"And you, Stanley. It has been a long time." He had been on the Continent as a soldier during her last visit to England.

"It will be longer still, I am afraid," he said. "Your brother is here to take you back to Sarvol House. He arrived just as I did."

Had the day passed already?

"Do you have to go?" Mater asked, seeming truly sad at the possibility.

How she wished she could stay. She loved being around this family. Nothing awaited her at her uncle's home but isolation.

"I do have to go," she admitted. "Scott must have expended a great deal of effort to arrange this. My uncle does not like the conveyances to be taken out—" She stopped herself before finishing that sentence with "for me." Her time with these ladies ought not end on so sad a note. "I had best take advantage of it."

"Do come visit again," Mater said.

"Yes, do." Sorrel's request brought momentary surprise to her sister and sister-in-law's faces. She, apparently, was not always keen on visitors. Whether this change was a reflection on Sarah in particular or simply the result of facing so long a confinement, Sarah didn't know. She wasn't discouraged by the second possibility. She would call on Sorrel as often as she was permitted. They would both benefit from the company.

"And please ask Scott to come visit me when he is able," Mater added.

"I will."

She slipped out of the room and made her way quickly down the corridor, down the stairs, and to the front entryway.

Scott was waiting for her. "I am sorry to disrupt your visit. Uncle allowed me the use of the carriage, and I didn't think it would happen again."

She nodded. "Especially if he knew you were using it on my behalf."

He offered his arm and led her outside. The carriage sat in readiness, the coachman atop, waiting.

"The flowers look lovely in your hair," he said.

She brushed her fingers over them again. "I do like them."

He nodded. "You did always like flowers."

She did, indeed. She'd grown particularly fond of them after Harold's offering years ago. The simple beauty of a bouquet of blooms warmed her heart.

"The dowager countess sent her wish that you call on her when you are able," Sarah said. "I daresay she is fond of you."

A sad sort of smile touched his face. "She has been like a second mother to me for years. I so dislike that I'm forced by Uncle's dictates to neglect her."

"I believe she will be grateful to see you whenever you are able to slip away."

They were quickly situated inside the carriage. Sarah watched longingly as Lampton Park disappeared from view. How she hated returning to Sarvol House.

"Moving here has not proven quite what I expected," she confessed. "We were going to spend so much time together exploring the area, forging friendships with the neighbors. We were going to build lives here. Now you seldom leave the library, and I either hide in my room or wander about the area alone, looking for someone to talk with."

"We don't have a lot of freedom here," Scott acknowledged.

It was a sad and uncomfortable truth. "I was so eager to leave Mother's household because I was treated like a child. Yet here, I am treated like a fungus."

"Which is worse?" Scott asked.

"Both. Both are worse."

He set his arm around her, a comforting gesture he'd used since childhood when she was unhappy or worried. "What do you mean to do?"

"I don't know. But I will find an answer."

He smiled at her, though it didn't quite reach his eyes. "You always do."

"Somehow, we will be happy here, Scott. I will find a way. I swear I will."

CHAPTER SIXTEEN

Harold—*Holy Harry*—was pondering the very real possibility of walking away from his life in the church.

"You need to spend some time deciding who you are and what you wish to do with your life." Mater had been right on that score, but Harold was finding the undertaking daunting.

He rolled his shoulders a few times, working out the soreness there. He'd been climbing for nearly an hour, trying to calm his thoughts and work out his frustrations. Climbing usually did that for him and brought him pleasure as well. Today, he was struggling.

He slowly walked the length of the abbey wall. It was not part of the original building but was what remained of an outer wall enclosing the abbey yard. It was sturdy and thick, high enough to be a challenge but low enough to be regularly scaled. Over the years, he'd devised any number of ways to reach the top. He'd used a chisel and mallet several times and etched a few paths with chinks for his hands and toes beyond what occurred naturally in the weathered and battered wall. That was the easier section.

Another spot had ropes hanging from the top, ropes he brought with him each time so the weather wouldn't destroy them. An ancient set of stairs ran along the back side of the wall; the boring way of getting up. He carried the ropes up that way. Once atop the wall, he fastened the ropes with the rivets and metal straps he'd long ago attached to the top of the wall.

Perhaps instead of becoming a vicar, he ought to have built things. He enjoyed working with his hands. Sorting out the question of how to construct something he'd never seen before brought him tremendous satisfaction. But would he enjoy doing it day after day? Especially since there was no call for fitting ropes to walls and chiseling grooves in walls. He would have to build houses and such. That didn't hold enough appeal to pursue. Besides, he could not be a laborer *and* a gentleman. Losing his claim to the gentry would cause difficulties for his family and, should he be so blessed at some point, would cost his children their futures as well.

A respectable profession was best, one that brought him some happiness and fulfillment. That was supposed to have been the church. Was it still? Had it ever truly been?

Well, Harold. Time for a challenging climb. You ought to at least accomplish something today.

Over the past year, he had begun pounding various nails, thick, flattened spikes, and other things that were sturdy enough to do the trick into a far section of the rock wall. He used them to climb, grabbing them and standing on them. It had taken a little trial and error to determine how deep they had to be pounded to be reliable. They were a challenge but also made it possible to scale the wall in places where it was a little too smooth to do so unaided. When he grew tired, scaling to the top of the wall grew a little risky.

He couldn't figure out how to use a rope and the imbedded nails and spikes at the same time. He'd been pondering it for years.

He stretched his arms, testing their tightness. He needed to climb; it calmed him. But the idea of falling to his death didn't. He would climb only halfway this time.

He stood at the base of the wall, plotting a route. Having a plan was crucial; otherwise, he wandered about and got himself in trouble. An interesting parallel to his life.

Start with the spikes directly in front of me, then veer a bit to the left. He'd placed a few more aids there; it would make for a slightly easier climb, which his tired arms needed. Once he reached the sparser section, he'd come back down. It was a good plan.

He grabbed hold of the first spikes, ones he'd bent into something like hooks; it made for an easier beginning. He set the tips of his toes on the lowermost nails. How was it the simple act of getting his feet off the ground was so exhilarating?

He straightened his legs and reached up for the next handhold. Upward he went. Heart pounding with effort, joy expanding in his chest. He loved this.

He'd reached the height he'd intended to reach and stopped with his legs bent, arms stretched above his head, resting.

Collingham deserved better. That was the truth he could not escape. If he was unable to do better and be better, then he owed it to his neighbors, to his parishioners, to his family to step aside and let a better vicar take his place.

I need to sort myself out. I need to pursue these answers.

He retraced his path, lowering himself back down the wall. A few feet from the bottom, he let go and dropped to the ground, landing in a crouch. His lungs burned, and his arms ached with tension. But his mind, at last, was clear.

It was time to return to the vicarage and make some plans, to sort out his path.

He turned to make his way back to his pony cart. And there, not five feet away, watching him, was Sarah.

Immediately, the painful pounding started in his chest, his mind racing as he searched for the right thing to say. Holy writ wouldn't work this time.

Her wide-eyed gaze moved from him to the wall behind him. "You were so high off the ground."

"I only went halfway."

She looked to him once more. Shocked. "You climb to the top?"

He pushed past her, fetching his waistcoat, jacket, gloves, and hessians from the bush where he'd laid them. Not only had she seen him scaling a wall, but she'd also spied him dressed in only his shirtsleeves, pantaloons, and the dancing slippers he'd altered specifically for climbing. They were flexible enough for easy movement. After he'd replaced the slick soles with rough leather ones, they'd also provided a useful bit of extra grip. He did enjoy making things and solving puzzles.

"Do you do this often?" She kept pace with him as he walked back toward his cart.

"A few times a week." He braced himself for her declaration of victory in their competition. A vicar indulging regularly in such a thing was surely the unavoidable loser in any battle of suitability.

He kept his back to her and pulled on his waistcoat. "I would prefer you not whisper it about the community."

"Why?"

He spun around, arms flung up in frustration. "Vicars don't spend their time planning and practicing climbing walls in the most complicated way possible. They walk up the steps with dignity." Which reminded him . . . "I need to get the ropes down, or they'll rot."

He passed her again but didn't look in her eyes. He couldn't bear to see the mockery that would likely be there. He hid his true self from the world for a reason. A man could endure only so much ridicule.

She followed him around the wall and to the stone steps.

"I concede defeat, Sarah. You are better suited to serving this parish than I am. You do the job better. I admit it." He looked back at her as they reached the top.

"You are conceding on the basis of *this*?" Did she not see this as the victory on a silver platter that it was?

He walked along the top of the wall. She kept to the stairs.

"How long have you been climbing?" she asked.

"About an hour." He spoke as he detached the ropes.

"I don't mean *today*."

He wound the ropes into large loops, hanging them over one shoulder. They were heavy against his weary muscles. "I can't remember a time when I didn't climb, be it walls or hills or mountains. Even when I was really little, I sometimes climbed with my—" *Father*. He had a great many memories of challenging hikes with his father, sometimes involving scrambling up rocky crags and steep embankments.

He made his way back to Sarah. She was watching him with a bit too much curiosity. His very personal thoughts were not up for examination. He turned the topic, instead, to her. "What brought you out this far?"

She answered as they walked back down. "Scott convinced the stable staff to let me use a horse. I don't know that it will ever happen again, and I have ridden as long as I dare. I'm on my way back now."

Harold adjusted his heavy ropes. "Your uncle doesn't let you ride?"

"He is still angry with me for helping Layton and Bridget marry."

Years had passed since then. The two had been happy in their marriage, which had provided Mr. Sarvol with a granddaughter. Surely Mr. Sarvol had put his disappointment in his daughter's defiance of his preference behind him by now.

"He has told me that my presence in his household depends entirely on whether or not he decides to allow me to remain, and he demands further restrictions all the time." Sarah's trademark optimism was not evidenced as usual.

They reached the pony cart. Harold tossed his ropes inside and pulled on his jacket. He turned to face her more directly. "How bad is life at Sarvol House, Sarah? Truly?"

Her shoulders drooped. A breath whooshed from her. "Miserable."

"Does Scott not intervene on your behalf?" Surely her own brother did not allow her to simply be abused.

"I never see him anymore. I don't know if Uncle is monopolizing his time or if he, in an effort to spare me further suffering, is monopolizing *Uncle's* time."

Either could easily be the case. "Whatever the reason, you are being denied the company of someone you care about, someone you had intended to be part of your new life here."

A grateful sort of relief touched her features. "Yes, precisely. I've tried to pinpoint just what it was that pricked at me most about Scott's absence. It is more than just loneliness, more than just being so very isolated in that unhappy home."

He thought he understood, at least to a degree. "You are not merely being denied your brother's company; you are being denied the dreams you came here to claim."

She looked away, worry pulling at her brow. "I keep telling myself it'll all work out somehow, but I'm beginning to struggle to believe that. I have so little control over my life. No other family members live here who might offer me respite. I haven't wealth enough to find myself a home of my own. Should Uncle decide that tormenting me has lost its appeal, he is within his rights to simply toss me out. I could return to America, but . . ." She suddenly looked very tired. "My mother doesn't despise me the way my uncle does, but living in her home was miserable in its own way."

He leaned against the side of the cart. "I wish I had answers for you, but I haven't the first idea how to help."

"It is good just to have told someone how I'm feeling. I sometimes go all day without seeing another person." She turned back to him once more. "It's easy to feel forgotten."

Sarah Sarvol was not the sort of person one forgot. He knew that all too well.

"*You* always did listen to me though," she said. "No matter how mundane the topic or uninteresting it must have been to you, you always listened."

"I don't remember any uninteresting conversations."

Her eyes twinkled. "I suspect climbing to such drastic heights has somehow rattled your memory."

"It's not the most sensible thing," he said. "It's also not very vicarly."

"Does it follow, though, that climbing is *un*vicarly?"

"Could you imagine the Archbishop of York scaling the walls of Beverley Minster?" he asked dryly. "All of England would heap criticism on him day and night."

She watched him more closely. He found himself squirming under her scrutiny. "Why does it matter so much to you that people approve of you?"

"Maybe because so many don't." He stuffed his hands in his jacket pockets. "Jason's wife actually compared me to a rooster that her family ate for dinner. And everyone laughed. That's all they ever do. They laugh at Holy Harry." He motioned at the wall. "I will not give them further reason to disapprove of me and make me the permanent laughingstock of the family. And I'd rather not have that mockery coming from the parish as well."

"And that is why you are so adamant about acting the part of the perfect vicar?"

"'Act well your part; there all the honor lies.' My father used to say that."

"Alexander Pope, if I'm not mistaken," Sarah said.

Harold nodded. The quote did originate with that well-known poet. "Father lived that ideal, and he wanted us to as well. Doing our best to fill our various roles was the honorable thing and the approach most likely to succeed."

She didn't appear convinced. "'Act well *your* part,' Harold, not 'Act well *a* part,' or 'a part as defined by others.' I think your father meant to convey that whichever part you as a unique individual chose to take upon you, you should do it in the best way *you* can. What acting it well means will be different depending on the person assuming it."

"Some approaches are too different."

She reached out and took his hand. He'd not yet put his gloves back on.

"I'm sorry my hands are so callused," he said. "A gentleman's hands aren't supposed to feel that way."

"I'd wager Corbin's hands are rough as well and Stanley's." She wrapped her other hand around the back of his, sandwiching his hand between both of hers. "They are both gentlemen."

"They are not vicars."

"But you are."

He pushed out a breath and let the tension leave his shoulders. "I am at the moment."

Her brow pulled. "Do you expect that to change?"

He slipped his hands free. He'd not intended to make that admission. Sarah had always been that way. "Do you wish to ride back home, or would you care to be driven?" He indicated the cart.

She didn't answer immediately but studied him. He'd admitted a great deal already; he wasn't going to say more, not when he still lacked so many answers himself.

"I think I would enjoy continuing my ride. Uncle might never again allow it."

Her uncle was a stingy, difficult man.

"Enjoy the remainder of your ride, Sarah."

"Thank you."

He stood beside the cart, watching as she rode away. Here was another person insisting that he could be himself and a vicar without being a failure. He wanted to believe them. Sarah and Mater were intelligent and sensible. If he stopped trying so hard to be what he ought, if he started being truly himself and the mockery didn't stop—Harold pushed out a tense, uncomfortable breath. He needed answers but doubted he was truly ready for them.

CHAPTER SEVENTEEN

Sarah sat in Lady Lampton's sitting room, equally intrigued and nervous at the possibility that Harold might come to visit his sister-in-law. Her mind had been filled with him in the fortnight since she'd seen him hanging precariously from the side of the abbey ruins. She didn't know which emotion was her strongest when thinking back on that moment: fear that he might fall or relief at finally seeing him shed, however momentarily, the stiff façade he'd adopted. The Harold she had known was still there. She saw him now and then but never more than briefly.

She'd spent some time pondering his declaration that vicars don't climb walls. Though she personally would not be put off by a man of the church embracing such an odd pastime, provided he didn't neglect his duties, she could not deny that not everyone would likely feel the same. Had he earned enough of his parishioners' loyalty and trust to allow them to see this part of him? Was it even possible to?

"That purple is the perfect shade for that flower." Mater examined Sarah's embroidery. "This is going to be lovely."

She pulled her thoughts back to the moment. "And I have you to thank for it. I've wanted to make something to brighten up my rooms at Sarvol House, but I could not convince my uncle to splurge for fabric or embroidery thread."

"Is your pin money not sufficient?" Philip sat on a sofa across the way, Sorrel beside him, reclining against him. He had carried her from her bed to the adjacent sitting room but then hadn't had the heart to leave. There was an aching worry in his attachment to her, a way of looking at his wife that spoke clearly of his struggle to remain hopeful.

"He does not provide me with pin money," Sarah confessed, preferring to focus on her own difficulties if it would take Philip's and Sorrel's minds off theirs. "Scott, however, has managed to sneak me a bit of coin now and then, and I find flowers from him in my room regularly, the same sweet little purple ones each time. I'm not certain where he gets them; Sarvol House doesn't have a conservatory or hot house."

"Are you certain they aren't from the blacksmith?" Philip asked with a grin. "I understand he is still quite amused by your expertise in feats of strength."

Mater laughed. "How I wish I had been here to see that."

Sarah liked their reaction to her rather odd undertaking far more than her uncle's. "My uncle disapproved quite heartily. Apparently, so did the Hamptons."

"The Hamptons disapprove of everything." Sorrel spoke weakly, quietly. She was pale, her eyelids heavy, the darkness of illness and fatigue beneath her eyes. She looked worse every time Sarah visited.

Philip kept his arm around her, his usually jovial expression showing a bit of strain. "I'm certain they even disapprove of themselves, though they aren't sure what to make of that."

Sorrel smiled up at him. "At least they are in agreement with everyone else."

"Right you are."

Sorrel leaned against him once more, her eyes slowly closing. Mater's forehead creased as she watched her daughter-in-law. Philip's mouth turned down in a solemn line of worry. He looked across at his mother, such bleakness in his eyes. Mater offered an expression of empathy.

"I haven't seen Charlie about." Sarah hoped an innocuous topic would help ease the weight in the room. Sometimes a distraction was more welcome than anything. "I assume he is up to some mischief or another."

"He doesn't get himself in scrapes as often as he used to," Mater said. "I don't know what magic our dear Mr. Lancaster worked while Charlie was in Shropshire, but the boy came back far more grounded than when he left."

"He fell off a roof," Philip said. "That is about as grounded as one can get."

Even Sorrel laughed. She didn't open her eyes, but she spoke. "Charlie told me he is attempting to keep up with some of his studies despite being away from university. That is keeping him occupied."

"He is like a poorly trained puppy," Philip said. "Keeping him busy saves the furniture and neighborhood from destruction."

"What is your approach for keeping Harold from wreaking havoc?" Sarah asked.

"Simple," Philip answered. "We slip an open prayer book in front of him and he is distracted for hours."

"Be nice to your brother, Philip," Sorrel said. "He is a little lost."

Philip looked down at her, obviously surprised. "Why do you say that?"

"Because I pay attention, dear." Sorrel adjusted her position so she was lying flatter, her head now in her husband's lap.

Philip stroked her hair. Sorrel's hand dropped to her rounded middle, and she seemed to relax.

"I agree with Sorrel," Mater said. "You ought to be a little less teasing with Harold. I don't think you brothers realize the impact your needling has had over the years."

"Is something truly the matter?" Philip asked.

"Not 'the matter,' simply a little difficult. He is trying to sort some things and could use all our support and patience."

"I saw him the other afternoon," Sarah said. "While I cannot say he had his feet firmly beneath him"—the unintentional pun very nearly pulled a smile from her—"I saw a glimpse of Harold as he'd been when I knew him before, carefree and lighthearted."

Philip continued stroking his wife's hair, such a tender and gentle gesture. "'Carefree and lighthearted'? That does not sound like Harold."

That pricked unexpectedly at Sarah. "Then you do not know him very well."

Philip hooked an eyebrow upward. "That was your impression of him during your previous visits?"

"He was never frivolous," she acknowledged, "but he was not so stiff and sedate as he is now. It doesn't suit him, and it is an act, not the person he genuinely is."

Mater watched her closely. "It bothers you that he works so hard to be vicarly?"

"It bothers me that he works so hard to be something other than himself."

Mater reached over and squeezed her hand. "That weighs on me as well."

Sorrel made a quiet but unmistakable noise of pain. Everyone's attention was instantly on her. She appeared to be sleeping, despite her discomfort.

"She hurts all the time," Philip said quietly. "I do not know how much longer she can endure this."

"And yet we have to hope she can endure it for several more weeks," Mater said.

Philip swallowed so thickly Sarah heard the noise even from across the room. "Scorseby looked in on her this morning."

"What did the doctor have to say?" Mater asked.

"Being entirely off her feet has helped but not as much as he had hoped. She is not doing well." He took a wobbly breath. "I am terrified I'm going to lose her," he whispered.

"Oh, Philip." Mater spoke with such heartbreak. "I don't know how the two of you are enduring this for a third time."

He gently moved a strand of Sorrel's hair away from her face. A sheen of emotion glimmered in his eyes. "What am I going to do, Mater?"

"You are going to hold fast to hope," she said. "And you are not going to give up on her."

A shiver slid over Sorrel. Sarah slipped quietly from her seat. She took a light throw from the window seat and crossed back to the sofa, laying it carefully over Sorrel's sleeping form.

Philip offered her a fleeting smile and a quiet "Thank you."

Sarah nodded. "I am here quite often," she said. "If there is anything you can think of that would bring her some comfort, I do hope you will tell me." She looked to Mater. "And I hope you will as well. I so enjoy your company and would love to know that I am offering you something in return."

"You have offered your companionship and your presence," Mater said. "That is something I treasure."

Sarah laughed humorlessly. "My uncle finds my presence noxious. I am glad you do not agree."

"You come here as often as you can," Mater said. "There is no reason you should be holed up in a place where you are so poorly treated."

"I will try."

The conversation ended with the abrupt arrival of Harold, the Jonquil Sarah's thoughts hovered on more often than not.

"Why, Harold," Mater said. "How good to see you. Do come in."

Harold offered quick and excruciatingly proper bows to the room. He was back to Holy Harry, it seemed. That was disappointing.

His gaze rested on Sorrel. "Is she unwell?" he asked Philip. "Beyond the established difficulty, I mean."

Philip shook his head. "Things are simply growing more precarious."

"Then this is truly poor timing on my part."

Philip's curiosity visibly grew.

"I am called away," Harold said. "A matter of personal business."

"Personal?" Mater's voice was tight. "There is nothing the matter with any of your brothers, is there?"

"No." Harold sat beside her, setting his hand atop hers. "At least nothing of which I am aware. I simply need to . . . see to a few things."

His hesitancy caught Sarah's attention. Whatever was calling him away, he seemed reluctant to admit to it.

Harold addressed his brother once more. "I had come in the hope of begging a favor, which I realize is very presumptuous of me."

"Presumptuous but intriguing," Philip said. "What is this favor?"

"My business takes me to Cumberland, and I am hopeful you might grant me the use of a carriage and the services of one of your junior coachmen. I would be gone for at least a fortnight, perhaps a bit longer."

"A fortnight?" Mater's question was clearly an objection. "That brings you quite near to Christmas. Will you not be here to celebrate with us?"

"I have every intention of returning with time to spare before the holy day."

"What if the weather turns?" Mater pressed.

"We will hope that it doesn't."

"And what if we are in need of a vicar?" Philip asked.

"I understand Miss Sarvol is quite adept at vicar-ing," Harold said a touch too innocently. "I assumed she would take over my duties."

Sarah smiled broadly at the quip. Philip shook his head in amusement, an emotion she suspected he also benefited from in that moment.

"I have arranged for a particular colleague of mine to take my place while I am away. He is a good man with a kind heart, devoted to his duties. His parish has a curate, so he can be spared for a few weeks. He and his wife will be staying at the vicarage, and I can, without hesitation, recommend them to you should you be in need of anything, even a simple word of encouragement."

"He sounds like a saint," Philip said.

"Seems a fair trade to me," Harold answered. "You loan me a carriage; I provide you with a saint."

Philip laughed. The sound roused Sorrel a bit. Philip bit back the remainder of the laugh and set his hand gently on Sorrel's shoulder. She settled almost immediately back to sleep.

Sarah slipped closer to the door. She didn't intend to leave; she simply felt the family would appreciate a bit of privacy.

"You are welcome to use whichever of the traveling carriages best suits your needs," Philip told Harold. "I have no plans to go anywhere anytime soon."

Harold nodded. "I assumed as much."

"And," Philip continued, "if you are bound for Cumberland, you might consider staying at Brier Hill, assuming, of course, it is near to your destination."

Unmistakable relief touched Harold's face. "I had hoped you might be willing to offer that. Staying at a family holding will save me money and inconvenience."

"How soon do you intend to leave?" Mater asked.

"In the next day or two," Harold said.

"Do not neglect to come by and bid me a proper farewell before you go."

"Of course."

"And you'll write to me?"

"I will." Harold rose. He offered Philip an additional dip of his head and received an overly solemn head dip in return, complete with dancing eyes and a barely concealed smile. Philip did like to tease his brother.

Harold moved toward the door.

Sarah had been put out with him for so much of the first weeks she'd been in Collingham; however, the last few times she'd been with him, her heart had tugged.

He didn't walk past her as she expected but stopped and faced her. "May I speak with you a moment, in the corridor?"

"With *me*?" She couldn't keep the shock from her voice.

He nodded.

Absolutely unsure what to expect, she stepped with him through the door. Once in the corridor, he motioned her a little away from doorway. Apparently, he did not care to be overheard.

"I wanted to thank you for not telling them about my climbing." Was he actually blushing?

She couldn't entirely hide her amusement. "How do you know I didn't?"

He took her hand. "Because I know you, Sarah Sarvol. You gave your word. You're not one to break it."

It was one of the kindest things anyone had ever said to her. "I'll promise not to break my word if you promise not to break your neck."

A few times during their walks around the Park when they were younger, he'd smiled at her a little crooked, a little mischievous. Her heart had threatened to leap out of her chest then. Seeing that smile now, she felt that same pounding return.

"I'll do my best."

"Whatever is taking you away seems important." She didn't want to pry, but he had listened to her concerns. She wanted to give him that same listening ear he'd offered her.

"It is," he said. "I need to spend some time sorting out how I am meant to act well my part and what that part even is."

"And you'll remember that your part should bring you happiness?"

He, to her surprise, took her hand and lifted it to his lips, then pressed a kiss to her fingers. "I am working very hard to bear that in mind."

She set her other hand gently against his cheek. "Be safe in your travels, Harold."

"Do you suppose my family would miss me if my travels did not go well?"

Did he truly doubt that? "Of course they would."

He closed a bit of the gap between them, so close she could see the depth in his blue eyes. "Would *you* miss me?"

She suddenly couldn't seem to force her voice to function. Hardly breathing, she nodded.

He kissed her hand one more time, then pulled away. He made his way down the corridor and out of sight. She was seeing more and more of *her* Harold. Kind. Caring. Willing to acknowledge a degree of affection for her. Attentive. Seeing her unhappiness when so many others didn't. Wishing to help her and support her. He was coming back to himself by bits, and her heart was growing vulnerable in equal measure.

CHAPTER EIGHTEEN

Cumberland

Harold stood atop Long Crag in clothes he'd borrowed from the coachman whom he'd borrowed from Philip. The cold air bit at him, the sting invigorating. Hilltops were quiet and peaceful. The effort required to reach them added depth to the experience. The top of Long Crag hadn't been overly difficult to reach, but he'd managed to find a few sections that offered a bit of a challenge.

He took in a lungful of cold air. He hadn't realized until standing there just how much he had missed this, how much he had longed to be on a summit again. Father had sometimes taken him to the family holding in Cambria, Brier Hill, and they had gone on any number of hikes. They had, in fact, summited this very peak.

"I think mountains may be the most peaceful places in the world," Father had said while they were sitting on an outcropping, eating a lunch he'd packed along. "It's rather like a church, isn't it?"

Harold hadn't thought of that moment in years. Father had been more correct than Harold could possibly have realized at so young an age. Being inside the church brought him an inarguable measure of peace. It was the reason he arrived ahead of the choir on rehearsal night and so far ahead of the time for mass and evening prayers. It was the reason he sometimes went to the chapel to simply sit. That same feeling of contentment and home that he felt inside the church, he had found here, high above the world, so near the heavens.

Philip had teased him when he'd come to claim the traveling carriage. He'd asked if Holy Harry meant to make a pilgrimage. Standing atop Long Crag, Harold realized he ought to have answered in the affirmative.

He'd taken this abrupt holiday in search of answers, in search of himself, not knowing where precisely to look for either one. He needed to know if being more himself would lift the burden crushing his mind and heart.

But if he discovered it did, what path did that put him on?

The crag was empty except for him. He preferred it that way, with one glaring exception. He wished Father were there. He needed his wisdom, his insights, his reassurance.

"How do I reconcile all of this, Father? I like being a vicar. I like helping people, when I manage it. But who I am and who a vicar ought to be don't seem to match at all."

The wind blew fiercely against him. He closed his eyes and imagined his Father standing beside him.

"What do I do?"

That beloved voice, grown vaguer as the years had passed and time had taken its toll on Harold's memory, echoed in his mind. "Act well your part."

"Sarah says what that means depends on me and the way I'm suited to that 'part.' Do you suppose it's possible to rewrite a part as well defined as that of a vicar?"

No answers came by the time he made his way back down. Feet on flat ground once more, he popped his hands into his trouser pockets and whistled a jaunty tune. The excursion had improved his spirits despite the weight on his mind. It had helped.

His path back to Brier Hill passed directly in front of the local village inn. Music floated out of the public room, a familiar tune he'd learned from Mrs. Dalton.

His first inclination was to remind himself that vicars didn't generally frequent public houses. But then he shrugged. This holiday was meant as a chance to see if an *un*vicarly life would suit him better. He didn't intend to do anything untoward or risqué. Taking a meal in a public room fell precisely into that "probably not wholly vicarly but also not unsavory" category.

He stepped inside. The innkeeper welcomed him warmly.

"A bowl of stew, sir?" he asked.

"And a thick slice of bread, if you have it," Harold said.

"Right quick." He disappeared into the kitchen.

Harold turned to face the room. It was a lively space, though not a rowdy one. He appreciated that. Musicians sat in chairs near the fire, their tune filling the room. A few patrons sat about, tapping their feet to the music or bouncing a bit. A few others sat gathered around a table, laughing and talking.

In a dim corner sat Philip's coachman, a tankard in his hand, his posture slumped forward. He looked pensive. Heavens, Harold himself probably looked that way more often than not lately. Perhaps he could help.

He approached. "May I sit with you?"

"I've no objection."

Harold sat. "You'll forgive me if I'm being nosy, but you look as though you have a weight on your mind."

He nodded slowly, silently.

"I'm a good listener, John." Harold hoped calling him by his Christian name would help him feel more comfortable discussing what might be a personal matter.

John spun his tankard slowly on the tabletop. "Harriet's marrying someone else."

Harold wasn't certain who Harriet was, but he could easily piece together the situation. "I'm sorry to hear that."

"Courted her for more than a year, I did. She fell for the merchant's son though. Can't say I blame her for choosing him. He can give her a life I can't." John took a long pull of ale. Nothing in his demeanor spoke of drunkenness, simply sadness.

Harold suspected what John needed far more than the sermon a vicar might be expected to offer was a bit of sincere empathy. Harold could offer a plethora of that. "That is a difficult thing to realize, isn't it? That the woman you love would be better off without you."

The innkeeper approached and set a bowl of stew and a slice of bread on the table in front of him. Harold thanked him and pulled the food closer, his stomach reminding him that he'd worked up quite an appetite on that hilltop.

John looked over his tankard at Harold. "Did a woman pass you over too, Mr. Jonquil?"

"Not exactly." Harold took a bite before continuing. "We had a tenderness for each other, a growing attachment. But I had years of study ahead of me and no means of predicting how long it would be before I had a living and a means of supporting a wife and family. I knew it was better for her if she was free to give her heart elsewhere, so I ended things between us."

John watched him, genuinely curious. "How'd she react?"

"Let's just say I still have the scar."

John laughed so quickly and suddenly that several men around the room looked in their direction.

"We're discussing the dangers of disappointing a woman," Harold told them.

Glasses were raised. Words of support and agreement were offered.

"You see, John? You aren't alone in this."

"Doesn't make it any easier."

Harold shook his head. "That it doesn't. Sometimes life asks us to walk a difficult path."

"But don't the good book say that the Lord will light the path?"

It wasn't an exact recounting, but the sentiment was correct. "It certainly does."

John nodded before sipping again. He wasn't lighthearted by any means, but he did seem a little less burdened.

"Have you had anything to eat?" Harold asked.

John shook his head.

"Let me buy you a bowl of this stew. It's delicious."

"No, sir. Lord Lampton paid me for my time on this trip with money enough for feeding myself." John squared his shoulders. "I'll not be double paid. That wouldn't be honest."

"Would you consider allowing it in acknowledgment of loaning me these clothes?" Harold asked. "They were just what I needed today."

John shook his head firmly.

How could he convince the man? Harold was almost unspeakably grateful to Philip for paying John's wages during this journey, as well as the stabling of the horses and upkeep on the carriage. If Harold hadn't been so desperately in need of answers, he never would have undertaken the pilgrimage.

He had money enough, though, to buy John a simple meal in a humble inn. And it wasn't an act of charity but an effort to lift him from his sorrows, to demonstrate that he was noticed and valued. But a man who'd been passed over by the love of his heart in favor of someone better heeled than he was would feel it a blow to receive anything resembling charity.

"A wager, then?" Harold suggested. He truly was stepping out of his vicarly persona.

John was clearly intrigued.

Harold grinned. He turned to the musicians. "I have a challenge for you, if you're of a mind to accept."

"What is it?" one asked.

"I'd like to make a wager with my friend John, here, that you can't pick a tavern song that I don't know the lyrics to."

The flute player snorted. The others laughed.

"A gentry cove like you?" The fiddle player shook his head in amusement.

"It's madder than that," John tossed in. "He's a vicar."

The laughter that followed that declaration would have quelled anyone less confident in his repertoire. The musicians conferenced, discussing in whispers what they ought to choose.

"Make it challenging," Harold called out.

The other patrons paused in their activities and were waiting with palpable interest. After a moment, the musicians were ready. Harold was given three almost identical looks of pity mixed with amusement.

"I've a feeling I'm going to be hungry," John said.

"Have faith, John."

The musicians hit an opening note and watched Harold as their selection moved forward. Harold let his smile grow excruciatingly slowly. As the song reached its chorus, he sang with enthusiasm,

"So come what will, boys, drink it still
Your cheeks 'twill never pale.
Their foreign stuff is well enough,
But give me old English ale."

Amazement gave way to laughter around the room. Soon, everyone was joining in. The song grew gusty and heavy with joviality. As they sang on, Harold motioned to the proprietor.

"A bowl of stew for John," he requested. "And a thick slice of bread."

"Can't believe you knew that," John said. "I've sung it since I was a boy, but I ain't Quality, and I certainly ain't a church man. Do you know many others?"

"Quite a few," he confessed. "It's an oddity in me."

"And do you drink a great deal?"

He shook his head. "I have never seen the appeal of being tipsy."

John dug into his stew, which had been swiftly delivered. Apparently, the proprietor had not doubted Harold's ability to win the wager. "You ain't married, Mr. Jonquil. Is your heart still pining for the lady you disappointed?"

It was more personal a question than any of his parishioners had ever asked him. His first inclination was to pull back, to keep that formal distance.

But Sarah's words filled his mind, censuring him however gently. "I talk to people, Harold."

Part of the reason he hadn't married was his meager income. The living was not a miserly one, but the disrepair of his home and the chapel drained his finances. He simply couldn't afford the food, clothing, or basic needs of even one other person. How often he had bemoaned the lack of financial education given to future men of the cloth. With a little more training in that area, he might have known better how to address those particular difficulties.

A bigger part of the reason was, indeed, Sarah. He'd not met anyone he loved even half as much as he had loved her. Seeing her in Collingham the past weeks had been an exercise in contradictions. He realized the enormity of the chasm between them as well as the deep and abiding feelings he still had for her. There were no good answers.

John was struggling with the pain of heartbreak. Harold knew that pain all too well.

"I do still care for her," he admitted. "And though I don't know that anything would come of it, I hope she still cares for me as well."

John nodded slowly, knowingly. "The hoping is sometimes the most painful part. You can't always know if you're hoping in vain."

"I suspect I am."

John pointed a finger at him. "You still have a chance. I'd wager m' boots on it."

"I'd hate for you to be rendered bare-footed," Harold said with a small laugh.

John shook his head. "Is the lady married?"

"No."

"Is she near enough that you could see her again?"

Harold nodded. "She lives in the vicinity of Collingham."

"Does she have a suitor?"

"No."

A firm and decided nod from John. "Then you've a chance."

Harold finished off his last bite of soup. "She did seem a little sad when I told her I would be gone for a couple weeks."

"Ah, then. There's something to build on." John turned to the rest of the room. "Our vicar here has a lady he's pining for who needs a little convincing that he ain't a clodhead."

That was actually a very good explanation of the situation.

"What advice have we for him?"

Harold pushed his bowl a bit away, amused despite himself. "This hardly seems necessary."

"Nonsense, Mr. Jonquil. I've no hope of having my Harriet's love and devotion. I'll not let you lose your love."

This, then, had the potential to be healing for John. How could he not allow the bit of admittedly embarrassing fun if it would help?

I cannot believe I am about to encourage this. "What say you, men? How do I best re-secure my lady's affection?"

"Have you tried kissing her?" the flute player suggested.

Harold nodded. He pointed to the long white scar running along the underside of his jaw. "Kissing her is what earned me this scar."

"Then you didn't do it right, my friend."

They all laughed at that, Harold included.

"Did she give a reason for putting you off?" a man at the neighboring table asked.

Harold turned a little to face the room more directly. "She didn't at the time."

"What did she say *not* at the time?" another man asked.

"More recently, she disapproved of the way I fulfill my calling as vicar."

"Because you know tavern songs?" the fiddler asked.

He shook his head. "She doesn't know about that."

"No one in our parish knows about that," John said. "Until today, if you'd asked, I'd've assumed you were a regular sort of vicar. Boring and a little above your company."

Harold winced. "That is precisely her evaluation."

"Sing her a chorus of 'Old English Ale,'" the fiddler said. "She'll change her tune right quick."

"She'll change it to 'Farewell, Fair One,'" Harold tossed back.

Again, the room laughed. Harold was not at all accustomed to bringing smiles and amusement to people's faces. It was a far more satisfying accomplishment than putting them all to sleep, which was what usually happened.

"Do you do anything else that might change the lady's ideas about you?" a man asked.

Harold leaned back in his chair. "I climb mountains, walls, and bridges, and a great many odd things. I once had aspirations of learning to do tricks on horseback; I still sometimes think about it. And I enjoy reading novels." That was a peccadillo he hadn't admitted to anyone before.

"Those are stories, then?" a man asked. "Not the books about church or being a better person."

"They *are* stories," Harold confirmed. "But one can learn about being a better person from reading them, either by reading a story of someone who is working to be better or about someone who chooses very poorly and turns out not good at all."

"Sounds like one of them parables to me," John said.

"Yes. The parables were, essentially, very short novels, stories that taught a principle by letting the listener learn from another's experiences."

"Seems that isn't so bad a thing for a vicar to be reading, then," the flute player said.

"It is, unfortunately, frowned on."

"I'd guess tavern songs are as well," the fiddler countered.

"And climbing mountains, maybe," a man added.

"And performing feats on horseback," John said.

Harold sighed and let his posture slump, something he seldom allowed. "Therein lies my difficulty, men. This elusive lady thinks me boring and standoffish, yet the things about me that make me unique are not acceptable."

"If you're asking me, Mr. Jonquil," John said, "I like you better for knowing you've a few oddities about you. Makes me feel I could come to you if I had troubles and you'd not look down on me for it since you ain't a saint or one of those angel types."

"I wouldn't look down on you." He hoped John heard his sincerity. "I would want to hear and help in any way I could."

"I believe you," he said. "Now."

Being himself hadn't negated his influence as a vicar in John's eyes, but not everyone viewed the world the way this collection of jovial and friendly men did.

Sarah had been berated by her uncle and the Hamptons and likely a few others for her silliness with the blacksmith, no matter that it had been a bit of genius and had helped a great many people. How many would disapprove of him being "an odd sort of vicar" if he let himself be more the person he was? How many would turn away instead of draw nearer? Did he dare risk it?

If being himself meant losing his parishioners, he could not justify it. But neither could he continue on as he had been if doing so meant losing himself.

CHAPTER NINETEEN

"Then the happy little fairy took the hand of her sweet fairy friend, and the two fluttered away on the breeze in search of more grand adventures." The little ones sitting on Sarah's lap clapped enthusiastically.

"Another one," the older of the siblings, at only four years old, requested.

Sarah looked to Mater. She'd come with the dear lady to call on the Joneses, the Lampton Park tenants who recently added a newborn to their brood, one who'd had a difficult first couple of months. Sarah had happily accepted the task of keeping the other children occupied while Mater visited with and offered what comfort she could to Mrs. Jones.

"If you have no objections, I would like to call again," Mater said to Mrs. Jones. "But I also hope you will send word if there is anything at all that you need."

The visit, then, was coming to its conclusion.

Sarah pulled the little ones in closer and said conspiratorially, "I will think of a particularly wonderful adventure for our two fairies, and I will come again and share it with you."

Though they were clearly disappointed, they accepted the necessity of her departure. She stood once the children had scrambled down. They smiled up at her, and she winked back before crossing to Mater and Mrs. Jones.

"Thank you for coming, Miss Sarvol," Mrs. Jones said.

"I am so pleased you welcomed me," she said. "I do love spending time with children. And your new little one is so very handsome, even if he is giving his mother a great deal of grief."

"Mr. Jonquil visited before he left," Mrs. Jones said. "Told us you were likely to visit. Even said Miss Sarvol might."

"He did?" Sarah could hardly have been more surprised.

Mrs. Jones smiled. "Seems he knows both of you well."

"It does seem that way, indeed," Mater said.

Harold had predicted she would call? His interactions with her of late had been softer, kinder, more tender. Her faith in him was growing. His faith in her was as well, it seemed.

They all exchanged farewells, and Mater and Sarah slipped from the cottage. They walked side by side down the lane, past a few other tenant homes. They exchanged greetings with the children who were about.

"Thank you for coming with me," Mater said. "It was far easier to give Mrs. Jones the attention and care I wished to while the children were being so expertly seen to."

"I do not know about 'expertly,' but I do enjoy children. It was a joy to be with them and a pleasure to have offered an afternoon of service to Mrs. Jones."

"It is a very good thing we did, else Harold would have had our necks." Mater bit back a laugh.

Her humor allowed Sarah's to blossom as well. "I can hardly reconcile his certainty that *I* would call on Mrs. Jones. Harold has not always thought well of me these past few weeks."

They turned down the lane that led along the hedge lining Lampton Park's north lawn.

"You have pricked at him, Sarah," Mater said. "And that is an uncomfortable experience for any person. But I do not for a moment believe he thinks poorly of you."

Sarah tucked her scarf more closely around her neck against the bite of December's frigid breath.

"Do you dislike him?" Mater asked the question with too heavy a tone of innocence for the inquiry to be entirely off-hand.

To Sarah's horror, emotion gripped her heart. It did not go unnoticed. Mater slipped her arm through Sarah's as they walked onward. Mater didn't press for a response, but Sarah didn't believe for a moment she had lost her interest in the answer.

Sarah swallowed the lump in her throat. "He broke my heart," she said, her voice emerging, though barely audible.

"Would it help to talk about it? I realize I am the boy's mother, but yours is not nearby."

"I loved him." Had she ever admitted that out loud? "We spent a great deal of time together—always in appropriate settings, of course—though perhaps we spent more time in the gardens, a bit isolated, than was entirely acceptable."

Mater nodded. "I did notice you two seemed fond of each other."

"Scott told me that he and my parents had pieced that together as well. They were wiser than I though. They realized it would not end well, but I had too many stars in my eyes."

Mater squeezed her arm as they walked on. "In what way did it not end well?"

Heat flamed her cheeks, but she pressed on. Understanding all that had happened might help her heart finally heal. "He kissed me."

"And that was unpleasant?"

She laughed, and what a joy it was to be able to do so. "No. That part was . . . wonderful, truth be told." She glanced at Mater out of the corner of her eye. "That is likely an uncomfortable thing to have someone say about one of your sons."

"Oh, my dear. Their father used to kiss me in such a way . . ." She sighed. "I would be very surprised if any of his sons proved entirely inept at it."

"The kiss was not unpleasant," Sarah said. "I'd hardly had time to catch my breath, though, when he said, quite without warning, that he would not ever write to me nor should I write to him, as he would not accept my letters."

Mater's eyes pulled a little wide, but she did not seem inclined to interrupt.

"At first, I was too shocked to say or do anything. Then, I will admit, I grew angry." She left out the part where she'd shoved him into the stream. There was only so much a person could admit to at once. "Mostly, though, I was hurt. Deeply, terribly hurt. That is the emotion that has remained. Hurt and pain and heartbreak."

"I will let you in on a family secret, Sarah Sarvol. The Jonquil brothers are utter dolts in matters of the heart."

"Did they inherit *that* tendency from their father as well?"

Mater laughed. "Absolutely."

Sarah felt surprisingly better having spoken of that difficult time and having received such ready support from this beloved lady. "Scott said that

Harold, along with all my family, would have known from the beginning that the attachment growing between us could not be continued."

Mater nodded. "You were both too young."

"Yet, he pursued it, then so callously ended it."

Mater's features tugged in pondering. "And that has left you wondering if his attentions to you were fully sincere."

"I confess, those doubts have entered my thoughts."

"Then allow me to share something with you that I have not told any of his brothers, neither have I informed him that I witnessed it."

Sarah all but held her breath. What did Mater intend to tell her?

"Harold had been happier and more hopeful during those weeks you were visiting, something I assumed had a great deal to do with you. I never did ask, but I suspected. Then he grew very suddenly distant toward the end of your stay. I suspect that change came about because he had reconciled himself to the necessity of doing what he ought to have done from the beginning: end the growing connection between you that he could not honor."

Sarah kept her gaze forward, almost afraid to hear the remainder of Mater's retelling.

"He didn't talk much to anyone. He was aloof and morose. His brothers teased him mercilessly, something I am ashamed to say I didn't realize affected him as much as it did." Mater took a moment, perhaps reflecting on those days, perhaps regretting not intervening. "I remember the day you left, Sarah. I remember because it was the last time I ever saw Harold cry."

Sarah froze. With painstakingly slow movements, she turned to face Mater. No words emerged.

Mater's expression turned a touch sad. "You told me that you loved him. My dear, he loved you too. I suspect that is why, despite knowing the unavoidable ending that awaited your tenderness for each other, he could not manage to end it sooner. His honor as a gentleman required that he put a period to things before you left, but your departure shattered him. And though it will sound a touch melodramatic, I will tell you that he has not been the same since. He never returned to that happy and hopeful Harold he had been. He holds back every emotion, every vulnerability. Your leaving left a hole in his heart, and he protects it fiercely."

Sarah shook her head. She could not reconcile this. "Why, then, was he so unhappy when I returned?"

"I don't think he was unhappy."

On this score, Sarah knew herself to be on firm ground. "Had you been here for the dinner Philip and Layton invited Scott and I to the first few days we were in the neighborhood, you would know with perfect clarity that he was not at all pleased to see me."

Mater smiled a bit. "I would wager his brothers did not warn him you would be there. They like to torment him. I'm certain he thinks they do so because they dislike or disapprove of him."

"Why do you suppose they do it?"

They began walking again. "Because they love him, first of all. Secondly, because they miss him. He has been so unreachable these past years, tucked behind a façade of feigned perfection. I think they'd like to see that crack and fall away so they can have their brother back."

Sarah had felt precisely the same way since returning to the neighborhood. Harold had become something, some*one* he wasn't. No matter that he'd hurt her, she wanted the gentleman she'd loved so deeply to come back. The fleeting glimpses she'd had of him had been torturous in a way. She missed him as well. Missed him fiercely.

Mater continued. "I imagine what you interpreted as displeasure at being in your company was surprise and shock at seeing someone with whom he'd once had so personal a connection. When he doesn't know what to do, my Harold pulls into himself. He often comes across as almost unbearably confident, perhaps even a little arrogant. But there is so much doubt and uncertainty in him."

"Perhaps on this journey of his, he will find more reason to value himself. He truly does deserve to be happy."

"So do you." Mater patted her arm. "I suspect you hide from all of us just how unhappy you are in your current circumstances."

At the reminder, the tension in her shoulders increased tenfold. She hadn't spoken with anyone about her situation in detail, other than Harold. He had asked, had listened. That had been his way years earlier as well. He saw her when others didn't. He heard her when she struggled to find her voice. He had a way of showing her with ease that he cared. "Life at Sarvol House is more miserable than I expected it to be. I seldom see Scott, and when I do, he always looks so burdened and unhappy. He has stopped having flowers sent to my room. The house is growing almost unbearably lonely and unhappy, but what can I do? Ladies are, unfortunately, very much at the mercy of our male relatives, and my uncle happens to be a miserable person."

"The law and Society give so much control over our lives to the men around us," Mater said. "But, my dear, that does not mean we have no choices."

Sarah wasn't certain if Mater had something particular in mind or was speaking more generally. They continued onward toward the Park, now within view.

"I do have the option of returning to America, though I don't particularly wish to."

Mater's nod was more acknowledgment than agreement. It was also encouragement.

"Some ladies marry to improve their circumstances." Thinking through her choices aloud might help Sarah find one she could cling to. "Being a governess is acceptable work for a lady, and I do like children. Being a lady's companion is also a possibility. Or I could stay where I am but find reasons to be away from the house as often as possible."

None of the options were ideal, but the reminder that she had choices helped her feel more hopeful.

"If you ever need a reason to get away, simply say your presence has been requested at Lampton Park. I will happily corroborate your story, even with no warning."

"I wouldn't wish to impose on you," Sarah said.

"If I told you we have flowers in our conservatory, would that help?" Mischief twinkled in Mater's eyes.

"Are you bribing me?"

Mater nodded without a hint of shame.

"I will likely take you up on your offer more often than you bargained for," Sarah warned.

Mater patted her arm. "You are always welcome here, Sarah. Always."

A carriage sat at the house's front portico. The Park, it seemed, had visitors. It was the perfect excuse for Sarah to slip away.

After a quick embrace and a word of farewell, Mater moved toward the house while Sarah turned to make her way back to Sarvol House.

"The law and Society give so much control over our lives to the men around us, but that does not mean we have no choices."

She had choices. But which one was the right one?

CHAPTER TWENTY

"IF I'M BEING TOO FAMILIAR, Mr. Jonquil, you just tell me. I don't want to overstep myself." John tossed him a look of concern. They had been rather chummy since their time in the public room a few nights earlier.

"I have no concerns on that score," Harold said. "Though I would like to know where we are going."

John grinned mischievously. "George—you met him at the inn; he plays the fiddle—told me there's an old stone wall out this way that the people here have a tradition of climbing. Reaching the top is a feat they celebrate since not many manage it."

"You certainly have my attention."

They walked along a narrow footpath in the direction of what sounded like a gathering of people. A din of voices, in fact. Harold pushed down the nervousness that always surfaced when faced with large groups. Vicars were supposed to interact; he needed to do so.

"You said those nights ago that you like climbing things, bridges and walls and such."

Ah. "George wants to see if I can climb their infamous wall."

"Everyone wants to see," John corrected.

Up ahead was, indeed, a gathering of men and boys standing near the base of a large, incomplete stone wall, most likely a ruin of a structure built long ago. Not unlike the abbey ruins. But was this one safe? A crumbling wall ought not be climbed, no matter the applause one might receive for being successful. He'd have to assess things before agreeing to the challenge.

The waiting men met him with welcomes and handshakes. Those he hadn't met at the inn or from walking about the small hamlet near Brier Hill were introduced to him. George repeatedly referred to him as "the climbing curate," which was both clever and a bit ridiculous. Harold wasn't a curate, though he once had been. And climbing was not his defining characteristic, though it was certainly a notable one, considering how unusual it was.

"We call this Cuthbert's Wall," George said once Harold had been introduced to everyone. "Been here since our grandfathers' time, probably longer."

That could be a good or bad thing, depending on how well it was built and how poorly it had weathered.

"Climbing it is a matter of pride, though few reach the top."

Harold nodded his understanding as he inspected the wall. He had, on a number of occasions when he was young, climbed the walls of Lampton Park. This wall was not nearly as high as those. It was lower than many of the walls at the abbey as well. "Is it sturdy, or does it have a tendency to crumble?"

An older man standing among them spoke up. "I've not ever seen a single stone come loose, and I've been watching people climb it for sixty years."

That was reassuring. "How many people have reached the top in those sixty years?" Knowing the odds wouldn't be a bad thing.

"Not many," the man said. "Not many."

Harold could understand why. The wall was fairly sheer, without a lot of grooves for one's fingers and toes. And unlike a mountain or a steep hill or a bridge, it shot straight up with little angle of incline to ease the way. This would require a great deal of care. A casual climber, one who had not made any kind of study of it, would struggle tremendously.

"Have many been injured in the attempt?"

Several nods answered his question.

Hmm. He walked along the wall, studying it. He found a section that was a bit more uneven, a bit rougher. He could see several places that would serve as more than adequate toe holds and a good number of stones jutting out enough for him to grip with his fingers.

He spied a good gripping spot at eye level. *Left hand there.* Another good spot nearby would do for his right hand. He had a couple of good beginnings for his feet. He mentally picked out his next spot, then the next. The path he'd need to take upward meandered a bit, but that wasn't unusual. A climber had to go where the wall let him. This wall, he felt certain, *was* going to let him.

"I've a farthing that says the Climbing Curate can't conquer our wall," someone in the crowd said.

"I'll match that," John said, "but I'm betting he'll make it."

More wagers were tossed around, some in support of Harold, some in support of the wall. Harold couldn't help thinking back on the wagers surrounding Sarah's feigned feat of strength. He'd been so sure in that moment that she was in the wrong. He felt differently now. He'd seen the good she'd done.

Harold turned from the wall to face the crowd. "I'm not certain I can make a climb if wagers are involved. As a man of the cloth, I'm more or less required to frown on such things. However . . ." He let the word dangle.

A young boy took the bait. "However *what*?"

"If you'd care to change up those wagers a bit, agreeing that should I prove successful, any money wagered on me will be given to your parish poor box, then I think I could overlook the betting."

"Sounds like a vicar to me," someone said, the words filled with laughter. The gathering followed suit, tossing out a few teasing comments and grins of clear amusement.

While the crowd arranged their various wagers, Harold set himself to plotting his path. An unfamiliar wall brought some risk. Cautious planning helped to mitigate it.

Everything seemed to be sorted out amongst the observers. They were watching him now.

"I believe I have identified a workable path," he said. He pulled off his hat and set it on an obliging rock. His gloves came off next, followed by his jacket and waistcoat.

He looked over at the men. "None of you will be offended if I take my shoes and stockings off, will you? I am relatively certain I'd never find a place to put my feet if I have to make room for these thick, unyielding hessians." Not to mention he'd not be able to feel the wall in the same way. For such a precarious climb, he needed all the information he could get, and he did not have with him the dancing slippers he'd modified for climbing.

They all encouraged him to do whatever was needed, their curiosity growing visibly.

After a moment, he stood at the base of the wall in nothing but his shirtsleeves and pantaloons. It was quite possibly the least vicarly he had appeared in public since he was a boy. And yet, he felt more himself than he had in ages.

He set his hands around the outcropping of rock he'd chosen. The toes of his left foot found their spot. He balanced himself on that foot, gripped tight with his hands, and set his right foot in its spot. His legs bent out in either direction, his hips close to the wall.

He straightened his legs and reached up for the next left-hand hold, then the right hand. He moved his feet to spots he'd preselected. Again and again he followed the pattern, keeping himself tucked close to the wall, using his legs to lift himself up.

About three-quarters of the way from the top, his arms began loudly protesting. He found a spot on the wall with an easy grip, a stone large enough for both his hands to grip. He took tight hold of it and moved his legs to a good, comfortable position. He bent his legs once more, letting his arms pull out straight so they could rest a moment.

He shook out one arm at a time, all the while studying his next moves. Hanging there, he was able to determine the remainder of his route. Outside of his waning energy, it wouldn't be too difficult. He'd made much harder climbs at the abbey.

He pulled in a deep breath, shook out his arms one more time, and resumed his task. He moved quickly and confidently until his hand slapped the top of the wall. With a surge of effort, he pulled himself up.

He sat on top of the wall, conqueror. His breaths came hard, and his arms burned with the effort, but the elation he felt outweighed the punishment. He'd done it. Below him, the men cheered. He held up his hands in triumph, eliciting a renewed excitement below.

"That's nearly four pounds for the poor box," John called up to him.

Four pounds. The local vicar could do a fair amount of good with four pounds. Harold had helped, not by adhering to the strictest rules of expected behavior but by giving rein to his oddities. For once, he was glad he had risked being truly himself.

From his position so high up, he took in the vista, the expanse of hills and moorland, the distant village, a church spire barely visible. *It is rather like a church.* Father's words often returned to his thoughts in moments of struggle, but they also arrived in his rare moments of success.

I wish you were here, Father. I wish you were here to give me the courage I too often lack.

"Are you planning to live up there, Mr. Jonquil?" John grinned up at him.

Harold shrugged. "This is a view I could quickly grow accustomed to."

"It ain't so pleasant when it's raining." George's observation earned him hearty and amused agreement from all around him.

Harold could appreciate that. "It is a little cold."

"Especially since you're half naked."

More laughter and grins. Harold stood once more, examining the wall. Planning a route down would be tricky, especially since he was tired and his fingertips and toes had taken a bit of a beating. Perhaps this wall had steps along the back like the one at the abbey. Sure enough, he spied the weathered remains of a set of stone steps.

He motioned that way. "Did you know there are steps back here?"

That met with the most raucous laughter of all. They had, indeed, all known it.

"They're the reward for making the climb," the old man in the group explained. "We don't count the effort if a man uses the steps to get up, but he's more than welcome to use them to get back down."

"I will accept that offer gladly." Harold carefully made his way along the top of the wall.

The steps were a bit slick but far easier than climbing down would've been. He was on the ground in no time and made his way around the wall to the front side where the onlookers awaited. They greeted him with cheers, pats on the back, and words of sincere congratulations. Not a single one chastised or berated him. Not a bit of disapproval touched a single face.

Had this been undertaken amongst a gathering of Society, the response would likely have been quite different.

A few of the boys and younger men were attempting to climb.

Harold approached, watching their efforts. "Might I offer some information?"

A few hopped back onto the ground. Others clung to the wall, even as their gazes turned to him. None had gone very high.

Harold dove into a quick explanation of testing a potential gripping spot, of the necessity of being thoughtful and cautious when making so difficult a climb.

"I've been making these sorts of climbs nearly all my life," he told them. "It's not as easy as it likely seems. Until you've had a great deal of practice and can climb easily, you would be wise to keep very near the ground. Practicing a foot off the ground is just as effective as a meter, but you're less likely to desperately injure yourself from that distance."

"We won't fall," one of the boys insisted.

"Everyone falls," he said. "Best not climb too high early on."

He talked several of them through very brief climbs, only so high that they could jump back down without any danger. He offered suggestions on things they might do differently.

Over the course of that single afternoon, he built a comradery with these boys that he'd struggled to form with the small number of Collingham lads who had come to him now and then for tutoring. He might have made greater progress with his pupils if he'd taken them somewhere to climb.

He might have heard more often from his parishioners who were struggling if he'd spent some time in the inn's public room singing songs and swapping tales.

He might have better provided for the poor in his area if he'd been willing to take an unexpected approach to gathering funds.

And he would likely have been less uncomfortable interacting with people if more of those interactions involved him sharing things he enjoyed, things he had a talent for.

These good people clearly approved of his efforts that day and a few nights earlier at the public house. But the upper rungs of Society likely wouldn't. He had parishioners from both segments of the population, and he didn't wish to alienate either.

Somewhere in the balance of that lay the answers he was looking for.

CHAPTER TWENTY-ONE

"Fe, fi, fo, fum!" Philip did a ridiculous but enthusiastic impression of a monstrous giant as he lumbered down the portrait hall in belabored pursuit of his nieces.

Corbin and his family had arrived for an extended stay over the holy season. Little Alice was, as near as Sarah could piece together the connection, Corbin's wife's daughter from a previous marriage. He had two sons, but the older was connected to him and his wife in a more complicated way, one Sarah had not yet unraveled. It mattered very little in the interactions of the family. They clearly all loved each other. And no one watching Philip chasing Alice and Caroline around the hall could possibly miss the deep love *he* had for these children.

Both girls giggled and squealed and ran about in feigned shows of fear.

Caroline spotted Sarah first. "Save us, Sarah! The giant is going to eat our bones!"

Philip rubbed at his belly and licked his lips. "Bones are my favorite," he said in a deep, growling voice.

"Don't eat us!" Alice grinned broadly.

"You'll save us, won't you, Sarah?" Caroline pressed.

"Do not fear, ladies." She stepped fully into the hall, hands fisted on her hips, chin at a heroic angle. She pulled an invisible sword from its scabbard. "I shall vanquish the monster." She assumed the best fencing stance she could, considering she'd had no actual training and did not, in fact, have a sword in her hand.

Philip, who had always been one for a lark, played along brilliantly but in a very unexpected way. He screamed, his pitch nearly as high as the little girls' had been. "Save me, fair maidens." He did his best to hide behind his nieces, but being exceptionally tall, his efforts proved hilariously ridiculous.

"I thought the gentlemen were supposed to save the fair maidens," Caroline said.

In his normal voice once more and with a grin of bemusement, he said, "That is not how it has ever played out in my life."

Sarah allowed a smile. The Jonquil men never had been intimidated by women of purpose and capability. It was one of the things she loved about them. They understood that they could be strong and able and protective without requiring others to be weak, ineffectual, and subservient. The late earl had often spoken of Mater's tenacity and intelligence and had done so with an undeniable tenderness and appreciation.

Harold had shown himself cut from the same cloth as his father. He'd never attempted to prove himself superior to her nor treated her with dismissal. That was, sadly, a somewhat rare thing amongst gentlemen. He had also never appeared to feel the least threatened when she'd known more than him about a particular topic or disagreed with his view on a matter. Even now, when she had challenged him to their ridiculous vicaring competition, he'd not lashed out nor treated her unkindly no matter that she'd struck at a particularly vulnerable piece of his puzzle.

He was good. In his company, she felt safe. And when he was truly himself, he felt like home in a way she hadn't experienced with anyone else.

Caroline held little Alice's hand and looked from Sarah to Philip and back, clearly unsure what to do. "Do we save the ogre, or do we defeat him?"

Sarah pulled herself from her startling moment of realization and returned to the game playing out in front of her. "Our next course of action depends entirely on whether or not you think he truly means to eat your bones."

Philip pulled himself up in his hunched monster's posture and assumed his low, gargly voice once more. "Bones are my favorite."

Alice jumped up and down and began to giggle again. "Our bones!"

"Quick." Sarah motioned them over. "Let's go to your aunt Sorrel's rooms. She will help us vanquish him."

She took Caroline's free hand, and the three of them rushed down the corridor. She had looked in on Sorrel just before passing the portrait hall and knew that lady to not only be awake and alert but also to be feeling a bit discouraged. She would appreciate the visit and jovial antics.

Behind them, Philip continued his lumbering, grumbling pursuit. He really was wonderfully good to the children with whom he interacted. She could not help but be put firmly in mind of his father in these moments. The late Lord Lampton had endeared himself to every child in the neighborhood.

They poured into Sorrel's sitting room, a bit out of breath but in good spirits. The ladies present watched their arrival with amused curiosity.

"What is this?" Marjie Jonquil asked.

"The monster is coming for us." Caroline pulled away and climbed onto the footstool in front of the sofa where Sorrel was lying. "The monster is really just Uncle Flip, but he is pretending, so we are pretending we don't know."

Sorrel smiled and nodded. "And are you hiding in here?"

Caroline shook her head. "Cousin Sarah says you know how to vanquish the monster."

"If anyone does, it's her," Lady Marion said.

Alice had climbed onto her mother's lap. Clara Jonquil was very quiet, more so even than Lady Cavratt, which was an accomplishment. Sarah had come to know, a little, at least, Corbin's and Crispin's wives. She liked them very much. But as more and more of the daughters-in-law arrived, Sarah felt less a part of the gathering. She had no actual claim on any of them.

Philip came inside in the next moment. Alice and Caroline squealed on cue.

"Bones," he growled.

Caroline turned an expectant gaze on her aunt.

Sorrel raised herself up on one elbow and leveled a fearsome look at Philip. "Horrid Monster of the Park, I order you to stop trying to eat these girls' bones."

Philip lumbered to her. "Maybe I'll eat your bones instead." He knelt on the floor in front of her sofa and placed a kiss on her neck.

"Philip," she scolded.

"Hmm." He kissed her again, closer to her ear.

Sorrel bit back a smile. "Philip, really."

Another kiss along her jaw. "I've changed my mind. Eating bones is no longer my favorite."

Caroline looked over at Sarah, brow pulled in confusion. "Is she vanquishing him?"

Sarah could not hold back her laughter. "She most certainly is."

The other ladies in the room smiled as well. Philip, however, took pity on his wife's potential embarrassment and ended his attentions, instead turning to face the room. His eyes fell on the little boy sitting on Lady Cavratt's lap.

He crossed to her and asked if he could hold the child. Having obtained permission, he picked him up and tucked him in close. He looked to Sarah.

"Have you met this little one yet? He is named for me, you know. Philip Robert. His bacon-brained father means to call him Robert, completely forgetting the much preferable first given name the boy bears. Never fear, though. I call him Phrobert, which is much better."

Lady Cavaratt shook her head. "Phrobert is not an improvement, Philip."

"Henry and William agree with me," Philip said.

"Henry and William are infants."

Philip shrugged. "They still agree with me." He looked to the girls. "Shall we tiptoe up to the nursery to see if your little brothers are awake?"

"If you rouse them from their naps, their nursemaids will strangle you," Lady Marion warned.

Philip only grinned. "I'll take my chances."

Caroline took Alice's hand once more, and they followed Philip out, Phrobert still in his arms.

"He does love those children," Clara said. "Reminds me of his brother."

"*All* his brothers," Marjie added. "Mater says their father was the same way."

"He was," Sarah said. "I never knew a gentleman with so tender a place in his heart for children. I doubt there was a single child in the neighborhood who didn't feel cherished by him."

"Philip would be a wonderful father," Sorrel said, lying fully flat once more and appearing quite done-in by the miniscule effort she had exuded. "Breaks my heart that it seems destined never to happen."

Reassurances were offered immediately and quite vocally. Sorrel accepted them with the slightest easing of her burdened expression. She was worried, not only about the outcome of her pregnancy but also about the heartache of her husband. Having her sister and sisters-in-law around her would help, but after Christmas, they would leave, and loneliness, Sarah knew all too well, amplified one's worries. She vowed to herself in that moment to call on Sorrel as often as she could.

"Miss Sarvol."

Sarah turned toward the door, where a maid stood. "Yes?"

"Your brother's sent word that you're to return to Sarvol House directly. Messenger said it was urgent."

"Thank you." She offered very quick farewells to the ladies before slipping from the room.

Though her return had been deemed urgent, no carriage had been sent for her. She requested one of the Lampton Park butler and waited in the entryway like a petitioner. She so often felt that way: forever the guest, never truly belonging. Returning to the Collingham neighborhood was not supposed to have been this way.

She'd known some very happy times here, had been cared about and connected to so many in this area. But most of them were gone now or had families of their own.

She missed her mother, though not enough to return to her household and assume the role of a child for the rest of her life. She couldn't imagine leaving Scott anyway. No matter that she hardly saw him any longer; he was here. They were as close as twins, never apart for more than a few days. Undertaking this adventure together had been a dream come true.

But what had happened to that dream? They were both unhappy and running out of hope.

She intertwined her fingers, letting her arms hang in front of her. There had to be an answer, just as Mater had assured her.

Her mind spun throughout the ride back to Sarvol House. These questions were precisely the sort she and Harold had easily discussed before he'd broken her heart. They had talked of their futures, their dreams, their concerns. Neither of them had necessarily had the answers—they had still been so young—but they'd listened to each other. They'd offered hope and support.

Where are you now, Harold?

He had genuinely loved her; Mater had said as much. There was some peace to be found in finally knowing that with some degree of certainty. Theirs had been an impossible connection, but at least it had not been feigned.

Her mind lingered on the brief moment in her sitting room when he'd held her, on the concern she'd heard in his voice as she'd told him of her struggles that day she'd found him out at the abbey ruins, of the quiet way he'd asked if she would miss him while he was away. Perhaps in some way, he loved her still. An aching hope began to bubble at the idea. She pushed it away. Until she knew who he was *now*, she could not entertain such errant thoughts.

The carriage came to a stop in front of Sarvol House. Her heart dropped at the sight. She dreaded returning here each day.

"There is an answer to all of this. There has to be," she said aloud before exiting the carriage.

Mrs. Tanner met her in the Sarvol House entryway. "Best hurry to the library, miss. Your uncle is in a rare taking. He is quite put out that you were not at home."

Odd. "I was at Lampton Park. He has never objected to my visiting there before."

Poor Mrs. Tanner looked frantic. "He has insisted you present yourself in the library as soon as you arrive."

Sarah squared her shoulders. "Then I had best appear there." She hoped her show of confidence was convincing. Her uncle might not be as belligerent if he believed she couldn't be browbeaten. If nothing else, she might offer Mrs. Tanner a temporary reprieve from Uncle's temper.

She stepped into the library.

Uncle sat at the desk, his wheelchair pushed up to it. "You were gone again."

Stay calm, Sarah. "I was calling on Lord and Lady Lampton and the Dowager Countess. Lord and Lady Cavratt were there as well." Her uncle put a lot of store by titles.

Uncle's anger, however, did not appear the least bit assuaged. "If I wish you to be here, you should be. Poor relations should not inconvenience those offering them charity."

"I am here with my brother, and he is your heir. We are hardly poor relations."

Uncle's gaze hardened. "*He* is my heir. I didn't ask *you* to come." There was something different in his grumbling. Something even angrier than usual. Something more threatening.

"Where is Scott?"

"He and Clark are seeing to a tenant issue," Uncle said. "He knows his place, something you would do well to learn."

"I have caused you no true inconvenience," she insisted.

"You cost me my daughter."

"She was happy at Farland Meadows."

"And now she is dead." He spat the words at her, accusation heavy in his tone. "You will return to your rooms and remain there."

"For how long?"

"I am master of this house and all who live in it. Do not push me."

Gentlemen were granted tremendous control over ladies' lives, but that did not eliminate their choices. Sarah clung to that as she stood there watching the anger and hardness grow in his glare. She had done absolutely nothing to deserve his wrath, yet he piled it on her day after day. Her choice, her escape, would be to continue spending time with the Jonquils.

"I intend to visit Lampton Park again tomorrow." She kept her tone calm and collected. "Is there any message you would like me to deliver on your behalf?"

"You will not be going."

"Why not?"

"You will stay in your room until I say otherwise." He took up a small stack of papers, though he continued speaking to her. "Do not attempt to convince the servants to undermine my orders. Every one of them can be replaced if they defy me."

"All of this simply to stop me from visiting the neighbors?" It made no sense.

"You will learn your place, Sarah."

"What place is that?"

His eyes met hers again. "Your place is wherever I determine it is."

He was making little sense.

"You clearly don't actually wish me to be here. Would you not rather I be away, then you needn't have me nearby since my presence seems to—"

"You will go directly to your room and not leave it until I give you permission to do so." He spoke calmly, a little *too* calmly. "Do not attempt to defy me in this."

"You and I seldom see each other. How would you even know if—"

"There are those among the staff who are unfailingly loyal to me. They know who controls their employment and their futures."

He meant to spy on her?

"Those who might be willing to assist you in thwarting my dictates will find themselves unemployed."

She swallowed against the growing dryness in her throat. He would punish the servants if they helped her. A servant let go by an unhappy employer often struggled to find new positions. She could not do that to them. And yet, to be at her uncle's mercy for something as simple as coming and going would make her already unhappy situation awful.

"Scott will not accept this."

Uncle's expression only hardened. "Do not for a moment believe I don't control every aspect of his life. He knows as much and toes the line accordingly. Should you drag him into any rebellion you might be planning, he will suffer for it."

"You will punish Scott and the servants as a means of hurting *me*?" How could he be so heartless?

"You took my daughter; now you have the audacity to claim a place in the home that was once hers. That I have not tossed you out on your ear is a charitable act for which you ought to be grateful." Spittle flew from his wrinkled lips as he spoke. His eyes snapped with frigid anger.

"You don't need to punish anyone," she said. "I'll go to my bedchamber."

"And stay there," he added sharply.

She nodded.

Uncle looked past her. "Norwell. Escort the girl to her room."

Sarah looked over her shoulder and directly into the face of Uncle's formidable valet. She had seen him only once before. He worried her then. He rather terrified her now. "I know the way," she insisted, moving quickly past him.

She heard Norwell's steps behind her all the way out the library and up the narrow back stairs. She rushed through the doorway of her little sitting room and slammed the door shut. She leaned against it, praying he would make no attempt to open it. The door didn't lock without a key, which she didn't have.

Long minutes passed. No shadow passed beneath. She heard no footsteps. The doorknob was never rattled. She began to breathe again.

I cannot stay here. But where would she go? How would she get there? Uncle had vowed to punish anyone who assisted her. She could not do that to the servants. She would not contribute to Scott's unhappiness.

She was on her own, but she refused to be defeated.

CHAPTER TWENTY-TWO

Harold did his utmost to not ever break his word to Mater. The roads back to Nottinghamshire had been poor at best, impassable in places. His return had taken longer than he'd expected. He arrived at Lampton Park only a few short days ahead of Christmas.

John, atop the carriage, tipped his hat with a grin before driving in the direction of the stables. He and Harold had come to know each other well. Through him, Harold had learned a lot about his parishioners, those with whom he had not previously interacted. He was returning to the neighborhood better equipped to serve them and, more importantly still, convinced at last that he truly could make the difference he'd always wanted to make. He'd managed it through unconventional means during his time away, and he meant to change a few things about his approach in the parish now that he was returned. Nothing shocking or unseemly. He simply meant to stop trying so hard to be perfect and start being a little more *himself*. Mater would approve. He felt certain Sarah would as well. His brothers were a different story altogether. They would think what they would; he would simply endure it. The Lampton Park drawing room was filled near to bursting when he stepped inside. All the family appeared to be present, except Jason and his family. Had the roads given them difficulty as well?

"Uncle Harry!"

Caroline. She ran to him, and he scooped her up.

"Papa and Uncle Flip said you would not be here for Christmas. But Grammy said you promised and so you would be."

"And so I am." He adjusted his arms so he could hold her more comfortably. "It seems to me your papa and Uncle Flip owe Grammy an apology."

Caroline nodded firmly. "And they owe you one too."

"I think you are correct, Caroline." He turned to face his oldest brother. "I am most certainly owed an apology."

Philip responded with instant drama; he was nothing if not predictable.

He attempted to get down on his knees but made a show of being thwarted by his close-fitting silk pantaloons. "May I make my pleas for absolution from a standing position? My valet will murder me if I ruin my clothes."

"I suspect, Philip, that you are at the mercy of a tyrant," Harold said. "Perhaps save your breath and apply it to the apology you are likely to owe him when he realizes your partner there"—Harold motioned to sweet little Alice—"has left a smudge on your waistcoat."

Philip pulled Alice closer. "If he speaks ill of my darling Alice, I will call him out."

Alice smiled up at him, clearly besotted with her flamboyant uncle. Nearby, Corbin and Clara sat watching their daughter, equally pleased looks on their faces, their boy Edmund tucked up beside them.

Harold looked at Caroline, still in his arms. "Will you serve as your uncle Flip's second? I intend to back his valet."

"I like Wilson," Caroline said. "He helps me match my ribbons to my dresses when I stay here. He says I'm beautiful."

"And so you are, my dear."

Caroline beamed at them all. Harold set her on her feet once more, and she skipped off to join Charlie, sitting in a wingback arm chair. Sorrel was lying on a fainting sofa. Marion sat with Marjie and Catherine not far distant. Stanley and Crispin stood near the fireplace.

"Where's Mater?" He couldn't imagine she wouldn't be present when so much of her family was.

"She stepped out just before you arrived," Philip said. "Scott Sarvol came and seemed very anxious to speak with her."

"I hope nothing is the matter."

Philip took a seat beside Sorrel's sofa. "All things considered, I would assume something is decidedly the matter."

That was certainly cryptic. Harold watched Philip in anticipation of the tremendous amount of information he was clearly leaving out. Philip simply took Sorrel's hand in his and looked for all the world as if there was nothing more to say.

"Do stop torturing him, dear." Sorrel sounded far frailer than she had when Harold had left.

"No one has seen Sarah Sarvol in two weeks," Philip said. "And the Sarvol staff is being entirely mum about the whole thing."

She'd been missing for a fortnight? Why hadn't something been done? "Where did Mater meet Scott?"

Sorrel's feeble smile was an empathetic one. "The east sitting room."

Harold didn't bother with a bow or nod of farewell but made his way directly there. Scott and Mater sat on a window seat, deep in conversation. Harold's entrance did not immediately draw their attention. He moved nearer.

"I don't know what to do," Scott said. "Uncle has already dismissed two maids who have attempted to assist her. He will cut me off if I make any attempt to free her. Not that I value the income more than my sister; I am simply trying to accumulate enough savings that I can find us a temporary home of our own until Uncle . . . until Sarvol House is a more welcoming place."

Mater's attention didn't waver. Harold had always cherished that about her. She offered her undivided attention when someone needed her.

"Has something happened to make Sarvol House even less welcoming than it has been?" Harold asked.

They both looked up at him, startled.

Mater's face immediately transformed into joy so palpable Harold felt it in his bones. "Harold, dearest." She rose and stepped to him, putting her arms around him in a firm and loving embrace. "You are home."

He returned her hug. She was the sure foundation in all of their lives, especially his. She loved him at times when he struggled to love himself.

"It is good to be home again." He kept an arm around Mater but turned his attention to Scott. "What has changed to render you so worried about your sister?"

Scott rubbed at his temples. "My uncle has confined her to the house these past weeks. None of his arguments against her activities away from home make the least sense, yet he cannot be dissuaded. He has always disliked her, but I suspect he has actually begun to hate her."

Harold motioned for Mater to resume her seat. He pulled a chair over and sat as well.

"What has changed today?" he asked.

"Today?" Mater apparently hadn't made the connection Harold had.

"This has been ongoing for two weeks, yet Scott is here *today*. Something must have changed."

Scott sighed and leaned back against the window frame. "He locked her in her room. His valet must have been involved; our uncle does not get about unaided."

Mater looked horrified. "Will no one unlock the door?"

"There is only one key, and obviously, my uncle has it."

Harold's jaw tensed, freezing to the point of making speech difficult. "Surely the door could be opened with a bit of ingenuity. The blacksmith is particularly fond of your sister; I daresay he would provide you with whatever tools were needed."

Scott met his eye, both offense and pleading in his expression. "I swear to you, we are not simply shrugging and saying, 'Well, isn't that unfortunate.' He is cruel to her, and any time she has attempted to take a stand for herself or, early in her ordered confinement, slip out anyway, it has made her situation all the worse. One of the maids accompanied her the first time she left in violation of Uncle's edict, and that maid was let go without references. A second maid he accused of having distracted him from noticing Sarah's departure suffered the same fate. Everyone wishes to help her, but we don't know how to do so without making the situation everlastingly worse."

It was a difficult situation, indeed.

"Is there any means of getting her meals?" Mater asked. "I understand from Caroline that her room is isolated, with only one entrance."

"Sarah's door has a gap underneath. I've managed to slide a few things to her. She won't starve, but neither can she stay locked in there indefinitely. The staff have said that if this goes on much longer, they will find a means of getting through the door regardless of the punishment. I'd rather it not come to that. I am absolutely convinced Uncle would subject every last member of the staff to the same treatment as the unfortunate maids he's already dismissed. They would be left destitute."

"And if you help her, you will be as well," Mater said.

He nodded. "Which leaves me in no position to help her."

"Oh, Scott." Mater's expression fell. "We simply must think of a solution."

Scott's lips pressed in a tight line. Emotion tugged at his features. "I should never have brought her here. I was worried how she would be treated, but I wanted her company. My selfishness put her in this situation."

Mater put an arm around Scott and tugged him to her. He laid his head on her shoulder. The gentleman, who was Harold's age, looked so young in that moment.

A vicar sees the needs around him. Addresses them. Relieves suffering.

But what could Harold do in this situation? What power did he truly have? He could talk with Mr. Sarvol, try to soften his edicts and show him the error of his behavior. But that seemed unlikely to be successful, at least not quickly. Sarah needed an answer now. Scott needed to know his sister was safe. The Sarvol staff needed to be free of the impossible choice they were facing.

"How can a man be so cruel to his brother's daughter?" Scott asked, still leaning against Mater. "It is unfathomable."

"I wish it weren't so common. Our own Catherine was subjected to absolute horrors at the hand of her uncle. Arabella Hampton—you'll remember her—was treated quite unkindly by her relatives." Mater shook her head in exhausted disapproval. "I suspect our laws contribute to these tragedies. With inheritances designed to benefit one brother and not the other, it is not difficult to see how resentment can grow, extending to the other's children."

"But my uncle was the fortunate brother," Scott said. "My father did not resent him for his inheritance; at least he never mistreated Bridget out of frustration with his situation."

"The resentment does not always flow that way, Scott. Your uncle knew that his estate would pass to his brother's son since he had no heir of his own. I believe that is what he resented."

Scott looked at her more closely, clearly still confused. "Wouldn't his unkindness be directed only at me if that were the source of his resentment?"

"I believe it does fuel his treatment of you, which you have admitted is often cruel and demeaning," Mater said. "But Sarah hasn't the promise of an inheritance. She is entirely at his mercy, and he knows that."

"Which made Sarah particularly vulnerable." Scott sighed. "He was punishing my father by proxy, choosing the person he could hurt most."

"I fear that may be the case."

Harold's heart sank at the truth of Mater's evaluation. Sarah was the whipping boy for her uncle's disappointments and miseries.

"We simply must bring her here," Mater said.

Scott hesitated. "My uncle would never agree."

Mater arched an eyebrow, an expression all the Jonquils knew how to make. "I hadn't intended to *ask* him."

"There are perks to being a dowager countess," Harold said, biting back a grin. Mater was fearsome when she needed to be.

"First things first." Mater looked from one of them to the other. "How do we get her out of her room without requiring the staff to be involved? There's no point ruining their lives while we're saving hers."

Scott nodded, his expression distant, as if thinking. "If we break the door down, he'll notice and they'll be blamed. Taking a more delicate approach would require more time, adding to the possibility that we'd be discovered. His valet is not the only minion Uncle has amongst the staff. Others are reporting her movements to him, but I do not know who the informers are."

A delicate situation indeed.

Mater shook her head. "We must somehow protect the innocent servants from those willing to double-cross them while hiding our efforts from those waiting to tattle despite not knowing who they are and all while slipping Sarah out of the house unnoticed."

Scott's expression grew ever wearier. "And we know we will be caught if she so much as steps into the corridor of the house. The few times she has tried, she was found out quickly."

"So we take her out the window," Harold said.

They both turned shocked looks on him.

"I've been to Sarah's sitting room. The window there overlooks a small grassy area enclosed by a wall. It appeared fairly secluded."

"It is." Scott's tone was hesitantly curious.

"This gap under Sarah's door, is it large enough that you could slip a rope to her?"

Mater's mouth dropped open in an O.

"You want her to climb out?" Scott shook his head. "She's never done anything like that."

Harold set his shoulders. "But I have."

CHAPTER TWENTY-THREE

Harold led his brothers around the side of Sarvol House. They'd needed the remainder of the day to plan their strategy and procure enough dark-colored clothing for all seven of them. Jason was not present, of course, but Crispin had volunteered his efforts.

"I cannot believe we are doing this," Layton said, a laugh beneath his quiet words. "We are grown gentlemen."

"Are you daft?" Philip shot them all a grin, barely visible in the dimness of dusk. "This is my favorite day ever."

They reached their predetermined spot around a corner of the house, inside the isolated, grassy courtyard beneath Sarah's window.

Harold faced Philip, who had always been the leader in these efforts. "We'd best get to it."

Philip gave a quick nod and motioned the others closer. "Brothers, there's a prisoner in this house in need of our special skills. It will not be easy. There will be danger. Charlie will likely fall off the roof."

Their youngest brother shook his head. He probably even rolled his eyes, but it was too dark to tell.

"Crispin, Charlie, you've spied your lookout posts?"

They both nodded.

"Bird whistles," Philip reminded them. They needed to know if someone unexpected came too near but couldn't risk calling attention by shouting. Though he was very nearly giddy at the opportunity to enact a bit of mischief, Philip was also taking this very seriously. Harold could not have been more grateful. "Stanley is waiting with the horses. Layton, Corbin, and I know our part. Harold most certainly knows his."

Nods. Were they not about to undertake something clandestine and a little dangerous, they probably would have teased him mercilessly.

"Do not fail Miss Sarvol." Philip set a fisted hand to his heart, the gesture they had long ago decided on when undertaking this type of mission. "We are the Jonquil Freers of Prisoners."

In unison, they joined him in finishing the well-known motto, fists pressed to their hearts, voices quiet out of necessity. "No one is abandoned. No one is forgotten."

Crispin and Charlie moved stealthily in the direction of their posts. Harold allowed himself only a moment to notice how much better Charlie was walking. He was nearly healed.

Corbin slipped the looped rope from his shoulder and handed it to Harold. "Be certain you"—He took a breath. Sentences seldom emerged whole from their quietest brother—"you don't start until—Let me check the fit one more time."

Philip had wisely suggested Corbin be the one entrusted with devising some kind of harness Harold would wear while climbing up. He'd never climbed this wall before, and the brief evaluation he'd been able to do earlier hadn't been promising. He wasn't about to climb it without something to catch him if he slipped. Corbin's vast experience with horses had taught him to tie knots expertly.

He and Harold had pored over Father's copy of *A Voyage to St. Kilda*, reading again and again M. Martin's brief description of the fowler's climb he'd witnessed and the harness-like contraption the climbers had used. They also found in another book about the history of the Far East wood-carving prints of the mountain crossings the people in those distant lands had undertaken by way of ropes and rope harnesses for more than a thousand years. Stanley had supplied what he had seen during battle when soldiers had scaled the fortified walls of cities using ropes.

Philip had jokingly suggested they ought to reference the holy book since the climb would be undertaken by a vicar. Harold had, admittedly smugly, pointed out that the spies who had entered Jericho in the book of Joshua had done so by climbing the wall assisted by rope. He'd meant the remark to give his brother back a bit of the teasing he so often tossed in Harold's direction, but it had proven a moment of revelation for himself. Climbing was not the purview of a vicar, but it was referenced in the Bible and not in terms of disapproval. He'd not ever thought of that.

"Thank you for helping with this," Harold said.

"No one is abandoned," Corbin said.

"No one is forgotten."

Corbin stepped back but didn't leave. He, Layton, and, though likely no one realized it, Harold were the strongest of the brothers. Corbin and Layton, along with Philip, would be holding the other end of the rope, keeping Harold—and Sarah, when it was her turn—from falling.

Though his eldest brothers often tormented him, Harold could not mistake the concern he saw in Philip's and Layton's eyes.

"Are you equal to this?" Layton asked. "This is not a short climb."

"It's less daunting than the ascent to the nursery when we were children, and I made that many times. *Without* Corbin's magic harness, I'll add."

Philip slapped a hand on his shoulder. "We did make good use of our monkey, didn't we?"

Layton fought a smile but lost the battle. "How long has it been since we called you that?"

"Years."

"Why did we stop? It's perfect." Did Philip truly not remember?

"You decided 'Holy Harry' was more to your liking."

Layton watched him closely. "But I suspect it was not more to *yours*."

"'Monkey' was devised to praise something about me. 'Holy Harry' was only ever meant to mock."

"Well then." Philip gave him a light push toward the wall. "Make your upward journey, Monkey. And we'll do our best not to let go of the rope."

"I would really prefer if you didn't, just so we're clear."

Philip nodded. "We won't let go, Harold. None of us would."

There was something more in the declaration than a promise to safeguard his upcoming climb.

Harold grabbed a small pebble and lobbed it upward. It hit the window with a tap. He watched. Waited. Had she heard? Scott said he would tell her to listen and to be ready to escape.

Her window opened.

"Are you ready for this, Harold?" Philip asked.

"I've been climbing all my life." Sarah appeared in the now-open window. The bit of Harold's heart that had ached for her the past weeks, the past *years*, warmed and softened at the mere sight of her. "For the first time, I think I know why."

She gave a quick, silent wave, then disappeared inside again. A moment later, one end of a long rope dropped down to them. Shortly after, the other side followed. Her window had a middle bar dividing the two halves. The rope looped around that thick iron bar.

Harold pulled off his jacket, undid the cuffs of his shirtsleeves, and put on his climbing slippers. He needed every bit of help he could get. He grabbed the harness Corbin had fashioned for him and slipped his legs through the two large loops. He tied another section at his waist. Two other loops hooked over his shoulders.

Philip and Layton retrieved one end of the long rope, while Corbin snatched up the other. Corbin worked with a confident swiftness that was deeply reassuring. After a moment, he had his end of the long rope tied to the ropes looped around Harold's body.

"This will hold?" Harold pressed.

"If I had any doubt, I would *never* let you go up."

After everything his brothers had put him through over the years, receiving repeated assurances tonight that he mattered to them was a new experience. Did they have any idea how much he needed to hear that?

"Be careful," Philip said.

"You be careful lowering her back down. If you drop her, I'll kill you. All three of you."

"Up with you, Monkey," Layton said. "The longer we wait, the more likely it is we'll be caught. None of us wants to risk the consequences that would fall on the servants or Scott."

They knew without a doubt Mr. Sarvol could not actually prevent them from simply walking into the house, up to Sarah's room, and back out with her. The man was frail, and there were a lot of Jonquils. But Mr. Sarvol would likely dismiss the butler for letting them in, the housekeeper for not preventing their departure, and any maids anywhere near Sarah's room. Scott might even be punished under the assumption that he had been involved.

This was for the best, no matter that it was a little risky and a little ridiculous compared to the far easier approach. But none of them wished to see the servants' rendered destitute by the evening's efforts.

Harold tugged at the knot in his rope, testing the tightness. He approached the wall, wishing he'd had a chance to practice rather than making his first attempt in the dark.

Corbin lit and positioned the lanterns they'd brought, each equipped with mirrors that directed the light with great intensity. That light now illuminated the wall.

With care, Harold planned out the first five moves of his climb. He'd have to judge the rest as he got higher. Corbin had set the lanterns to light a good amount of the wall, but some of it was quite dark. Thank the heavens for the harness and rope.

He found hand and foot holds and pulled himself onto the wall. One hand and foot at a time, he made his ascent. His hands slipped a bit now and then, though he managed to stay on the wall. He reached a darkened section.

Where next? He couldn't see as well as he would have liked.

He curled his right toe and dug it into a small but well-positioned crevice where a bit of mortar had weathered away over the years. He reached up for a stone he ought to be able to get his hand around.

His fingers slipped. Then his left foot.

Harold's heart flew to this throat. The harness yanked hard against him, not letting him drop more than a couple of inches.

He pushed out pent-up breath. His brothers had caught him. They wouldn't let him fall, just as they'd vowed. He didn't have to cling as hard and desperately as he had.

His confidence renewed, he set himself upward once more. He didn't take unnecessary risks, but he wasn't as paralyzingly cautious as he had been. One hand movement, one foot movement at a time, he climbed upward toward Sarah's window, all the while feeling the unfailing tension in the rope and the reassurance that his brothers would not abandon him.

At last, his hand reached the edge of the outside windowsill. He set his other hand there as well. He pulled himself through the open window and sat on the sill, his legs dangling inside the room. His breaths came tight and belabored, but he'd done it. He'd reached her.

There she stood, within reach, watching him, pale and visibly shaken. He slid off the sill and the rest of the way inside the room. Before he could take a single step toward her, she closed the distance between them and wrapped her arms around him.

He didn't hesitate but held her close. A mixture of relief and awareness filled him. He'd held her a few times when they were younger, fleeting embraces during their leisurely afternoons together. His arms had longed for her ever since.

"Sarah," he whispered.

"I knew you would come. Even before Scott's note explaining this plan, I knew *you* would come for me."

He lightly kissed the top of her head. "You have more faith in me now than you did a few months ago."

"That was before I knew you could climb walls."

His chest shook with a silent laugh. "The climbing won't win me any vicaring competitions, but it can be very useful."

"I was so afraid you would fall." Horror filled her words.

"My brothers wouldn't have let me."

She pulled back, smiling up at him. "Are they also dressed as thieves?"

"We have decided to take up a life of crime," he said. "I thought I'd best begin dressing the part."

She stepped from his arms but didn't go far. "Is that the conclusion you came to during your travels? That thievery is your true calling?" She spoke very seriously. *Too* seriously. Sarah always had been quick with a jest or a light comment yet so very good at posing it with brilliant subtlety.

"Indeed." He began pulling off the rope harness. "Of course, I did spend the entirety of my weeks away posing as a highwayman. That may have influenced my decision." He stepped out of the leg loops and hung the contraption over his shoulder.

Sarah's momentary amusement faded. "You took a tremendous risk, Harold."

They stood near enough each other for him to clearly see the uncertainty in her eyes. He took her hand. "We are the Jonquil Freers of Prisoners, a merry band of miscreants with a long and storied history of breaking unfortunate souls free of their imprisonments. Of course, most of the captives we freed were *each other*, but we were always entirely innocent and undeserving of our punishments. Freeing our brothers was an act of justice."

The smallest bit of lightness returned to her face. His heart warmed to see it.

"I had forgotten how funny you can be," she said. "I always liked that about you."

He had all but forgotten that about himself as well. Though he would have enjoyed spending a moment basking in the compliment, they hadn't the luxury.

"Did Scott explain the odd . . . clothing adjustments you needed to make?"

She blushed a little and nodded. Harold knew it was a somewhat indelicate thing, requesting a lady wear a pair of men's trousers under her dress, but using the harness in a dress without trousers underneath would have been humiliating for all of them, especially her.

"And he told you we'd be lowering you down?"

She took an audible breath. "I will confess, I'm not entirely happy about that bit."

He set his hands gently on her upper arms and looked into her eyes. "If you absolutely can't do this, we will try to think of something else."

She shook her head. "I am ready to get out of this room and this house, but I will not risk the servants being punished for my escape. If this is the best way to manage that, then I will do it. I will be part of my own rescue, Harold. Don't think I won't be."

"I never thought it for a moment," he said. "I know your determination well enough."

A clunk sounded nearby, pulling their attention back toward the window. A small pebble skidded along the floor.

"I suspect my brothers are growing impatient." He slipped away from Sarah and moved to the window. He called down, keeping his voice low. "She needs to get the harness on."

"We could see you embracing," Philip called back. "I've been retching repeatedly."

"Hold yourself together, man," Harold called back. "If you grow ill, we'll leave you behind."

"I'm still in charge," Philip answered.

"I'm with Harold on this point," Layton said.

Corbin, true to form, kept out of the bantering.

Harold looked out over the darkened landscape. Charlie and Crispin were out there, keeping an eye on things. That set his mind at ease. "Any bird whistles?"

"None." Layton was usually more sensible in these situations than Philip. Yet Harold would not have felt at all confident in the plan without his eldest brother.

"She'll be ready to climb down in just a moment." Harold looked more closely at his dimly lit brothers. "Does Philip have my jacket on his head?"

"It's cold out here," Philip tossed back.

Harold sometimes forgot how entertaining Philip really was. "If Wilson could see you now, he would likely tender his resignation."

"Or finally begin trusting *my* fashion sense," Philip countered.

"If you two chatterboxes are finished," Layton said, "we've a lady to help escape and detection to avoid. You're not helping either cause."

"Yes, Mama," Philip answered.

Harold turned away from the window.

Sarah studied the rope harness. "This is safe?"

"It caught me on the climb up. I trust it."

"Is there a different way?" she asked.

"None that wouldn't have dire consequences for the staff."

She took in a deep breath and pushed it out through tight lips. "What exactly do I need to do?"

No one would ever accuse Sarah of lacking courage. "We'll make sure the harness is good and tight. Then you will climb out of the window backward. You'll hold the rope right here at this knot." He indicated the one that connected the rope to the harness. "Philip, Layton, and Corbin are beneath you, all holding the rope. They will lower you slowly."

"I'm to be Don Quixote descending into Montesinos's Cave?"

"More or less." He slipped the harness off his shoulder.

She looked out the window. "How will you get down?"

"They'll hold the rope still for me, and I'll use it to climb down. I descend a section of the abbey wall that way all the time."

"And you haven't died yet." She nodded as if slowly growing more convinced.

"Not yet. And I don't intend for that to change tonight."

"Neither do I." She indicated the harness. "Let's see how well this works."

He explained to her where the various loops went, and she pulled it on. Harold helped her tighten it, careful to keep his gaze away from the havoc it would wreak on her dress or the trousers that would be peeking out beneath them. Outside was dark enough; little would be visible.

Sarah sat on the windowsill. "Is there a particular way to navigate this part?"

He held his hands out. "Grab hold of my wrists, and I will hold yours while you lower your legs out. Once you're in position, take hold of the rope."

"You have surprisingly large arms," she said. "Strong, I mean."

His arms were unusually large. No shirts ever fit comfortably. "I climb walls. That builds a great deal of strength. No one ever sees it though."

"We see your strength, Harold. We just don't tell you often enough."

This was quite the night for compliments. He didn't at all know how to respond to them all. "Are you ready?"

She set her shaky hands over his, grabbing his wrists. He held tightly to her wrists. With careful movements, she turned enough to lower her legs out the window. Harold tightened his grip even more. Heavens, if she fell—He wouldn't let himself finish the thought.

The rope was tight on the other side. His brothers were holding firm below.

"Grab the knot," he told her.

"I won't fall?"

"You won't fall."

She let go of him, but he kept hold of her wrists until her hands were wrapped around the knot.

"I'll see you down below," he told her.

She nodded.

"Go," he called down to his brothers.

Sarah pushed away from the wall with her feet, just as he'd instructed her, and slid down. Bit by bit, she descended lower and lower. Harold held his breath, watching and praying. At last, she was on the ground. Layton was at her side on the instant, helping her slip free of the harness.

She was safe, and she would soon be free of her uncle's tyranny. His brothers would likely not tell anyone how it had been managed. No one in Collingham would learn the truth about the Climbing Curate.

He would not yet be required to discover if the role of vicar was truly flexible enough to include someone like him. That would come soon enough.

CHAPTER TWENTY-FOUR

Sarah was not a crier. Still, she wept when Mater greeted her at the door of the dower house with a fierce and protective embrace. Every drop of loneliness, every fruitless longing for a sense of belonging these past weeks, every disappointed hope of the previous years simply poured from her in the form of soul-deep tears.

"You consider this your home now, Sarah," she said. "For however long you wish it to be. And consider us part of your family."

That made her cry even more. In her uncle's house, she had been anything but family, and it had never felt like a home. Mater's kindness and caring was opening wounds she'd spent so many years hiding from the world.

Sarah looked back at Harold. "Thank you for this." His brothers stood not too far distant. "And thank the others as well."

"They are the Jonquil Freers of Prisoners," Mater said. "They leave no one behind."

Harold's eyes widened in surprise.

Mater laughed. "Did you boys really think your father and I weren't aware of your mischief? There's a reason we had that trellis installed so near the nursery window and had it anchored far more solidly than any simple trellis ever was. We wanted to be certain our precious 'Monkey' did not fall to his death for want of something to hold fast to."

A lopsided smile tugged at Harold's lips. He stepped up to them and pressed a kiss to his mother's cheek. His gaze shifted to Sarah. "You'll look after her as well, won't you?" He motioned with his head to Mater.

"If, when you say 'look after' you mean 'get into mischief with,' then yes. Yes, I will."

Harold took her hand in his and raised it to his lips. He lightly kissed her fingers, lingering over the tender gesture. A thickness started in Sarah's throat, her heart pounding against it. He had held her hand before; he'd even kissed her fingers. But it was different this time. His touch tugged at her from a place deeper in her heart.

"We've been apart a long time, Sarah," he said quietly.

"You were away for almost a month," she acknowledged.

He shook his head. "I've been away for years."

"I wish you would come back," she whispered.

"And I think you should be on your way, Harold," Mater said. "Sarah needs to settle in and sleep."

He offered a small bow, then turned and walked to where his brothers stood. They, as a group, offered waves and farewells to Mater before traipsing down the lane leading away from the dower house.

"Quite a group of remarkable gentlemen, though I say it myself." No one could miss the affection in Mater's voice. "Their father would be proud of them."

"I still cannot believe all the trouble they went to on my behalf," Sarah said. "And to manage it without implicating the servants so that they would be safe as well. I'm amazed to the point of near speechlessness."

"They are Jonquils, my dear. Jonquils save people."

Sarah leaned into Mater's one-armed hug. "Do you think Harold really is coming back to us—the *real* Harold, not the whole-cloth version of him he's been presenting to the world?"

"I see more of him peeking through all the time."

"I do hope so."

They stepped inside the dower house, moving slowly toward the stairs.

"I still cannot get past the sight of him scaling that wall."

Mater nodded knowingly. "His brothers called him Monkey. I always thought he was more like a spider. His climbing scared the life out of me, but I couldn't deny he was remarkably good at it."

Sarah's heart flipped. "It was very impressive, I will admit."

With mischief in her eyes, Mater said, "You found him rather dashing, did you?"

Heat spread over Sarah's face.

"His father was a climber as well. Not walls, as Harold does, but mountains. I saw him undertake a dangerous climb early in our marriage. It was both terrifying and . . ." Her voice trailed off, even as a slow smile spread across her face. A deep sigh slid from her. "Lucas was remarkable in so many ways."

"I loved him," Sarah said.

"Everyone loved him," Mater said quietly.

They walked up the stairs to a serenely appointed bedchamber, complete with a washbasin of warm water, a vase of freshly cut hot-house flowers, and a burning fire. A maid waited inside.

"This is Hannah; she will be acting as your lady's maid."

Sarah said little the remainder of the night beyond expressions of gratitude for Hannah's kind ministrations and apologies to everyone who made such effort on her behalf. She felt torn between feelings of relief and guilt.

She awoke the next morning feeling both as though she'd slept for ages and hadn't slept at all. She was tired to her bones but determined to make this new start a good one.

As it was Sunday, she had a difficult dilemma to sort. Uncle had not permitted her to leave her room to attend services the past two weeks. She wished to go to mass that morning, but he would most certainly be there. Her uncle might not even know yet that she was gone. The longer her escape remained undiscovered the less likely he was to assign blame to anyone in particular. For him to discover in church that she had defied his orders might very well end in disaster.

She hadn't the least fear that he was capable of forcing her return to Sarvol House. One did best to never underestimate the Jonquil family when they were united in support of a common cause. She knew she was free of her uncle's household, but she also knew with clarity he would see her escape as an affront and would respond with anger. She would be humiliated. Scott would be as well. She wouldn't put it past Uncle Sarvol to lash out at the servants while the entire congregation looked on.

What was she to do? She could avoid services, but she so wanted to attend. She found such peace in the chapel. And she wished to see Harold undertake his duties after his journey, to see if he had changed and how.

"Oh, Miss Sarvol." Hannah stood in the doorway. "I'd meant only to peek in and see that your fire was still burning. I hope I didn't wake you."

She shook her head. "You did not."

Hannah came the rest of the way into the room. "Have you looked outside yet? What a snowing we had last night. Must've come in right late, long after you arrived."

Sarah slipped from her bed. The floor was frigid against her bare feet. Without the influence of the fire, the air would have been almost unbearably cold. She crossed to her generously proportioned window and looked out on a blanket of pristine, glistening snow. Everything was covered. Every tree branch, every shrub, every wall. And the snow lay so deep not a single blade of grass could be seen.

"Quite a snowing, indeed." She turned back to Hannah. "It looks very deep."

Hannah nodded, pulling open the armoire. "So deep, in fact, the vicar has sent word around the parish that there'll be no services today. He doesn't wish anyone not having a carriage or horse to have to walk in all this snow. Good man, our vicar."

"Yes, he is."

Bless, Harold. He'd saved the local people from a miserable walk in the snow. He'd saved her from having to face her uncle. He'd always said he wanted nothing more than to help people. He was managing precisely that.

"I pressed your gown, Miss Sarvol." She pulled out the dress Sarah had worn when she'd left Sarvol House. She'd come with nothing else. Even her night dress was borrowed from Mater. She hadn't the first idea what she would wear while they waited for Scott to devise a means of sneaking a few of her things from her still-locked bedchamber.

Mater sat at the table in the small dining room when Sarah arrived downstairs nearly thirty minutes later. She looked up from her tea and book. A smile bloomed on her dear face. "Good morning, Sarah. You look lovely."

Sarah felt more beautiful than she had in all the months she'd been away from America. It was miraculous what having a lady's maid could do. No longer was Sarah fumbling to fashion her hair in some way or another when she had no practice creating a flattering coiffeur. And she was no longer rushed through the effort to dress so the maid helping her could return to her actual duties. The fashions of the day did not lend themselves to hastiness.

"Thank you for Hannah," Sarah said. "She is such a welcome help, and so kind."

Mater nodded. "I knew you would like her. And I suspect she already adores you. She's kind to her very soul, and her taste is impeccable."

Before Sarah could take a seat at the table, Charlie wandered inside. "Morning, Mater. Sarah." He stopped abruptly. "Am I allowed to call you that? I know it was permitted when we were little, but—"

Mater looked to Sarah. "That is really for you to decide, dear."

"I do not mind." Indeed, she did not. The Jonquil brothers felt like *her* brothers in a very real way.

"Perhaps you can be Sarah when it is just the family," Mater suggested, "and Miss Sarvol when amongst others. Some people are very particular about observing the niceties."

Sarah agreed. Charlie looked instantly more at ease.

"Since Harold has decided to shutter the church and pretend it is not Sunday," Charlie said, "I've been sent to invite the ladies of the dower house to spend the day with the gathered Jonquils at the Park."

"'Shutter the church and pretend it's not Sunday'? Did Philip charge you with using that exact phrase?" Mater seemed to already know the answer.

Charlie tipped an eyebrow upward. All the brothers employed that exact expression now and then and in nearly identical ways. Harold's version of the "Jonquil eyebrow" had too often tended toward censure these past months. She hoped it would begin to look more mischievous like the others'.

"Very well." Mater held her hands up in a show of surrender. "I will not require you to tell tales on your brother." She looked to Sarah. "Would you care to toss yourself in amongst this madcap family?"

"More than anything."

"I suspect she's as mad as the rest of us," Charlie said. "Agreeing to be lowered down the side of a house simply because Harold told her it was safe. Mad as a hatter."

"Perfect. She'll fit right in." Mater rose. "I mean to fetch a few things, then we can be off." She paused to give Sarah's shoulders a squeeze. "It is so good to have you here."

Sarah inwardly smiled as Mater left the room. "I've been here twelve hours, most of that spent sleeping, yet she is convinced my presence here is a blessing from heaven itself."

Charlie, to her surprised, looked saddened by the declaration. "She's lonely. We all see it, but we don't know what to do. Most of my brothers have families of their own now. Harold has his parish duties. I need to get back to school. She's alone, and we can't fix that."

Sarah crossed to him, this dear young gentleman who had been like a little brother and cousin to her all the years she was growing up. "She is not alone now. I will stay as long as she wishes me to."

Charlie didn't appear reassured. "The last lady who joined her here and who was meant to alleviate some of that loneliness was married within six months."

Sarah grinned, slipping her arm through his and walking with him out of the dining room. "I do not suspect I'm in much danger of following in her footsteps."

Charlie snorted.

"Do you know something I don't?"

His mouth twisted in wry amusement. "Apparently."

They moved to the entryway. Charlie clearly meant to offer no more explanation than that. Either they would stand there in silence, or Sarah could choose a different topic.

"When do you return to Cambridge?"

"Next month for Lent Term. And I've been invited to spend the time between Lent Term and Easter Term with Mr. Lancaster and his family."

Sarah held back the observation that Mater would be rendered even lonelier if her youngest didn't return home during school breaks. She did not wish Charlie to feel guilty for spending time with a friend.

"I do not know the Lancasters, but I believe he is the gentleman you were with when you had your accident."

Charlie grinned. "Testament to my forgiving nature that I'm voluntarily returning, isn't it?"

"You're a saint," Sarah said.

With a laugh, he said, "Mr. Lancaster's sister would vehemently disagree with that declaration."

Sarah had heard something about Charlie not getting along with a member of the Lancaster family. "Does she dislike you as much as I've heard she does?"

"It is a mutual dislike."

She was intrigued. "I have never known you to truly dislike anyone. Well, perhaps George Finley, but everyone dislikes him."

"Except George Finley," Charlie added.

Sarah could not deny the truth of that. "Why, then, has young Miss Lancaster earned your very rare disapproval?"

He shrugged, no longer looking at her. "I don't know. She's—Being around her is like watching a play. She's acting a part all the time. It irritates me, but I don't know why I even care. We're not friends. We're not family. Whether or not she glides about Society pretending to be something she isn't shouldn't matter to me in the least." He shook his head. "But it does, and that bothers me."

Now, that was decidedly interesting.

Mater returned, ending any further prodding Sarah might have undertaken. The front walk of the dower house had been cleared of snow, but it was at least six inches deep on either side. Not unpassable, by any means, but certainly a miserable depth for someone to walk through all the way to church. Those with access to carriages would have managed the journey none the worse for wear, but the less fortunate would have endured a dreadful trudge. And that many cold, wet feet would likely spark an epidemic of illness. Harold was wise to have cancelled services.

Sarah, Mater, and Charlie were handed up into the Lampton carriage and whisked off to the main house. The path between the two buildings must have been cleared of snow as well; the horses didn't seem to struggle at all to make the journey. Mater spoke again and again of how delighted she was at the prospect of spending the entire day with her family. Sarah made note of that. She would make certain Mater was afforded that opportunity as often as possible.

The drawing room was full to bursting when they stepped inside. Mater moved directly to her extended family, receiving embraces and kisses on the cheek.

Charlie leaned a bit closer to Sarah. "This is a lot of Jonquils, isn't it?"

"You're nearly overrun."

"What would one call a gathering of Jonquils?" Charlie wondered out loud. "We're not a herd or a flock."

"A gaggle?" Sarah suggested.

Charlie grinned. "A pack."

"An escargatoire."

A laugh burst from him. "We're not snails."

A delighted squeal of "Charming!" reached them over the din of voices. Caroline rushed toward them.

"Careful, dear," Charlie warned her. "I'm walking better, but my balance is not very sure yet."

Caroline skidded to a halt, finishing her approach with utmost care. She slowly, cautiously wrapped her arms around Charlie's middle. "Grammy said you would come back, but I told her, 'What if you fell off a roof again?' and then Uncle Flip said that Harold was the one who probably would do that next because he has started climbing houses. But I think he is being silly with me."

Charlie set his hand on Caroline's back, her arms still wrapped around him. "Harold has been climbing houses. I saw him."

"Do vicars climb houses?" Far from shocked, Caroline sounded hopeful.

"Our vicar does."

Caroline giggled. "Our vicar is the best vicar."

"Yes, he is," Charlie said.

The best vicar. How she hoped Harold's family said that *to* him now and then.

"Poppy says we can play jackstones if you'll play with us."

Was there yet another member of this growing family Sarah did not yet know? "Who is Poppy?"

"Sorrel's brother," Charlie said.

"Her *brother* is named Poppy?" That seemed unlikely.

Charlie laughed quietly. "His name is actually Fennel, but Philip has called him Poppy from more or less the moment they met. Caroline has adopted the habit as well."

Sarah looked to the little girl. "Is Poppy a very skilled jackstones player?"

"I don't know. We haven't played yet." She tugged at Charlie's hand, pulling him toward the family gathering. "Edmund is very good at jackstones," she told her uncle. "If I get very good, he might play with me."

Sarah watched this family enjoying each other's company. Her home hadn't been devoid of affection—her father, especially, had been very tender in his regard for his family—but this scene was something else altogether. This was the very picture of love.

Many of the sisters-in-law had gathered near each other, talking and laughing. Philip, as she'd discovered was not unusual for him, was fully occupied playing with many of the grandchildren. Sorrel lay on the fainting sofa directly by him, watching with amused tenderness. Mater was deep in a whispered conversation with Corbin.

Harold was not present. Had he been unable to leave the vicarage? That didn't seem likely. It was not so very far away, and he had access to a cart and pony. He must be somewhere in the house. The pull of the loving family vignette was strong but not powerful enough to keep her in the drawing room.

She slipped into the corridor. Where might the elusive vicar be? Her footsteps carried her around the house as she attempted to be unobtrusive but meticulous in searching every public room she passed. Only upon reaching the door to the conservatory did she hear another voice. Two others, in fact. One, she knew with perfect clarity, was Harold's. The other, she felt certain, was one of his brothers. The Jonquils not only looked shockingly alike, but their voices were also remarkably similar.

"I didn't mean for her to feel neglected," the unidentified brother said, "but there's so much peace out in the fields, Harold. I spent most of the past years convinced I'd never feel that again. I need it. I need it like I need air, but the long hours I spend out there have left Marjie alone and lonely. I don't know what to do."

"Have you told her all of this?"

"We've spoken a lot since I followed her here. I know she needs more of my time."

"I suspect what she needs more of is *you*."

Sarah slipped back out into the corridor. She wished she'd realized sooner how personal the conversation she'd stumbled upon was. Harold was listening to Stanley's concerns, helping him sort out his worries, like a good brother and an excellent vicar. While Sarah was beyond pleased to hear Harold acting in the role she knew he was well-suited to—he had listened to her worries and concerns, her hopes and dreams often enough over the years—she had no desire to eavesdrop.

She wandered down the corridor, intending to make her way back in his direction after a time in the hope that she would find him on his own. Was that inexcusably bold of her? The rules were more stringently adhered to here than in America, though propriety had never truly been lax amongst the society she'd grown up in.

Surely she would be permitted a short, private conversation with him. They'd be in a public room, the door left open. As she'd discovered only moments before, anyone might wander in without warning. They'd ridden alone in the dark on quiet, abandoned lanes the night before. He'd been in her room, for heaven's sake. If that was permissible, surely this would be.

The tap of a cane on the tile floor sounded enough warning for her to step into a darkened doorway. Stanley moved past, a look of thoughtful contemplation on his face. Seeing him with his wife the day he'd arrived at Lampton Park, Sarah had known there was difficulty between them, though she'd not known the exact cause. There had also been unmistakable devotion.

Once the way was clear, she stepped out again and quickly moved toward the conservatory. She hadn't seen Harold pass. He might yet be inside.

There was something miraculous about a conservatory. The air was always warm, no matter the bitterness of the outside world. The smell of earth and life filled the vast space. It was bright with sunlight, even in the dim of winter. And there were always flowers.

Flowers. She stepped closer to the spray of flowers she was just then walking past. Delicate, deep-purple flowers. The exact flowers she'd received from Scott so many times. He'd not ever delivered them personally, but she'd found them in her rooms time and time again. He had apparently obtained them here.

Harold came upon her a moment later. "Sarah." He stepped up closer to her. His gaze fell on the flowers. Color stained his cheeks. "You—you recognize them."

Recognize them? She did, of course. But why did he? And why did he seem embarrassed for her to discover them there?

"Mrs. Tanner assured me she would not be in any kind of trouble for delivering them," Harold said.

"They were from you?"

His expression was a little flustered. "You always liked flowers, and that little sitting room of yours was so tiny and bare. I hoped a few sprigs would brighten it a little."

Of course the flowers were from him. How had she ever thought otherwise? Harold, who had climbed a bridge to pluck blooms for her, who had, when she'd known him before, been the most thoughtful person of her acquaintance, who'd dedicated himself to quietly serving people, was precisely the sort of gentleman to offer an anonymous bit of happiness. And the flowers had stopped coming during the weeks he'd been gone. How had she not pieced that together?

"I am sorry if I overstepped myself," he said.

"You didn't at all. I am simply so touched."

He laughed lightly. "I have not always been the best vicar, but at least I'm not a terrible person."

"You've always been a very good person, and you are showing yourself to be a fine vicar."

"Spoken like someone who did not have to go to services this morning." He sounded so much lighter than he had the last months. "I was sorry not to hear the choir sing today; I have missed their music these past weeks. But I could not clear my mind of the thought of Mrs. Jones and her new little one making that trek in the snow." He shook his head. "They would not be the only ones in that miserable situation. I could not help thinking the Lord would wish me to look upon their circumstances with compassion rather than insist upon a rigid and unwavering schedule."

She pressed her fingertips to her lips, swallowing down the emotion rising in her throat.

His expression turned alarmed. "What?"

She shook her head.

He set his hands on her arms. "You look as if you're going to cry." His mouth turned down. "Has something upset you?"

"No."

"Sarah." The tender way he said her name nearly undid her. "Please tell me what's happened."

"I'm not upset," she said. "I swear to you. This is one of those odd moments of tears arising from... happiness, relief, likely a little exhaustion."

"I know perfectly well why you're exhausted, and I can guess the reason you're feeling relieved." He smiled, his hands sliding down her arms and wrapping around hers. "I would dearly love to know what has made you happy."

"You gave me flowers." Her heart lodged firmly in her throat, thickened with joy and amazement. "Just as you used to."

"I wish I could have sent you flowers while you were in America. I wish—" He closed his eyes. "I wish a lot of things, Sarah."

Emotion bubbled inside. This was the Harold she longed for. The *real* him. The Harold she had loved and missed.

He kissed her hand just as he had the night before. Her heart fluttered again, even as tears pooled anew.

"I've missed you," she whispered.

"And I've missed you." He spoke as quietly as she had. "The heavens know I've missed you."

She swallowed back her emotions and offered a smile. "I'm no longer confined to a dim corner of Sarvol House. We should be seeing a lot of each other."

His smile grew as well. He had always had a beautiful smile, though it had become a rare sight. "I would like that very much, indeed, Sarah Sarvol."

Her heart pounded, telling her in no uncertain terms that it was beginning to grow attached to him again.

"For now, though, we should likely join the rest of the family," he said. With a formality that, at last, did not grate nor frustrate, he offered her his arm. "My brothers tend to grow very protective of any ladies who enter the sphere of the family."

She tucked her arm around his. "And your sisters-in-law? Do they grow protective as well?"

"They mostly grow terrifying."

They walked from the conservatory, neither saying anything of significance, yet something significant between them had changed. Harold was coming back to the person he'd once been. She was relaxing the defensive position she'd tucked herself into since arriving in the neighborhood. Finally, they were seeing each other without masks, without walls. Where there had been little but heartache and regret, she could now see wonderful possibilities.

CHAPTER TWENTY-FIVE

Harold held Sarah's arm all the way back to the drawing room. He'd have continued doing so, but she'd slipped free as they'd stepped inside and had crossed to Mater. When he'd first seen her in this very room a few months earlier, he'd been panicky, wishing for nothing short of escape. Now having her nearby brought him greater peace and happiness than any other person. He could not imagine not having her in his life.

Beck, the Lampton Park butler, stepped inside, saying something quietly to Philip before the both of them stepped out again. Fennel noticed the departure and moved to sit by Sorrel.

Harold took a seat in a vacant armchair. His eyes wandered, as they often did when in this room, to the family portrait above the fireplace.

Father, I wish you could see this family now. He would have loved being surrounded by his grandchildren. He would have cherished his daughters-in-law. And there was no doubt in Harold's mind he would have treasured Mater's company as deeply as he always had. If only he were here.

Stanley and Marjie sat on a nearby sofa, his arm around her. He pressed a light kiss to the top of her head. Harold hoped they truly were working through their difficulties. He knew how very much they loved each other. After all the sorrows they'd passed through, those two deserved their "happy ever after."

Across the way, Sarah brought Mater a throw, tucking it around her and little Alice, who sat on her lap. Mater smiled a thank you. Having Sarah at the dower house would be good for Mater. Being there would be good for Sarah.

The Jonquil family was not without worries. Harold knew with certainty they had difficult times ahead, but he felt hopeful.

A footman stepped inside and crossed to Harold. "Begging your pardon, Mr. Jonquil. Lord Lampton has requested that you and Miss Sarvol join him in the servants' dining hall."

"The servants' dining hall?" An odd place for Philip to have gone.

The footman nodded. "You and Miss Sarvol."

Harold rose, thanking him for delivering the message, then crossed to Sarah, who stood near Mater. "Philip has asked you and me to join him in the servants' dining hall."

She looked as confused by the request as he felt. He offered his arm, and she accepted. They walked together into the corridor.

"I can't decide if we're about to discover something is horribly wrong or that Philip is up to some mischief or another," Sarah said.

Harold grinned. "With him, one never knows."

Philip was not alone in the dining hall. Everything about their attire and posture identified the others as servants, yet Harold didn't recognize any of them.

"Janey? William?" Sarah eyed the others in the gathering with surprise. "Why are all of you here?"

Philip answered. "Your escape has been discovered, and your uncle is furious. He has begun dismissing anyone he thinks was involved."

Sarah paled. "Have all of you lost your positions?"

Ah. These were Sarvol House servants. Good heavens. There must have been fifteen people in the room.

"We have, Miss Sarvol," one of the women said.

"But none of you was involved in my leaving."

"Don't matter. He won't listen to anyone trying to tell him they're innocent. Insists you couldn't've left without help."

"She did have help," Harold said, "but not from any of you."

One of the men, dressed like he plied his trade in the stables, spoke up. "Young Mr. Sarvol told him as much, but it didn't do any good. The master's dismissing anyone who crosses his path. There'll be more."

Sarah took a shaky breath. "I was so afraid this would happen. No matter how careful we were not to involve any of you, he is punishing you anyway."

Philip caught Harold's eye. "I'm willing to tell him I was part of this, but I suspect he won't be satisfied unless we tell him how we got her out right under his nose."

There was a great deal of warning in his tone. "I am not afraid of Mr. Sarvol's disapproval."

Philip shook his head. "If you make known our methods, all the parish will learn about your . . . pastime. Seeing as you haven't yet shared it with anyone beyond the family, I thought perhaps it was something you preferred not be widely known."

He was not wrong. "I have been very careful not to share this oddity in me, and I cannot pretend it wouldn't complicate how I am viewed as the vicar. But Mr. Sarvol will never believe the staff was not involved unless he knows how we managed it." He turned to the gathering. "If we explain what happened, showing that you weren't involved, would he change his mind?"

The stable hand shrugged. "Might."

Harold looked to Sarah and lowered his voice. "Explaining all of this means people will know *you* climbed out a window. There are certainly some who will disapprove."

She actually laughed. "I am the mad American who bested the blacksmith. No one will be the least bit shocked."

Harold nodded and met Philip's eye once more. "I'll not let these good people suffer simply because it might save me a bit of embarrassment. Let's go speak with Mr. Sarvol and explain to him what truly happened."

"Mrs. Beck." Philip addressed the Lampton Park housekeeper. "Will you please see to it these men and women are fed? I will return shortly."

"Of course, my lord."

Philip led the way out. Harold and Sarah followed.

"I have every intention of coming with you," Sarah said, "so don't bother wasting your breath arguing with me about it."

"He will likely be unkind," Philip warned.

"I would likely not recognize him otherwise."

That earned a laugh from Harold's oldest brother. Philip swung his quizzing glass about on its ribbon, shaking his head in amusement. "I do like you, Sarah Sarvol."

"So do I," Harold said.

Sarah beamed. She ought always to look so happy. She deserved to be.

Layton stood in the front entrance when they reached it.

Philip hooked an eyebrow. "Let me guess. You've discovered the plight of the Sarvol House staff, have guessed our destination, and intend to join the effort."

Layton answered with a single crisp nod.

Philip sighed dramatically. "Your jacket clashes with mine, but I suppose I can endure that."

"Shall I ask Wilson for advice on my 'confront my father-in-law' attire?" Layton asked dryly.

Philip pursed his lips and shook his head. "Wilson is unfailingly loyal to me. He won't lend his genius to just anyone."

Layton shrugged. "Then I suppose I'll have to beard the dragon dressed as I am."

"Are they always this ridiculous?" Sarah asked with a laugh in her voice.

"They have not even begun to be ridiculous."

Philip managed to keep the tone among them jovial all the way to Sarvol House. Though his dandified manners had always pricked at Jason, even that brother had come to appreciate Philip's ability to lighten a tense situation. And more and more of Philip's responsible and dependable nature peeked through the layer of frivolity.

The housekeeper answered the Sarvol House door, her expression frenzied. She sputtered a bit, stumbling over her words of welcome. "Forgive me. We are in utter chaos here just now."

Sarah stepped in. "We are aware of the havoc my uncle has wreaked upon you. We are here, we hope, to soothe some of that."

"Miss Sarvol, he will be so cruel to you. You ought not to have come back."

Sarah set her hand on the woman's arm. "I will not allow him to keep hurting people. None of us will."

Harold nodded to her. "Allow us to see if we can bring a bit of peace back to this home, Mrs. Tanner."

Her shoulders dropped. "Thank you. He is in the library."

"While we manage that business," Philip said, "will you have whoever from the staff can be spared gather up Miss Sarvol's things? She was unable to take them with her last evening, but we would like for her to have them."

"Of course, my lord."

They did, indeed, find Mr. Sarvol in the library. He sat alone at a broad table. His grizzled eyes rose to them as they approached. Harold's brothers led the way. He didn't cower, but he did remain a bit behind. Sarah kept to his side. She looked nervous but determined.

Philip sauntered toward him; there was really no other way to describe it. "Sarvol." His tone was casual, but no one listening could miss the underlying sharpness there.

"Lampton," Mr. Sarvol grumbled back. His eyes fell on Layton. "How dare you come into this house, Farland. How dare you."

Layton didn't so much as flinch. He was built like a tree and stood as solidly as one. "We're not here to discuss me."

"We're hearing a great many whispers around the neighborhood." Philip inspected his fingernails. "Would you care to shed any light on anything in particular?"

"I—"

Harold took an involuntary step in front of Sarah at the absolute hatred that suddenly entered Mr. Sarvol's eyes, eyes that were now focused on her.

Sarvol let forth a string of profanity and shockingly vile insults at his niece. It came with no warning, no instigation. They all stood in mute shock.

Philip found his voice first. In tones entirely devoid of the frivolous dandy he often portrayed, he made himself heard over Mr. Sarvol's vile spewing. "That is quite enough, sir. No matter your age, no matter your frailty, should you let one more offensive phrase fall from your lips, I will call you out."

Mr. Sarvol's eyes pulled a bit wide.

"I will stand his second," Layton said. "I doubt anyone will stand yours."

Mr. Sarvol pointed a gnarled finger at Sarah. "She—"

"Careful," Philip said.

"She disobeyed me. Left home without permission. No true lady does that."

"You are tiptoeing mighty close, sir, casting such aspersions on her character." Layton inched the tiniest bit toward Sarah, clearly placing himself as a shield. "You did that often enough with Bridget for me to know you're perfectly willing to insult a lady no matter that you consider yourself a gentleman."

"Do not dare to speak her name in this house. You stole my daughter from me."

"Enough," Philip snapped. "We are here to discuss the matter of your dwindling staff and the misconceptions under which you are operating."

"My staff is none of your concern."

"On the contrary." Philip turned to Sarah. "I am certain you have endured enough of your uncle to last a lifetime. If you would rather not burden yourself with his company, you are welcome to help Mrs. Tanner gather your belongings."

"Would it be cowardly of me to jump at the escape he is offering?" she asked Harold.

"Not in the least."

She took a deep breath and, with a quickly dipped curtsy, slipped from the room.

"Brothers." Philip motioned to the chairs around the table.

They all sat. Mr. Sarvol's expression turned almost petulant.

"You dismissed your staff for defying your orders and helping Miss Sarvol escape," Philip said, "but they had nothing to do with her departure."

"She could not have escaped alone," Mr. Sarvol said.

"She didn't," Philip said. "We helped her, and we did so without a single member of your staff knowing anything about it."

Mr. Sarvol shook his head. "Couldn't have. Someone had to have let you in and out. Someone had to have helped you get the door open."

"No one had to," Philip said. "We had the vicar with us."

Mr. Sarvol's mouth twisted sardonically. "He prayed her door open?"

"I didn't have to," Harold said. "I went in through the window."

"A story above the ground?"

Harold nodded. "I climbed up, then she climbed back down. No door needed opening. No servant needed to help."

"I don't believe it."

Harold rested his elbows on the table and steepled his hands. "Are you calling me, a man of the church, a liar?"

"Vicars do not climb things."

"Vicar Hohenwart was the first to reach the Kleinglockner summit," Philip said. "It was an accomplishment hailed far and wide. I would say vicars most certainly do climb things."

Harold wasn't aware of that. He wasn't well versed in mountaineering. The idea of another vicar climbing anything, even if it was a mountain and not a wall, helped further settle his worries about this odd pastime of his.

"You broke into my home?" Mr. Sarvol growled.

"You locked your niece in a room," Harold said. "I don't think *my* behavior is the most shocking."

"None of your staff was involved in Miss Sarvol's escape," Philip said. "Dismissing them without references was entirely unwarranted. I assume that will now be corrected."

"You have no say in how I run my household." Mr. Sarvol's eyes hardened. "They deserved their dismissal."

"They did not," Philip countered.

Mr. Sarvol sat with jaw set. He didn't look at any of them. He likely would not be convinced to change his mind on this point.

The sound of rustling skirts pulled their attention to the doorway. Sarah rushed inside. A franticness showed in her eyes. She looked directly at her uncle. "Where is Scott?"

"I will not be interrogated in my own home."

She crossed the room toward a far door, speaking as she walked. "Mrs. Tanner said there was shouting this morning, and no one has seen Scott since." She stepped through the door but returned almost immediately. "His belongings are gone." She turned to Harold. "Where is he? What could have happened?"

"Likely the same thing that happened to the servants."

Sarah shook her head. "He would toss his heir out into the cold?"

"I would put almost no act of cruelty past him," Layton said, rising. He crossed to Sarah. "We'll find Scott. He likely took shelter with someone."

Realization lit Sarah's face. "He will have sought out Mater. I know it. He likely went to the dower house first, which is why we didn't see him."

Layton set a gentle hand on her arm. "I'm certain you are correct." He looked to Harold. "I think Sarah has spent enough time in this horrid house. Will you see to it she returns to Lampton Park safely? There are a few things I've been needing to say to my father-in-law for a number of years, but none of them are appropriate for a lady's ears."

Harold and Philip both stood. Harold moved to Sarah's side.

Philip slapped a hand on Layton's shoulder. "Do you want me to hold the carriage?" he asked.

Layton shook his head. "This will likely take awhile."

Philip's shoulders set. His expression turned earnest. "I'll stay here if you want me to."

"I need to do this on my own," Layton said, a bit of emotion in his voice. "Bridget deserves for him to finally hear what she was never permitted to say."

Philip nodded. He motioned Harold and Sarah out of the library.

Mrs. Tanner and a couple of maids stood in the entry hall with a trunk and portmanteau, as well as a couple of paintings. "Forgive me for even asking," she said, "but would you gentlemen help us get these things in the carriage? Both of the footmen and our stable hands were dismissed."

Harold took up the trunk. Philip tucked the paintings under his arm and took the handle of the portmanteau in his other hand. Sarah reached for the small frame one of the maids held. Harold recognized it: the bouquet he'd given her.

Their eyes met. She blushed adorably. Harold didn't bother hiding his smile.

The coachman held the horses still as Philip and Harold packed Sarah's things in the carriage. Poor Mrs. Tanner apologized again and again, embarrassed at the sight of two gentlemen doing the work of a servant.

Harold pulled her a bit to the side. "I don't know what can be done to appropriately restaff this house, but Lord Lampton and I will do all we can to help. I cannot like the idea of you being so overburdened."

"The servants who were let go?" she pressed.

"We'll do what we can for them as well."

Mrs. Tanner pressed a hand to her heart. "Thank you, Mr. Jonquil. It's good to know you care about us."

"I do, indeed." He only wished he'd done a better job of communicating that to the parish before now. He'd worried so much about being the perfect vicar that he'd neglected that most basic of duties.

They were loaded in the carriage and on their way. Sarah sat forward facing. Harold and Philip sat facing her.

"I worry about the servants Uncle dismissed," she said. "What will they do without references?"

"I wish I could simply employ them all," Philip said. "The Lampton estate is profitable but not enough to take on fifteen servants we don't actually have positions for."

Harold rubbed at his weary face. "I'll make inquiries. With luck and a good amount of prayer, we might manage a miracle."

Sarah's expression remained drawn. "We tried so hard not to implicate them. It breaks my heart to see them suffer."

"Do not give up hope, Sarah," Harold said. "You bested a blacksmith. I would say you are rather an expert in miracles."

She closed her eyes and took a deep breath. Some of the tension left her posture. She pressed her palms together, touching her fingertips to her lips. It was very nearly a posture of prayer.

Please, he petitioned the heavens. *She deserves a miracle.*

CHAPTER TWENTY-SIX

Harold had undertaken Midnight Mass on Christmas Eve before, but he hadn't, on that previous occasion, been legitimately worried. He had no doubt many in the congregation had heard about his climb, but he wasn't at all certain what they thought of him in light of that. Further, he would that morning be instituting the changes he meant to make in his approach to serving this parish. What would they think of that? Would it all simply be more than they were willing to accept? Would he be laughed at? Rejected?

The earliest pieces of the service were nearly rote, the processional, the reading of scriptures from the lectionary. The portion of the mass over which he had the most discretion was the sermon; he knew perfectly well that it was the part his parishioners disliked most.

His legs shook beneath him as he climbed the steps to the pulpit. He set his prayer book in front of him and took a calming breath. He looked out over the congregation, the familiar and beloved faces there. These people were important to him. Did they know that? Had he sufficiently shown them that?

Never in his years as curate or vicar here had he, while standing at the pulpit, allowed his gaze to touch the space where Father had once sat. Though the family did not leave it entirely empty, there was always a bit of a gap. Harold turned his eyes there now.

I've tried to make you proud, Father. I'm going to do better. I'm going to be better.

The congregation sat in silent anticipation. Nothing about their postures or expressions spoke of excitement. He had noticed it before but had assumed it was the result of him not being dedicated enough to the exactness required of a vicar, of him falling short of the mark of required perfection. He now realized he'd missed the mark entirely.

He cleared his throat. Swallowed. Pushed out the words. "Let me begin by thanking our choir for the carols they have touched us with tonight." He could only just see Mr. Felt far to his left. "Thank you."

He received a shocked nod in return. Sarah had been right about that: he didn't praise or thank the choir as much as he ought. He intended to do so more.

The congregation didn't look as confused as Mr. Felt. Harold would guess they weren't paying enough attention to have even realized he'd veered from the usual approach.

"This is the point in our service when I am charged with determining what is the best message to share with you. I have given that a great deal of thought. Tonight, I feel the best I can do is be brief."

Surprise filled the chapel. Philip pretended to clean out his ears, as if certain he'd heard wrong.

Harold smiled, something he didn't think he'd ever done at the pulpit. "I am certain there are many among you who came here tonight expecting to indulge in the usual nap. I apologize that there will not be time to do so and hope you will feel some degree of forgiveness when I assure you I will expound long and monotonous in the morning at our Christmas service."

Someone in the chapel laughed, light and quiet but genuine. It did Harold's heart good.

He let his gaze settle on Sarah, seated between Mater and Scott, watching him with what could be described only as approval.

"I will limit my remarks to this." He looked out on the congregation once more. "Honor the Season by being kinder and more generous, forgiving, and loving to each other. Give of yourself. Do not overlook those in need. Love each other. That is the best gift we can give at Christmastime."

He took up his prayer book again and turned from the pulpit. One glance at the congregation told him they did not at all believe his sermon was complete. He leaned back, facing them sideways. "That really is all. We'll proceed to the rites that remain, but I truly am finished with the sermon."

Whispered conversations erupted immediately. He had no idea if their comments were of happiness or disapproval. Time would eventually tell.

The remainder of the service was predetermined: rites and sacraments and blessings. All proceeded as it usually did, other than the looks of closer examination he received. He simply smiled, nodded, and moved forward.

The usual words of farewell were as baffled as the looks he'd received earlier. Harold took it in stride. Change was always a little jarring. In time, he would know better if this new approach was the best one. His sermons would not all be so short, but he meant to make certain they were what was best for his congregation.

Mater, Sarah, Scott, and Philip were the last to leave the chapel.

"That was the best sermon you've ever given, Monkey. I request a repeat performance in the morning."

"A sermon is not a performance," Harold said.

Philip tugged foppishly at his cuffs. "Would be if I were undertaking it."

Mater swatted at him. "Behave. We're still in the shadow of the church."

Philip shrugged and made a sound of dismissal.

Harold met Sarah's eyes. "My brother is a heathen. It's a shame, really."

"Well, his wife is a saint," she said. "I suppose they even each other out."

Harold shook his head. "Rather, she *cancels* him out."

"Behave, Harold," Philip said. "You are in the shadow of a church."

"I cannot go anywhere with you boys." Mater slipped one arm through Philip's and the other through Scott's. She looked back over her shoulder at Harold. "We will see you at the Park when you are done here."

"Of course." He turned to Sarah once more as Mater and the two gentlemen walked away. "Though it is likely horrible of me to say so, I am grateful your uncle was not here tonight. I have very little confidence he would not lash out at you and Scott, as well as those dismissed servants who were here."

"I am equally guilty. I confess to a very loud, very audible sigh of relief."

"Was Scott equally happy?"

Her shoulders drooped a bit. "I know he is glad to not be subject to Uncle's vitriol, but Scott is not as light and relieved as I would expect him to be. He is weighed down, and I don't know how to help him."

Harold wanted to reach for her hand, to offer that gesture of support, but doing so in a public setting, no matter that most of the worshipers were gone already, could not truly be permitted. He was being a bit more lax in his adherence to the strictest of expectations, but he didn't intend to do so in ways that embarrassed other people.

"You had best hurry," he told her. "Mater will wish to return quickly to the Park to make certain all is in readiness, and Philip is no doubt anxious to be with Sorrel. And though he may not show it, I believe Scott is happier with you nearby."

"I hope so," she said.

"I *know* so."

"It was good to see you at the pulpit today," she said.

"You've seen me there before."

She shook her head. "I've seen Holy Harry. It is good to finally see *you*."

* * *

"I have something for Caroline," Sarah told Layton and Marion the next evening during the Jonquil family Christmas gathering. "But I wished for the two of you to see it first and decide what you feel is best to do."

Marion tipped her head to one side, gaze a bit narrowed. "Why do you think we would object to your gift?"

"Not object. Not exactly." She looked to Harold, having asked him to join them in this small sitting room, away from all the rest of the family. He knew better than she what Layton had passed through the past years. She wanted him there to help her gauge how his brother was responding. Layton was special to her; she wouldn't cause him grief for all the world.

"I think you will understand better Sarah's concern if she shows you what she has for Caroline."

Layton and Marion exchanged glances but didn't object.

She took up the painting she'd leaned against the wall, its subject facing away from Layton and Marion. "This once hung in my uncle's house, but when I returned here from America, I found it relegated to the attics. It ought to belong to Caroline, though I leave it to you to determine the how and the when."

She turned it around so they could see it.

Layton took in a sharp breath. "Oh, merciful heavens." His next breath shuddered from him. "Oh, heavens." His was not an expression of pleasure but of grief.

Sarah looked to Harold. This was what she had worried about.

Harold set an arm around her waist, keeping close to her side. "He is strong enough for this," Harold whispered. "And he is not alone."

Sarah took a deep breath. Layton wasn't alone, and neither was she. "This is how I remember Bridget," she said. "Smiling. Happy. Lovely. I want Caroline to know the Bridget I knew, and this will help." She blinked back the emotion rising in her. "I want you to give it to her when you are ready for her to have it. And I will help any way I can. I love Caroline, not only for my cousin's sake but for hers. She is a dear and kindhearted and loving child."

Layton's pained gaze did not leave the portrait.

"Caroline loves so freely because she has been loved so fully," Sarah continued. "Thank you. Both of you."

Layton met her eyes for the first time since she'd shown him the painting. "I have been a bit cold to you since you returned. I hope you know I wasn't *un*happy to see you. It's only that . . . you . . . you look so much like her."

Sarah nodded through the tears she couldn't entirely hold back.

"Seeing you tore at wounds I didn't realize hadn't healed." A tear fell from the corner of his eye. "I miss her. The grief is sometimes terribly close to the surface."

"I miss her too," Sarah said. "And so does Caroline, though she never knew her. Please give her the portrait when the time is right."

Layton nodded silently.

Marion took his hands in hers and led him to the nearby sofa, silently urging him to sit. He did, and she kissed the top of his head. She turned back to Sarah and accepted the painting. "This will help," she whispered. "I promise you, he is grateful for it. We both are."

This was the very reason she'd wanted to give them the picture away from the others. She had suspected it would be an emotional thing for Layton.

Giving Layton the privacy he needed when seeing it for the first time was the only gift Sarah had to give him.

She looked up at Harold. "We should probably leave them."

Harold agreed silently, walking with her from the room. As they slipped into the corridor, he took her hand in his. "Thank you for doing that for Layton and Caroline. They have grieved for so long. Having a bit of Bridget to keep will do them both a world of good."

She leaned her head against him. "It can be difficult to know how to help when someone is hurting that much."

"I know." He stopped. So did she. "Not knowing the right way to help stopped me from trying for far too long. But you showed me the importance of doing what I can in whatever way I can. Have I thanked you for that?"

She could feel a little warmth creep over her face. "You haven't."

"Thank you for finding me when I was lost," he said quietly, tenderly.

"Thank you for coming back to us. To me."

His arm moved tentatively around her. Warmth spread through her at his touch. "That day at the stream—"

She swallowed, trying to keep her breathing steady.

"I shouldn't have—I didn't mean to—" His gaze dropped. "I wasn't trying to hurt you."

"I know."

He might have said more. She might have as well, but a shout of excitement sounded from the drawing room, one too loud and enthusiastic to be ignored.

Harold stepped back, his arm falling away. "We should see . . ."

"We should."

An awkwardness settled between them as they walked slowly to the drawing room.

The Jonquils were decidedly in a celebratory mood. Harold dipped his head to her, face still a little flushed with embarrassment, and moved away. She sat on the chair beside Sorrel's sofa. "What have I missed?"

"Word has come from Norfolk." Sorrel's weakening state became more obvious every time Sarah interacted with her. It showed in the gauntness of her face, the weakness of her voice.

Sarah did her best to hide her worries. "Who is in Norfolk?"

"Jason."

"And what was so important that he sent word at Christmas? Well, a few days before Christmas, I suppose." With the weather being what it had been, the messenger had likely needed quite some time to make the journey.

"He is a new father."

The smiles and excitement around the room indicated the delivery in Norfolk had a happier conclusion than was anticipated here. "And is Jason father to a son or a daughter?"

"A daughter," Sorrel said. "They've named her Isabella. Philip had teased him that it would be twins. Mater is a twin herself and has twins of her own."

"One of whom is Jason." Sarah laughed lightly. "I can see how Philip would enjoy pestering him a bit over that."

"He enjoys teasing all his brothers. Laughter is a tonic to his worries."

"Is there any tonic I might offer for your worries?" Sarah pressed.

Sorrel met her eye. The weight she saw there nearly stole her breath. "You have helped Harold find himself and his strength. Philip will need that from him. For that, I will always be grateful to you."

Not too far distant, Philip had Henry in one arm and Phrobert in the other while Alice sat on his foot, her arms and legs wrapped around his leg. Caroline might have joined in the game, but she was in the corner, talking ceaselessly to Corbin's boy Edmund.

"My foot has grown oddly heavy, Mater," Philip said in a theatrical voice of confusion. "What could possibly be the cause?"

Alice giggled and giggled. Philip tromped about, jiggling her as he went. The silly faces he made at the two tiny boys made them laugh as well.

"It is some comfort, however thin, to know that someday down the road, long after—" Sorrel paused, though whether she was out of breath, out of strength, or pushing down her emotions once more was not clear. "After I—He may yet one day be a father, as he was always meant to be. He'll be happy."

Though Sorrel hadn't said as much directly, Sarah understood the tragic possibility the dear, suffering lady had, it seemed, accepted as probable: that she would not survive the coming delivery and that Philip would eventually marry again. What could Sarah say? She could not offer words of reassurance that all would end in the best possible way, that Sorrel had nothing to worry about, that she and Philip would have a long, happy life together with all the children they could hope for. Sorrel would know that for the empty platitude it was.

"He really does love you," Sarah said. "It is obvious to anyone who sees him so much as look at you."

"I know, and his love is the greatest blessing of my life. His love is a light in my darkest moments, hope when all other hope is gone." Sorrel watched Philip playing with the children. Her eyelids grew heavy, and her weak smile faded. After a brief moment, she was dozing, though likely not deeply, considering her pain and discomfort.

Layton was struggling in a distant room. His daughter was grieving a mother she'd never known. Stanley and Marjie had not entirely sorted their difficulties. Philip and Sorrel had all but resigned themselves to a near future of sorrow and pain.

Sarah desperately hoped Harold was equal to what was coming, and she prayed she could find a way to help him help his beloved family.

CHAPTER TWENTY-SEVEN

Harold felt a little ridiculous sitting at the top of the vicarage stairwell in his "thinking place," but he no longer saw it as proof of his failure to be the person he'd tried to be. He was odd, yes. He had more than his fair share of quirks, but in the week he'd been back in the neighborhood, he'd embraced the changes he meant to make and had received acceptance, support, and approval, though not without a good amount of wariness. He felt hopeful.

After receiving an unexpected letter that morning, however, he was also feeling torn. How was it that after finally setting himself on a course toward a future he could be excited about, that future suddenly became far less certain?

Mrs. Dalton took the stairs to the midfloor landing and looked up at him. "Still thinking, are you?"

"Always."

"Do you ever worry you'll think so hard you'll fall?"

He smiled a little at that. "I'll be careful. I promise you."

Sarah stepped up beside Mrs. Dalton, eying him with curiosity. "Do you promise me as well?"

He probably should have been more embarrassed than he was. Instead, he felt mostly relieved. Sarah had done that for him all those years ago and was now doing it again. When she had been with him, he'd worried less and hoped more. Heaven knew he needed a dose of that now.

He turned enough to hang his legs over the ledge. "Have you any commitments for the next hour?"

She shook her head.

"I'm trying to sort through something," he said, "and I could use a listening ear."

"That is very convenient because I am here for the same reason."

She'd come to him with a concern, to talk through and sort things. What a change from their earliest interactions a few months earlier when she'd found him to be so utterly lacking. He lowered himself over the banister and hand-crawled along the ledge.

"Does he always get down this way?" Sarah asked Mrs. Dalton.

"He does. And I have heart palpitations every time."

Harold dropped onto the step just a few below them. He tossed Mrs. Dalton a grin. "My goal is to get you to swoon over how very strong and agile I am."

Sarah shook her head and offered an exaggerated look of disapproval. "If you keep torturing this woman, she'll spread it about the neighborhood that our bachelor vicar and the dowager's very unmarried houseguest spent an afternoon alone, spilling their worries into each other's ears, and then we'll both be in the suds."

"Mrs. Dalton is discreet as a statue."

Sarah smiled kindly at Mrs. Dalton. "You have been good to our vicar and good *for* him."

"He's a good lad, though I say it. Cares about everyone but doesn't know how to show it. And he knows every drinking song ever written, which is a fine thing, if you ask me."

Sarah looked at him once more, wide-eyed. His heart lurched, waiting for the condemnation, the disapproval.

"Do you know 'Down among the Dead Men'?" she asked. "I learned that one onboard ship during our journey here."

Harold was momentarily too shocked to respond.

Mrs. Dalton snorted a laugh. "Well, if you aren't two peas in a pod." She slipped past him. "Have a good gab."

"How long have you had an interest in drinking chanteys?" Harold asked.

Sarah shrugged. "They make me laugh. They always have."

Harold motioned her down the stairs. "Why did you never tell me?"

"I can't say it ever occurred to me *to* tell you. And in my defense, you never mentioned your interest either."

They stopped in the entryway. "Do you have any objection to a walk around the Park? It's not far from here, and we'd have a bit of privacy without pushing the bounds of propriety too far."

"That would be lovely, provided there are a few paths clear of snow."

"The formal gardens are cleared. I walked out along the edge of the east field yesterday; the pathway is clear there as well."

He helped her put her coat on. It was such a commonplace gesture, something that happened dozens of times over in every house throughout the kingdom, yet it struck him in that moment. His mind filled with the image of the two of them in this exact arrangement day after day. A simple, quiet, but happy domesticity.

Harold shook it off. He was hardly in a position to be entertaining those thoughts. Too much was yet uncertain, both between them and in his own life.

Beyond a few off-hand remarks on the weather and the Christmas season, they said very little as they wound their way toward the back entrance to the Park.

A few steps out into the east field, Sarah spoke. "What is it you hoped to talk with me about? You seem very pensive, whatever it is."

"I received a letter this morning."

Her attention was fully on him. He would need to keep an eye on their path so she wouldn't stumble.

"Was the letter unsettling? Something worrisome?" she asked.

"No. Far from it, actually. It was an offer."

"What sort of offer?"

He still hardly believed what he'd read. "The Duke of Hartley anticipates a vacancy in the living he has the advowson of. It is possible the living will be vacant in the next few months."

She squeezed his arm. "He offered it to you, didn't he?"

"I am as amazed as you are."

She rubbed his arm. "I am not the least amazed, Harold Jonquil. I always knew you would be a fine vicar."

"His Grace, apparently, has faith in me as well." Harold couldn't explain it. He'd done nothing to garner the duke's notice, and he had only just begun making important improvements in his approach to his duties. "The duke has offered me three parishes, all of which have been overseen by the current vicar via the employment of curates."

"Three parishes? That seems a great deal to be in charge of. Are they near each other?"

Harold shook his head. "Not terribly near, but that is not unusual for vicars with multiple livings. It is the main employment of curates to see to parishes the vicar cannot or, sadly, *will* not."

"You were a curate in this parish for a time, I believe."

"I was," he said. "Philip convinced Mr. Throckmorten to give over the running of this parish to me."

Sarah looked ahead once more. Her expression had hardened. "Though it is likely uncharitable of me to say as much, I am grateful Philip talked him into stepping aside. He was hard and unfeeling in a way I am certain hurt people."

That was precisely what had happened. Throckmorten had told Layton he was not welcome in the church because, in his grief after Bridget's death, Layton had drifted from the faith he had once embraced, the horrid man ignoring pointedly the role he had played in pushing Layton away. Removing a vicar was not an easy thing to do, nearly impossible in fact, but Philip had found a way to rid the neighborhood of the man, something for which Harold was grateful.

Sarah's brow pulled. "You are the vicar now though."

"Throckmorten's passing allowed Philip to bestow the living on me, which gave me a livable income, provided I have only myself to support." He had worried over that. "Adding this new living would give me income enough to live with a degree of ease I could not know otherwise, enough to begin thinking of a future beyond the lonely one I have now."

"That is a good thing," she said. "Why, then, do you seem so concerned?"

Though he *was* concerned, speaking with her calmed him. It always had before. How had he managed in the years since she'd left? "One of the parishes is quite large and could not be run by a curate alone. The vicar would need to be there, reside there."

"You would have to leave Collingham." How quickly she had sorted his dilemma.

"I, of course, would select a curate who would care for this parish in the best possible way. I would never allow the people here to suffer in my absence—"

"But you care about them and don't know that you would be happy away from them." She leaned a little more toward him as they walked on. "I've watched you, especially since your return from your holiday. You love the people of this neighborhood. You grew up among them. You know them in a way you don't any other parish. And your family is here. Taking charge of a different parish would mean leaving them behind and leaving the care of them to someone else."

"You always did understand me better than anyone. I suppose that is why your criticism of me when you first returned stung as much as it did. From anyone else, I could have dismissed it. But not from you."

She rested her head against his upper arm, he being too tall for her head to reach his shoulder. "Seeing you broke my heart. I felt as though every hint of the Harold I had known was gone."

"He wasn't gone. He was simply adrift." He chuckled a little. "Do you know, Sorrel once told me precisely that."

"That you were adrift?"

He nodded. "I scoffed at the time, but I knew she wasn't wrong."

"I visited her this morning." Sarah spoke too quietly for his comfort. "She looks awful, truly and honestly awful. I don't imagine it will be much longer before her time comes. I am praying for a happy outcome, but my hope is all but gone."

"They lost another child this time last year. Sorrel was not nearly as far along then as she is now. There is a greater possibility of the baby surviving, though that is still quite slim without more time."

"Yet, the longer this continues, the greater the chance that *she* won't survive." Sarah's heavy tone matched the difficulty of the situation.

"Life is difficult, Sarah. It asks so very much of us."

She slipped her arm from his and tucked it around him instead. "I'm cold," she explained.

He set his arm around her as well. "You're cold," he explained with a grin.

She laughed a little.

How was it that even when discussing topics as difficult as those they'd covered during this walk, she still managed to lift him and lighten him? He had needed her every moment since the first time they'd been together all those years ago.

"What was it you wished to talk with me about?" he asked.

"Mater," she said.

His heart dropped on the instant. "Is something the matter with her?"

"No," she assured him. "But I wanted your thoughts on something regarding her."

"I'll certainly help if I can."

She adjusted a little, pulling her arm back and rubbing her hands over her chilled arms. Harold tucked her in more closely.

"Though I doubt she realizes it, Mater has mentioned more than once a vague wish to do some traveling. She always very quickly brushes it aside with an acknowledgment that she has many responsibilities here. Charlie told me he means to spend the term break with Mr. Lancaster and his family. He will not be at the Park. I think it is the perfect opportunity for her to pursue her wish to travel."

All of this was news to Harold, every last bit of it. *I talk to people, Harold.* She talked, and she listened, and she remembered. A wonder. An absolute wonder.

"I don't know this country very well. Where is someplace she and I—and Scott, if he is able—might go, not too far distant but far enough that she would feel it a bit of an adventure? And how would I go about making some of those arrangements so that she needn't worry over it? I think if given the opportunity to pursue that still-vague dream with minimal obstacles, she would do it. And, Harold, I think it would bring her some much-needed happiness."

Something in the way she said that made him wonder if there was more to be worried about where Mater was concerned than he realized. "Do you suspect she is unhappy?"

"To borrow a word from Sorrel, she seems *adrift*. Her boys are all grown. She has dedicated the last dozen years of her life raising the lot of you alone, and now that chapter in her book is finished. I think she doesn't know what comes next. She needs a purpose, and she needs something to look forward to."

He shook his head in amazement. "I have lived among my family all my life but have missed so much. That you see what we don't is a blessing to us all."

She looked up at him. Mischief danced in her eyes. "Are you finally conceding that I am a remarkably good vicar?"

"We Jonquils don't concede defeat very easily."

She laughed as he'd hoped she would. It always had been a joy to make her laugh.

"A stubbornness," she said as if having pieced something together.

"A *what*?" He laughed in spite of his confusion.

"Charlie asked me what a gathering of Jonquils would be termed. We decided against herd or flock. I believe you would be called a stubbornness."

"A stubbornness of Jonquils?"

She laughed again, setting his heart flipping about. "Accept it, Harold."

He shook his head at her very welcome banter.

"I will talk with Layton and Philip about places you and Mater might visit. Your options will expand if Scott is available. I'm sure both of my brothers would happily lend her the use of a carriage, coachman, and footman, and whatever else she might need."

"You all love your mother. It is the thing about you that reminds me most of your father. He loved her."

"Yes, he did." An unexpected lump rose in his throat. Father had most certainly loved Mater. Theirs had been a love story for the ages. If only the fates had granted them more time together.

Sarah's gaze shifted to the landscape beside them, something like confusion in the pull of her features. "This is the east field?"

"Mm-hmm."

She motioned toward the narrow rivulet of water nearby, patches of it frozen, the middle still running, but slowly. "Then this is the stream where—" Her face was red from the cold, but he swore her color deepened further.

This was the stream where he'd kissed her, the stream he'd landed in when she'd shoved him rather quickly afterward.

She slipped a bit ahead of him, closer to the stream. "You kissed me here."

"Believe me, I remember."

Her eyes remained on the icy, encrusted water. "And then you told me you would never write to me, you wouldn't receive any letters from me. And you said it as if it was not at all surprising, as if it didn't bother you at all to sever the connection between us."

He shoved his hands into the pockets of his heavy outercoat. "It seems I should have pursued a future on the stage instead of in the church."

She looked back at him, her gaze a bit softened. "Did you regret it?"

"Of course I did, but I'd created the situation. I was making commitments I couldn't keep." He was evermore ashamed of himself each time he reflected on those weeks they'd spent together. "My future was still entirely up in the air. It was wrong of me to not step away when I first began feeling a pull to you, but you gave me strength and kindness and—and you believed in me when no one else did. I needed that." He hadn't intended to make such an enormous confession. It was all simply pouring from him. "It was wrong of me though. I knew it was. You needed to be able to leave without the weight of impossible promises. I had done everything wrong during those weeks, and I was afraid I would simply make it worse. Remaining distant and unfeeling was the only way I knew of to get through that farewell."

She watched him closely. "Did you ever wonder what might have happened between us if we'd been a little older, if you had been completing your education rather than beginning it?"

"Constantly."

"We are older now, Harold," she said. "You are not beginning your education. Aren't there possibilities now that weren't available to us then?"

"Yes." Confessing that nearly brought a blush to his face, something that didn't happen often. But they were being honest with each other. He wouldn't be anything less than truthful about this. "There are very real possibilities. Hoped-for possibilities. Yet, there are also many of the same obstacles. Once again, I don't know where my life is going. Your efforts, and Mater's, and my own discoveries have helped me realize I do want to continue my life in the church, but the duke's letter has sent so much back into uncertainty once more."

She nodded, watching him with a hopeful intensity. How he wished he had something more encouraging to tell her.

"If I accept the livings he is offering, I would have the income I need to support a family, to begin building a future that could include something more than perpetual bachelorhood a breath away from poverty."

"Is your current living so insufficient?"

"Throckmorten neglected the vicarage and the glebe. He left so much in need of repair that my living is being stretched beyond bearing. A vicar's education focuses on theology, not the more practical concerns of life. There might be a better answer to these troubles, but I haven't the first idea what it might be."

She set her hand on his arm, the gesture one of support and empathy. "I am sorry."

"I could have a less lonely future, but it would mean leaving Collingham. I very much fear I would be miserable if I did, no matter the increased comfort of my financial situation."

She nodded her understanding. "And you being miserable would be a terrible foundation on which to build a new family."

"Precisely."

"Here we are again, then," she said, "on the banks of this stream, your future uncertain once more. This time, though, there is honesty between us."

"Honesty, but not a great deal of hope."

She leaned in and placed the briefest of kisses on his cheek. "There is more hope than you know."

"You don't mean to give up on me, then, while I sort all of this out?"

"I mean to help you sort it, if you'll let me."

He took in a lungful of frigid air. "There isn't an easy answer," he warned her.

"But there is an answer," she said. "And you will find it. I have every hope you will."

Hope. Where was she finding that elusive promise? If he accepted the living he was being offered, he would have income enough to build a life with the woman he'd never stopped loving. But she would be away from her brother, and Harold would be away from his family and the people of Collingham he cared for so deeply. He would have her, but he would once again be pretending to fit the role he'd taken on. Yet, if he remained here, where he was learning to be himself as vicar and serve in the way best suited to him, he would, out of necessity, be alone.

No matter what he chose, he would lose something essential.

CHAPTER TWENTY-EIGHT

At Sarvol House, Sarah had been often alone and isolated, and those had been the best days she'd spent there. Living at the Lampton Park dower house, on the other hand, was utterly joyful. Scott was with her. He was returning to himself by bits. She saw more happiness in his face. She watched with deep gratitude the maternal care Mater offered him and the transformative quality of it.

How very much they owed that dear woman.

Sarah had begun discussing with Marion places Mater might enjoy visiting. The suggestion had been made, and it was a wise one, that travels be postponed until summer. The roads would be less problematic and the weather more likely to be predictable. More importantly, whatever the outcome of Philip and Sorrel's next few days or weeks, Mater would not be gone when that difficult time arrived. That a month had passed since Christmas without Sorrel's time arriving was both hopeful and troubling.

Sarah and Harold had spoken many times since their walk down to the stream. They'd discussed Sorrel, the neighborhood, Scott, but not ever again the topic of his future.

She sat in the chapel as the choir practiced, occupying her usual pew. Harold sat in his usual spot as well. He still spent his time during practice doing his work, but he made absolutely certain to express aloud his sincere appreciation of their effort and to praise them when a piece was performed particularly well. Sarah had seen a profound change in the choir members since he had begun encouraging them. She had seen a change in many people in the neighborhood. She had seen a change in him.

He had his eyes closed now, not in sleep but in concentration. A small smile of enjoyment touched his lips. She saw that more often, proof that he was happier at his core. Harold deserved to be happy. Choosing the livings the Duke of Hartley offered was the only chance they had of building a life together, but she couldn't bear the thought of him being miserable again, not when he'd come so far.

Should he choose to stay in Collingham, rendering himself too poor for them to create a life with each other, she would be heartbroken. She would find herself living near him, seeing him regularly, without the possibility of a future together.

She felt like her younger self again, all the heart-fluttering anticipation tempered by the heartbreak that had brought that previous connection to an abrupt end. Things were different this time though. They were both older, both wiser. He had told her of the difficulties they faced. He was being honest. She was keeping her feet firmly on the ground while doing her utmost to remain hopeful.

She didn't know all the turns in the path ahead of them, but she wasn't afraid to walk it. If fate chose to be kind, she would not need to do so alone.

He opened the eye closest to her and looked at her sidelong. Sarah dropped her gaze to her clasped hands. She hadn't intended to be caught longingly watching a gentleman whose future might not include her. Again.

Harold rose and moved to where she sat. He carefully shifted the stack of music sheets away and sat beside her. "Is something the matter, Sarah?" he asked quietly.

She shook her head.

"There was worry in your eyes," he said.

He had always been able to ascertain her mood. It had been something of a challenge between them when they were younger. She would attempt to hide her thoughts, and he would still manage to sort them out. She saw little point in requiring him to guess now.

"I was wondering if you had made a decision about the duke's offer."

He didn't answer for a long moment. She looked at him once more. The worry he'd said he saw in her eyes she now saw in his.

"I still don't know what to do," he admitted. "The income would allow me to have a future, but I find myself recoiling at the idea of leaving this place that has always been home to me and the people I love."

Was she one of those people?

"I wish I had known all those years ago when I set myself to a future in the church that I would be choosing between serving in the way I wished and avoiding poverty. You see, I take great delight in my work, but I also really enjoy eating."

There was her Harold, the gentleman who had laughed and smiled even in difficulty. She saw him nearly constantly now. Such a change from the stern, unreachable Harold he'd pretended to be.

"I suspect you have spent a great deal of time lately sitting on the railing in your stairwell."

He nodded. "Mrs. Dalton is beside herself. She finds the precariousness of my perch not at all to her liking."

"Have you considered the possibility that your housekeeper is rather fond of you?"

Oh, how she loved his smile. "I most certainly have."

Quick footsteps sounded on the flagstone floor, pulling both her attention and Harold's to the back of the chapel. A stable hand from Sarvol House, one of the only servants still employed in that house, was rushing toward them.

"Miss Sarvol." He addressed her in rough breaths. Apparently, he'd rushed through more than the chapel. "Your brother's sent for you. Mr. Sarvol's in a bad way. Real bad." The stable hand looked to Harold. "You're being asked for too, Mr. Jonquil."

If Scott was sending for her *and* the vicar, it could really mean only one thing: her uncle was dying.

"Allow me a moment to gather what I need to administer to him," Harold told her. "We'll go over together."

"Thank you."

Sarah remained in the pew, attempting to settle her spinning thoughts and feelings. Her uncle was a decidedly horrible person. He had treated her cruelly. He had caused Bridget a great deal of misery as well. Scott had been rendered heavy and unhappy in the time they'd been in Collingham, and she knew that was owing to the tyranny of Uncle Sarvol. Yet she grieved to think he was nearing his end. Death was a difficult thing.

She rose, breathing calmly and setting her thoughts to the night ahead of her. When Father died, there had been very real and deep grieving. Mother had been devastated, as had she and Scott. This passing would be different. She and her brother were Uncle's only remaining family, and while they would grieve the way one did with the ending of a life, there was not the closeness between them that brought soul-deep mourning.

Harold returned, a small leather case in his hand, just as she slipped from the pew. He offered not his arm in the formal manner but his hand in a gesture of very personal support. She walked with him out of the church and into the cold. A Sarvol carriage waited for them at the gate to the churchyard. They were settled quickly. The door closed, and the carriage rolled forward.

While Harold had initially taken the rear-facing seat across from her, as was strictly proper, with the conveyance in motion and the two of them alone, he moved to sit beside her. He took her hand once more.

"What do you need from me, Sarah? This will be a difficult night. I will, of course, see to it your uncle receives his final rites, but you weigh heaviest on my mind just now."

"And Scott weighs heaviest on mine. His life is about to change very drastically." The oddity of worrying over Scott's sudden inheritance and responsibilities when a man was dying struck her. "Am I a terrible person, Harold? I should likely be more heartbroken than I am to know my uncle is dying."

"No one is obligated to mourn someone who abused her."

"I still do, a little." The realization surprised even her. "It is an odd sort of grief though, mourning the person he might have been and the relationship we might have had."

"And perhaps mourning for the happier days you might have known if he hadn't done what he did."

Sarah leaned her head against him. He set his arms around her. She closed her eyes and shut out all the world, allowing her mind to process nothing beyond the comfort he offered.

"My father was a good man," she said after a time. "Uncle could have been as well, but he chose not to be. I think that is what grieves me the most."

Harold pressed a tender kiss to the top of her head. Sweet, loving Harold. She wanted him to have the steady and comfortable future he deserved, but what would they all do if he left?

* * *

Mrs. Tanner hung the black mourning wreath on the front door of Sarvol House just as the sun rose the next morning. Sarah sat in the sitting room, looking out over the front lawn. Harold watched her a moment from the sitting room doorway, knowing he had no more legitimate reason to remain but not wishing to leave her.

"He hurt so many people." Sarah spoke without looking at Harold. "Bridget never knew life without him. I wish she had."

He stepped inside and sat beside her. Her gaze remained on the vista through the front window. A tear hung at the corner of her eye. He pulled a handkerchief from his pocket and slipped it into her hand. She didn't dab at her eyes but simply sat with the square of linen in her grasp. She rested her head against him.

"He cannot hurt anyone any longer," Harold said. "And in the end, we managed to find positions for every one of the servants he so heartlessly dismissed."

That had been a struggle. Without references, they had needed to be very creative. Most of the servants were from this area and didn't wish to leave their families and friends behind. But Sarah had been indefatigable, and they had proven themselves a very good team.

Her eyes met his at last, regret and pain etched in their brown depths. "I wish he hadn't caused you so much difficulty. You had enough on your plate as it was."

He cupped her face with his hands. "Helping people is a pleasure and an honor. And knowing you were free of this house relieved a crushing burden on my mind and heart." He pressed a kiss to her forehead. "I only hope that, in time, the pain he caused you will lessen."

She closed her eyes and took a slow, deep breath. "I believe it will."

He dropped his hands to hers. "What can I do?"

She opened her eyes. Though grief remained, some of the weight there had lifted. "Look in on Mater. I won't be there with her for the next week or so."

"After that? Do you mean to return to the dower house or stay here as mistress of Sarvol House?"

"I don't know. I'm not going to worry about that yet."

Wise. "Please tell me if you or Scott need anything. I'll visit either way, but . . ."

She smiled, a tremulous expression, but genuine.

"Mr. Jonquil." Mrs. Tanner stood just inside the doorway, a folded missive in her hand. "This has just arrived for you."

He stood and crossed to her, accepting the letter with a brief word of gratitude. He unfolded it.

Harold,

Sorrel's time has come. Scorseby's been sent for. Please do not delay.

Yrs,
Philip

No banter. No jesting. Not a single unneeded word. The situation, Harold surmised, was already perilous.

He turned back to Sarah. "I have to go."

Her alarm was obvious, but she didn't press for information, likely wishing to preserve the confidentiality between a vicar and a parishioner, not knowing from whom the letter had come.

"Sorrel," Harold said.

Sarah took a sharp breath. She nodded, somber. "Have things only begun or . . . ?"

"Only begun."

"Mater and Dr. Scorseby will look after Sorrel," Sarah said. "Go be your brother's sure foundation. He will need you. Desperately."

He did not wait even another moment. The last time Sorrel had come to the end of a pregnancy, the situation had grown dire extremely quickly. He would not leave Philip to endure that alone.

Harold had visited Sorrel the morning before. It had been clear she'd had little time left before her body would simply be unequal to the enormous strain on it. She had been pale and weak and in such obvious pain. The next hours would bring her to whatever conclusion awaited. He pointedly ignored the fact that he had with him all he needed to perform the final rites, having brought it to Sarvol House for that purpose and having no other choice than to carry it to Lampton Park in his haste.

CHAPTER TWENTY-NINE

Harold had discovered a newfound bit of confidence in his ability as a vicar during his weeks of self-reflection. His new approach felt more natural, more fitting, and he had already begun to see the fruits of that change. He could believe, at last, that he was where he was meant to be, doing good in the way he'd always wanted to. But every ounce of assurance fled as he watched Philip's tense pacing. His brother was facing the loss of yet another baby and, in a way too real and too probable to dismiss, the almost-inevitable loss of his beloved wife, his dearest friend, the person who meant most to him in all the world. All of Harold's study, his admittedly limited experience, his soul-deep desire to touch lives felt entirely insufficient.

"This will be agonizing," Scorseby had told Harold. "Your brother is strong and stalwart, but the look in his eyes is one I've seen before. He's nearing his breaking point, and were he to witness what his wife is about to endure, it would shatter him. I will be attempting to save two lives I am not certain can be saved, and your mother and Lady Cavratt need to be able to focus on helping Lady Lampton without worrying about him. Lord Lampton simply cannot be in the room until this is over."

Harold had understood, yet he worried. "If he loses her and he's not there to make his goodbyes—"

Dr. Scorseby had nodded a little impatiently. "I promise to send for him if we are reaching that point."

"And should the baby be born alive, they will both wish it to receive the baptismal rites as quickly as—"

"I am fully aware of all that would need to happen and how quickly it would need to be seen to. I swear I will not neglect that." Urgency had added frustration to Scorseby's tone. "But I need you to take him away from here and keep him there. Somewhere near enough that he can return quickly, but far enough that he cannot hear her cries."

Harold had chosen the sitting room on the east end of the house. They couldn't hear anything. Though Harold understood why Scorseby wished for the distance, the silence was proving deafening.

"This didn't take as long the last two times." Philip turned back from the window where he'd been standing for all of five seconds. He crossed to the fireplace. "Taking longer—that's a good sign, don't you think?" He turned and moved across the room again, tapping the closed door as he passed. "It could also mean things are going badly. It could mean that." He dropped onto the sofa opposite Harold's chair. He slumped low. Wouldn't London be shocked at the sight of their most famous dandy, the gentleman all of Society thought valued appearance above all else, dressed in wrinkled clothes, his jacket long discarded, slouched like a street urchin, his hair likely not even combed that morning, stubble rough on his face.

"Scorseby said he'd send for me before—" Philip cut himself off. They'd had this exact abbreviated conversation many times already. "He'll make certain I'm there before she—"

"You chose well when you recruited Scorseby to take Dr. Habbersham's place here in Collingham." Harold knew Philip had invested untold hours and a significant sum of money in convincing the doctor, who had established a successful practice elsewhere, to relocate to this corner of the kingdom when their resident physician had decided to retire to Tunbridge Wells. Knowing Sorrel's health would never be great and would, at times like this, be dangerously poor, Philip had left no stone unturned finding the very best man of medicine available. "Scorseby is thorough and thoughtful, competent, compassionate. He'll not neglect either of you. Worth every penny you paid to bring him here."

"I'll give him every penny I have left if he can save her." Emotion broke Philip's whispered words.

"I have every confidence in him," Harold said. "And though the past weeks have taken a toll on her, Sorrel is the strongest person I think I have ever known. That gives me hope."

Philip eyed him, not with reassurance, not with relief, but with pain. "Don't think I am unaware of what is in your leather case, Harold. I saw you come in with it."

"I came here directly from Sarvol House. There was not time for returning the case to the vicarage."

"Would you have?"

Harold felt certain honesty was best, no matter how uncomforting it might be. "I still would have brought it."

Philip leaned forward, his elbows on his legs. He set his head in his upturned hands. "She's going to die, Harold."

"She has survived this twice before," Harold reminded him.

But he shook his head without looking up. "Not like this. She was less frail, less fragile. She started the other deliveries stronger than she is now. She was not so broken already, so worn down. She had to fight with every ounce of strength she had, and it was very nearly not enough. She doesn't have that reserve this time." Philip's breath trembled even as his body shook. "I'm going to lose her; I know I am."

Harold left his chair and sat instead beside his brother.

"Do not offer me empty platitudes," Philip muttered. "This pain is not a lack of faith or something that can be erased if I just believe more."

"I hadn't intended to say anything remotely resembling that."

Philip didn't sit taller, didn't look up. He sat with his head in his hands. "Throckmorten would have lectured me. He apparently did that to Layton over and over again."

"Throckmorten was a bell swagger of the worst sort."

Philip appeared utterly shocked. "I didn't think I'd ever hear you use cant like that."

Harold waved that off. "I'm a vicar, not a saint."

"You're a blasted good vicar. I don't think we tell you that often enough."

Harold allowed a small smile, quick but sincere. "I don't think I've deserved it often enough."

Philip's gaze shifted to the cherrywood clock on the mantel. "This is taking too long." He stood and paced away. "Something's gone wrong, and I'm not there with her."

"Scorseby will send for you."

"Once it's too late," Philip said. "Once there's nothing more to be done. I ought to be there now. She shouldn't be alone."

This was why Scorseby had told Harold to stay with Philip. The worry, the panic, the anticipatory grief would override his judgment, and Scorseby knew he'd not be able to do all that needed to be done to give Sorrel her best chance of survival if Philip's panic sent the sickroom into chaos.

"Mater and Catherine will not leave her," Harold reminded him. "She will not ever be alone or neglected or left comfortless."

Philip pressed his forehead to the wall. He tapped the wall with the side of his fist.

Harold had no words of comfort, no reassurances. There were none to be offered. He had seen Sorrel's deterioration for himself, and he had been in the room after the last delivery and had known how close she had come to not surviving. Philip's assessment—that he was about to lose his wife—was Harold's as well.

"She is my whole world, Harold. Every bit of it. Everything that matters. If she leaves me . . . I can't recover from that."

"I am sorry, Philip. I truly am. Life asks too much of us sometimes. It leaves us broken. No matter how we put those pieces together again, we are never the same."

Philip turned to face him, his back against the wall. "What if I can't put those pieces back together? What if everything is simply broken forever?"

"Then you let us help you." Harold crossed to him. "You let Mater and Layton, Corbin, Jason, Stanley, Charlie, and I hold you together for as long as you need. We're family, Philip; we love you." He set his hand on Philip's shoulder. "No one is abandoned. No one is forgotten. We find our strength in each other."

Philip's chest rose and fell with a trembling breath. *"Fortitudo per Fidem.* Strength through loyalty."

"*Fidem* is not exclusively interpreted as 'loyalty.' It also refers to 'faith.'"

"Faith in what?" Such pain filled his eyes.

"In this moment, faith in your own endurance, faith in your family."

Philip closed his eyes and breathed, slowly, deliberately.

The door to the sitting room opened. Philip's stiff posture and almost unnerving stillness spoke volumes of his bone-deep worry.

Sorrel's lady's maid peeked inside. "You're being asked for. Both of you."

Philip took an audible breath but didn't move. The maid turned a pleading gaze on Harold.

He nodded. "We will be there directly."

She slipped back out. Philip pushed a breath through his tense lips. "Best bring your leather case, Harold," he whispered.

Harold fetched it quickly, catching up to Philip in the corridor. Neither of them spoke. Philip kept his gaze ahead of them, his brow furrowed and his mouth tight. His pace picked up steadily.

He had made this walk before but never with so little hope. If Harold was being asked for specifically, Philip was likely about to lose his wife and child. Being a vicar had always been about helping people, but Harold felt helpless in that moment.

The door to Sorrel's sitting room was open when they reached it. They stepped inside. Not far distant was the door to her bedchamber, also ajar. Philip paused. Breathed. "I don't know if I can do this."

"Sorrel needs you to."

Philip nodded. He took only a moment longer, then squared his shoulders and rid his expression of his panic and worry.

Harold's oldest brother's ability to slip on a mask had often bothered Harold. He saw in that moment, however, the gift it actually was. Philip would present to his wife a calm and strong façade. It might ease some of her suffering.

The bedchamber was lit by a small scattering of candles, with one very near the head of Sorrel's bed. She lay there, propped up a bit by a stack of pillows. She had been brought low by her condition before this day's work; she looked far worse now.

Philip must have noticed as well. Every ounce of bravado fled his expression. He simply crumbled, kneeling on the floor at her bedside. Philip, who, despite his theatrical prancing and preening, had always been, at his core, a solid and unshakeable presence in the family, dropped his head against the blanket.

"Sorrel." Misery filled the whispered name.

Her hand, shaking a bit, brushed over his hair. "Do not fall apart now, Philip." Sorrel's voice was weak. Her expression spoke of tremendous pain.

"You can't leave me, Sorrel." He didn't move; he simply knelt with his head buried on the bed beside her. "Please don't leave me."

An ache filled Harold's heart at the pain in his brother's voice and posture.

"If you give up on me now, Philip Jonquil, I will never forgive you." Sorrel spoke firmly but quietly.

He raised his head enough to press a kiss on her hand, offering for the first time a view of his teary, broken expression. "Harold told me to have faith."

"You really ought to listen to him more often." She pulled in a tense breath, pain tugging at her features.

Philip looked to Scorseby.

"She will need time to heal, but I have more confidence than I did before today."

A painful hope touched Philip's face. "Then you do have *some* confidence?"

"I do, now that I have a better understanding of what was making this so very difficult." He pulled a tin from his bag. "Her best chance of recovery lies in rest, which she will not be able to do without powders to ease her agony. Taking them means she will sleep most of the time and be more or less insensible when she is awake. And still, there is no guarantee she will recover."

"But there is a chance?" Philip pressed.

"There is a chance."

Sorrel brushed a tear from Philip's face. "Do not cry, dear."

He turned enough to press a kiss to her palm. "I love you, you know."

"I know." She took a sharp, tense breath. "This doctor you brought here means to render me insensible for days on end. I need you to hold me before I fall asleep."

"You don't even have to ask, my love."

A trembling smile tipped the corners of her mouth. "But first, your mother wishes to make some very crucial introductions."

Mater? Harold's attention had been so focused on the scene before him he'd not even stopped to think that his mother had to have been somewhere nearby. The room was too dark for easily spotting anyone else. But in the far corner, a silhouette moved closer, slipping into the spill of light from a candle on the bureau.

She held a baby in her arms.

Philip's face froze. His entire frame did. "Alive?" The whispered question was almost silent.

Mater nodded.

"Healthy?"

"Quite," she said.

Philip rubbed at his upper lip before wrapping his hand around his mouth and chin. Tears spilled unchecked from his eyes, which remained firmly focused on the child Mater held. He kept his other hand in Sorrel's.

Mater motioned to someone else in the dim corner of room. Harold had forgotten Catherine, though he'd known perfectly well that she'd been present for the delivery. She stepped into the same spill of light that illuminated Mater. In her arms was another blanketed bundle.

"Oh, blessed heavens," Harold whispered. *Twins.*

Sarah's voice echoed in Harold's mind from across the years and one of their many conversations about the life he meant to live as a vicar. "You will be part of people's joys and sorrows. You will walk with them through the most difficult and beautiful moments of their lives."

This was one of those moments. Powerful. Heartbreaking. Hope affirming. And he, as Sarah had said, was *blessed* to be part of it. This was what had drawn him to the church. This was the reason he served.

"Both healthy?" Philip asked the same question again but slightly modified.

Mater nodded. "They are tiny but nearly the healthiest little boy and girl I have ever seen." Tears clogged the declaration. Not tears shed in grief but in joy.

Sorrel set her free hand atop her other, squeezing Philip's hand between hers. "Go greet your children, darling. They have wanted to meet you all their lives."

Gaze heavy, he looked at her once more. "But you are—"

"Not going anywhere," she said with a feeble laugh. "I put off my powders specifically so I could witness this. Do not disappoint me."

Philip rose but without his usual fluid grace. He was actually shaking. Harold didn't think he had ever seen that before. Mater, crying as well, carefully laid her blanket-wrapped bundle in Philip's arms.

"Which one is this?" Philip's voice shook.

"The oldest," Mater said. "Your son."

"My son," he whispered.

Catherine approached. Philip adjusted his tiny boy into one arm, and Catherine set the baby girl in his other one. "Your daughter," she said.

Philip shook his head, amazement and awe and utterly raw emotion in his face. He looked to Sorrel. She smiled and nodded.

He turned to Scorseby. "They're healthy? We needn't be terribly afraid for them?"

"They were born a bit before their time," Scorseby said. "And they are very small. But I can honestly say I've never seen two healthier infants under those circumstances. I am a man of medicine and do not often speak in terms of miracles, but this comes as near to one as ever I've seen."

Philip's gaze dropped to his bundles. "Twins," he whispered.

Mater set an arm around him, her head resting on his shoulder. Catherine watched with her hand pressed to her heart. This room, where so much heartache had been anticipated, was filled in that moment with joy and hope.

Sorrel locked her gaze with Harold's. She motioned him over. He obeyed.

"I need you to do something for me," she said.

"Of course." He sat in the chair nearest the bed, leaning near enough to hear her without requiring that she strain her obviously diminished strength.

"I want the babies to be christened as soon as Crispin arrives. Catherine sent word to him this morning. I may very well be unconsciousness, thanks to the powders. There is yet a chance I will not be—" She paused for a breath, though whether to clamp down emotion or because she lacked the strength he did not know.

"Christenings do not need to be performed so soon," Harold reminded her. "There is time enough for you to regain your strength."

"We lost the others, Harold. Little ones for whom there was not time enough." Her next breath shook. "I cannot rest easy until I know all is—I need to know all is in order, that everything is seen to for these dear little miracles. I need to know."

"If you wish for it, I will make certain the rites are performed the moment Crispin gets here."

She still did not look relieved. "Philip will object. He will insist on waiting until I am able to be present."

"He wishes to share that moment with you, just as you wished to share this one with him." Harold's gaze returned once more to his brother holding his tiny children in his arms.

"There is every possibility I will not ever be able to share that with him."

"Please, do not—"

"You are a vicar, Harold. You know better than any of us that death is part of life. I will not pretend otherwise."

"For Philip's sake, I think you ought to pretend at least a little."

Her gaze, though clouded with pain, pierced him. "You will not speak as bluntly of this to Philip as I have to you. If I hear that you have, I will either beat you to a pulp when I recover or haunt you mercilessly if I do not. And do not think for a moment I don't mean that."

Harold nodded, even smiled a little.

"Crispin and Catherine have been chosen as godparents. Philip and I have already discussed names, though we did not anticipate needing both." She sucked in a breath through her teeth. "See to it the christenings are performed. I need you to promise me."

"I give you my word."

Her eyes fluttered closed for a moment, and a look of peace settled over her pained features. "Your brothers like to torture you about your profession, but you have the heart of a vicar, Harold. Do not allow them to torment you into doubting that."

"I am only now beginning to know what the heart of a vicar really is."

She nodded, her eyes still closed. "Miss Sarvol?"

"Sarah has proven a demanding and enlightening tutor."

"She is good for you, Harold."

He leaned closer and lowered his voice. "And you are good for Philip. Please do all you can to not leave him here alone."

She slowly opened her eyes once more. "Too much has been demanded of him already. I do not believe the heavens mean to ask this."

"I will petition them thoroughly," Harold said.

She nodded slowly, the tension in her jaw growing noticeably. "Ask that horrid doctor to come over here again. I cannot bear this any longer."

Harold rose and stepped away from the bed. He passed, not directly to where Dr. Scorseby was stirring powder into a glass of water but via a path that took him to Philip and Mater first.

"You had best go rejoin Sorrel," Harold said. "Scorseby will need to administer her powders soon."

Philip wasted not a moment. He returned to the bed and carefully laid one of the children in Sorrel's arms. He kept the other in his own. He placed himself beside her, and she rested her head against him.

Mater remained at Harold's side. She put her arms around his middle and embraced him. "Thank you for being here with them."

"Witnessing this moment," he said, "I consider myself deeply blessed to have been here." Dr. Scorseby looked over at him. Harold motioned to Sorrel and nodded. The doctor took up his concoction and crossed to the bed.

"She will be able to rest now," Mater said. "And she will heal."

"I believe she will." He would move forward with unshaking confidence in the mercy of heaven. Though he knew good people too often slipped away far sooner than seemed fair—his own father's passing had come at a cruelly young age—having faith in the possibility of a miracle was a source of strength.

He would believe, and he would help his family find reason to believe as well.

CHAPTER THIRTY

When Sarah's father died, all the household had mourned deeply and sincerely. The neighborhood had grieved his passing. Having spent the last few days at Sarvol House, watching as the trappings of mourning were donned and displayed, Sarah could not help but note the difference. Father had been beloved for his kindness and his generosity. Uncle had been despised for his arrogance and cruelty. While no one was crass enough to celebrate his passing, there was no real feeling of loss. Indeed, Sarah sensed a great deal of relief among the staff.

She saw very little of Scott but understood. He was charged with making arrangements for the funeral and burial. He, as heir, would meet with solicitors and debtors and any number of people as he officially assumed the reins of the estate. Servants would also need to be hired to fill the gaps in the staff left by Uncle's shortsightedness. And the household budgets would need to be re-evaluated. Those fell to the mistress of the estate, the role she had come to England with Scott to fulfill. The time had come to do so.

That, however, meant leaving the dower house. She grieved that; Mater had become like a mother to her in many ways, as well as a friend and a companion during a time when Sarah had felt very alone. And now she was leaving Mater alone.

Knowing she could delay the inevitable no longer, Sarah made her way back to Lampton Park to make her explanation and gather her belongings.

All of Collingham was abuzz with the news that Philip and Sorrel were the proud, and likely shocked, parents of newly arrived twins. Though no one seemed entirely certain of Sorrel's condition, all were firm in their belief that the tiny newborns were hale and hearty. Knowing all of that, Sarah did not need to be told where she would find Mater.

The sight that met her in Sorrel's bedchamber would have warmed even a frozen heart. Philip sat beside Sorrel's bed in a rocking chair, a new addition to the room, holding a tiny, blanket-wrapped baby in his arms. Mater sat not far distant in a high-back armchair holding an identically-bundled little one. Sorrel slept under the vigil of her husband and mother-in-law.

Philip spotted Sarah first. "Come in," he said eagerly. "You haven't met my children yet."

A glow of amazement and pride shown in his eyes when he spoke those words: *my children.*

"I haven't," she said, "though they are the talk of the neighborhood, I assure you."

"As well they should be." Philip pulled his gaze away from his armful and back to her. "This one, you understand, is bald, which will cause any number of whispers in Society."

"A tragedy of immense proportions," Sarah said with a laugh. She crossed to him, gazing down at the tiny baby. "Which of your dear ones is this?"

"The oldest." Philip tucked the blanket back enough for Sarah to see the baby better. "I wish I could say he was the better behaved of the two, but he woke his mother earlier, which I think was inexcusably inconsiderate of him."

Oh, this was one besotted father. Sarah could not hide her amusement and delight. "What is his name?"

"Kendrick Lucas Crispin Jonquil."

Sarah shook her head solemnly. "His hand will cramp every time he signs a letter."

"Harold managed to say the entire thing during the christening without falling asleep once. I was impressed, I tell you." Philip managed to make the absurd declaration with an entirely solemn expression.

"You should never have doubted our vicar," Sarah said.

Philip nodded, even as he began rocking his chair back and forth. "You are right on that score." He smiled up at her. "You should meet my daughter. She's an angel."

Sarah turned to face Mater, who clearly held back a laugh. Understanding the amusement for what it was—pleasure at seeing Philip so incredibly happy—Sarah grinned and rolled her eyes.

"Don't think I don't see the two of you over there," Philip said, "enjoying yourselves at my expense. It is not my fault I have two perfect children."

Mater met Sarah's eyes once more. "Shall we remind him of that declaration when they are both three years old and wreaking havoc on his household?"

"Yes, and again when they rub their jam-covered hands all over his silk waistcoat or manage to untie in mere moments what his valet labored over for hours and his irreplaceable Wilson storms from the house never to return."

"Nonsense," Philip said. "They won't ever do anything wrong."

Mater simply laughed. Sarah closed the rest of the distance between them, wishing to meet Philip and Sorrel's second little miracle. Mater adjusted so Sarah could better see the tiny girl.

"This one is not bald." Sarah spoke loudly enough for Philip to easily overhear. "I think you should keep her."

"She is too well behaved to do anything but keep her," Philip said. "Which is a good thing. Scorseby informs me he does not permit his patients to change their minds about these things."

Sarah shook her head at his teasing. The baby was not sleeping, but neither was she fussing. She simply lay in her grandmother's arms as content as anything.

"This is Lady Julia Elizabeth Jonquil." Mater brushed the tip of her finger over Lady Julia's thick, dark hair. "She is named for me, you realize."

"I bet you thought Mater's name was actually 'Mater,' didn't you?" Philip said from across the room. "That is a common mistake."

Sarah lowered her voice. "It is good to see him back to his old jesting self, isn't it?"

Mater nodded. "The weight of the last months was crushing him."

Sarah pulled over a nearby chair. "How is Sorrel?" She kept the question quiet, not wishing to upset Philip should the answer be distressing.

"She is in a great deal of pain, which is expected. Scorseby is concerned about her hip; it is apparently very far out of joint, something he had known was possible but had hoped to avoid."

"Can anything be done?"

Mater nodded minutely. "Once we know better how well and how quickly she will recover from the toll of the past months and the delivery itself, Scorseby means to recommend some remedies. None are guarantees, and some are apparently far more difficult than others, but he assures us there are options."

"And he feels she will survive?" Sarah held her breath, waiting for the answer.

"Yes. The first day afterward was touch and go. Heavens, I thought Philip was going to lose her after all. But she rallied. Her strength never ceases to amaze me." Mater looked over at her son once more. "Both their strength. Life has taken so much away from them."

"And has, at last, given something back."

"At last."

Sorrel stirred a little. Philip, keeping Kendrick in one arm, set his hand atop Sorrel's. She settled again.

"You have raised good sons, Mater," Sarah said. "Every last one of them."

"That is their father in them."

"It is," she acknowledged, "but it is *you* as well. Your influence, your efforts, your love."

Mater pressed a kiss to her little bundle's head. "How is Scott? What a burden he must be carrying."

"He is a little overwhelmed, yes, but you would be very proud of how well he is carrying it all."

Mater watched her a moment, pondering, piecing things together. Sarah had discovered that about her during their weeks together: Mater sorted people's puzzles very quickly.

"He needs you to fill the role you came here to fill." Mater nodded. "Having a mistress of the estate will be invaluable to him right now."

"I hate the idea of leaving the dower house," Sarah said. "And I was so looking forward to our journey when summer came."

Mater shook her head. "You will have finished your mourning period by then, and your household will have made its transition. We can still make our journey if we wish to."

"I would like that very much indeed," Sarah said.

Echoing from the corridor came the jaunty strains of "Down among the Dead Men," the tavern song Sarah had hoped Harold knew. It seemed he did.

"Who is that?" Philip asked with a deep chuckle.

"Harold," Sarah said.

"Harold?" Philip sputtered out the name.

"He enjoys tavern songs," she said. "His housekeeper has confirmed it."

Philip shook his head. "Sometimes I think we never knew a thing about him."

"Sometimes," Mater answered, "I think you're right."

Harold stepped inside in the next moment. Sarah's heart threatened to simply burst from her. It did that when he entered a room or smiled at her. Sometimes all she had to do was think of him and her pulse pounded an anticipatory rhythm that filled her entire being with a tingly sort of hope. She'd loved him for years, but somehow, that love simply grew day by day.

He stood a few steps inside the room, watching them all with quiet mirth. "I thought I might discover a soiree in here. Our Sorrel is so remarkable a hostess, she can sleep through the gathering and still be the belle of the ball."

Sarah shrugged. "At the moment, I believe she is sharing the spotlight with Lady Julia and the bald one."

Philip laughed out loud, which set Sorrel stirring and Kendrick fussing in his arms. He held his son against his chest, rocking him and rubbing his back even as he continued to grin. "'The bald one.' He will never live this down."

"Well, if he had been born with hair, none of this would have happened." Harold shook his head in mock scolding. "I think that makes this Kendrick's fault."

"I agree," Sarah said solemnly.

"I see you two have joined forces." Philip had managed to settle his son once more. "I can't decide, though, who is the good influence and who is the bad."

"I am the good," Sarah declared at the same moment Harold said, "Sarah is the good." That set the room to laughing again, which made Kendrick cry, which woke Sorrel.

Philip looked over at his wife. "Harold did it."

She smiled vaguely, her eyelids heavy and half closed. "Did Harold keep his promise?"

"What promise is that?" Philip asked.

"The christening," Harold supplied.

"He performed it yesterday," Philip told her. "Over my objections, I will point out. Even a small delay meant you would be able to be there."

Sorrel looked to Harold, a firmness in her gaze despite her continued grogginess.

"I gave my word," Harold told her. "I would never break it, no matter Philip's thoughts on the matter."

Philip looked to Sorrel once more. "He told me that given the choice between siding with you or with me, he hadn't the least hesitation in choosing you."

"As I will do every time," Harold answered.

Philip's expression softened. "Good."

Harold turned to Sarah. He had a way of looking at her lately that melted her to her core. It was equal parts tenderness and a deep sort of longing she had a hard time describing. Whatever the exact emotion beneath this renewed pull she felt, she yearned for it when he was gone and cherished it when he was nearby. "How are you? This week has not been easy for your family."

"Nor for you." She rose from her chair and moved to where he stood near the doorway. "A funeral two days ago and two christenings yesterday."

"Serving can be exhausting, but it is also fulfilling. I would rather be very busy in good works than bored."

"Spoken like a Jonquil," she said with a laugh.

He looked at her with confusion.

She slipped her arm through his. "I don't know a single Jonquil who can bear not being busy. And not one of you can resist helping anyone and everyone who needs it."

"A fine compliment." He set his hand on hers and looked over at Mater. "I am going to steal your visitor. And what is worse, I will not feel the least guilty about it."

Mater arched her brow. "What is even worse than that . . . she will not be coming back anytime soon."

Harold once again looked confused.

Sarah tugged him toward the door. "I'll explain while we walk. We've missed our time together these past days."

He went with her. "Have you enjoyed our walks, then?"

"Immensely."

They stepped out into the corridor.

"What is this about you leaving?"

"Mater only meant I will no longer be living at the dower house," she said. "I came from America to serve as mistress of my brother's household. That household is now his, and he needs me. So much has fallen to him so suddenly."

Harold nodded. "You must be happy to be assuming the role you'd meant to assume all along."

"Not as happy as I'd expected to be."

He took her hand. He always used to do that when they talked of their lives and worries and hopes. "Do you know why you aren't happy?"

These were the moments she could almost believe no time had passed since their walks around the Park years ago. He listened, and he cared. She'd always loved that about him.

"I have treasured my time with your mother. I will miss her. And I will worry about her."

"And what else is interfering with your happiness?" he asked.

She had her suspicions but wasn't willing to examine those thoughts in detail. Sarah lifted her head enough to look at him. "Have you decided what you mean to do about the livings you've been offered?"

"I've decided what I *can't* do, which I suppose amounts to the same thing." He held her hand more firmly as they walked down the wide staircase. "My family is spread out all over the kingdom, but two of my brothers are settled here. And though I suspect Mater will find her opportunity to travel, her home is here as well. Corbin is settled within a short distance. When the family gathers together, it is always here at the Park." He paused a moment, both his words and his steps. "My father is buried here, and his memory fills that chapel every time I am there. No matter that this living is not a grand one and I will never be wealthy, no matter that I would struggle to support myself, I cannot leave. This has always been and always will be home."

A warm feeling of peace spread through her at the look of contentment on his face. That had been missing for so long. "There are some things a large income cannot replace. Being home and among family is chief among them."

He clasped both his hands around one of hers, holding it to his chest. "But without that income, we have no . . . we couldn't . . ."

"Surely your father would not have wished for you to assume a living insufficient to have a family of your own." She had known the late earl well enough to be absolutely certain he would have wanted Harold to be happy and would never have resigned him to a lifetime of loneliness. "Could the parsonage's fields be farmed again, do you think?" The glebe would be a source of income if properly attended to.

"With effort. It would need to be cleared and prepared, and I would need to find a family looking to work it in exchange for a portion of the proceeds. There is a small tenant home out in the glebe, but it—"

"Is in disrepair, brought on by neglect." Sarah set her other hand lightly on his cheek. "I wish I had the answers, Harold."

"As do I."

"How long would you need, do you think, to put the parsonage and the chapel and the glebe land and cottage to rights so you would have the entirety of your income to live on?" She wanted him to be secure, but she asked for her own sake as well. She felt very nearly certain he would consider a future between them if he felt his situation were settled.

He turned his head enough to kiss her hand. "It could be years, Sarah."

"Have you spoken with Philip about any of this?" she asked.

"He has endured enough worry of late. He doesn't need to worry about this as well."

"You are good to wish to spare him," she said.

Harold looked at her sidelong, a smile tugging at his lips. "But a fool not to pour my worries in his ear?"

She let herself grin back. "He might know something, Harold. He is considerably older than you are, and a father now. He has likely grown wise in his old age."

"Suppose instead of wise, he has grown inadvisably generous and simply makes me his next charity case."

She shrugged. "Then you punch him in the mouth."

He turned wide eyes on her.

"I'm an American," she said. "We're a little violent."

Heavens, she loved the sound of his laugh. "I will consider divulging to him how very penniless I am, but I reserve the right to respond to any patronizing bits of charity in as American a way as possible."

"I would be disappointed if you didn't."

He kissed her hand again as they walked on. "I am so very glad you came back to England, Sarah."

"So am I."

He sighed but not with despondency. He had worries, but he was not beaten down by them. "It will be years before my living is set to rights."

"Years is not so long," she said. "I'll have my brother's household to run, and you'll have a parish to serve. When your situation is stable at last, then . . ." She let the sentence dangle unfinished.

"Then, maybe you will meet me by our stream once more and, perhaps, this time *not* shove me into the water."

She bumped him with her shoulder. "That would depend a great deal on you, Harold Jonquil."

He nodded. "I will plan my words and deeds accordingly."

"Deeds?" She allowed a hint of a smile.

"There were more than words exchanged that day, you'll remember," he said.

"Believe me, I remember." She'd used the exact phrase he had when they'd last spoken of their ill-fated encounter on the banks of that stream.

He laughed again lightly. Sarah rested her head against his upper arm. She often imagined herself walking with him exactly that way day after day, crisscrossing the parish, serving the people they both loved, happily building a life together. How easy it was to indulge in those visions and forget for a few moments his straitened circumstances.

If you've any miracles left, she petitioned the heavens, *we could use one. I cannot bear the thought of spending years without him.*

CHAPTER THIRTY-ONE

"I am in desperate need of a meat pie." Harold likely could have thought of a more elegant way to enter the kitchen, but he was tired, frustrated, and hungry.

"Have you finished your sermon, then?" Mrs. Dalton nudged a plate of pies across the worktable to him.

He'd been holed up in his study all afternoon, bent over impossible ledgers, hounded by seemingly impossible dreams, and doing his utmost to ignore the aroma of meat pies slowly filling the house. He'd finally given up.

"I wasn't writing a sermon." He gingerly set a hot pie on a tea towel, letting the warmth of it seep through to his fingers.

"Now, that is a relief. You were in there so long I was beginning to fear you were returning to your long, prosy sermonizing."

He smiled a little. "I wasn't so bad as all that, was I?"

"I'll just say this: I'm not complaining that you're preaching to us more with your heart than your mind now and not merely because your heart isn't so longwinded."

Harold laughed out loud; he couldn't help himself. "'Longwinded.' How was I so oblivious to the congregation's misery?"

"You weren't." Mrs. Dalton always did speak her mind. "I heard you bellyaching often enough about all the parish sleeping through your sermons."

"'Longwinded' and 'bellyaching.' You don't paint a very flattering picture."

She shrugged. "I'd rather you not climb up the banister again because your mind's heavy. Being direct seems the best approach."

"And your best chance of keeping my feet on the ground."

Mrs. Dalton nodded solemnly.

Harold took a careful bite of the meat pie. It was still hot but not scalding. How was it a mouthful of good, familiar food could help settle a person's mind? Perhaps Scorseby had an explanation. Whatever the reason, Harold was grateful.

"If you weren't writing a sermon, what were you working on?" Mrs. Dalton bent over her sewing, something she often did while they talked.

Harold sat on a stool at the table, nibbling at the steaming pie. "Mathematics, which was never my best course in school."

Mrs. Dalton glanced at him doubtfully. "Do vicars have much use for 'ciphering and such?"

Harold nodded. "Mostly in matters of balancing ledgers and making a tight income stretch as far as possible."

"Ah." She nodded. "Your money troubles." Most servants wouldn't feel comfortable speaking so freely. Harold was grateful Mrs. Dalton had no such qualms. He appreciated having someone to talk to.

"I've made do with what I have after seeing to repairs and such, and it was sufficient for a single gentleman who didn't wish for any of the trappings of luxury or even all the comforts of life. But it isn't—I no longer—"

"Say no more." Mrs. Dalton nodded knowingly. "You're needing that income to stretch enough to support another person, one you'd want to have all those comforts and a few of those luxuries."

"I want her to be happy. And *not hungry*, if that can be avoided."

"Hunger can make happiness harder to come by. But if you could manage to feed her and secure her happiness . . ." Mrs. Dalton made no attempt to hide her expectation of more information.

"Then I would consider myself the most fortunate gentleman in all the world."

Mrs. Dalton leaned forward and snatched a meat pie for herself. Settling back once more, she joined him in the very informal meal. "Does Miss Sarvol feel the same about you?"

"I never said I was speaking of Miss Sarvol."

"You also didn't tell me you'd be wanting meat pies today, but I knew that, didn't I?"

"'Oh'"—Harold pulled the note out long—"'Give her a drop of the whiskey brew—'"

Mrs. Dalton joined him to finish the musical refrain. "'She'll tell your future and 'twill all be true.'"

Harold committed himself to the remainder of his meat pie. Mrs. Dalton's cooking combined with her joyful company was the best antidote Harold knew for a case of the blue devils.

"What are Miss Sarvol's thoughts on your situation?" She was more than willing to keep at a fellow if he didn't give her the information she wanted.

Harold smiled to himself. "She said, 'Years is not so long to wait.'"

"Years? Are you thinking it'd take that long?"

He wiped his fingers on the tea towel. "Based on my wrestle with numbers earlier, I would say two or three years, if I am both fortunate and careful."

Mrs. Dalton finished her pie. "When Mr. Dalton asked me to marry him, we hadn't two pennies to rub together. We had a greater claim to poverty than you do. But we knew something you don't seem to: that a challenging life together was far better than a life of comfort spent apart. There were difficult times, but we faced them together. That was worth a lot."

There was wisdom in that, and yet it was not an ironclad argument. "Miss Sarvol has many choices besides the poverty of a struggling vicar's wife. She has never truly known want. It would be a tremendous change for her, one I am not certain would be welcome."

"Have you asked her?"

"One doesn't simply ask—"

"Why blasted not?" Mrs. Dalton actually sounded upset.

Harold had not been expecting that.

"You've done enough hemming and hawing trying to decide what you mean to do with your life; meanwhile, she's kept coming back, she's kept pushing you to be better and happier. That's not a lady who'll shrink at a challenge."

"She has no experience with economizing." Harold had made all these arguments to himself often enough to know them without thinking.

"I do." Mrs. Dalton was not one to be easily shaken. "And I'd do all I could to see the two of you happy here."

"You think you could get along with her, then?"

"All the town gets along with her. She's one of the best things to ever happen to Collingham."

Harold couldn't argue with that. "The blacksmith certainly thinks so."

"*Everyone* thinks so."

There was a pointedness to that remark that couldn't be ignored. "And they likely all think I'm a fool for dragging my feet."

"Not one of us has missed the way you look at her, nor the way she looks at you." Mrs. Dalton's expression softened. "You're happier since she came. Things between you were difficult at first, but her being here's changed you for the better. And, heavens, the way she smiles when you're near. You're good for her too."

"I'd be asking her to give up a great deal." Harold couldn't deny that.

"Give her a chance to make that choice rather than making it for her."

A surge of energy pulled him to his feet, even as his mind demanded to know what in the world he was doing. "I can't believe I'm even considering this."

"I can," Mrs. Dalton said. "A man who'd climb walls and bridges and mountains, who'd take a hard look at himself and change what he saw because it needed doing isn't a man who'd shrink from something simply because it was a risk."

"What if she turns me down?"

"She won't." Mrs. Dalton spoke without the least uncertainty.

"You know that for a fact?" He shook his head at her surprising degree of confidence.

"I know what it is to be a woman deeply in love. I know how that feels, and I know what that looks like. I see it in her every time you're together."

Harold took a breath, squaring his shoulders. "I certainly hope you're correct."

"I'll have a fruit tart waiting for you to celebrate when you return."

"I'll accept, whether it's eaten in celebration or commiseration."

She snapped her hand towel in his direction. "Enough dithering. Go claim your future."

He had gone only as far as the kitchen door before turning back. "You really believe she'll accept a life of straitened circumstances and struggling to stretch every pound when all I have to offer her . . . is me?"

Mrs. Dalton rose and moved to him, holding his gaze with a firm one of her own. She set her hands on his upper arms. She was more of a mother figure to him than most housekeepers were, a bit of nursemaid tossed in too.

"You are a good man, Mr. Jonquil," she said. "You don't think that of yourself often enough. But she sees it. Have faith that she does, and have courage enough to give her the chance to show you as much."

"And you'll help me see that she's happy here?" He didn't want to cause Sarah more pain than she'd already experienced.

"I suspect she's one who finds her own happiness, but I'll do all I can to make this a good and happy home for the both of you."

"I don't thank you enough for all you do, Mrs. Dalton." He needed to do better about that. "I certainly don't pay you enough."

Mrs. Dalton spun him around and gave him a nudge. "Go."

He practiced his words all the way to Sarvol House. Though most gentlemen would wish to find a tender way to declare their affection, he felt it best to be very upfront about his situation. That he loved her but understood if the life he had to offer wasn't enough. That he would wait until he had money enough if that was what she wanted. That he would marry her tomorrow if he felt his situation wouldn't bring her misery.

However, all his carefully rehearsed words dissipated as the Sarvol House housekeeper bade him follow her up the narrow, isolated stairwell to Sarah's former rooms, the ones in which she'd been a temporary prisoner.

"Has she not been moved to the mistress's rooms?" Harold didn't mean to criticize the household, but it seemed odd to require Sarah to continue on in this corner of the house.

"She has," the housekeeper said, "but she has come to like her little sitting room and spends much of her day there."

If she could feel at home and content in a small room filled with mismatched secondhand furniture, then perhaps she would not be entirely miserable in the small spaces of the parsonage, with its humble rooms and offerings.

The housekeeper preceded him, announcing his arrival before stepping to the side and allowing him entry. Sarah stood in the middle of the room, a mere few steps away, talking with what appeared to be her lady's maid. He offered a bow. She curtsied.

"I'll see to this," the lady's maid said, taking up a basket at their feet. "I'll use the chair just on the other side of the bedchamber door."

"Thank you, Hannah."

The maid slipped through the door to the side and, barely visible around the doorframe, took a seat. She wasn't in the room, but she was near enough for propriety while still allowing a bit of privacy.

Harold did his best to breathe. He and Sarah had spoken about the difficulties in his future but had come only to the conclusion that they could not make plans or discuss anything more between them until his finances were in better condition. He felt certain she cared for him. More than once she'd given him clear indication that she very deeply cared. Yet, taking this leap was proving more daunting than expected.

Sarah turned to face him. Her smile was soft and welcoming, and his tension eased under its influence. "First things first," she said. "How awful do I look in black?"

She indicated her mourning dress. Though there was undeniable jesting in her tone and expression, he also sensed more sincerity than she was letting on. Black was a somber color. Not many appreciated wearing it in unrelieved constancy.

Harold took her hand. "You are beautiful no matter what color you wear."

"I hope you like black, then, because that is all you're going to be seeing me in for the next three months."

That was encouraging. "Does that mean I will be seeing you?"

"Would you like to?" Every now and then, Sarah managed a tone that was utterly flirtatious.

"I would very much like that. I would, in fact, really like to see you *all* day each day. Every day."

She threaded her fingers through his, watching him closely.

He firmed his resolve. "I have spent the morning and a good part of this afternoon looking for a way to address the neglect at the vicarage while not draining my income as quickly as I have been."

She nodded silently, not looking away.

"I don't think it can be done," he said. "My situation will be difficult for a long time. I cannot change that." He saw disappointment tiptoe over her. He pressed forward. "I've lived years without you, Sarah. I was lost, wandering, broken. I used to pray—literally pray—that you would come back."

"You did?" She spoke almost breathlessly.

"Then I heard you *were* returning, and I was terrified. I knew—I knew you would be disappointed in me."

"I—"

"And you *were*," he pointed out. "Rightly so. And your disappointment shook me from my yearslong stupor." He tucked both his hands around hers and pressed them to his heart. "When I am with you, I feel like I can be better, I can be more than what I've let myself become. You make me whole in a way nothing else and no one else ever has."

She watched him with such tenderness.

It was all the encouragement he needed. "I have almost nothing to offer you. You would have far more comforts and ease here in your brother's home."

She tucked herself against him.

One of his arms slipped free and wrapped around her. "I would love you, Sarah, but that is all I have. No comforts, no promise that we wouldn't have days when food was scarce. The vicarage is cold in the winter to save on coal. There'd be no new clothes, no jewels. Only my devotion and my love."

"That, Harold, is all I've ever wanted from you. It is all I have dreamed of."

"I'm offering you a life of poverty." He needed to be certain she understood that.

"You are offering me your heart. That is a treasure." She stretched and placed a kiss on his cheek. "I have hoped ever since our discussion of your finances that you would simply ask me if I was willing to accept a life on a small income, if it was enough for me. I didn't want to push you, but I hoped."

"I finally found the courage to ask." He leaned his forehead against hers. He brushed his fingers along her cheek. "I have loved you all these years. I never stopped. I never could."

"And I love you," she said. "I always have."

He tipped his head enough to press a light kiss to her lips. Her arms slipped around his neck. He pulled her to him, holding her close as he kissed her more fully, more deeply.

He'd lost her once to his own doubts and uncertainties, every hope he'd had disappearing in a single afternoon. Yet here she was in his arms, loving him as he loved her, accepting what little he had to offer.

Never again would he doubt that the heavens could work miracles.

CHAPTER THIRTY-TWO

Watching Harold fill his role was a joy. He smiled now. He laughed. He was loved. And his family had, at last, begun showing him the appreciation and acceptance he needed from them. Jason and his wife had come with their tiny daughter, and Stanley and Marjie had returned with their new son, both wanting their infants to be christened in the Collingham church by their brother. Others who had witnessed the rite likely hadn't realized how deeply touched Harold was to have been asked to perform it, but Sarah had seen it in his eyes.

She had been invited to join the Jonquils for a family gathering afterward. Scott had left for Town a few days earlier. He'd not elaborated, but some matter of business related to the estate had pulled him there with noticeable earnestness. She was grateful to see him no longer forced into a position of subservience to a meanspirited and angry man, but he was very busy, and she missed him.

Harold met her in the entryway. He put his arms around her, pressed a kiss to her temple, and held her to him.

She held fast to him. "Scott said that before he left for Town, you spoke with him about our wish to be married."

"I did. And he laughed."

She pulled back and looked up at him. "Laughed?"

Harold grinned. "He said that he knew it was customary for me to ask his permission and he knew that the two of us would have to work out the particulars of the arrangements but that he found it rather ridiculous that his 'permission' played any role in this at all since you have always been one to do exactly what you felt was best."

"He knows my stubbornness all too well."

Harold kept his arms around her. In the week since they had chosen the future they meant to claim together, he had grown very affectionate. She loved this change in him.

"I intend to tell my family today," he said, "now that all is settled with your brother. I should warn you though: the laughter that will follow will put your brother's little chuckle to shame."

"You think they'll laugh?"

"I am nearly the youngest. That puts me in the perfect position to be teased by all of my older brothers, and every last one of them is here today."

"If you need someone to stand as second, you simply tell me." She felt him chuckle, and she held tighter to him. "I missed this all those years we were apart: being with you, hearing your voice. I don't want to ever have to miss that again."

He slipped his hands to her face, holding her tenderly. He pressed a light kiss to her lips. "Let us go face the horde."

"Did we decide on 'a horde of Jonquils,' then?"

He shrugged. "It'll do for now, at least."

"The horde it is."

He nodded. "The sooner we tell my brothers about our plans, the sooner they will finish tormenting me over it, and the sooner we can begin planning our forever."

"I love you, you know."

"And I am more amazed by that every day." He kissed her again, lingering over the moment of affection.

His sigh when he pulled back spoke of regret. She understood; she too wished they could stay just as they were.

The drawing room was a study in beautiful chaos. The five oldest Jonquils, plus Crispin. All their wives. Their ever-expanding families.

"Sorrel has joined the gathering tonight." Sarah was so pleased to see her future sister-in-law sitting amongst the family. Clearly, she had not fully recovered from all she had passed through—her coloring remained pale and her posture spoke of continuing weakness—but she was there, enjoying the gathering.

"The twins are down from the nursery as well," Harold said. "They've been passed from one aunt or uncle to another all evening. I suspect the poor babies are growing seasick."

"Those two will not want for attention; that much is certain."

Harold smiled. "No one does in this family."

"I cannot believe I get to be part of it." Sarah could not hide her amazement.

"I cannot believe you want to be." His grin brought out her laugh.

Philip and Layton turned at the sound. Layton smiled warmly. Philip looked ready to burst with amusement, a common thing for him these days.

"Are you ready?" Harold asked out the side of his mouth.

"Absolutely."

Harold slipped his hand around hers. She held fast. She wasn't truly nervous, but there was enough anticipation tiptoeing over her to make his touch and his comfort very welcome.

"I don't know what you see, Layton," Philip said, "but I spy a Jonquil looking to make an announcement."

"I see the same." Layton could be every bit as mischievous as his older brother when he chose to be.

"Am I so transparent?" Harold didn't seem the least offended.

"Let us just say, this moment has played out a few times." Philip rolled his eyes. "Did you want this to be announced to the entire gathering, or were you hoping for a more personal moment?"

"If everyone already knows, secrecy hardly seems necessary."

Philip turned to face the crowd, who were paying him no heed. He let out a long, shrill whistle, and the room fell silent, all eyes on him.

"Holy Harry means to sermonize."

Amusement, eye rolls, disbelief. Nearly every reaction was accounted for amongst the gathering.

Harold was not put off by any of them. He had at last reached the point where he felt sure enough of himself to not be overset by his family's tendency to tease. "I have no intention of preaching," he said to them all. "I simply wanted you to share in my joy. Sarah and I"—he looked at her as he spoke, love filling his eyes—"mean to build a life together. She has agreed to marry me."

Caroline spoke before anyone else could. "She was always going to marry you, Harry. You just hadn't asked her yet."

Snickers followed that pronouncement. Marion eyed them both with amusement but also with a look that clearly said, "The girl is not wrong."

Harold lifted Sarah's hand to his lips and kissed it. "Is that true, my dear?"

"I would have married you years ago if you'd asked me."

He pressed their clasped hands to his heart. "We have wasted a great deal of time, my love."

"Speaking of wasting time," Philip jumped in. "Do you have any other announcements you want to *not* shock us with?"

Harold pushed out a dramatic groan. "This is not at all the warm, heartfelt congratulations I was expecting."

"How long have you known this family?" Stanley asked dryly. "Mockery was a given; congratulations never are."

Harold met Sarah's eye. "I still can't believe you are willingly joining this throng."

"As long as you're part of it," she said.

Philip joined them, nudging them a little away from the others. "Are you meaning to marry by license or post the banns?"

"It had best be the banns," Harold said. "I haven't enough for a special license."

Philip's brow pulled in confusion for only a moment. "Consider it a wedding present, Harold. You have kept Sarah waiting long enough."

"Would you consider a different present?" Harold asked. "Because I could use advice more than a license."

"Advice on what?"

Harold kept her hand in his. She suspected he was finally going to ask his brother about the insufficiency of his living. "Vicars aren't educated on matters of budgets and finances. I am hopeful you'll know something I don't about stretching an income."

Philip motioned for them to walk with him into the corridor. "Are you struggling, Harold? The income attached to this parish is not enormous, I grant you, but it isn't meager."

"I have no complaints about the size of the living," he assured his brother. "If not for the impact of Throckmorten's neglect of the vicarage and church, I would have far more of my income at my disposal still."

Philip's brow pulled low. "The vicarage is in disrepair?"

"Not as much as before, but there is still much to be done. It will require a significant portion of my income for a couple of years."

"Confound it, Harry. Did they teach you nothing at Cambridge?" Philip didn't sound angry. Exasperation hung in his amused tone. "The upkeep of the vicarage is the responsibility of the estate that controls the living, you beefhead." Philp laughed. "If the vicarage is falling to bits, that's for the Lampton Estate to put to rights. Your income was never meant to cover that."

Harold stared for a long moment. He shook his head. "The parish tithes repair the chapel and bridges and roads," he said.

"Yes, the parish oversees those things. The *estate* maintains the vicarage."

"Mercy," Harold whispered.

Philip took pity on him. "I ought to have spoken with you about this when you first took on the role of curate. You always seemed so sure of your role it never occurred to me you might have some gaps in your understanding."

Harold looked to Sarah, amazement and emotion in his expression. "The *estate* maintains the vicarage."

"I knew you should tell him."

"You were right," he said. "Philip does know something."

Philip laughed. "Make an accounting of what you have spent putting the vicarage to rights, and I'll see to it you're reimbursed, and for heaven's sake, let me know what else needs to be done there. I'll have to fund it out of Kendrick and Julia's inheritance, but as long as you don't have guilt about leaving infants destitute . . ." Philip shrugged.

Sarah patted Philip's arm consolingly. "The bald one will struggle, but I suspect Lady Julia has her mother's resolve."

"The bald one." Philip shook his head. "I'll have you know, even Wilson approves of his bald little head."

"Well, Wilson has a bald little head," Harold said.

Someday, Sarah hoped to meet this legend of a valet.

Mater peeked through the drawing room doorway. She shot her oldest son a look of warning. "I mean to gush over these two, and you had best not interrupt."

"I'm in the suds now," Philip whispered. He crossed to Mater and pressed a kiss to her cheek, then left the three of them in the corridor.

Mater looked back at Harold and Sarah. Without another word, she pulled them both into a hug. "I couldn't be happier. I have waited for this since the last time Sarah was in England. I had hoped you two would find your way to your happy ever after."

What a joy it was to be part of this loving family.

After a long embrace, Mater released them. "Do allow Philip to procure you a special license. You've waited quite long enough, and I would so love to see you married while so many of my boys are here to be part of such a special day."

"I believe I will accept his generosity," Harold said. "As soon as Scott returns, we can hold the ceremony."

Sarah met his eyes, her heart warming and glowing inside. "I couldn't be happier, my dear."

Mater walked with them back into the drawing room. They were instantly flooded with Jonquils offering well-wishes. No one seemed the least displeased, and absolutely no one appeared surprised.

"Will you be my aunt *and* my cousin now?" Caroline asked.

"I will."

The little girl smiled broadly. "I am glad. I like that you're in my family."

"I like it as well," Sarah said. "It is my very favorite dream come true."

EPILOGUE

According to his brothers, Harold Jonquil was born a vicar. According to his new bride, he was her champion, her companion, her dearest love. She made him feel as though he could conquer the world.

Harold sat on the doubled-back section of banister in the quiet stillness of the house he now shared with Sarah. He'd always liked the Collingham vicarage, but it finally felt like a true home.

He heard her footsteps before he saw her.

She leaned around the corner of the wall and looked at him. "Why are you in your thinking spot? Has something happened?"

He shook his head. "I was only sitting here, realizing how very fortunate I am and how very much I love you."

"Would you care to ponder your good fortune over here with me?"

"I am always pleased at the prospect of spending time with you."

She held her hand out to him. "Come join me on solid ground, Harold. I don't climb on banisters."

He scooted down the wood and hopped onto the floor beside her. His arms slipped around her almost of their own accord. "I love you, Sarah Jonquil. I love you so very much."

She smiled broadly. "You tell me that often, Harold."

"You had best grow accustomed to hearing it." He kissed the soft spot just below her right ear. "I don't intend to stop telling you. Over"—he kissed her neck—"and over"—he kissed her just below her jaw—"again."

Sarah leaned into his embrace.

He closed his eyes, committing the perfect moment to memory. "I love you, Sarah."

She shook with a silent laugh. "You really are going to keep telling me that, aren't you?"

He bent low and whispered in her ear. "For the rest of our lives."

ABOUT THE AUTHOR

SARAH M. EDEN IS A *USA Today* best-selling author of witty and charming award-winning historical romances. Combining her obsession with history and her affinity for tender love stories, Sarah loves crafting deep characters and heartfelt romances set against rich historical backdrops. She holds a bachelor's degree in research and happily spends hours perusing the reference shelves of her local library. She lives with her husband, kids, and mischievous dog in the shadow of a snow-capped mountain she has never attempted to ski.